DISCARDED

mys.

BITTER LEGACY

ALSO BY H. TERRELL GRIFFIN

Matt Royal Mysteries

Wyatt's Revenge
Blood Island
Murder Key
Longboat Blues

Thrillers: 100 Must-Reads
(contributing essayist)

BITTER LEGACY

A Matt Royal Mystery

H. Terrell Griffin

Oceanview Publishing

Longboat Key, Florida

ISBN: 978-1-933515-96-0

Published in the United States of America by Oceanview Publishing,
Longboat Key, Florida
www.oceanviewpub.com

2 4 6 8 10 9 7 5 3 1

PRINTED IN THE UNITED STATES OF AMERICA

For
Johnnie Ray Allred
The man from Exxon

There is a strange charm in the thoughts of a good legacy.
— Cervantes

Truth is always bitter.
— St. Jerome

ACKNOWLEDGMENTS

My thanks to the Oceanview crew who work so diligently to turn my scribbles into books.

To my readers who make all this possible, I value your thoughts and criticisms. You make me a better writer. I know you invest your valuable time in reading my books and I take seriously my duty to ensure that your time is not wasted; that you finish the book and feel that you have had a brief and enjoyable sojourn into a world that is partly real and partly imagined.

The suggestions of John Allred, Jean Griffin, Peggy Kendall, and Debbie Schroeder enhance the final product immeasurably and provide me with a sounding board and plain old friendship and support during the writing process.

The people who inhabit my slice of paradise, Longboat Key, Florida, are a continuing source of stories, ideas, and friendship. Aside from the fictional murders that my books foist upon Longboat Key, I try to remain true to the reality of the island, its residents, and its place in the sun.

And most of all, thanks to my best buddy, Jean Griffin, who has been married to me longer than she likes to remember and who has always supported me, loved me, and soothed my soul.

SATURDAY

CHAPTER ONE

The killer shot Logan Hamilton in the chest. Not from close range, but from a long way off. Maybe from the rooftop of one of the high-rise condos that line Main Street in downtown Sarasota. Logan had been walking east and crossed Gulfstream Avenue, staying on the north side of the street. He was coming from a boat docked two blocks away at Marina Jack, ambling toward a restaurant on the corner of Main Street and Palm Avenue. He had a lunch date with Bill Lester, the chief of police of Longboat Key, an island lying off Florida's west coast just across the bay from Sarasota.

The chief had arrived early and was sitting at a sidewalk table, idly watching the downtown workers scurrying off to lunch or errands before returning to their desks in stock brokerages, banks, or law firms. Their lunch hours were used for a lot of things, not always lunch. It was Friday, and there was a hint of expectancy lingering in the thin spring air, relief that another week was about over, that the weekend beckoned.

Lester was wearing a pair of jeans, a white golf shirt, sneakers, and a ball cap. He was not tall, five eight maybe, and still carried nearly the same weight as when he had signed on with the police department twenty years before. A small belly protruded over the waist of the jeans, but most of it disappeared when he stood. He was on his way to Ed Smith Stadium to see a spring training game. Marie Phillips, Logan's girlfriend, had left word at the police station that Logan wanted to meet for lunch, so here he was. The game didn't start until two.

A breeze blew from the west, bringing a slight chill off the Gulf of Mexico. It was late March, the sun bright and warm on the chief's face, the wind blocked by the planters situated along the curb. He raised his hand, signaling to Logan, who was just across Palm Avenue waiting for a motorcycle to clear the intersection.

A slight cracking sound assailed the chief's ears, a sound his professional senses immediately identified as a rifle report coming from behind him. Logan crumpled to the sidewalk, going over backward, no attempt to catch himself. He was down and still as the chief came out of his chair, moving fast, running toward the body, pulling his badge from his pocket, jerking the pistol from the ever-present holster at his waist. *No*, he thought. *Not Logan. Please, not Logan. Logan was his friend, his drinking and fishing buddy. Who would kill Logan? Why?*

He crossed Palm Avenue at a dead run, stopped, and stood over Logan. He looked up the street from where he thought the bullet had come, his pistol pointed at the sky. Nothing. No movement, except pedestrians running toward him. No threat, just curious people. Death had come to a quiet street in Sarasota on a spring day that made people smile and gave them purpose, a day that rivaled the ambrosia of the gods in its sweetness. *Not Logan, not on this day, not now.* The chief's breath was shallow, quick, the onset of hyperventilation threatening to overcome his professional instincts.

He fell to his knees beside Logan, tears welling in his eyes. He was fighting off the panic that struggled to overcome the detachment he would need to get him through the next minutes. Logan wore a pair of cargo shorts, boat shoes, shirt, and a windbreaker bearing the logo of the University of Tampa Spartans. His sparse graying hair was tousled by the wind, his middle-aged face flaccid, benign looking, bereft of life. Hope was deserting Lester as he tore open Logan's shirt, exposing a patch of reddened skin that would become a bruise, but no entry wound. He saw movement in the victim's chest, the lungs filling and deflating rhythmically. Logan wasn't dead. *Where had he been hit? Where the hell were the medics?* Lester pushed back the panic, striving mightily to purge himself of the deluge of adrenalin that gushed through his body. Logan was alive, but for how long.

The chief looked more closely at Logan's chest, trying to find a bullet hole. Nothing. He moved the windbreaker back over the bruise. He noticed something heavy in the inside pocket of the jacket. A thick paperback book, five or six hundred pages at least. Lester pulled it out and found the bullet lodged in the book. Relief spread through him. Logan hadn't been shot. The bruise was not lethal. A few days in the hospital and he'd be as good as new. He chuckled, a nervous reaction to the relief. Saved by Ayn Rand, he thought.

A sniper rifle bullet travels at about three thousand feet per second when it leaves the barrel. The friction caused by the air through which it travels slows the projectile. The farther the distance between the rifle and the target, the slower the bullet is traveling when it impacts the victim. The slower the bullet, the less damage it does. It was impossible to determine the distance the bullet in Logan's book had traveled, but it had to have been a long way, or the slug would have penetrated his chest.

The chief scanned the street, looking east, trying to see any movement, any clue as to where the bullet had come from. Where was the sniper? There were a lot of possibilities. The tall condominiums that had sprouted like weeds along Main Street, a couple of high-rise office buildings. All would have provided the shooter with a place from which to bring sudden death to interrupt the rhythms of a spring day in a quiet seaside town.

Only a few seconds had elapsed since Bill had reached Logan. It seemed like an eternity. The chief bent over the body, saw slight movement of the head, and then Logan's eyes popped open. "You're hurt," said Lester. "Stay down."

Logan stirred. "Bill?" He shook his head, trying to clear it. He was trying to focus his eyes and his mind, trying to understand what had happened. "What the hell is going on?"

The chief put a hand on Logan's chest. "Somebody took a shot at you. You're okay. Stay down. For now. Trust me."

Logan closed his eyes, let his body relax. Concern etched its way across his features, an eye popped open, glanced at Bill as if to reassure himself that the chief was still there, still had his gun out. The eye closed, opened again, closed. Logan was trying to comply with Lester's order, but it was obvious to the chief that he was scared. With good reason. Somebody had tried to kill him. A man came out of the bar in the middle of the block, holding a cell phone aloft. "Paramedics are on the way."

A siren wailed, the sound bouncing off the buildings. An ambulance was leaving the downtown firehouse a couple of blocks away. Two police cruisers were three blocks east, turning onto Main Street, traveling in tandem, their sirens yelping, light bars flashing, engines roaring, coming fast. They fell in behind the ambulance as it screamed to a stop at the curb. A paramedic hurried from the passenger seat, carrying a case, his whole body conveying a look of urgency. He started toward the chief and Logan. The driver opened the back door of the ambulance, removed a gurney, and stood quietly on the sidewalk as if waiting for some sign to proceed.

"He's okay," shouted Lester.

"Let me check," said the paramedic.

He leaned over Logan, put his finger on his carotid artery, inserted the ear pieces of his stethoscope and listened for a few moments to Logan's heart, nodding his head. Logan's eyes were open, a bemused expression on his face.

"I tried to tell him I'm okay," Logan said. "Let me up."

The paramedic shook his head. "We're getting you to the hospital."

Lester waved his badge at the man. "No. We're not going to the hospital."

"Sorry, Chief. I've got to take him in."

"Somebody just tried to kill him. He can't go to the hospital."

"I don't have any choice. He's going to Sarasota Memorial."

"Call your chief. Tell him Bill Lester wants to talk to him."

The paramedic stopped, uncertainty flashing across his face. He looked at the chief's badge and his gun and reached for his cell phone. He spoke into it and in a few seconds spoke again. Then he handed the phone to Lester. "It's Chief Fulcher."

"Les," said Bill Lester, "I've got a situation here. One of my citizens has been shot on your street. He's a good friend of mine. Do me a favor and tell your man to do what I ask him to do."

The police chief was quiet for a moment or two and then handed the phone back to the paramedic. The man spoke again, listened, clicked the phone off. "What do you want me to do?"

"Take us to the medical examiner's office."

"You want to go to the morgue?"

The chief nodded his head. "Doc Hawkins can check him out."

The cops had tumbled out of their cars behind the paramedic, then pulled up short. They recognized Lester, backed off a step or two, looked about, puzzled. One spoke quietly into the radio microphone attached to the epaulet of his shirt, leaned in to hear the response, spoke softly to the cop standing next to him, his body language indicating indecision. They both pulled out notebooks and began to question the onlookers who always gather to gawk.

The chief took a sheet from the gurney, covered Logan, and helped the paramedic load him onto a stretcher. He crawled into the back of the ambulance and told the driver to take them to the county morgue. Lester picked up his phone and made another call as the meat wagon sped on its way to the last place anyone ever wants to escort a friend.

The chief medical examiner for the Twelfth Judicial Circuit, Dr. Bert Hawkins, was standing by the door as Logan was unloaded from the ambulance. He didn't look happy.

"I'll take it from here," Hawkins said to the paramedic. "I'll bring your gurney back as soon as I get him on the table."

"Do you want any help?" asked the paramedic.

"No, thanks." He turned to Chief Lester. "You might as well come with me."

"Wouldn't miss it."

They pushed the gurney down a long corridor and turned into the autopsy room at the end. The place smelled of disinfectant and ancient medicinal odors that the air-conditioning was unable to purge. The fluorescent lights reflected off the highly polished tile floor and bounced off the expanse of white walls unbroken by pictures or other decorations. The morgue was not a pleasant place.

Hawkins removed the sheet from Logan, saying, "Let's get this piece of shit onto the table so I can start cutting."

"Cutting, my ass," said Logan as he sat upright. "What's going on, Bill? My chest hurts like hell and I'm lucky I'm not dead. Who shot me? Why am I in the morgue?"

"We don't know who shot you. I called Bert from the ambulance and told him I was bringing you in, alive and well."

Bert cleared his throat. "You know that the Sarasota PD is going to be swarming this place in a few minutes. They'll want a statement from the victim."

"I still don't know what the hell is going on," said Logan. "Who wants me dead, and why?"

"I'm kind of making this up on the fly," Lester said. "When I saw you go down after the shot was fired, I thought you were dead. The shooter probably thought so, too."

"He was almost right."

"Yeah. If we keep you under wraps for a few days, you'll be safe and we might get a line on who's trying to kill you and why. If you end up in a hospital, whoever is after you might try again."

"Somebody just tried to kill me. I don't have any idea who or why," said Logan. "Is that the best idea you can come up with?"

"For right now."

Bert said, "I've got to get this gurney back to the ambulance guys. You stay here."

"Logan," said the chief, "I'm glad you're okay. Your girlfriend's message said it was important that we meet for lunch. What's up?"

"When did you talk to Marie?"

"I didn't. She left the message with our dispatcher."

"The dispatcher called me on my cell and said you wanted to meet for lunch," Logan said. "At the Sports Page."

Lester opened his phone, dialed, identified himself, and said, "Did you call Logan Hamilton and ask him to meet me for lunch today?" When he hung up, he said to Logan, "The dispatcher got the call from Marie and called me. That was all he knew about our meeting. Somebody was setting you up. But why did they want me on the scene?"

"I don't know. Why the hell would somebody want to shoot me in the first place?"

"Good question. Maybe the CSI people will turn up something on the shooter. We'll get you into a hotel for tonight and figure out something more permanent tomorrow."

"I'm hungry," said Logan. "Never did get lunch."

"Let Doc Hawkins take a look at you and we'll grab a sandwich."

"Somewhere safe," said Logan.

Hawkins returned. "Want to tell me what's going on?"

"You know everything we know," said Lester.

"Okay. Let me take a look at you, Logan."

Hawkins did a cursory examination. He shined a penlight into Logan's eyes, palpated the back of his skull where it had hit the sidewalk when he was shot, looked closely at the bruise left by the bullet. He finished and said, "No signs of concussion or anything broken. You've got a knot on the back of your head and you're going to be sore for a few days in the area where you took the bullet. All in all, you look better than most of my patients."

"You're the medical examiner," said Logan. "Your patients are all dead."

"Yeah. That probably explains it."

CHAPTER TWO

I eased my boat slowly into its slip, adding power as I fought the current flowing through the lagoon with the outgoing tide. A brown pelican sat on the outboard piling, watching nervously. As I laid the boat gently against the dock, the bird took flight, rose a few feet, and landed on a nearby pier.

Jessica Connor stepped from the gunwale onto the dock and looped a line around a piling. I shut down the big outboards and walked another line to the bow, lassoed a cleat, and pulled the boat in snug against the pilings. I would loosen the lines after we unloaded, giving the boat a little room to float away from the dock with the wind and current.

It was mid-afternoon on Saturday. We'd had a good run the sixty miles from Boca Grande Pass, staying about two miles offshore on a sea of glass, the autopilot engaged, the engines humming, and Jessica sitting nude next to me enjoying the sun and my reaction. She put the bikini on as we came into Longboat Pass and idled under the bridge. Just inside, I turned south and then east, rounded Land's End, and came to my cottage clinging to the edge of Longboat Key, facing the lagoon and Jewfish Key.

"Matt," said Jessica, "you'd better check this line before you go up. I'm never sure I've got it tied right."

"No sweat. Let's haul the junk up to the house and then I'll secure the boat."

The sun was warm as we worked at unloading a week's worth of dirty clothes and the other detritus of a vacation well spent. Jessica made several trips, carrying the gear to the end of the dock, while I washed down the boat. She was a twenty-eight-foot Grady-White with a small cabin, powered by twin Yamaha 250-horsepower outboards. A sweet piece of machinery that I called *Recess*.

Jessica and I had spent the week boating around southwest Florida, stopping at likely looking places in Charlotte Harbor, Pine Island Sound, and points south. We stopped for cheeseburgers at Cabbage Key and I was glad to see a portrait of the longtime dockmaster, Terry Forgie, hanging in the restaurant. He'd been an institution, and the place was a little less lively with his passing. We had dinner with my friends Dan and Cher Clark in Punta Gorda. We stayed two nights at Everglades City and spent Friday night at the old Miller's Marina just inside Boca Grande Pass.

We'd made a pact that we'd tune out the world. We turned off our cell phones and refused to watch TV or read newspapers. If somebody dropped the big bomb on New York or Washington, we'd probably hear about it from somebody at the marinas we visited. Anything less than that wasn't worth our attention.

We'd had more than our share of wine and beer and good seafood and outstanding sex, but our idyll was about to end. Jessica would leave the next day for Paris and her job at the American embassy there. I would rejoin the slow rhythms that make up life on my slice of paradise, Longboat Key. My buddy Logan Hamilton and I would fish, walk the beach, eat good food at the island establishments, drink our share of beer, ogle the women, fish some more when the mood struck us, and on occasion talk of things deep or amusing or silly. We'd spend time with our friends at Tiny's, the bar on the edge of the village, eat lunch at Mar Vista or Moore's, and gobble up the days that seemed to stretch endlessly before us.

My name is Matt Royal. When I was a young man, I'd been an officer in the United States Army Special Forces, the Green Berets, the toughest fighting men on the planet. I'd been to war, killed some people, lost some friends, got shot up, and came home and tried to put it behind me. I was mostly successful, but some nights the dead visited me, the ones I'd killed and the ones I'd lost. The ones I'd killed didn't have faces, but I knew who they were. My men came dressed as they were on the day they died; grimy jungle fatigues, floppy hats, boots, and belts full of gear. Their faces were stubbled with several days of beard, and sweat pooled at their necks. They carried their M-16s with an ease born of repetition. The rifles were the only thing about them that was clean.

During those dark nights in my sweaty bed, they'd discuss their lives with me, just as they had on the long evenings of boredom that interspersed the firefights. But their lives had ended on a hot day in a jungle far from home. Mine went on. I never remembered what the dead enemy said and, truth be told, I did not want to know, could not bear their opprobrium.

The government that wouldn't let us win the war gave me some medals when I got out of the military hospital and helped me finish college and law school with the G.I. Bill. Those medals were stashed somewhere in a drawer with a piece of the shrapnel the docs had dug out of my gut and a picture of my team standing in front of a Huey, the helicopter that took us into that last patrol. They were all there, those tough young men, grinning and cavorting for the signal corps guy with the camera. For five of them, it was their last flight, if you didn't count the one that brought their bodies back several days later.

I found a career as a trial lawyer, but over the few years became disenchanted with the profession that was becoming a business. Finally, I tired of the rat race, retired early, and moved to Longboat Key, a barrier island off the southwest coast of Florida just below Tampa Bay, about half way down the peninsula. Life is easy in our latitudes, where it never gets cold in the winters and the Gulf breezes cool the summers enough to make them bearable. Island living was pleasant and tranquil and fulfilling. I wasn't rich, but I had enough money to live modestly without working.

I'm a bit of an exercise nut, trying to keep the old body going as long as possible. I try to run four miles a day on the beach, work out in the island gym a couple times a week, and take martial arts lessons once a week. I'm six feet tall, weigh the same 180 pounds I did when I got out of the Army, and have a face that has been described as nice, not handsome mind you, just nice. My nose is bigger than I'd like it to be and a little off-center and I think my eyes are too small. My hair is still dark and covers my head the same way it did twenty years ago. I have a mouthful of good teeth and a smile that I like to think melts the hearts of the young ladies. That may not be true, but I do smile a lot, because living on my island makes me happy. I tend to grow on people, it seems, and the women don't find me completely unattractive.

Our island is small, about ten miles long and a quarter-mile wide. Life is easy on the key, one day rolling into the next, the sun diligent about its daily arrival. Our pace is slow, without stress, our lives filled with friends and good food and beer and booze and fishing and beachcombing. We are separated from Sarasota by a wide bay, and one has to cross two bridges and another island just to find the mainland. We like it that way and live with the conceit that the real world seldom finds its way into our bit of paradise.

I'd met Jessica some months before when I was in Europe. She'd visited me on Longboat Key at Christmas and had wrangled another week away for what she called her spring fling. She'd arrived on Saturday and we'd left on the boat on Sunday morning. Our six days of idleness seemed to reenergize her, and she was anxious to get back to work. And as much as I enjoyed her company, I was looking forward to some time alone and to readapting to the ever-present rhythms of island idleness.

We piled our stuff on the patio that ran the width of the back of my cottage. I went around to open the front door. There was a note taped there:

Matt, call me on my cell ASAP!!! Very damned important!!!!!
Bill Lester

Bill was a good friend, but he was also the Longboat Key police chief and he wouldn't have left such a note unless it was urgent. Jessica followed me inside and went toward the bedroom, shucking her bikini as she walked. I heard the shower in the master bath come on as I dialed Bill's cell phone. He answered on the first ring.

"Matt, are you back?"

"Yeah. What's up?"

"Meet me at the Market in five minutes."

"What's this about, Bill?"

"I'll tell you when I see you." He hung up.

I put the phone down, confused by his abruptness. I went into the bathroom and stuck my head into the shower. Jessica's sleek body was soaped up and she was standing under the water, her head thrown back letting the shampoo rinse out of her hair.

"Come on in."

"Can't. Gotta meet Bill Lester at the Market. I'll be back soon."

"What's that all about?"

"I don't know."

CHAPTER THREE

Jason Blakemoore closed the office door behind him, jiggled the handle to make sure the lock was engaged, and trudged off into the mid-afternoon heat, warm for late March. He wore a white shirt, red tie, and navy pants over wing-tipped shoes. He was about six feet tall, two hundred pounds, blond hair, early thirties. He looked back at the squat cinder-block building that housed his office. It was small, nondescript, flat roofed, its white paint glaring in the South Florida sun. A large sign over the door announced that the building was a law office.

Belleville wasn't much of a town, but then Jason Blakemoore wasn't much of a lawyer, so it all seemed to fit into the cosmic plan. The town was small, its few buildings old, decrepit, many of them empty. One could walk from the town square to the edge of the Big Cypress Swamp in under ten minutes. The Tamiami Trail ran near the southern edge of town, lightly traveled since the opening of I-75 through the Everglades.

Blakemoore had grown up in this dismal place, the son of a waitress over at the truck stop on the Trail and a fishing guide out of Everglades City. Jason wasn't real bright, but he knew how to play football. He'd been an outstanding linebacker in high school and was recruited by several colleges. His academic credentials were nil. He'd made the same score on the SAT that he would have if he'd just written his name and walked out. He missed almost every question.

The glaring lack of college preparation doomed his chances of playing for a major university. A coach at the University of Florida managed to get Jason a scholarship to a junior college in Kansas, where he excelled in football and made passing grades in class. As long as he played well, his grades were good. Good enough to allow him to transfer to the University of Florida for his junior year. He was red-shirted, which meant that he didn't play his junior year, but his eligibility would not be threatened. He could still play two years at Gainesville. Again he excelled on the field and his grades were mediocre, not bad for a guy with no intellect. Against all odds, he graduated. He still had a year of football eligibility left and the Gator coaching staff thought this would be his year to shine. They talked the law school into taking him.

Jason's last year of football was indeed stellar. He made all conference as outside linebacker and his law school grades, while very low, were enough to maintain his eligibility. When football was over, a grateful university administration ensured that he could stay in law school. When he graduated, he took the state bar exam and failed. He took it again, failed again. On his last try, he passed with the minimal grade needed. Apparently, some of the bar examiners were Gator alumni.

No firm would hire him, so he came back home, back to Belleville. He opened his office and managed to survive on the crumbs cast off by the area law firms. He represented the occasional Seminole Indian from the nearby reservation who ran afoul of the local law. He took assignments from the courts for misdemeanor cases that the public defender was too busy to handle. He lost most of the trials, but he always figured the people he represented, or at least most of them, were guilty anyway, so the conviction didn't upset the delicate balance of his universe.

Jason's parents were dead now, and he'd never married. It wasn't that he didn't like women; it was just that he had a very low sex drive, perhaps the result of certain steroids he'd taken daily while playing football. He also liked his solitary life, didn't need a woman to nag him about being home for supper, to slow down on his drinking, to work harder, make more money.

Jason Blakemoore was a happy man. He whistled as he walked across the square, heading for the town's only bar, the Swamp Rat. He'd been into Naples to visit a client in the county jail, an unusual event for Jason on a weekend. The judge had called on Friday afternoon and said the public defender had assigned the case to Jason and the client needed a bail hearing at ten on Saturday morning. Jason went and got the judge to release the man without bail. It was a petty theft charge, shoplifting from a Wal-Mart.

The old guy was eighty years old and this was his first offense. He was confused and didn't understand where he was or why he was there.

Jason had stopped by his office to check his mail for any checks that might have come in, but there had been none. The Swamp Rat Bar was beckoning him. People he'd known all his life would be there, drinking the afternoon away. He usually scored a few free beers from those who remembered him as the high school star.

He stopped at the curb waiting for a car to pass before crossing the street for the air-conditioned refuge offered by the bar. A black Mercedes was driving slowly down the street, two men in the front seat. Jason was watching them idly, wondering why such an expensive car was in Belleville. The car slowed more as it approached Jason. A shotgun poked out of the passenger-side window, a blast cut the air, sending to wing the pigeons that inhabited the park in the square. A red splotch appeared on the white shirt worn by Jason, his tie turning to ribbons of red, his face showing surprise and consternation and puzzlement. He stumbled, fell, and was no more.

CHAPTER FOUR

The Market was a unique place, part grocery store, part delicatessen, coffee shop, ice cream shop, butcher shop, and meeting place for the village residents. It took up one end of the small shopping center at Whitney Beach on the edge of the village near the north end of the key, sharing a parking lot with Tiny's bar, a video store, two restaurants, an art and framing shop, dog grooming parlor, and a T-shirt shop.

The village itself is formally known as Longbeach Village and it is the oldest residential area on the key. It's a place of small cottages and homes, many built in the 1920s and '30s and a few before that, a couple of restaurants, and a world-class art center; a place where working people and retired middle-class folks can still afford to live in houses they bought long before the price of island real estate climbed into the stratosphere. They are an eclectic bunch, the villagers, proud and stubborn and against the change that seems to be a constant condition on our key. They take life as it comes at them, with a certain stoicism that is absent in the key's higher rent precincts. They're my kind of people.

I'd recently moved to my cottage in the village from a bayside condo just to the south. I hadn't intended to make the move, but life sometimes throws you a curve ball. And that curve ball, on occasion, will provide you with the opportunity for a home run. Such was my case.

Rose and Ed Peters had come to our island when he retired from a distinguished career in the U.S. Army. They bought a small home in the village and settled in to live out their lives.

Ed, or the Colonel as he was known to most, became a regular at Tiny's, my favorite little bar that sat on the edge of the village. He was always home by six in the evening to have dinner with Rose. His daily hour at Tiny's, he often said, was the substitute for his officer's club routine, honed during the thirty years he'd spent doing his duty for all of us.

For twenty years after he retired from the Army, Ed gave himself to the community, serving for six years on the Town Commission and for a two-year term as mayor of the Town of Longboat Key. Shortly after he retired from the commission, on a bright morning in December, while taking his morning walk, he dropped dead of a massive stroke.

Rose's grief was overwhelming. They had no children, and each was an only child. They were the only family each other had. The people of the village came to the rescue and Rose slowly recovered. Her smile came back and her kindly disposition once again radiated over the North End.

She called me one day about a year after Ed's death and asked if I had time to stop by her house. She had a problem she wanted to run by me. I told her I'd be there in an hour.

Rose's cottage hunkered under an ancient Banyan tree, its limbs shading the house. Tropical plants flanked the crushed-shell walk, a large bougainvillea painted the spring air with its red blossoms. The bay shimmered behind the house, the sun reflecting off the still water in a blinding burst of light.

She met me at the door, a small trim lady in her seventies. Her gray hair was cut short, a pixyish styling that set off a face that was still beautiful, the few wrinkles providing a sense of character. She was wearing white shorts, a sleeveless pink blouse, and sandals. She made the attire look elegant, because she was a lady of grace.

She hugged me. "Thanks for coming, Matt."

"It's good to see you, Rose."

She escorted me into the living room. Bookcases lined one wall, the titles running to military history and Florida crime fiction. A large flat-screen TV sat on a shelf amid the books. A fireplace with a brick hearth dominated the other end of the room. Two photographs sat on the mantel, one of the colonel in a dress blue uniform and the other of a young couple in wedding attire, the man in the uniform of a second lieutenant and the woman a beauty in a white gown and veil holding a spray of flowers. A matching sofa and love seat and a recliner took up space on the Oriental rug spread over the hardwood floors. Sliding glass doors opened onto a patio overlooking the bay. A dock ran along the seawall enclosing an empty boat slip.

Rose motioned me to a seat on the sofa. "Can I get you something to drink, Matt?"

"No thanks. How have you been?"

"Not too good. I've done something really stupid, and I'm about to lose my home. I know you're retired, but you're a lawyer, and I'm hoping you can show me a way out of this. I can pay you a fee."

"Tell me about it."

"Do you know anything about reverse mortgages?"

"A little," I said. "If your house is paid for you can get most of the equity out of it in cash paid in equal monthly installments. When you die, the house is sold and the mortgage holder gets its money back, plus interest, and the remainder of the sales price goes to the heirs."

"That pretty much sums it up. I got one of those after Ed died. But this one paid me a lump sum in cash, not monthly installments."

"Then you should be pretty well set up. When you die, the house will be sold and the loan paid off."

"Supposedly. I'm afraid I didn't read the paperwork too closely."

Her story was shameful. Shortly after Ed's death, a young man came to see her, told her about the reverse mortgage, and explained how the money would help her live out the rest of her days worry free. Ed's pension from the Army died with him, and she only had Social Security to live on. The Army is not a generous employer, and like most who dedicate their lives to the country's service, Ed did not retire wealthy.

Rose signed the papers, got the cash, invested some of it, and gave pieces of it to several charities. Some of the investments didn't do well, and she lost a lot of the money. She moved what was left into a savings account and would be able to live frugally for the rest of her life.

She handed me a letter. "This came in yesterday's mail."

According to the letter, her mortgage was now due, and she was required to begin making monthly payments. In the event she did not, a foreclosure action would be filed and she would lose her house.

I shook my head. "This doesn't sound like a reverse mortgage. Have you got the paperwork you signed?"

She handed me a file folder. I began to look through the documents, my heart dropping a little with each page. She'd been swindled. All the correspondence from the mortgage broker discussed a traditional reverse mortgage, but the documents themselves provided for a standard mortgage with an extremely high interest rate. The payments would be delayed for one year, but then the loan would have to be repaid over a period of ten years with an interest rate of 12 percent. I knew that standard mortgage rates were running about 6 percent for thirty years, and less for a shorter time period.

I raised my head. "You've been taken. Let me see what I can do. May I take these with me?"

"Certainly. Thanks, Matt. Keep track of your time and I'll pay you."

CHAPTER FIVE

Predators stalk the elderly and infirm, targeting the least resistant, not unlike the lionesses who roam the African veldt in search of food. The lioness does it for survival, the human predator because he's a lazy son of a bitch without a conscience. In Florida, where there are more elderly people, there are more predators trying for the easy buck. I had the name and address of this particular predator, and I would have his ass. I made an appointment for the next morning to discuss a reverse mortgage, and went to see him in downtown Sarasota.

His office was in a high-rise building overlooking Sarasota Bay and New Pass, the view reaching to the horizon. He had a small office, no receptionist, no outer office, just a door with his company's name, Managed Investments, discretely etched on the glass. I knocked and went in.

A man of about thirty rose from behind the desk. He was five ten, two hundred pounds, with a hard belly hanging out of his unbuttoned coat. He wore a white shirt, green tie, and blue pinstriped suit. He had a big head, blond hair, an open Irish face set off by a nose that was too long, and a toothy smile. His had his hand out. I shook it.

"You must be Matt Royal. I'm Jim Corrigan. I must say you don't look old enough for a reverse mortgage. You have to be at least sixty-two to qualify."

I wasn't old enough to qualify. Not even close. They say that youth is fleeting and I can attest to the fact that much of my youth has fled. I'm not yet a member of the senior citizen crowd and although I know the days of gray hair and arthritic aches are relentlessly chasing me, I resist them mightily. I was a bit insulted that the guy even thought I would be interested in a reverse mortgage.

"I don't want a mortgage," I said. "I want you to release Rose Peters's mortgage and remove the lien from the public records."

He looked puzzled. "Why would I do that?"

"Because you swindled her, and I'm going to sue the pants off you if you don't fix this thing."

He chuckled. "Lawyers cost a lot of money, Mr. Royal."

I reached over the desk and laid one of my business cards on his blotter, the one that identified me as a lawyer. "They do, Mr. Corrigan. But Mrs. Peters is a friend of mine, and I'm not going to charge her a dime."

"Wait a minute, Mr. Royal. I couldn't do anything about that mortgage if I wanted to. It was sold on the secondary market. I don't have any way to change the terms."

"You can pay it off then."

"No way. The old broad got the money. She owes it."

"Let me put it this way, Mr. Corrigan. If you haven't paid off that mortgage and released Rose from all obligations by the end of business tomorrow, I'll be filing suit. I'll also have a little discussion with the state attorney in this circuit, who, I might add, is a close friend of mine. I imagine that the U.S. Attorney would also be interested in mail fraud charges. You did use the U.S. mail now, didn't you Mr. Corrigan?"

"Whoa. I don't want any trouble."

"You square things with Mrs. Peters's house, and you won't hear anything else from me."

The idiot blustered a bit more, but in the end he agreed to pay off the mortgage. The next day, I checked with the clerk of court in Manatee County, where Rose's house was located, and found that a satisfaction of mortgage had been filed at the opening of business that day. The house was once again free and clear.

Then I called the state attorney for the Twelfth Judicial Circuit, a man I'd never met. I identified myself and explained Corrigan's scheme. The law was interested and I promised to drop the documents off the next day. I'd lied about knowing the state attorney, but I'd kept my promise. Corrigan never heard from me again. However, he did hear from the police and the postal inspectors, and he was now doing five to eight years in state prison and would face another five years in a federal pen when his state time was up.

Rose insisted on paying me for my help, and I insisted on not accepting anything. Life moved on, the rhythms of the key unbroken by the events surrounding Corrigan. I read in the newspaper that a number of elderly people who had been swindled by Corrigan got their money back.

CHAPTER SIX

Over the next year, I would see Rose occasionally at the Market. Once or twice we shared a cup of coffee and enjoyed each other's company. Then one day I heard that Rose had died in her sleep. A neighbor noticed that her morning paper was still in the driveway at noon, and went to check on her. She'd apparently had a heart attack and died peacefully.

We had a memorial service for her at Tiny's. It was the island way of mourning our lost ones. Rose would have enjoyed seeing so many friends. There were a lot of laughs and a few tears, and then we put her away, back in the memory banks with all the others we'd lost over the years. Longboat Key has a large population of elderly people. Death is a regular visitor, and while we never get used to losing one of the good ones, we have learned to live with the losses.

A few days later, I got a call from a lawyer in Bradenton whom I knew casually. "Matt, I'm the personal representative of Rose Peters's estate. She left all her cash to various charities and she left her house to you."

"To me?" I was dumbfounded. "That doesn't make sense."

"She also left a letter for you."

"Can you read it to me?"

"Sure. 'Dear Matt, I'm sure you'll be shocked at the news that I've left my house to you. But I wouldn't have the house if it weren't for you, and I have no family to leave it to. You were a friend of my dear Ed and he always spoke so highly of you. When I needed help, you didn't hesitate. You were there in a jiffy and you wouldn't accept any payment, and you saved my home.

'Take good care of the house. It was a place full of love during the twenty years Ed and I lived there. Treat it kindly and think of us some-times. Thanks for being my friend. Love, Rose.' "

"What can I say?"

"Nothing, Matt. She wanted you to have this place. Enjoy it."

CHAPTER SEVEN

I parked the Explorer and entered the Market by the door next to the newspaper racks. Bill Lester was sitting at a table, sipping from a cup of coffee. He waved me over.

"Enjoy your trip?" he asked as I walked up.

"I sure did. Why the urgent summons?"

"Let me get a refill. You want one?"

I nodded. He went to the counter and filled two Styrofoam cups with the black liquid, brought them back to the table, and took a chair. "Somebody took a shot at Logan today. Downtown."

Alarm spread through my body. Logan was my best friend on the island, a man who'd retired as an executive in the financial services industry and moved to our key. "Is he okay?"

"Yeah. The slug got stopped by a book he had in the inside pocket of his windbreaker. He's just bruised up a little."

"Bill, talk to me. Who shot him? Why?"

"We don't know. No arrests, no suspects. The slug was from a rifle, fired from a long way off. It was about out of steam when it hit Logan. Good shot, but I don't think it was a professional hit. A pro would have known that the distance was too much. Logan got lucky."

"Is he in the hospital?"

"No. I figured if somebody was after him and realized he wasn't dead, he might not be safe in a hospital. We've got him in a hotel."

"Is that necessary?"

"There's something else. Last night a security guard at Logan's condo complex saw two men on the property. He asked them to identify themselves and one of them pulled a pistol. The guard turned and ran before the man could shoot him. He called for backup from the Longboat Key Police, but by the time the cops got there, the men were gone."

"You think there's a connection?"

"Don't know, but I think I'd rather have him safe in a hotel than at his condo."

"What was Logan doing downtown? Somebody had to have set that up."

"Logan moved onto Bill Gallagher's boat at Marina Jack for a couple of nights. He had some kind of leak in his condo unit and the carpets are wet. He's got people in there drying them out with those big fans and heaters." Lester told me how the meeting had been set up. "Marie did not call our dispatcher. Somebody knew enough about Logan to know about Marie and that if she called I'd meet him for lunch. I just don't know why they wanted me there."

"Maybe you were part of the setup somehow. What did the dispatcher say Marie told him about where you were to meet Logan?"

"I was supposed to sit outside and wait for him. That was it."

"If the shooter was trying to lure Logan into a kill zone, he might have had to place you so that Logan would come toward you. If you hadn't been visible, Logan may have come another way, or ducked into the restaurant from the side and wouldn't have been where the shooter needed him to be to get his shot."

"That's as good a theory as any. I doubt we'll ever know for sure."

"Why would anybody be after Logan?"

"We don't know. Logan doesn't know of anybody who would want to kill him, and we haven't found any evidence to help us."

"Did you find out where the shot came from?"

"Yes, but there was nothing there. The shooter was on the rooftop of an unsecured building. The door to the roof was not locked, so anybody could have gone up there. We didn't find the first piece of physical evidence."

"Where's Logan now?"

"He's in a hotel out on I-75. We'll move him into a safe house as soon as we can get it set up. In the meantime, a Sarasota County deputy is with him."

"Can I see him?"

"I don't think that's a good idea. I'm concerned that whoever is after Logan might be after you as well. If they follow you to Logan, we could have a bad situation on our hands."

"Come on, Bill. Who'd want to kill me?"

"I can think of a few people. You've been in some scrapes with some pretty bad folks."

"Yeah, but I don't think any of them are still alive."

"Maybe not, but you need to be careful. I want your permission to run an electronic sweep on your house. The reason I didn't talk to you on the phone is that your house might be bugged."

"Bugged? What are you talking about?"

"One of my patrolmen saw a couple of men in front of your house last night, just after dark. He didn't think much about it. They were walking away from your front door, and my cop didn't know you were out of town. He'd been on vacation himself until yesterday. Anyway, the men he saw matched the description of the ones at Logan's."

"Why would you think they planted a bug? They might have been Jehovah's Witnesses or salesmen or something."

"We found a small box near where the men at Logan's scared the shit out of the security guard. It contained a listening device. I don't know if it even belonged to the same guys, but I can't imagine where else something like that would have come from. If they were planning to bug Logan, they may have done the same thing to you."

"It won't hurt to find out. Jessica's here and I don't want to alarm her. I also don't want to sleep in a bugged house. Can you have your whiz kids debug my place while I take Jess to dinner tonight?"

"Not a problem, but why don't you wait until tomorrow to go see Logan?"

I agreed.

"There's something else," said Bill. "I'm assigning my new detective to the case."

"New detective? What happened to Martin Sharkey?"

"I promoted him. He's the new deputy chief."

"Who'd you promote to detective?"

"I didn't. I hired from outside."

"Name?"

"J.D. Duncan."

"Where'd you get him?"

"Her."

"What?"

"Her. J.D. is a woman. Jennifer Diane Duncan. Never call her Jennifer or Diane."

"You hired a woman detective? Isn't that taking affirmative action a little far?"

"She has a degree in criminology from Florida International and was with Miami-Dade PD for fifteen years, ten of those as a detective. She worked vice and narcotics, a lot of the time undercover. Her last assignment was second in command of the homicide division. She also owns a black belt in one of those Eastern martial arts."

I blew out a breath. "Forget the affirmative action comment. She sounds way too good to be on this island."

He gave me an exasperated look and slowly raised his middle finger in my direction. "When her parents died, she inherited a condo on the key. She wanted to move here, get out of the big city. So I hired her."

"When do I meet her?"

"Soon."

CHAPTER EIGHT

It was late. The streets of Belleville were dark and quiet, a small town where people worked hard all day and went to bed early. Lieutenant Charlie Foreman stood on the sidewalk in front of the Swamp Rat Bar, listening to the sounds of people talking, laughing, enjoying themselves. It was the only place open in the whole town, and it didn't shut down until the last drinker left or 2:00 a.m. rolled around, whichever came first.

Foreman knew this town and he knew its people. He'd grown up in Belleville, gone to college over in Miami, and then to the Police Academy up in Orlando. He'd joined the Collier County Sheriff's Department twenty years before, patrolling the back roads of a county that stretched well into the Everglades. He'd chased illegal poachers, moonshiners, drug addicts, and those who made their living purveying drugs to the unwary or the duped. He'd busted farmers growing marijuana, fishermen importing pot from mother ships out in the Gulf, crabbers trapping out of season, and a few gun-toting miscreants who came into his county to do harm to its citizens.

Charlie was a creature of Belleville, and through all his years in law enforcement, he'd never gotten the hardscrabble little town out of his system. He had worked hard and achieved success. He rose through the ranks until he made lieutenant. One day the sheriff called him into his office and offered him the job as resident deputy in Belleville. Charlie grabbed the opportunity and moved his wife to the little town hard by the swamp. Their only son was in college in Gainesville, so it was just the two of them.

Belleville had some years before disbanded its small and unprofessional police force. The town contracted with the sheriff to provide law enforcement. The contract called for a resident deputy who would be the de facto chief of police. He would be supported by other deputies who patrolled the vast area surrounding the isolated village. It was a good fit for Charlie Foreman and he planned to finish out his career right here, in the place where his life had begun.

His tenure as resident deputy had been smooth. There were the occasional fistfights, domestic disturbances, juvenile pranks, public drunks, speeders, and other miscellaneous misdemeanors. Once, there had been a hold up at the convenience store on the edge of town, out by the Tamiami Trail, and the perps were still at large.

There had never been a murder, not during Charlie's time. In fact the last murder recorded in Belleville had happened when Foreman was a boy. One of the sugar cane cutters who lived in the camp on the edge of town had hacked up his girlfriend with a machete. He stayed with the body until the police came and then tried to slash the officer with the same machete he'd used to kill his girlfriend. The cop shot him dead. Case closed.

Charlie was as surprised as anybody when the town's only lawyer was shot to death in a drive-by shooting that afternoon. It made no sense. Jason Blakemoore was essentially a harmless fellow, not too bright and kind of lazy, but he certainly wasn't the type to generate the kind of animosity it would take for someone to kill him.

Was it random? Big cities were used to that kind of violence, but Charlie didn't think it had come to his town. Yet, gratuitous murder was not uncommon in other parts of Florida. Gang novitiates in Miami killed in order to earn their membership, show their manhood, prove their psychopathology. Maybe the big city law was clamping down on the gangs, putting a damper on their murderous impulses. Maybe the little bastards were being herded into the small towns where the authorities weren't ready for them, not expecting city-bred violence to taint the essential peacefulness of isolated villages.

Foreman was a big man, standing six foot four and weighing 230 pounds. He was in his mid-forties, with dark hair going to gray at the temples. His face bore the remains of a teenaged bout with acne, his mustache clipped short and shot with gray. There was no fat on him, a testament to his wife's near obsession with healthy foods and his routine of morning exercises. He was dressed in jeans, a powder blue short-sleeved button-down sports shirt. A nine-millimeter Glock was in a holster on his belt. His usual attire. He didn't need a badge or a uniform. Everybody in town knew him and knew what he was. A cop.

He took a deep breath, knowing that the next few minutes were going to be difficult. He had to talk to the late night drinkers about what they'd seen that afternoon. They wouldn't know much, and what they knew had by now been confused with what they had heard or wanted to believe or simply made up in their booze-addled brains.

The sheriff's lab boys were good. They'd combed the area and found almost no evidence. Jason had been killed by a twelve-gauge shotgun and had died almost instantly. That's all they knew. Other deputies had canvassed the area, taking statements from the witnesses. All they'd gleaned from this was that the car driven by the shooters was black or gray or dark green, that there were two or three or four people in the car, that it was a Mercedes or a Lexus or a Chevrolet. In other words, they had nothing.

Charlie hoped that somebody in the bar would know something, and because Charlie was one of them, would tell him things they wouldn't tell the other deputies. He knew these men, most of them unemployed or underemployed. They picked up odd jobs when they could, working the truck farms and fish camps, crewing on the commercial boats out of Everglades City, sometimes moving on for a few months or years, looking for work out of state, supporting their meager lives, ashamed to be on the dole, not willing to accept the government's charity. They were hard men, proud in their way, perhaps an anachronism in this day of federal and state largesse. And they were mostly honest, although some of them couldn't understand why providing a commodity, like marijuana, to people who wanted it could constitute a crime. Some of them had done prison time for hauling the bales in from the Gulf, but they'd not taken to the prison culture. They didn't consider themselves criminals, although they understood that the law took a dim view of some of their activities. They knew that going in, and figured they'd gambled and lost. They'd pay the price up at Raiford or over at Glades Correctional Institution, and then get on with their lives.

No matter where they went, prison or to another state for work, they always found their way back to Belleville. They had felt the same magnetic pull home that Charlie Foreman had. Maybe they weren't that different from the great sea turtles that came year after year to lay their eggs on the same small piece of beach on which they'd hatched. Another deep breath, and he walked through the front door into the fanciful gaiety of a bar with patrons deep into the evening, their brains already pickled to one degree or another.

"Hey, Charlie," roared one of the men at the bar. Others turned to look at the deputy and joined the chorus of greetings, smiling, laughing, as if Charlie were the bringer of good cheer.

SUNDAY

CHAPTER NINE

I pulled into the parking lot of a downscale chain hotel next to an off-ramp of I-75, out east of town. I'd driven Jessica to the Tampa airport, hugged her goodbye, and watched her board the plane to Atlanta, the first leg of her trip to Paris. I headed south toward Sarasota, nursing a sense of relief I didn't want to feel.

We'd had a quiet evening, dining at a small Italian restaurant near a shopping mall on Tamiami Trail. I told her about the attempts on Logan's life. She was concerned, but didn't know what to do or say. Our conversation became awkward, the verbal meanderings of accidental lovers who had shared a fantasy and were now moving inexorably toward reality.

We'd met in Europe in the fall, and she'd visited her friends Patti and Russ Coit on Longboat Key at Christmas. We'd become lovers, or at least we'd made love, while she was enjoying the holidays. She'd accepted my invitation to come back in the spring. Here we were, our trip finished, and she was off to France, and her actual life. I think we were both a little relieved. It'd been fun, but neither of us was cut out for a long-term relationship, especially an intercontinental one.

Our last night together was sedate. We made love, but it seemed more like an obligatory denouement after our explosive week on the water. I hoped Bill Lester had removed the bugs from my bedroom. I didn't want his guys thinking this was my best effort.

We drove to the airport in the early afternoon, making small talk, interspersed with silences that filled the car. We planned to keep in touch, to see each other again. I think, though, that we both knew that wouldn't happen. We'd put the past week back into that lockbox of memories that we all have, those bits of joy that we occasionally examine and wonder briefly why we didn't make more of them.

I went directly to Logan's room and knocked. Marie Phillips opened the door. She was wearing shorts, a sleeveless blouse, and was barefoot. She was tall, blonde, and had a ready smile, a rangy body, and a warmth of character that drew men in like the tentacles of a friendly octopus. She was Logan's girl.

"I'm glad you're back," she said, as she hugged me. I looked over her shoulder to see Logan lying on the bed, eyes glued to a ball game on the flat-screen TV sitting atop a cabinet, his beloved Red Sox playing an exhibition game. He was wearing nothing but shorts and I could see a large bruise in the middle of his chest. He was five feet eight inches tall, gray hair turning to bald, maybe ten pounds overweight, a face that radiated good cheer and friendliness, a smile that reminded you of his Irish genes, a voice that carried the accents of his native Massachusetts.

" 'Bout time you got here," he said, never taking his eyes off the game.

"I've missed you, too, buddy."

Two double beds took up most of the room. There was an easy chair in the corner with an ottoman tucked in front. An open suitcase lay on a stand under the window overlooking the interstate.

"Palatial outpost you have here," I said.

"I asked for a suite at the Ritz-Carlton and Sarasota PD offered me a cell at the county lockup. We compromised on this."

"What happened?"

"I got shot."

"Yeah. Who'd you piss off?"

"Nobody that I can think of. Except Ham Jones. I told him the Gators are going to suck this year."

Ham was a mutual friend, a local restaurateur who loved his wife, Lorraine, his dog, Gator, and the University of Florida football team, not necessarily in that order. He wouldn't hurt a fly, but I made it a point to never say anything negative about Gator football. Logan had no such restraints after a few Dewars.

I laughed. "Tell me what happened."

"I don't know, Kemo Sabe. Somebody's taking shots at me. I don't know who or why. You got any ideas?"

A knock on the door interrupted us. Marie went to the door, opened it to the length of the security chain and said, "Yes?"

"Maintenance, ma'am. We've got a leak in the bathroom above you. I need to check your bathroom for any problems."

Marie shut the door and undid the security chain, opened it wide and said, "Come in."

A man entered the room. He looked around, holding his tool kit at his side, his eyes scanning the room. He had an equipment belt around his waist, a leather one that maintenance men wear, screwdrivers and wrenches sticking out of the pouches. He reached into it and pulled out a pistol. He pointed it at my chest, and said, "Hello, Mr. Royal."

CHAPTER TEN

The man was not tall, about five feet eight, and slender. He had the wiry look of a runner, or of someone who doesn't get enough to eat. His skin was dark, tanned to almost brown by the relentless sun bouncing off water. His hands were scarred, thick with calluses, nails bitten into the quick, some yellowed by nicotine. He had a shock of sandy hair falling toward a face that seemed a little off center. His nose, broken sometime in the past, leaned to the right, his mouth, when he spoke, curled on the left showing large yellow teeth, his lips cracked by the sun, his eyes, one smaller than the other, were the deep blue of frozen seawater, and as cold. A small dollop of spittle collected at the ends of his lips.

"I didn't get your name," I said.

He grunted. "Didn't give it."

Snappy comeback, I thought. "What do you want?"

"You need to come with me, Mr. Royal."

"Why would I do that?"

"Because I'll shoot you if you don't."

"Okay. Where do you want me to go with you?"

"Some guys I know want to talk to you."

"About what?"

"They didn't tell me."

"How did you find me?"

"Wasn't hard. I followed you when you left your house. Didn't know you were going to take me on a ride through Tampa."

"What about these other people?" I gestured toward Logan and Marie.

"Don't know them and don't care. They just told me to bring you."

I knew the pistol he was holding on me. I had one just like it. Unfortunately, mine was in my house. The gun was a Walther PPK .380 ACP that weighed little more than a pound. He was holding it in his right hand, and I could see the safety lever on the left side of the gun just above the trigger. The safety was still on. Either he didn't know much about guns, or in his excitement he'd simply forgotten to take the safety off.

I took a step toward him. He backed up, raising the gun. I took another step. He backed into the closed door, his gun pointed at me. I took another step and he tried to squeeze the trigger. I reached out, grabbed his wrist, twisted it hard while grasping the pistol with my other hand. He let go, crumpled to the floor, put his head in his hands and sobbed.

I was stunned. I sat on the bed, the gun pointed at the sandy-haired man, the safety off. Logan and Marie were quiet. I said, "He forgot to take the safety off."

I leaned down to the assailant. "This isn't your regular job, is it?"

"No."

"Who are you?"

"Jube Smith."

"You're a commercial fisherman." It wasn't a question.

"Yes."

"Cortez?"

"Yeah. But there ain't much running out of Cortez these days."

Cortez was an old fishing village that sprawled across either side of Cortez Road at the foot of the bridge leading from the mainland to Anna Maria Island. It had once been a prosperous place inhabited by hard-working men and women who made their livings from the sea. Changing times, new fishery regulations, and farm-grown fish were slowly killing off the village. Many of the fish houses had disappeared, victims of a failing economy, and the boats had moved elsewhere or were simply left to rot at their anchorages, their usefulness ended with the demise of the ancient fishing culture that had sustained this part of Florida for generations.

"Who hired you?" I asked.

"I don't know. Some guy in a bar gave me a hundred bucks and told me there was nine hundred more if I brought you to him. Never said his name."

"What bar?"

"Lil's. The one what used to be called Hutch's."

"On Cortez Road?"

"Yeah."

"I thought that was closed."

"The county took the property from some guy who got busted and then sold it to Lil."

"Describe the guy."

"Lil? She's a woman."

"I mean the guy who hired you to come after me."

"I dunno. Tall, taller than you, early thirties maybe, shaved head, two hundred pounds or so."

"Have you ever seen him before?"

"No."

"Why did he pick you to do his job?"

"I dunno. We talked at the bar for a while. I told him I was looking for work."

"Where were you supposed to take me?"

"To my house. He said he'd come by this evening to see if I had you."

"How were you to contact this guy?"

"I wasn't. He'd come to me."

"Where'd you get the gun?"

"He gave it to me."

"What in the world would make you do something like this?" I asked.

"I haven't worked in six months, and my wife's got cancer. I need the money."

"Do you know Captain Cobol, runs the *Mary T* out of Cortez?"

"I know who he is."

"All right. Get your sorry ass out of here," I said. "You tell whoever sent you to come himself next time. I'd like to meet him. I'll hold onto his gun for him."

"You're letting me go?"

"Go see Captain Cobol. Tell him I sent you. He may have some work for you."

The man rose slowly, his feet under him, sliding his back up the wall where he had been huddling, his hands in front, palms up.

"Don't let me see you again," I said.

"No, sir. Thank you, Mr. Royal. I won't forget this."

He turned, opened the door, and was gone.

CHAPTER ELEVEN

Charlie Foreman sat at the desk in Jason Blakemoore's office, a stack of files on either side of the scarred blotter. He'd been going over them, one by one, looking for a thread, a clue, something to go on. The men and women at the Swamp Rat Bar the night before had nothing to give him. No one saw the shooting. They heard the blast of the shotgun and some of them had run outside to see what the noise was all about. A few of these saw a retreating car, but their description matched those given to the deputies who had canvassed earlier. Everybody had seen something different.

There'd been a cabinet full of files, some of them going back five or six years. The file drawers were open, the files dumped haphazardly. The desk drawers had been pulled out, emptied into the growing pile of litter spreading across the floor.

He'd been in Jason's office all morning, a space adorned with an ancient shag carpet, the color faded into an indeterminate mess of spilled coffee, sodas, and God knows what else. The walls were covered with a walnut veneer that had been fashionable thirty years before. His diplomas from the University of Florida hung from nails, their heads rusty. Pictures of Jason in the football uniform of the local high school and the university were hung from the other walls. The single window that looked over the Dumpster in back by the small parking lot was filthy, dust and bird droppings partially obscuring the view, such as it was. Hot air and the smell of garbage wafted through a broken pane in the window.

Charlie had checked the office the day before, soon after he'd identified the dead man across the street from the Swamp Rat Bar as Jason. He'd called for the coroner and his meat wagon. He'd retrieved a rain slicker from the trunk of his car and covered the body, taking only Jason's key ring from the pocket of his trousers. As soon as one of the road deputies arrived, Charlie walked over to the office. Everything was in order. He looked around quickly, locked the door and returned to await the coroner and the crime-scene technicians.

When he'd returned to the office early the morning after Jason's death, Charlie was surprised to find the place in a mess. Somebody had been there during the evening, probably while Charlie was in the bar, drinking beer, schmoozing the locals, looking for a lead. That lead must have come in through the window, waltzed into Jason's office and turned it upside-down. He was looking for something. That was obvious. But what?

Charlie set about putting the files in some order. He was sure he hadn't gotten every piece of paper where it belonged, but he'd look at everything. Most of the paper was tacked into the file with Acco clips, but there were still a lot of loose pages spread around the office.

The lawyer never discarded anything. It had been a poor practice, and Blakemoore had never hired a secretary. That was clear from the mess in the files, notes without order, pleadings and letters stuffed without thought to chronology, an occasional bill marked paid, many apparently still owing.

Charlie had taken a break for lunch, ate a hamburger at the small café down the street. It hadn't set well on his stomach and the onions had given him heartburn. He popped another Rolaids and continued to read. He still had a large pile to dig through. He scanned one and put it in the stack that he'd finished. Most were thin files, a testament to the meanness of a law practice in this one-lawyer town.

Charlie was tired and had decided to call it a day. It was mid-afternoon and with the exception of the lunch break, he'd been closeted in this dim office all day. He pulled a final file from the stack, glanced at the name. Abraham Osceola. *Must be one of the Indians from the reservation,* he thought. Another misdemeanor of some sort, traffic stop, public drunkenness, something like that.

He opened the file. There was one piece of paper, a yellow lined sheet from a legal pad, paper clipped to the edge of the file. The client's name was written at the top and a date, five days before, a Wednesday. The notes didn't mean much. They read:

> Moultrie Creek Treaty
> Large Res.
> Black Sem.
> Mineral rights
> Codicil?
> Matt Royal, Longboat Key

Nothing else. It didn't mean anything to Charlie. He had no idea who Matt Royal was and wasn't even sure where Longboat Key was. Somewhere down in the Keys, he figured, but he could never keep those little islands straight. Maybe Royal would know something. He picked up the phone, dialed 411, and got the information operator for Longboat Key. She gave him a number with a 941 area code. That surprised Charlie. The Keys were in the 305 area code; 941 was up in the Sarasota area. He'd check out the map when he got home and find out just where the hell Longboat Key was. When he had a little more information, he'd call Royal, see if he knew anything.

Charlie rubbed his face, stretched, felt the need for a beer. He surveyed the office. Still a mess. He'd come back tomorrow. Finish looking at all the paper. He didn't expect much, but he had to start somewhere.

He pulled the lone sheet of paper from the Osceola file, folded it, tucked it into his shirt pocket, turned out the lights, locked the office, and walked toward the town's lone bar.

CHAPTER TWELVE

Logan hadn't moved. He was still lying on the bed, a quizzical look on his face. "What the hell was that all about?" he asked.

"Guy looking for a job," I said.

"Huh. Messy way to do it. He could've gotten killed."

Marie, who had sat on the side of the bed when Jube appeared with his gun, was pale and a little shaky. "Matt, that guy could've killed you."

"Not with the safety on," I said.

"Why did you let him go?" Marie asked. "Shouldn't we call the police?"

Sometimes a load of crap falls on a guy's head and no matter what he does he can't get out from under it. He gets sick for a week and can't work. He gets fired and can't find another job. It's a dreary progression, a downhill spiral. His life is tenuous at best, living from payday to payday. Miss one paycheck and he never catches up. His wife gets sick and the medical bills roll in like a calamitous tide, inexorable in their crushing power. He has no money, can't pay, so the wife doesn't get the medicine that takes the edge off the pain. There's no safety net. No family, friends tapped out. Hopelessness rides his shoulders. Desperation hangs like a miasma, thick, impenetrable, unyielding, and ultimately deadly. So he shows up in a hotel with a borrowed pistol trying to make enough to cover the next pharmacy bill.

I shook my head. "I don't think cops are necessary. He didn't seem to recognize Logan, and I believed him about his wife being sick. He's just a guy at the end of his rope. Sometimes all a person like that needs is a chance. I heard Nestor Cobol was looking for another hand. Maybe that'll work out."

"Matt," Logan said, "what the hell is going on around here? Why would somebody take a shot at me and then come after you?"

"Who knows," I said. "I don't like it."

"Are the two connected?" asked Marie.

"They have to be," I said. "I can't imagine that different people are after us. They think Logan's dead and I've been gone. I'm back and they came looking for me. It's got to be the same people."

My cell phone rang. I looked at the caller ID. Bill Lester. I answered.

"Matt, where are you?"

"I'm in Logan's palatial hotel suite. You guys aren't spending a lot of money on this."

"It's better than he deserves."

"You're probably right."

"I just got a call from Sarasota PD. They've got a guy down at Sarasota Memorial they think you might know."

"Who is he?"

"Don't know. He had a piece of paper in his pocket with your name and address written on it. Logan's, too. No ID. Somebody hit him on the head with something hard. Tossed his hotel room. He's still in a coma."

"Where'd they find him?"

"He was in one of those old motels over on the North Trail. Checked in with a false name. Paid cash. Somebody heard a commotion, called the manager, and they found him in his room."

"Nothing else?"

"Nope. But he might be from the Caribbean."

"Why do they think that?" I asked.

"The woman who owns the motel said he spoke English with an island accent."

"White or black?"

"He's a black man."

"What name did he use to check in?"

"Abraham Royal. Any relation?"

"No. But I might know him," I said.

"One of my guys was on routine patrol Friday night and found a black man at the front door of Logan's condo building. That door has a code that you need to punch to get in. The guy didn't have the code and wouldn't or couldn't give us a good reason for being there. He identified himself as Abraham Osceola and said he had come to the key looking for you. You weren't here and somebody told him to ask Logan when you'd be back.

"He said something that didn't make a lot of sense. He wanted you to help him with some kind of big money deal. One of my officers drove him across the bridges to Cortez and let him out. We had no reason to hold him. Now I wonder. Do you know this Osceola guy?"

I paused for a beat. "I met him once. Last year, down in the Keys. Do you think there's a connection between Abraham and the guys gunning for Logan?"

"I don't know, but I'm figuring the guy in the hospital must be the same Abraham who was at Logan's"

"He probably is. But I can't imagine why anyone would try to kill him."

"What about the big money deal he mentioned to my officer?"

"Abraham isn't the kind of person to get into big deals. Maybe he was just putting your guy on for some reason."

"Could be. The officer who took the black man from Logan's is on his way to the hospital to see if he can identify the guy. You'd better get over there too. Check in with a Detective Kintz in the ER."

CHAPTER THIRTEEN

The scent of orange blossoms floated on the soft spring air, the night closer now, a time for owls and other predators, of human garbage who visit their sickness on the unsuspecting, who stalk the innocent and the unwary. The old house sat deep in the grove, hidden from the roads that traversed the area. It had a tin roof, rusted by years of summer downpours, and a sagging front porch that ran the width of the house. The windows were large, built to catch the minimal breeze that stirred the heat of a Florida summer. A crescent moon hung high in the sky amid a million pinpoints of light, suns for other solar systems, emitting energy that took thousands of years to reach this dark spot on a ragged peninsula hanging from the bottom of the continent.

The house smelled of age and decay and ancient family quarrels. The bare boards of the floor had not seen wax in a generation and they creaked with every step. A single bulb, suspended from the ceiling by a braided electric cord, cast its frugal light over the figure of a man hunched at a computer terminal. He was in his fifties, his thinning gray hair at odds with his head. He was paunchy and wore the pallor of a man too long away from the sun. His face hadn't seen a razor in several days, the stubble gray and itchy. He wore a pair of faded jeans and a plaid shirt found in the mission box at a local church. He was barefoot, his toenails hardened and yellow, his soles gray with callouses.

He sat alone in the night, wandering the Internet, trolling for bits of information, for customers and victims. He stared at the monitor, occasionally scratching his face or stroking the keyboard. The stale odor of his unwashed body permeated the room, vying with the smells of fried food, beer, and whiskey. A box with the logo of a local fried chicken chain rested on the floor beside his chair, bones from several meals overflowing the container.

A cell phone sat on the table next to the keyboard. It rang. The man picked it up, looked at it, opened it, answered. "Yeah?"

The voice on the other end was raspy and ancient. "You get Royal?"

"Not yet."

The voice came again, breathless, wheezy, deep southern accent. "I'm not paying you to sit there with your thumb up your ass."

"I'm working on it."

"What happened today? I thought you were going to bring him in."

"My subcontractor fucked up. Sent in an amateur."

"What about yesterday? Can't you do anything right?"

"It was a long shot. I'm told we had the best marksman money can buy."

"Hamilton's still alive."

"Yeah, but we went through his apartment last night. No documents. My people are going to grab Royal tomorrow."

"Forget Royal. Just kill him. Hamilton, too."

"Okay."

"Get your ass in gear, boy. You hear me?"

"I hear you."

"I'll be in touch." The phone went dead.

"Pissant," muttered the man at the computer. He lay the phone down and returned to his keyboard.

CHAPTER FOURTEEN

Night had fallen by the time I reached Sarasota Memorial Hospital. The buildings of the campus were awash in the light pouring from every window. I parked in a lot near the emergency room. A red neon sign above the entrance told me where I was. An ambulance in the driveway, its stern against the loading dock, rear doors open. Quiet now, its run finished, its patient delivered. The engine ticked as I walked by, the sound of a cooling motor, tired from its dash to the hospital.

I'd been told to meet a Sarasota detective in the emergency room waiting area. When I walked through the automatic doors, I saw a man in a suit standing at the counter, chatting idly with the woman who sat at a computer. I walked over. "I'm looking for Detective Kintz," I said.

The man turned to me. "Mr. Royal? I'm John Kintz."

We shook hands. "I appreciate your coming down," he said. "I'll get us a conference room. A little privacy, you know. Have a seat and I'll be right with you."

I had one of those fleeting moments of déjà vu, or something like it, a swelling of near recognition of the man, but not quite. He was a stranger, a man I'd never seen, as far as I knew. Yet my subconscious was clanging alarms, trying to tell me something that my conscious brain needed to know. Then recognition dawned. I didn't know the man, but he looked uncannily like Bill Lester, the Longboat Key chief of police.

The detective disappeared through another set of doors that led into the bowels of the hospital. I took a seat. There were several others in the waiting area, some trying to nap, their heads against the backs of the uncomfortable chairs. They were waiting. Waiting for news of loved ones, those who had disappeared into the maw of the ER, the sick or injured friends or relatives. It was a feeling of powerlessness, of impotency and fear, and of dread and hope.

I remembered how scared I was when I was thirteen and my mother had to go to Orlando to the hospital for what we thought was a brain tumor. I prayed a lot that summer. I thought about this as I sat in the cheerless waiting area in Sarasota. Everything was gray: carpet, furniture, the waiting patients. A soap opera played on the TV in the corner. A map of the world decorated one wall. A blonde woman with dark roots, late middle age, wearing a gray dress, and packing an extra thirty pounds, dozed on one of the chairs. Her husband, a dark Hispanic of indeterminate age, came by now and then to hug and kiss her, worry etched on his face.

The detective returned in ten minutes, apologized for keeping me waiting. I followed him through the interior doors, down a hall, and into a small conference room. A table, one end stacked high with journals and other loose papers, took up most of the room. A large portrait of a pretty blonde lady with a pronounced widow's peak, wearing a pink blouse and white skirt, stared from the wall. A small bronze plaque dedicating the room to the woman was affixed to the frame. I wondered who had loved her and when and where and how she had come to have this poor space named for her.

"Do you know Chief Lester out on Longboat?" I asked the detective.

He laughed. "Oh, sure. People get us mixed up all the time. He called to tell me you were coming. Said you were old friends."

"Yeah."

The detective gestured me to a seat. He sat across from me and pulled an eight by ten photograph from the file he carried. It showed a black man lying in a bed, an IV in his arm, an oxygen cannula affixed to his nostrils, his eyes closed as if sleeping. "Do you know this man?"

"Yes. His name's Abraham Osceola. He's a Seminole Indian."

"Mr. Royal, this man is black and he apparently has an island accent."

"Mr. Osceola is one of the Black Seminoles who left Florida in the nineteenth century and went to the Bahamas."

"I don't understand."

"It's kind of complicated and not something you read about in the history books. During the eighteenth and nineteenth centuries a number of escaped slaves joined the Seminoles in Florida. They lived among the Indians and intermarried. The children of those marriages were part of the tribe and were considered Seminoles. At the end of the First Seminole War, and again after the Second Seminole War, many of the Indians' black relatives fled in canoes to Andros Island in the Bahamas, where slavery had been outlawed. Their descendants are still there, and in most ways are indistinguishable from the other Bahamians."

"Does this man live in the Bahamas?"

"I think he lives in Key West."

"How do you know him?" the detective asked.

"I met him briefly in the Keys last year. I don't really know him or anything about him."

"Why would he have your name and your buddy's name in his pocket?"

"I don't know. Hamilton is my best friend."

"Did you know that Osceola was in Sarasota?"

"No."

"Could he have come to see you?"

"I suppose. He told the Longboat police that he had come looking for me to help him with a deal. But I don't know why he would."

"How did you meet him?"

"I was in a boat off Key West, and he was in a kayak. We chatted for a while and he told me his name and that he lived in the area. He used to work the fishing boats. He's retired now."

"Did he know that you're a lawyer?"

"I might have mentioned it. Why?"

"That may have been the reason he was looking for you."

"Maybe."

"Any other contact with him? After Key West?"

"No. That was the only time I ever met him."

"Were you expecting him to come visit?"

"No."

"A Longboat officer left just before you got here. He said this guy was at your friend's condo on Longboat the night before last. Can you think of any reason why he'd be after Hamilton?"

"No. I doubt that he was after Logan. He may have been visiting. He might have been looking for Logan to find out when I'd be back in town."

"To your knowledge, did Hamilton know Osceola?"

"I don't think so."

"Then why would he be looking for you at Hamilton's home?"

"I've been off-island for several days. Boating down south. If Osceola had come looking for me, most anybody could have told him that I was gone and that Logan was my best friend. Abraham told the Longboat officer that somebody had told him to look up Logan to find out when I'd be back in town. Maybe he went looking for Logan to find out where I was."

The detective looked skeptical. "It's a theory."

"And at least as good a one as yours," I said.

CHAPTER FIFTEEN

I left the hospital more confused than I'd been all day. And this had been a confusing day. The more I thought about it, the better I liked my theory. If Abraham had come looking for me, he would have gone to the condo complex where I had lived until recently. That would have been the only address he had. I'd seen the condo manager at Tiny's with her husband the week before Jessica and I left on our trip. We'd talked about some of the lesser-known anchorages in Charlotte Harbor, so she knew I was going to be off the island for a week or so. If Abraham had asked, she would have told him I was out of the area and would probably have given him Logan's address. She wouldn't have yet heard about the shooting in downtown and Logan's absence from the key.

But why was Abraham looking for me? I'd only met him briefly in the Florida Keys the previous fall. He'd done me a favor, and I gave him my address in case he was ever in the Sarasota area. I didn't really expect to see him again. He didn't strike me as the traveling kind. If he really had some deal involving money and needed a lawyer, why hadn't he hired one in Key West?

I hadn't eaten all day and was starving. I stopped at St. Armands Circle and went into Lynches Pub and Grub for a hamburger and a beer. I knew the place would be full of locals and everyone would want to know about Logan. There had been a small article in the morning's paper about the shooting. I didn't want to get into it, but I needed a little food and some conversation.

Much to my surprise, the place was almost empty. There were a few tourists enjoying a beer or wine, but no locals. Except for Jill, the manager. She came over as I took a stool at the bar. A look of concern sharpened her facial features. She put her hand over mine on the counter, said, "Matt, I'm so sorry about Logan."

"Me too, Jill. Thanks, but he's going to be fine. Can we talk about something else?"

"Sure," she said, flashing a sad smile. "Miller Lite?"

"Yes. And a burger, too, please."

"Coming up." She pulled a beer from the cooler, opened the bottle, poured it in a frosted glass, and set the glass on a coaster on the bar. She went back to the kitchen to order my food.

I listened to the slight rumble of traffic on the street in front of the bar, the laughter of people strolling the circle, the buzz of conversation from a tableful of sun-reddened visitors. Minutes went by and Jill returned to the bar with my burger. We talked as I ate, conversation between two old friends, nothing of importance, just chatter, but hers was overlaid with a sadness born of Logan's near death.

I left the bar and headed north for home. My sunroof was open and the soft night air enveloped me, a tincture of sea and distant orange blossoms floating on the breeze, stirring memories of youthful evenings at the beach with a pretty girl who daubed citrus scented perfume behind her ears.

I turned onto Broadway and found my way to my new home beside the bay. I parked in the driveway, walked to the front door, opened it, flipped on the light, and discovered chaos.

CHAPTER SIXTEEN

My house was a mess. Books pulled off their shelves and thrown haphazardly on the floor, TV screen shattered, desk drawers pulled out and emptied in random piles. I backed out of the front door and pulled my cell phone from the pocket of my shorts. I called Bill Lester at home.

"Bill, sorry to bother you. Somebody trashed my house."

"Bad?"

"Pretty bad." I told him what I had seen. "I haven't been into the house. I'm hoping your crime-scene guy can find something."

"Hang tight, Matt. I'll start people moving on this. I'll see you in a few minutes." He hung up.

I stood on the sidewalk, curious about who would vandalize my home. It didn't look as if anybody was searching for anything in particular. It appeared to be some sort of rage-induced need to destroy. I wanted to go inside, to see how they had gotten in, but I didn't want to disturb any evidence.

I looked at my watch. Nine p.m. I walked next door and rang the bell. Cotty Johnson answered, wearing a bathrobe. She looked at me and said, "Come on in, Matt, but don't get any ideas just because I'm half-dressed."

Cotty was an eighty-something-year-old widow, a good friend of many years. I laughed and followed her into her living room. A sitcom of some sort was playing on her TV, the sound turned low.

"Want something to drink?" she asked.

"No, thanks. I just got home. Somebody trashed my house."

"Trashed your house?"

"Yeah. It looks pretty bad. I called the police."

"I'm sorry to hear that. It's kind of scary. We don't have much of that on the island."

"I know. Did you see anybody hanging around?"

"There was a guy in a go-fast that tied up at your dock and went inside early this afternoon. I assumed he was one of your buddies."

A go-fast is what the islanders called a cigarette-style high-powered boat, a kind we see a lot of in our area.

"Can you describe the boat?"

"Sorry, Matt. I didn't pay that much attention. Besides, I don't know a lot about boats."

"What about the man driving it?"

"He was a big white guy. Shaved head. He was wearing jeans and a tight T-shirt. Sunglasses, the kind the aviators wear. Probably six feet two or three. That's about all I can tell you."

I laughed. "Nothing much gets by you, huh Cotty?"

I heard a car drive up out front, saw blue lights flickering in the darkness. "Thanks, Cotty. The cops are here. I'd better go. They may want to talk to you later."

"Anything I can do to help, Matt."

I walked back outside and met the uniformed policeman as he was getting out of his car. "Hey Matt," he said. "The chief said to get my ass over here pronto. He's called out our CSI guy. What's going on?"

"Vandals, I think. But it may be more than that."

"You think it's tied into Logan's shooting?"

"Could be. Cotty Johnson saw a guy in a boat come into my dock this afternoon. He went inside the house. The back door wasn't locked, so that wouldn't have been hard to do."

"I'll wait for CSI before I go in. If there's any evidence, we'll find it. Chief's lit a fire. You know how he can be when he gets riled."

I knew. As I stood chewing on the question of who the tall bald guy was, the chief pulled up in his unmarked Crown Vic. He motioned me over to a streetlight and took out his notepad. "Talk to me, Matt."

I told him what I'd found when I opened my door, what Cotty had told me about a large bald man and how that description fit the man who had hired Jube Smith to find me. I told him about Jube accosting me in Logan's hotel room.

"Did you call the sheriff's office?" Bill asked.

"No. I don't think Jube is dangerous. He just needs to get back on his feet. The description of the bald man isn't enough to help find him."

"Any idea who he is?" he asked.

"None. I'd think this had something to do with Logan's problem, except Jube didn't seem to have any idea who Logan was."

"That doesn't mean it's not connected."

"No. Jube probably doesn't read the newspaper. He might not have known about Logan."

"What about the black guy in the hospital?"

I told Bill what I'd told the Sarasota detective. "By the way, Kintz could be your twin."

"Yeah, but I think I'm better looking."

"I don't know, Bill. He's pretty stunning."

"Yeah, well, I'm the chief and he's not. Kintz pisses me off."

"Why?"

"How'd you like to have people mixing you up with somebody all the time?"

"That's not Kintz's fault."

"Right. He could move to California or something."

"You're just jealous because he dresses better than you do."

A car turned into my street and parked behind the chief's cruiser. The CSI guy. He came over to us, carrying a large case. "Hey, Matt, Chief," he said. "Anything I should know before I get started?"

"No," said Lester. "Go on in and do your thing."

"How long before I can get in the house?" I asked.

"Give me an hour," said the CSI guy. "By then, I'll have a pretty good idea of whether there is any recoverable evidence." He turned and headed for the front door, leaning a little to his right as the heavy case pulled on his arm.

"Let's get some coffee," said Lester. "The Market's still open."

CHAPTER SEVENTEEN

The Market was quiet. Andrew, who owned the place and worked sixteen hour days every day, was behind the deli counter. Two older men sat on the stools arranged along the length of the counter, sipping coffee and talking quietly.

"Chief, Matt," said Andrew. "Coffee?"

"Please," I said.

"Anything to eat?" asked Andrew.

I looked at Lester. "No," he said, "just coffee. Black."

We took our cups and retreated to a table in the corner. Bill blew over the top of his cup, took a sip, smiled, and said, "Hits the spot. Why couldn't you have discovered your problem while it was still daylight?"

"Because you told me to go to the hospital to meet your buddy Kintz."

"Right. What were they looking for, Matt?"

"You mean in the house?"

"Yeah."

"I don't have any idea. None. I don't understand why anybody would want to kill Logan or Abraham or screw up my home."

"These things don't just come out of the blue. There's got to be a connection. You and Logan have been hanging out for years, so Abraham would seem to be the new factor in the equation. Any thoughts on what he was doing here?"

"He must have been coming to see me for some reason having to do with the money thing he mentioned to your officer. Abraham's not the type to lie to a cop. I'll go see the manager at my old condo tomorrow; see if Abraham went there. It makes sense that if he couldn't find me, someone would send him to Logan. He'd never met Logan, so that's the only reason I can think of for him being at Logan's condo on the night of the shooting."

We sat for an hour, talking about old friends, fishing, the weather, and occasionally veering back to the problems at hand. Who would want to kill Logan? Did they want to kill me, too? I thought so, since somebody had sent Jube Smith after me with a gun. This thing had to be tied in to Osceola and his money issue. That was the only connection, but even if somebody was trying to kill Abraham over money, why were Logan and I in the line of fire? It was a puzzle.

The chief's cell phone rang. He answered, hung up, and said, "The CSI guy says you can go home."

The house was an even bigger mess than when I'd last seen it. The CSI guy was waiting by the front door when the chief and I drove up. "Sorry about the mess, Matt. I used a lot of dust trying to get a good fingerprint. Nothing."

The chief said, "In all that mess, you didn't find anything?"

The CSI guy shook his head. "I'm afraid we don't know any more now than we did an hour ago. Whoever the guy was, he wore gloves. He was a careful son of a bitch. He went through every drawer and nook and cranny in the house. Looked like he was in a hurry."

"So it wasn't just vandalism," I said. "Somebody was looking for something."

"Looks that way," the CSI guy said.

I stood at the threshold, hesitant to go in. The disaster was reflected off the dark floor-to-ceiling windows overlooking the bay, a mirrored effect caused by the darkness on the other side of the glass. A double mess. Finally, I moved forward, beckoning to the chief to follow. We toured the house. The place looked as if a tornado had blown through.

"You need some help cleaning this crap up?" Lester asked.

"No. I'll call Joy Fitzpatrick tomorrow. She'll get some women from her cleaning service in to take care of things."

"I've got an idea."

"What?"

"Beer. We need beer and Tiny's is just down the street."

"Can't hurt."

"Might help."

"Probably will."

"Then, let's do it."

And so we did.

MONDAY

CHAPTER EIGHTEEN

The coffeepot was where I'd left it. The coffee was in the refrigerator. I stumbled around trying to get coffee and water into the maker. It was touch and go. The beers at Tiny's had turned into more than was good for me. I was feeling a little numb as I stumbled across the debris-strewn living room into the kitchen. The early morning light streaming through the windows did nothing for my mood. My head hurt, my hands shook, my stomach growled and did flip-flops when I moved. A monumental hangover. Never again. I'd never drink again. Right. Well, at least not that day. Damn Bill Lester and his bright ideas.

I threw some bacon and sausage into a frying pan, thinking that a little grease and coffee would help me regain some semblance of life. When the meat sizzled to a well-done hue, I took it out of the skillet, put it on a paper towel to drain, cracked four eggs into the pan and fried them over easy. Bread went into the toaster. When it was all done, I sat at the table and ate. I was feeling better. I went to the front door to get the morning paper, took it to the patio in back with a second cup of coffee, and breathed in the clean salt-laden air blowing gently off the bay. I was going to survive.

I'd slept on my mattress on the floor, a blanket thrown over me. Everything was in a shambles, but to be honest, I hadn't really cared by the time I got home from Tiny's.

The phone rang. I answered. Joy. "Two of my girls will be there in twenty minutes."

"What?"

"To clean up the mess."

"How'd you know?"

"Tiny's telegraph."

I groaned. I should have known. There are no secrets on the key, and if you want something done, you just need to mention it in Tiny's. I must have said something to somebody while working on all those beers.

Joy laughed, a big laugh. "Patti said you were feeling a little chipper last night. Bet you're not doing too well this morning."

"Tell the girls to come on in. I'm going back to bed." I hung up. Patti Colby was Joy's friend and I knew I'd talked to her at some point the night before. Oh well, the house would get cleaned up and they didn't need me. I looked at my watch. It was a little after eight. I headed for the bedroom.

The phone woke me at noon. Logan. "You still in bed?"

"Yeah."

"Went to Tiny's last night?"

"Yeah."

"Feeling bad?"

"Yeah."

"Get over it. I need you to come pick me up."

"What's going on?"

"I need to get my ass out of this hotel. Marie saw some strange look-ing guys in the lobby when she went down to get some stuff out of her car."

"Strange? How?"

"Two of them. Both wearing jeans and T-shirts. Lots of tattoos."

"Logan," I said, "you're not exactly staying at the Ritz-Carlton. Maybe they're just guests."

"Marie heard them ask about me. By name."

"Uh-oh."

"Yeah. The desk clerk doesn't have me registered, so he couldn't tell them anything."

"Where's Marie now?"

"I just sent her home. I figured if there was going to be trouble I didn't want her anywhere near it."

"Maybe they were just checking all the hotels."

"Then why are they sitting out in the parking lot on a couple of Harleys?"

"I see what you mean. I'll be there in half an hour. Did you call the sheriff?"

"A deputy's been outside my door since last night. Apparently Bill Lester called and told them about the guy that came after you yesterday. I'm supposed to stay put."

"But you don't think that's a good idea."

"Not a chance. I'm a sitting duck here, deputy or no deputy."

"I'm on my way."

I threw on some clothes and left in a hurry. I was only vaguely aware that my living room had been put back together, the mess cleaned up. I'd have to buy a new TV. Maybe they'd get the rest of it done by the end of the day.

My best bet was south on Gulf of Mexico Drive, around St. Armands Circle, out Fruitville Road to Interstate 75, then south a couple of exits to Logan's hotel. That took almost forty-five minutes.

I pulled into the parking lot. Two tough looking men were sitting on motorcycles, drinking from green beer bottles. A radio was blaring rock music. I continued on around the building. I didn't want anybody to see my Explorer in case someone recognized it. I parked in a loading zone next to a door near a large Dumpster that overflowed with garbage. Today was probably the pickup day. The door was locked. A sign said: No Entrance. Deliveries only.

I picked up the phone hanging on the wall next to the door. No dial. I put the receiver to my ear. A ringtone. Then an answer, "Front desk."

"This is Hugo," I said. "I've got sodas to deliver for the machines."

"Where's Buddy?"

"Out sick today. I'm covering his route."

"Come on in." There was a buzzing sound and I heard the lock click open.

I went through the door into a small vestibule. Steps led upward. A push bar was on the door below a sign that said Emergency Exit Only.

ALARM WILL SOUND. I started up the stairs, found the third floor and opened the door into the hallway. I saw a Sarasota County Deputy Sheriff in a chair outside Logan's room. He was leaning back, the chair cocked against the wall. He was reading a book. A David Hagberg thriller.

He looked up as I approached. The chair came down on all four legs. He stood, wary. "May I help you, sir?"

"I'm Matt Royal to see Mr. Hamilton."

He took a piece of paper from the breast pocket of his shirt. A list of names. Looked at it. Looked at me. "May I see some identification, sir?"

I pulled out my wallet and gave him my driver's license. He looked closely at it and handed it back to me. "Thank you, sir." He reached around and rapped on the door. "Mr. Royal's here, Mr. Hamilton."

The door opened. Logan was dressed. Golf shirt with the logo of the Red Sox on the pocket, chinos, sneakers, and a ball cap with a Dewars label embroidered into the fabric. "Come in," he said.

I did and closed the door behind me. "You ready to go?" I asked.

"Yes. But what about the cop in the hall?"

"Nothing. You're not under arrest. We'll just tell him we're leaving."

"We can do that?"

"Let's go."

Logan picked up a small suitcase and we opened the door. The deputy stood again, his face posing the question before his mouth formed the words. "What are you doing?"

"We're leaving," I said. "I'll call the sheriff and tell him we checked out against your wishes."

"Mr. Royal, I can't let Mr. Hamilton leave."

"Deputy," I said, my face stern, "I'm a lawyer, and unless and until Mr. Hamilton is under arrest, he's free to come and go as he pleases. We're leaving."

"Sir, I can't let that happen."

"Deputy, if you try to stop us, I'm going to sue you for false arrest, false imprisonment, assault and battery, and several other things I'll think about later. Your career is going to be over. Now, I'd suggest you call whoever you report to and tell him that some smart-ass lawyer just took his client out of your protective care and the only way you could stop them leaving was to shoot one or both and you didn't think that'd be a good idea." I turned and walked off, Logan following.

We went through the door to the stairwell. Logan chuckled. "I love it when you get on your legal high horse. You always sound like an ass."

"I know. I'll make sure Bill Lester smoothes any ruffled feathers and gets that young deputy off the hot seat."

We got to the bottom of the stairs and I hit the push bar on the door, moving fast. As advertised, an alarm sounded, echoing up the stairwell. We got into my Explorer and headed for the exit nearest the Dumpster. I didn't think the bikers would be able to see us leave. I was mistaken.

CHAPTER NINETEEN

I drove I-75 north, exiting onto Fruitville Road. Traffic was light and I was doing a steady forty-five miles per hour, I was vaguely aware that there was a motorcycle behind me, but I didn't think much of it. I caught a green light at Cattlemen Road and as I approached Honore Avenue, three more bikers fell in behind me. I was in the middle lane, getting a little nervous.

"Logan, there are four bikers behind us. It might be some of the same bunch who were at the hotel."

"I doubt it. I think we gave them the slip."

The two lead bikes accelerated. One moved over into the right lane and the other into the left lane. They had me bracketed. I could see both in my side mirrors. The one coming up on my left was holding something down beside his leg. As he moved up even with my left rear tire, he got into my blind spot. I looked over my left shoulder. The rider was holding a shotgun, moving it up into a firing position. I reacted instantly, jerking the wheel to the left, sideswiping the bike. I heard the sound of gunfire as I swung the wheel abruptly back to the right. I heard more metal grinding into the Explorer as it collided with the other biker. Another shot. I could see the bikers down in the road, skidding along on the pavement with their motorcycles. I didn't think they'd be alive when they stopped.

I slammed hard on the brakes, thinking I'd get rear-ended by the two remaining bikes. That didn't happen. They peeled off, roaring around me at high speed, concentrating on escape. If they had weapons, they didn't show them.

A very small moment had passed since I swung the wheel to the left. Logan was beginning to react. "What the hell?" he said.

"Are you hit?" I asked.

"No. Was that a gunshot?"

"Twelve gauge, I think."

Logan had spotted the wreckage in the road, cars slamming on breaks, trying to dodge the carnage. The bikes had stopped their skids. The riders were still, blood seeping out of torn jeans and jackets. I brought the Explorer to a stop in the middle of the road. Traffic was still moving in the eastbound lanes, but our lanes were at a standstill.

I pulled my cell phone from my pocket, dialed 911. "This is Matt Royal," I said to the emergency operator. "Some bikers just tried to kill me on Fruitville Road at Honore. In front of the Comcast studios. You'd better send ambulances and cops."

"Sir, where are you calling from?"

"I think two of the bikers are dead."

"Sir, I need your name and a phone number where I can reach you."

"I'll wait here for the cops."

"Sir, calm down and talk to me. Do you see any blood? Who are the victims? What is your phone number?"

I hung up. "Friggin' bureaucrats," I muttered.

"Matt, what the hell just happened?"

"I don't know, but those guys were going to shoot us."

We sat quietly. People were out of their cars, milling around, telling each other what they had seen. A sheriff's department cruiser came around the corner of Honore, siren blaring, light bars flashing frantically. He stopped on the shoulder, went to the bikers lying on the street, felt for a pulse, spoke into his radio. He saw the shotguns lying on the road a few feet from the wrecked bikes. He went over, peered at them, but didn't pick them up. He was a good cop. Leave it for the crime-scene folks.

I got out of the car, started walking toward the deputy. "Get back in your car, sir," he said.

I kept walking toward him. He stiffened a bit, on guard. "Deputy," I said, "I'm Matt Royal. I called this in. These guys were trying to kill me and my passenger. Call your boss. He'll fill you in."

"Who's your passenger?"

"Call your boss, Deputy. Give him my name. He'll tell you what he can. I'll be in my car." I turned and walked back to the Explorer. I could see body damage near the right rear wheel well. I walked to the other side. There was a gash in the metal just forward of the rear wheel, running along the side almost to the front door. My insurance company wasn't going to like this.

I got into the car. "What's going on?" Logan asked.

"I don't know." I pulled out my cell phone and called Bill Lester.

"Matt," he said. "Where the hell are you and Logan and why did you take him out of the hotel? The sheriff is all over my ass."

"Bill, we've got bigger problems than that. Some people just tried to kill Logan and me. I think they were the same people who were at the hotel." I told him what I knew about the morning's events.

"Marie is at the courthouse," he said.

"Why?"

"She was on her way back to the key when a couple of bikers came up behind her. She thought they might be the same ones she saw at the hotel. She turned off Fruitville and stopped in the middle of traffic in front of the courthouse. She went inside and told the security folks she needed help."

"Where is she now?"

"In a witness room on the first floor. A deputy is guarding the door. She's fine."

"Bill, I don't like being out in the open. We're sitting ducks. Can you get the sheriff's office to let us go on and we'll talk to them later? And I want to get Marie."

"I'll handle it." He hung up.

I related all this to Logan.

"Those sons of bitches," he said. "They're after Marie."

"I think they somehow found out where you were hiding. I don't understand who these bikers are, though."

"Hired guns, I'd guess."

"Probably so. But who's doing the hiring? And why?"

"I don't know."

The deputy walked over to my side of the car. "Is it drivable?"

"I think so," I said.

"The sheriff said for you to go on home. Somebody will be in touch about this mess."

"Thanks, Deputy. I hit them on purpose. They were trying to shoot us with those shotguns."

"Well, you took 'em out, Mr. Royal. These two won't be giving you any more trouble."

I cranked the Explorer, pulled slowly around the dead bikers, and headed west.

CHAPTER TWENTY

I called Bill Lester and told him we had left the scene and were on our way back to the key. He was alarmed about the attempt on our lives and wanted us to come directly to the station to give a statement to him and his new detective. "It's about time you met her anyway. And the Sarasota sheriff's office will want a statement from you."

"I'm on my way to pick up Marie. I'll call you when I start back to the island."

"Don't forget, Matt. This is important."

"I know. I promise."

I drove to the Judicial Center on Ringling Boulevard and found a parking place. "Pull your hat low," I said, "and stay here."

"If somebody's after Marie, I think it'd be better if there were two of us."

"I doubt that the bad guys stuck around after Marie dodged into the courthouse. Besides, somebody wants you dead. Let's wait until we get a reading from Bill Lester."

He reluctantly agreed, pulled the hat low on his face, and slunk down in the seat. I walked to the front door, identified myself to the deputy at the security point, showed him my driver's license, emptied my pockets into a basket, walked through the metal detectors, got my stuff, and followed the guard's directions to the witness room where Marie waited.

Another deputy was at the door. I identified myself again, showed my license again. He was expecting me. I went into the room. Marie was sitting in a chair reading a magazine. She did not seem frazzled at all. She looked up, smiled, and said, "Is Logan okay?"

"He's fine. Waiting in the car."

"Then let's go."

"You okay, Babe?" asked Logan as I put Marie into the backseat.

"I'm fine. What happened to Matt's car?"

Logan told her about our day as I drove out toward Longboat Key. As we were rounding St. Armands Circle, I said, "Guys, you can't go home. People are looking for you."

"I don't think your house would be much better," Logan said.

"No. Let's go to Sam Lastinger's. You'll be out of sight there."

Logan laughed. "It's only three o'clock. Sammy's probably still asleep."

"He usually gets hungry around noon," I said. "He should be up."

Sam was the bartender at one of our favorite places on the key, Patti-george's. He lived in an old house next to the restaurant, fronting on the bay. He joked about his long commute. He had a dock behind the house and kept a crab trap on the bottom of the bay, secured to a piling. He didn't pay too much attention to whether crabs were in season.

I called Sam. He was awake. "Hey, Homey," he said. "When are you coming in?"

"I'll be at your house in ten minutes. I need a favor."

"I'll be here."

I called the chief again. "I'm on my way to Sam Lastinger's house. Do you want to meet me there?"

"I'll send J.D. She needs to get into the loop."

I wasn't too happy about getting J.D. into the loop. I didn't know her, didn't know if I could trust her, and wasn't looking forward to pinning my future to an ambitious woman who was new to our community.

I pulled into Sam's yard, right up next to his back door. He opened it as Marie and Logan got out of the Explorer. He stopped dead still, a look of relief on his face. "Logan?"

"You got any Dewars in this shack?" Logan asked.

Sam let out a whoop. "Logan, my God, I heard you'd been shot."

"Sort of," Logan said.

"Come in. Come in."

We followed Sam into the interior of his tidy little house. He gave Logan a big hug and then Marie. "What the hell's going on?"

"Have you met the new Longboat detective?" I asked.

"No," said Sam. "I didn't know we had one."

"She'll be her shortly," I said. "Let's wait for her, and I'll fill you in."

"She's a woman?"

"Yeah."

"Good looking?"

"Don't know. Haven't met her. Does it matter?"

"It might"

I just shook my head. Sam's mind often seems to work in a very linear fashion.

We sat quietly and sipped our drinks, nobody saying anything. A lull in a day filled with danger, a time to enjoy the friendship of people I knew and trusted. No more than three or four minutes had elapsed when there was a knock on the door. Sam went to answer it.

I heard a female voice with a slight southern accent say, "I'm Detective Duncan. I was told I could find Mr. Royal here."

"Come in, Detective. I'm Sam."

I watched as a tall woman, perhaps five eight or nine, walked into the room. She was a beauty. Mid-to-late thirties. Dark hair, cut just above shoulder length framed her face, startling green eyes, a quick smile that revealed even white teeth. There were small lines at the corners of her eyes. If she wore makeup it was so subtle as to be invisible. She was dressed in navy slacks, a white blouse with short sleeves, black low-heel pumps, and a demeanor that oozed confidence. A Sig-Sauer nine-millimeter pistol was holstered on her left side, butt facing forward, her badge fastened to the front of her belt. Her body was trim, long neck, a slight swell of breasts under the blouse, a delicate rounding of hips. She was a lady who stayed in shape, aerobics probably, maybe some light weights. There was no muscle mass of the kind that dedicated weight lifters build.

Logan and I stood, introduced ourselves and Marie. She smiled again. "I heard you've gotten yourselves into a bit of trouble."

Logan laughed. "If you consider two attempts on my life a 'bit' of trouble."

She nodded. "The chief filled me in up to a point. Tell me what happened."

"Sit down," I said. "This is going to take a while."

"Sam," said Logan, "get me a Dewars first."

"Coming up. Detective?"

"I could use a glass of water."

Sam moved toward the kitchen.

He returned with a tall Scotch and water for Logan, a Miller Lite for me, and a glass of white wine for Marie. Sam was drinking bottled water and handed the detective one.

"Bad night?" I asked.

"Yeah. They've got to start closing the Haye Loft earlier. Eric pours a heavy drink, and I stay way too late."

"All their fault," said Marie.

"Detective," I said, "I don't yet know what's going on, but somebody tried to kill Logan and they took some shots at me today." I told her the whole story, stopping once to refresh my beer. At some point Logan wandered into the kitchen and returned with another tall glass of whiskey.

When I finished talking, and Logan and Marie had told their stories, the detective said, "There's got to be some connection to Abraham. Chief Lester told me that Abraham wanted you to help him with some kind of big money deal. What kind of money would he be talking about?"

"I don't know. He always worked the fishing boats out of Key West. I'm sure he never made a lot of money, so I don't think he'd be talking about an investment. Maybe he stumbled over a sunken Spanish galleon. A treasure ship."

Logan shook his head. "That's pretty far-fetched. Besides, if it was treasure, why would he need you?"

"I don't know. Maybe he thought he needed a lawyer to handle the contracts with salvors. Deal with the government. You know the feds always get a piece of the action on any treasure found. Sometimes they want more than their share."

"Do you know anything about that area of the law?"

"No, but Abraham wouldn't know that. And the thought of money like that brings out all kinds of bad guys. Maybe he mentioned it to the wrong people."

"Who?" asked Sam.

"That, my friend, is the question we have to answer before it gets us killed."

We sat quietly, sipping our drinks, the sound of cars passing on Gulf of Mexico Drive intruding into the silent room. I was facing the back windows, staring at the bay. We had eaten up the afternoon. The water had taken on the golden hue of the sunset over the Gulf reflecting off low-hanging clouds. I could see a boat moving slowly into the cove behind one of the mangrove islands, a fisherman in a flats skiff. The water was still, the late afternoon calm of a Florida spring. We were nearing nightfall, the darkness creeping over from the mainland, blanketing the bay in its soft opacity. I was not sorry to see the end of this day. I wondered briefly what the morrow would bring. Why was someone trying to kill Logan? Why Abraham? Why me? What the hell had we gotten ourselves into?

"I have a plan," I said.

"Mr. Royal," said Detective Duncan, "I appreciate your cooperation, but you need to forget whatever plan you have. This is my case. I do the planning and the execution. You sit tight and stay out of my way."

I was a little surprised by the steely tone in her voice. "Look Detective," I said, "I'm not exactly a novice at this sort of thing. I think I can be of help."

"You can't, sir. The chief told me a lot about you. I know about your war record and some of the other scrapes you've been in, but this is now my case. I'll work it and I'll solve it and I'll put the bad guys in jail. You stay out of my way."

I shook my head. "You're new here. You don't know the island or the people. I do."

"I've been a cop for fifteen years," she said. "I worked all over Miami-Dade County. I was in lots of places where I didn't know the people or the neighborhood. I'll handle this."

She stood to leave. "Come by the station in the morning to give a statement." She looked at Logan and then me. "Both of you."

She turned abruptly and walked out the front door.

"That," said Logan, "is a hard woman. What do we do?"

"I wonder what she looks like naked," said Sam.

"My God," said Marie. "Do you ever stop?"

"I was just saying," said Sam.

Marie shook her head. "Geez. Will you ever grow up?"

Sam grinned. "I hope not."

Logan laughed. "Okay, Matt. What do we do about the lady detective?"

"We'll just ignore her. As I said, I've got a plan of sorts."

"Talk to us," said Logan.

"Marie," I said, "don't you have a sister in Orlando?"

"Yes."

"I think you should go stay with her until we sort this mess out."

"That's your plan?" she asked derisively.

"Part of it. I want you out of the way so that Logan and I don't have to worry about you. We can operate a little better on our own."

An argument ensued, with Marie enumerating all the reasons she should stay, and me being obstinate. Logan sat and smiled.

CHAPTER TWENTY-ONE

The lights were low, giving little reflection off the sliding glass doors leading to the balcony. The city of Sarasota glowed across the bay, its lights reflecting off the water. The ancient man sitting in the recliner could see the graceful bridge that tied the city to Bird Key. Red and green lights atop channel markers blinked rhythmically in the dark.

The old man was alone, his mind wandering over the years of his life, a sense of ineffable sadness pervading his thoughts. He would die soon, and that knowledge brought with it memories of lost opportunities, of old friends now gone, of women he had bedded and the one he had loved. He wasn't afraid of death, but he resisted it, tried to keep the unknown at bay, uncertain of what the end of life would bring. Another life? Heaven? Hell? He didn't know, and that was the only thing in his life that he'd ever questioned.

He had been so certain about everything else. And now, when he was weak and nearing the end of the road, they were trying to take it away from him. He couldn't have that. It didn't matter to him personally, but there was a principle involved. His grandfather had taken the land, farmed it, eked out an existence, and died land poor; lots of land, little money. His dad had found the family fortune under the grass that had fed livestock for fifty years, and he, the last male of his line, had turned that fortune over many times, so that now he was rich beyond wealthy.

He sighed, and stirred in the chair. He scratched his cheek, feeling the day-old stubble, the thin skin of age, the wrinkles that multiplied every year that he breathed. He was a slight man, small and wizened, his hair mostly gone, the remainder gray wisps of what once had been. He'd never been big in stature, but his mind had been outsized, his intelligence higher than most, his drive to achieve constant. He'd bested them all, all those bright Ivy Leaguers who'd never understood that they'd met their better. Because he *was* better, better than them all put together. And he'd left a lot of bodies, figuratively, in the ditches beside the road of life. He liked that metaphor, understood that it was trite, but thought it apt. He'd never killed anyone, not in the physical sense, but there were a lot of men, and some women too, who'd thought they could outsmart the little man with the big southern accent. So he proved them wrong, killed their futures, their dreams, their beliefs in their own superiority. And now, in his dotage, he sat in his recliner and thought about them, remembered every one, and wondered if he had been too tough, too harsh, too unfeeling. Well, too late to do anything about them now. But he'd paid a price for his success, in loneliness and isolation. Too late now to change anything, even if he wanted to.

Where the hell was Donna? She'd been with him for years, taking care of his houses, and now nursing him in his last days. He had to pee. Where the hell was that woman?

He heard footsteps on the stairs. "Donna?" he yelled.

"Coming, sir." A woman in late middle age came into the room. She was all white. White hair, white skin, white dress, white stockings and shoes. Her skin had the pallor of one who never took the sun, who ventured out only after darkness. Her eyes were the pink of the true albino.

"Where've you been, woman?"

"I told you I was going to the Publix."

"Right. I forgot. I need to pee. Help me up."

The woman came to him, took his upper arms, and pulled him from the recliner. He stood unsteadily, balanced by the strength of his helper. She reached out and took the walker from beside the chair, handed it to him. "Can you do this alone, sir?"

"Are you asking me if I can take my pecker out and pee without help? Goddamnit, yes. So far. When I can't do that anymore, you just go ahead and kill me."

She smiled. The old man was rough and cantankerous, but he had his moments of humor. She had been with him for thirty years, since she was in her late twenties. She was his maid, his traveling companion, and she took care of all his homes when he was in residence. As he aged, he sold off the houses, so that now he only had the one, a grand mansion on the bay side of Longboat Key.

She had been born with a mutation in an enzyme called tyrosinase that resulted in the most severe type of albinism. She was used to living with it and had learned to cope. She no longer paid any attention to the stares she elicited from unfeeling boors. She stayed out of the sun by choice, but if she had to go outside during daylight hours, she slathered herself with sunblock and covered every inch of skin with clothing. It was simply easier to do her shopping and outside chores after dark.

"If I have to kill you, can I do it slowly?" she asked.

The old man grunted. "You'd like that, wouldn't you?"

"It'd break up the boredom of living with a shuffling old codger."

The old man laughed, a wheezing sound. He knew the woman loved him in a filial sort of way. They'd never been friends. Their relationship always that of employer and employee. But she was important to the man, perhaps more important than any other living person. He'd never married, never had a family of his own. His father had died when he was a teenager and his mother had followed him to the grave when their son was in college. He had no other relatives.

He used his walker to hobble to the bathroom, stood before the toilet, urinated, zipped himself back up. Some urine escaped into his pants. Damn nuisance, getting old, he thought as he moved back into the living room.

Donna was in the kitchen preparing his supper. He sat again in the recliner, looked at the lights of Sarasota, and thought about what he had to do, perhaps the last act of a long life, and the most ruthless thing he'd ever done. And he didn't even have a good reason for doing it. Except that he didn't want to see the empire he'd built crumble into some great welfare sump.

CHAPTER TWENTY-TWO

It was time to talk to the manager at my old condo complex. I still owned the apartment and used it to house visiting friends. I didn't expect her to be there this late, but I needed her phone number. I'd left the list of numbers at the condo. Whoever was after us knew where I lived, so maybe I'd be safer at the condo than at my cottage.

Night had crept across the island, shrouding us in a dark blanket. There was no moon, but the stars dappled the sky with bright pinpoints. I opened the sunroof on the Explorer and enjoyed the flow of salt-scented night air. Far out on the Gulf, lightning bursts were playing in the dark, providing subdued flashes of brilliance that defined the horizon. Heat lightning, the locals called it, but I knew there was a terrible storm way out, over toward Mexico, and it would be churning the sea into a ferocious beast. I hoped it wasn't headed our way.

I'd left Logan and Marie at Sam's. I had to do a little legwork, and I needed to be careful. I didn't know if the assault on my car was just an attempt to kill Logan or if there were people after me as well. Perhaps my death on Fruitville Road would have been nothing more than collateral damage. Or maybe somebody wanted me dead.

How did the bad guys figure out where Logan was staying? Why were they trying to kill him? Or me? I called Bill Lester and told him that Logan and Marie were safe and at Sam's.

"How'd you like J.D.?" he asked.

"Can't say that I did."

"Why?"

"She has what you might call a controlling personality."

"Yeah."

"She told me to stay out of this."

"Yeah."

"That's not going to happen, you know."

"Yeah."

"Where are you in this?"

"Matt, I've always told you to stay out of it. You've never listened to me, so I don't imagine you're going to listen to J.D."

"Right."

"Just try to stay out of her way. This is her first case with our department, and I don't want her thinking I'm encouraging civilians to solve cases."

"Bill, if somebody wasn't trying to kill me, I wouldn't be interested in your case."

"Be careful, Matt. The press is already nosing around. That mess on Fruitville today got their dander up. By tomorrow, they'll know you and Logan were the targets. We're going to have to tell them something."

"I wish we knew something."

"Yeah. I'll release a story tonight. The papers can run it tomorrow. I'll talk to Sarasota PD and the sheriff and figure out how to play it."

"Okay. I'll let you know what I find out."

"Yeah."

"I'm still in the game."

"Yeah."

"You say that a lot."

"Yeah."

"Bye, Bill." I hung up.

I parked in the visitor's area at the condo complex. If somebody was watching, I didn't need to give them too much notice that I was there. The parking lot was dimly lit with security lights. The island was a quiet place, and nobody needed much security. Until tonight.

I walked in the shadows, staying close to the building. I avoided the elevator, went to the end of the building, and took the stairs to the second floor. A walkway ran the length of the building, doors to the units opening off it. A large hedge of schefflera reached above the second floor and partially shielded me from the parking lot. I ducked into my apartment as quickly as I could.

I turned on the lights. I was alone. I went to the safe in the closet of the master bedroom and pulled out my .38-caliber pistol. I probably wouldn't need it, but I felt better having it on me. I clipped the holster to my belt and changed into a Hawaiian shirt that I wore outside my pants. It covered the pistol nicely.

I found the number and called Marcia at home.

"Hey, Matt. Are you back?"

"I'm back."

"I'm so sorry about Logan. I know how close you guys are."

"Logan's fine, Marcia. Somebody took a couple of shots at him but didn't hit anything vital."

"That's real good news. I'm happy for you. For Logan too."

"Marcia, did anybody come looking for me while I was gone?"

She was quiet for a moment, thinking. "You know, somebody did. Actually two people were looking for you at different times. A man came by on Friday about noon, a white guy, and then a black man with an island accent came the same day, late in the afternoon. I was working overtime trying to get the books ready for the board meeting on Monday."

"Did either one give you a name?"

"No. I told both of them that you didn't live there anymore and gave them your address. I said you were out of town, but that Logan could probably get hold of you. I told them where Logan lived and they left. Did I do something wrong?"

"No. The black guy's an old friend. Can you describe the white guy?"

"He was tall and muscular. Had a shaved head. That's about all I remember. What's up?"

"Nothing, really. The black man's in the hospital, and I wondered if he'd come to see me. I'm not sure who the white guy is. You did exactly right."

"Oh, that's a relief. Tell Logan I'm glad he's not dead."

"Thanks, Marcia." She hung up.

I snuck out of the condo the way I'd come in. I opened the door at the bottom of the stairwell and stopped, scanning the parking lot. I saw a figure leaning against my Explorer. I wondered if it was one of my neighbors, but that didn't make sense. I eased out the door and slipped quietly around by the large room that held the Dumpster. I went past the bicycle rack and around the end of the line of covered parking spaces. I slipped quietly down the row of cars, my gun in my hand. I crouched down beside a parked car, raised my head slowly above the hood. The Explorer was parked three cars down the line. The figure was leaning against the driver's door on the far side facing away from me. I could see shoulders and a head above the roof of my vehicle. The outline was clearer now, illuminated faintly by the parking lot security lights. Hair almost to the shoulders, smaller shoulders, not those of a man.

The figure's hands went up into the air, a gesture of surrender. A slow turn to the right, one hundred eighty degrees. Facing me now, the figure said, "I hope you're not going to shoot me, Mr. Royal. First day on the job and all. That'd be kind of tricky to explain."

"Detective Duncan," I said, standing and walking toward her. I put the pistol back in my pocket. "You following me?"

"Sort of."

"Why?"

"I get the feeling that you don't mind well."

"Yeah. My third grade teacher used to tell me that."

"You got a permit for that pistol?"

"Sure do. How did you know I was here?"

"I saw you coming out the door of the stairwell."

"Why are you following me?"

"Actually, I wasn't. I drove in and saw the banged-up Explorer, the same one I saw at the house a little while ago."

"Why are you here?"

"I live here."

I stared at her, completely out of words.

She smiled. "I moved in last week."

I continued to stare. I must have looked as dumb as a stump. "I don't understand," I finally mumbled.

"My mom's been in bad health for the past year. She's been with me in Miami. She died recently and I inherited her condo."

"I lived here for years."

"I know."

"Who was your mom?"

"Helen Monahan."

"I heard she'd died. Nice lady. I'm sorry for your loss."

"Thank you, Mr. Royal. May I call you Matt?"

"Sure."

"Good. Call me J.D."

"Not Jennifer?"

"Not unless you want me to shoot you."

"You still haven't told me why you were waiting for me."

"We need to talk. I'm afraid I came on a little strong earlier."

"You want a cup of coffee?"

"I'd like that."

I looked at my watch. "The Market is still open. You want to ride with me?"

She looked at the Explorer skeptically. "If you think this heap will make it there and back."

"Guarantee it."

CHAPTER TWENTY-THREE

Nine o'clock in the evening. The Market was quiet. Andrew was behind the coffee bar counter cleaning up. Two of our town commissioners were seated at a table in the corner talking quietly. A couple I'd never seen before sat at another table, sipping coffee and nibbling at pastries. The large ceiling fans turned slowly, barely stirring the air. It was a cool spring evening outside, but with the doors closed it got a bit warm inside.

J.D. and I both got coffee from Andrew and went to a table. The mile ride from the condo had been silent, the sunroof open, a slow jazz number playing on the radio. A police cruiser passed us going south. Routine patrol. Nothing much going on in paradise.

Easter had come early that year and most of the tourists and snowbirds had left the key. It was part of the annual migration. Easter marked the tail end of the northerners' stay and if Easter came early, they left early. They were as imprinted with that need to head north as were the white pelicans who wintered with us before heading back to northern Canada. We were entering the season that the locals cherished, the quiet of late spring. Summer would bring the younger crowd of tourists, those with kids enjoying their respite from school. The island would be busy again, not like in the winter, but more so than in spring and fall.

"I'm sorry about coming on so strong earlier," said J.D. "First day jitters, I think."

"There's no need to apologize. I wouldn't want strangers interfering in my job either."

"I've heard a lot about you from the chief. He says you're a stand-up guy who knows when to back down."

"Sometimes," I said, smiling. "I'm afraid not always."

"I'm new," she said, stating the obvious. "I know there're a lot of stories on this island, a lot of people with backgrounds in police work and the law. It was the same in Miami. The retired guys find it hard to stay retired, and sometimes they get in the way."

"I promise I won't get in your way. But there are things I have to do to protect myself and my friends."

"I'm supposed to protect you. That's what cops do."

"But you can't be with me every minute of the day and the bad guys can come anytime."

"The chief told me that you're a pretty good investigator and that you don't always stay inside the lines."

"What lines?"

"The lines that society draws around the bad guys. The parameters that the constitution guarantees every citizen. Even the bad ones."

"J.D., I was a lawyer for a long time. I believe in the constitution. There're bad cops who need to be reined in. Those constraints hobble the good cops sometimes, but it makes us a better country. But I'm not a cop, and those restraints don't apply to me."

"So you think you can just bull yourself through life? Do what you want to do?"

"No. I don't. But sometimes, when danger threatens, it's necessary to blur the lines, to color outside of them, if you will, to do what is necessary to protect yourself or those you love."

"Take the law into your own hands."

I shrugged. "I don't exactly see it that way. The law is your domain. Survival is my goal. Sometimes you have to break a few rules in order to continue breathing."

"I don't agree with you."

"I didn't think you would. Can we still be friends?"

She laughed. It was the first time I'd heard that. It was a sound that would have pleased the gods on Olympus. A bright, tinkling, infectious giggle that made my heart skip a beat. "We'll see, Counselor, we'll see."

I stuck out my hand to shake. She took it and held on, looked me in the eyes and said, "You'll share any information you get? You'll keep me in that loop the chief talked about?"

"Yes. I'm assuming that's a two-way street."

"It is." She shook my hand once and withdrew hers. A deal had been made, a bargain sealed, and I regretted that she had taken her hand back.

CHAPTER TWENTY-FOUR

I drove J.D. back to the condo where I'd spent so much of my last few years, watched her go up in the elevator. I drove south to Sam's house. I left the sunroof open and the slightly chilled breeze blowing off the Gulf filled the Explorer with the trace of brine that defined our sea air.

I mentally slapped my head, laughing at myself. I'd met a ball-busting woman whose steely exterior seemed to dissipate with one burst of laughter. I'd gone all squishy on the margins, thinking about her as a woman instead of a tough cop. One laugh was all it took. And Jessica had been gone less than two days. I was turning into a satyr.

I truly liked women. Each was as different from the other as the men I'd known. I respected them, trusted them, fought in courtrooms against them, made love to them, and had loved one of them more than my very life. I'd pushed her away, perhaps out of fear of the intense feelings she had engendered in me, and finally she left, slipped out of my life, and found happiness with another man. Then she died. Maudlin thoughts. I pushed them to the back of my mind, to the corner where I hid those memories that were too painful to relive.

I wondered who was trying to kill us and why. What had we stumbled into? Maybe nothing. Perhaps there was evil abroad on the island, a meanness that we couldn't fathom. My experience had been that most illegal actions were governed by real emotions. Murder was more often than not retaliation for a perceived grievance, or for money, or sex, or love. It was seldom random, and even then there was usually a purpose to it. The gangbanger making his bones, the terrorist blowing up innocent people because he was deluded or envious of other cultures, the religious fanatic who thought he was doing his Lord's work. But sometimes, it was just pure evil, a meanness of heart and mind that sane people couldn't comprehend. And the evildoers were the hardest to stop and the least likely to be caught and brought to justice.

I'd tuned the radio to an oldies station and my mind drifted into the memories brought back by the sounds of my youth. When I was a boy, I listened each week to the preacher at the church my mother took us to. Most days I was bored, fidgety, anxious to leave the sanctuary and stop by the ice-cream shop in the next block. That was the deal Mom made with my little brother and me. Go to church, sit still, pretend to listen, and you can have a double scoop of chocolate in a sugar cone.

My mother was a strange woman in many ways. She didn't like my father very much, but lived with him in sort of an armed truce. There were never the sweet kind words that seem to pass between most lovers. Acrimony was the norm; loud, complaining, bitter acrimony. My dad just sat and listened, never raising his voice. More often than not, he had fortified himself with cheap bourbon before he came home. He'd sit alone in the kitchen, sipping from a glass of whiskey that he kept in the refrigerator. No ice. That only weakened the drink. But he was in reach of the refrigerator and from my and my brother's room I could hear the rhythmic swoosh of the opening of the door as he retrieved the glass, took a sip, returned it, and closed the door.

On some Sundays, the preacher talked about evil. That always got my attention. I wasn't sure what evil was or how I would know it if I saw it. I was told that the devil, old Satan, was evil. I figured that if I ever saw a red man with cloven hooves, a forked tail, and a pitchfork I would recognize him and know the face of evil. In reality, it wasn't that easy.

I'm not a religious man. I think war cured me of that. I had finally seen evil in the war, the one that had almost consumed me. How could a good and merciful and omnipotent God allow evil to exist? Another paradox, a question that is unanswerable. I respect all religious beliefs and the men and women of faith who follow their teachings. It occurs to me that there are certain universal truths that are accepted by most religions. They all seem to support the dignity of man, his need to live in peace, safe from harm, insulated from evil. We have fashioned laws based on these almost universal tenets, the laws that grace our criminal justice system and those of most cultures. Some are harsh, much harsher than our Western minds will accept, and some of them seem so mired in the Dark Ages that I despair of their ever finding the light of modernity. But their basic laws, those that prohibit behavior, are very similar to our own. The Code of Hammurabi, first promulgated in the eighteenth century BC, almost four thousand years ago, is not that different from the proscriptions of certain behavior that are found in the modern Florida Statutes. Evil, it seems, is universal.

I'd read about evil. I knew about the Nazis and the Holocaust. I could never square the absurd contradictions presented by that terrible time. How could a nation that produced a Goethe, a Beethoven, and a Brahms also produce a Hitler, a Goebbels, and a Goering? How could a nation sink into such an abysmal pit of evil that it could not hope to recover its honor?

And I'd read about serial killers, those madmen who killed for the sheer excitement of murder. What drove them, if not evil? Yes, I knew evil existed, but I've never seen it. I'd seen meanness, knew men who were racists, heard terrible stories of ogres and trolls and monsters. But I'd never actually seen evil, not until I passed my nineteenth birthday in a faraway land. And then the evil I saw was to my amazement, homegrown.

I'd gone to war as a teenager. I'd killed men who were trying to kill me, but they weren't evil. I knew even as I shot them that they were simply patriots in a different uniform, fighting for their country and their buddies. They had families and friends who would mourn their deaths, and that made me sad. But I killed them just the same, because the alternative was for them to kill me.

One day when our A team was working its way from the landing zone back to base camp, crawling through thick and fetid jungle, killing a few of the enemy and getting shot at by other boys in different uniforms, we came upon a clearing. It was quiet there, the intense sun beating down through the opening in the trees. There were no bird cries, no rustling of animals, no shouts of soldiers. Only silence. Then I saw why, or perhaps I smelled it first.

Bodies were stacked in the middle of the clearing, the stench of decay rising like a cloud of steam. Two white men, big men, stripped to their shorts, were throwing another body onto the pile. There were men, women, and children in that pile, old and young, all small Asians. Not Vietnamese, but tribesmen who ranged in this country at the base of the mountains.

My men were alert, rifles ready. They spread out in a skirmish line, not sure what was going on in this dismal little place, but ready for anything, keeping their distance from one another, obeying the army axiom that you never bunch up or one round will get you all.

The men putting the body on the pile had not seen or heard us. We were on the very edge of the clearing, blending into the jungle behind us. A small hut squatted on the far side, a fire burning in a pit in front of the door. It was thatch, probably built in a hurry, no aesthetic value to it, simply utilitarian. A wooden totem, about four feet high, stood next to the door. I recognized it as the art of one of the hill tribes.

I called to the white men. "Hey."

They stopped in their tracks, turned, squinted at my team.

"Who are you?" I asked.

"We're Americans, First Cav. Who're you guys?"

"Special Forces. What's going on here?" I said.

"Just a little cleanup. Getting rid of some gooks."

"I'm Lieutenant Royal. I want your name and rank."

"Fuck you, Loot. I'm Major Harding and this is Sergeant Dill."

"Okay, Major. I need to see some identification. Sir."

"Tell your men to stand down, Lieutenant."

"Sorry, sir. No can do. Let me see that ID."

He came toward me, a slight smile on his face. He pulled a wallet from the pocket of his shorts, extracted a military ID card, and handed it to me. He backed off a couple of steps, watched me look at the card. He was indeed Major John Harding, Infantry, U.S. Army. I snapped to attention.

"Back your men down, Lieutenant," he said.

"Sorry, sir. Not until I know what's going on here."

He spit into the dirt. "We're killing these little bastards and letting their bodies rot in the sun."

"Sir," I said, "did you kill the children and old people too?"

"Bet your ass, boy." He turned to the sergeant, who was ten feet behind him. "Tell 'em, Dill. Ain't none of these gook kids going to grow up and kill Americans."

"Where're your weapons?" I asked. I had relaxed back into a loose posture, standing at ease, my rifle at the ready.

The sergeant pointed. "Over in the hut. We're taking care of them with knives. Scares the shit out of them."

"This on your orders, Major?"

"That's right, son. My orders. Me and old Dill here been taking the slopes out one at a time."

I wanted to kill the bastard. This was the evil I'd heard about in church, read about in the history books. It was strange. The major looked ordinary, like any other middle-aged soldier, dirty, ragged around the edges, a slight stubble on his chin. Yet he was killing without distinction, without remorse, with glee even. My finger tightened on the trigger, but in the end I couldn't do it. I would be a murderer, better only by degrees than this demented officer.

I saw Sergeant Dill in the background, his face stony, eyes squinting in the bright light.

I trained my rifle on the major. "Sir, you're under arrest."

He laughed. "Look, you little shit, I was in this man's army when you were in diapers. You aren't arresting anybody."

My voice was hard, not that of a nineteen-year-old, but of a weary soldier who'd seen too much death, too much fear, a teenager who would never be young again. "Keep your hands where I can see them, sir."

I called to one of my men, a boy named Tommy Abernathy, to disarm the major and restrain him. We would take him back with us to face military justice.

"Wait," Harding said, as Abernathy approached. "Stand at attention, soldier. You men, put your weapons down. I'm taking command here. I'm senior."

Abernathy kept moving toward the major. My other men didn't move. We stood there, staring, men weary of death and of killing and of jungles. Men who asked only that they be allowed to get home alive. And the two jackasses who seemed to enjoy killing.

Abernathy was within a couple of steps of the officer when Harding pulled his bloody knife from the sheath at his belt and stabbed Abernathy in the heart. I didn't think, didn't reason, didn't hesitate. I shot the major in the head, right above his left ear. He went forward, face into the dirt, no attempt to catch himself.

I saw Dill move, his hand coming from his back pocket, a .45-caliber semiautomatic in it. He was raising the barrel, pointing my way. I shot him in the chest. I saw surprise cross his face for an instant before it went blank with death. He was falling backward, limp as a noodle. He hit the ground hard, stirring up little clouds of dust. I heard the sound of my shots reverberate off the jungle canopy.

Jimbo Merryman, my top sergeant and the best soldier I ever knew, moved quickly behind me. I reached Tommy, felt for a pulse in his neck, looked up at Jimbo and shook my head. Abernathy was dead. He was nineteen years old, my age.

He was from Rochelle, Illinois, and had a girl waiting there for him, his high school sweetheart. I'd seen her picture many times, a sweet-eyed brown-haired girl in a portrait that must have been her high school graduation photo.

Abernathy was the son of a minister, a boy who grew up in the church, believing in God and in good and evil, redemption and forgiveness. He'd joined the army to prove himself and he'd done that over and over. He'd been a good soldier who planned to go home, marry his girl, and study to become a preacher like his dad. He was a gentle soul who had become a fierce warrior, a man who wanted little out of life other than his girl and the children they would produce and a chance to preach the gospel and tend to his flock of believers.

"L.T.," said Jimbo, using the nickname the soldiers had for young lieutenants, "I don't think these guys are dead." He shot the dead major and then went to the sergeant's body and shot him in the chest. One by one, each of my men, all twelve of them followed Jimbo, each taking a shot at the two dead men.

Jimbo turned around and loud enough for us all to hear. "I don't guess we'll ever figure out whose round actually killed these bastards." The men grunted in agreement.

We walked to the other edge of the clearing. There were five people still alive, all tied to trees, waiting like staked goats for their executioners. They began to moan as we approached. Jimbo, who spoke a little of their language, talked quietly, explaining that they were free to take care of their dead and to go home. We cut them loose and walked on into the jungle, headed for the base camp, carrying Tommy Abernathy's body on a makeshift stretcher.

I never did know who those American soldiers were. They were rogues, dangerous men who spit in the eye of every American serviceman who served with honor and decency. And almost all of them did. These two were aberrations. They liked the killing, the fear they saw in the eyes of their victims. They were serial killers with a key to the candy store. They killed with impunity, and enjoyed doing it

I had seen evil, perhaps for the first time in my life. I was never exposed to anything like that again, but now I knew it existed, that evil traipsed through our world, often with impunity, always ready in its maleficence to do harm to those least expecting it. Because evil is a coward, preying on the weak, the uninformed, the sunny people who go through life not believing in it. But the monster is always with us, searching out the weaknesses in others, preying on those least ready to defend themselves, the weak, the ignorant, the optimist who denies evil's very existence and is thus never ready to confront this terrible malignancy, this frightful malefactor.

There is that old conundrum that poses the question of what if someone had killed Adolf Hitler in 1933, and thus saved the lives of millions of people. Would the killer have been justified? Of course, that begs the question. One has to make decisions based on the evidence available at the time the decision is made. If I'd known that the major was going to kill Abernathy, I would have been justified in killing him, a preemptive strike to save a man who had entrusted his life to me. On the other hand, Hitler's putative 1933 killer could not have known what the future would bring anymore than I could have discerned the major's intention to kill Abernathy. Can we decide morality retrospectively based on facts that come to light after the completion of the act under consideration? Suppose I'd shot the major before ordering Abernathy to disarm him, and it turned out that the man had no intention of harming my soldier? I'd never know the answer to that, since I'd killed the only person who could have told me. Likewise, I could not have foreseen the actions that the major did take, because they were acts of a deranged man. He must have known that if he drew his knife, I would shoot him.

So on a soft spring evening beside a placid Gulf of Mexico, when the stars peeked through the open sunroof, I thought of good and evil and of the choices we make. If I'd followed my first inclination and shot the major on that hot day, Abernathy might still be alive somewhere in the Midwest, loving his girl, raising his children, giving solace to his parishioners. I would still be a murderer, but would that have put me into the same category as the major?

If I'd shot him, I would never have known his intention to kill Abernathy. Thus, I would have been the murderer, one without justification for the act. Can one evoke good by doing evil, by committing murder? Had I pulled the trigger, Abernathy would not have been killed, but a part of me would have died in that jungle, the part that I hold onto with such zeal, the core that I like to think is good and decent, even when I respond in ways that call that into question.

The wheels always turn, round and round, questions of moral judgment that are beyond my ability to answer. Still, I'd always wished I had just shot the bastard.

I wasn't sure if my friends and I were being stalked by true evil, but I suspected it was so. Knowing my adversary had kept me alive time and again, and I would keep in mind the ageless maxim, "Know thine enemy."

CHAPTER TWENTY-FIVE

I picked them up at Sam's, walking into an argument between Marie and Logan. She wanted him to go with her to Orlando. Logan was adamant that he was staying. Logan won, but Marie wasn't happy about it. She argued that she had no clothes, but I told her to buy some in Orlando. We couldn't take the chance of her being seen at her condo and followed. What about her job?

"Call in sick tomorrow," I told her. "You should be back in a few days."

She acquiesced, grudgingly. "It's a good thing I love Logan so much."

"What about me?" I asked.

"You're okay. A little bossy maybe. Like now. I sure do put up with a lot of crap from you guys."

I grinned. "Love is hard, sometimes."

She gave me the finger.

"I called Jock," Logan said. "He'll be here in the morning."

"Shit."

"Hey. He's a professional and if I let you get your ass shot off, he'd come after me. I'm just covering my bases."

Jock Algren had been my best friend since junior high school, more a brother than a friend. He was an agent with the U.S. Government's most secretive spy agency; so secretive that it didn't even have a name. To the rest of the world he was an oil company executive, but that was only a cover. He kept trying to retire from the intelligence business, but his boss kept dragging him back in. National security required it, he was told.

Jock spent a lot of time on Longboat, staying in my guest room. He always came running when I needed him. He'd helped Logan and me out of a few scrapes in the past.

"Okay. I guess it can't hurt."

Sam suggested that we take his car, since nobody would be looking for it. That was a good idea, and we accepted the offer. I told Sam we'd be in touch, and we drove back down the key, around St. Armands Circle, and crossed the John Ringling Bridge to the mainland. We were careful, taking more turns than we needed, making sure we weren't followed. We went to the Sarasota-Bradenton Airport and rented a car

Marie drove off toward the interstate and Orlando. She'd be safe there, out of harm's way, and we all breathed a sigh of relief.

As we were leaving the airport in Sam's car, my cell phone rang. Bill Lester. "Matt, Detective Kintz wants to talk to you first thing in the morning. He's working with the sheriff's department since we think the attacks on Osceola and Logan are all connected to what happened on Fruitville today."

"Do we know who those guys were?"

"We've got IDs. They were members of a real nasty bikers group up in Tampa, called the West Coast Marauders. Those guys are into drugs, prostitution, porn, you name it."

"I'll be at my house, Bill. Tell him to come by about eight. Logan will be there too."

"Are you sure that's wise? To go to your place?"

"I'm not going to let the bastards run me out of my own home."

"I'll put a cop on your street."

"Thanks, Bill. Jock will be here in the morning, so I think the three of us can handle things then."

"Shit. If the always-dangerous Jock Algren is coming to my island, I worry about the safety of the civilians."

"He's quite tame, Bill. When he's in a good mood. Piss him off and the Rottweiler comes out. Just be nice."

"Right. I'll stop by and have coffee with you when he gets in. I'm glad he's coming."

We stopped by the Judicial Center and Logan drove Marie's car back to her condo near the south end of the key and parked it in the lot. We drove on to my house. I walked around the place, looking for signs of entry. I didn't see any, but it was mostly dark, with only the glow of the streetlight giving any semblance of illumination.

I unlocked the door, pistol in hand, walked into the house, looked in all the rooms and relaxed. Joy's crew had finished cleaning the place and everything was almost back to normal. Logan went to the kitchen to get some coffee started. I stuck my head back out the front door and emptied my mail box.

There was only one piece of mail. An envelope addressed to me. The return address had only a name. Abraham Osceola.

CHAPTER TWENTY-SIX

There was no light in the old grove, other than a sliver that escaped a cur-
tained window in the ancient house that squatted in the middle of it. The
night was quiet, very quiet. No highway noises penetrated this far into the
trees, no jets flew over it. The only sound to break the silence was the occasional rustle of leaves made by a scurrying animal.

The man sat in front of his computer, his hands playing over the keyboard like a piano virtuoso. He'd stop now and then, read the content on
his monitor, move on. He made his living by delving into secrets held by
servers the world over, servers thought to be inviolate. But he could crack
them all, make them his, do as he wanted with them, and never leave a
trace.

His cell phone rang. He picked it up, answered, "What?"

"I lost two men today." The voice was low, guttural, the raw sound of
a heavy smoker, the words carefully rounded, squishy from too much
whiskey.

"What do you mean you lost them?"

"Dead. That bastard Royal killed them. They were good men."

"They must not have been that good if they let that pansy lawyer get
the drop on them."

"He ran over them. Out on Fruitville Road. With his fucking SUV."

"I don't need to know any more. Put them on the bill," said the computer man.

"On the bill? Two of my men are dead and you just want me to put
them on the bill?"

"Yeah. They'll be paid for."

"Both Royal and Hamilton got away without a scratch."

"I told you to kill them."

"I tried. Put some of my best men on it. I think Royal got lucky."

"Where are they now?"

"The county morgue, I guess," said the man on the phone, mumbling.

"No, you dumbass. Royal and Hamilton."

"I don't know. I guess they went back to Longboat Key."

"You find them. If they've gone to ground, get the girl, Marie whatever her name is. Hamilton won't let anything happen to her."

"Okay."

"You're probably not going to get that bonus for fucking this one up today."

"But I lost two men."

"You've got others." He hung up. Sat back in his chair.

God, he was surrounded by stupid people. The Sarasota Police Department's computer had been easy to crack. He knew from the start that Hamilton was in the hotel hideout, but the cops didn't know who they were dealing with. He was just smarter than most anybody else in the world. He ought to get a Nobel Prize or something.

Except that nobody knew who he was. He was known throughout the southeast simply as "The Hacker." Hard men bought his services, paid him in cash or wire transfers to his Cayman Islands bank account. He had never come to the attention of law enforcement. He knew this because he trolled the computers of all the agencies on a regular basis. No one ever knew he had been there.

He'd been contacted by his client in this case in the usual way. An e-mail to an account that went through several foreign servers before landing in the one he used in Germany. It would be almost impossible to trace him. When he finished one job, he waited for the next. He lived simply, didn't really need money, but enjoyed watching his stash grow. Maybe someday he'd move to an island, maybe buy one for himself and live there alone. He didn't need people, didn't really like them much, was uncomfortable in their presence. Yes, an island would do just fine.

Most of his work was simply finding somebody. It was usually someone that some very bad people needed to get rid of. All he had to do was point his client in the direction of the people he found and his job was over. He never knew what happened to those he put the finger on. And he didn't care.

Sometimes, like in this case, muscle was needed. The Hacker had established a working relationship with a biker gang in Tampa that had affiliates in many places in the world. When he needed to do more than find someone, when his client had the money to pay to get it done, but for some reason didn't have the resources to take care of it himself, the Hacker would call on the bikers. His anonymity was complete. He bought cell phones at Wal-Mart, paid cash for each phone and a certain number of minutes of talk time. The phone number he used was a one-time thing. When the job was completed, the phone was tossed off a bridge into the Manatee River.

Compartmentalization was the key. The Hacker never let one hand know what the other was doing. The bikers weren't his only resource for muscle, and sometimes he needed more than one outfit to handle different aspects of the same job. If one of the operatives got caught by the law, the only people he could give up were those in his own group. It was a neat and tidy way of doing business. The Hacker was very pleased with himself.

CHAPTER TWENTY-SEVEN

Headlights turned into my street. A Longboat Key police cruiser glided to a stop in front of my house, shut down its engine, turned off its lights. I walked out to the curb, leaned down into the passenger window. Officer Steve Carey sat behind the wheel. "Hey Matt. Glad Logan's okay."

"Yeah. Me too. Want some coffee? I just put a fresh pot on."

"Wouldn't mind if I do. It's going to be a long night."

"Come on in. Logan's brewing the joe."

I stuck Abraham's letter in my pocket as we walked to the front door. We sat at the kitchen table and sipped our coffee, talking quietly about the day's events. Logan and I had known Steve for a long time. The year before, when one of our friends had been ill, Steve had taken vacation days to drive him to the hospital and doctor's offices for treatment. He was a good cop, a quiet guy, compassionate and helpful to all who knew him. This past fall, the local Kiwanis club had named him officer of the year.

Have you met the new detective?" I asked Steve.

"No, but I hear she's hot."

"Pretty much," said Logan, "but she's a hard-ass."

"Well," said Steve, "I don't think that'll be a problem for me. She's too old."

I laughed. "It's all in perspective, Steve. What are you? Twenty-five?"

"Twenty-four. I'd better get back outside. I'm supposed to be keeping you guys safe."

"You can stay here," I said.

He laughed. "Not a chance. The chief would bust my balls if he thought I wasn't out there in the car standing guard. Gotta go."

After Steve left, I pulled the letter from my pocket. "Logan, I need to bring you up to date on something. Do you remember Abraham Osceola?"

"I never met him, but I know he's the guy who helped you out down in the Keys last spring. Is that the same one the police talked to at my place on Saturday?"

"That's him. I talked to Marcia, over at my condo. Abraham came there looking for me on Friday, just before he showed up at your place. Marcia told him that I was out of town, but that you might know how to get in touch with me. She gave him your address. He probably went to your house trying to find me. Later that night, somebody bashed in his head at one of those cheap motels over on the Trail."

"So you think that's connected to somebody taking a shot at me?"

"Probably. I'm guessing that the bad guys had your apartment staked out in case you came home. If they figured out you weren't dead, they'd probably think you might be treated and released. They could have followed Abraham to his hotel."

"So he never contacted you?"

"No. But tonight I found a letter in my mailbox from him."

Logan looked at the envelope in my hand. "Open it and let's see what it says."

I took the letter out of the envelope. There was one page that looked as if it had come from a copy machine. The writing was in black ink, a tight cursive, very legible. It read:

My dear Matthew,

I hesitate to bring my troubles to you, but I have nowhere else to turn. I tried to retain a lawyer in South Florida to help me, but he seemed baffled by the whole legal process. I hope you can help.

I have discovered a secret that will make my people rich beyond their dreams. As you know, the Seminole tribe is getting wealthy from its gambling enterprises, but we Black Seminoles have no part in those affairs. We are still poor and living mostly on Andros Island in the Bahamas.

I will need legal counsel to perfect our claim. I am in hopes that you will be able to assist me upon your return from holiday. You may reach me at the Jensen Motel on North Tamiami Trail in Sarasota.

Your faithful friend,
Abraham Osceola

"What the hell is that all about?" Logan asked.

I shook my head. "No clue."

"You don't think it's buried treasure?"

"I doubt it. Abraham is a smart, shrewd man. I don't think he'd go off after some kooky idea of buried treasure."

"I wonder if this has something to do with the people who're after us?" Logan asked.

"If it is, then Abraham must have stumbled onto something big."

"And real."

"Why are the West Coast Marauders involved?"

"Damned if I know," Logan said.

"What time does Jock get in?" I asked.

"Early. He's renting a car and will drive out to the key. He said he'd be here for breakfast."

"No surprises there. He always eats the same thing."

"A bowl of grits with fried eggs on top."

"Well, he worries about his weight," I said.

Logan stood, stretched, and yawned. "Been a long day. I'm going to bed. You got your gun handy?"

"Oh yeah. And the M-1 is in the closet in your bedroom. Locked and loaded. See you in the morning."

I got up and followed him down the hall, turning into my bedroom. I brushed my teeth, undressed, and fell across the bed into a dreamless sleep.

TUESDAY

CHAPTER TWENTY-EIGHT

I crawled out of bed, washed my face, brushed my teeth, and padded toward the kitchen. Light was just beginning to seep over the bay, a gray false dawn. There were no clouds, so the sun wouldn't be far behind. I stood for a moment in the living room, staring outward, ever awed by the splendor of the sunrises in our latitudes. In a moment, the first arc of the sun began to peek above the mainland, painting the sky in pastels of gold and yellow and burnt orange. Tuesday, another day born, the sun a happy precursor of what might prove to be a dangerous time for my friends and me.

I put the fixings in the coffee maker, went to get the paper off the front stoop. The police car was disappearing around the corner, headed out of the village. Steve, or somebody, had stayed until dawn.

I went back to the living room to watch the day unfold from the night. I opened the sliding glass door that led to the patio, drank in the light air that blanketed the bay, the scent of the sea tickling my nose. The water was flat, without a ripple, reflecting the pastoral scene of trees that hugged the shore of nearby Jewfish Key. My boat rested in her slip, inviting in her stillness, as if she were beckoning me aboard, needing to run with the dawn, like a good horse in an open pasture, just for the hell of it. I was sorely tempted. But not this morning. Jock would be here soon, and we'd go about the dirty business of ferreting out those who would harm us.

I flopped onto my favorite lounge chair on the patio, read the paper, and sipped at my coffee. A front-page article recounted the deaths on Fruitville Road on Monday. There were few details, and the names of the witnesses, Logan and me, were not printed.

There wasn't much else to the paper. The usual problems in the Middle East, drought in Africa, floods in Bangladesh, a terrorist cell unearthed in London. I put it down in disgust. Our little island, so isolated from those problems, was in the paper, right beside the tragedies. Sometimes, real life intrudes into our slice of paradise.

I thought about the treasure Abraham had mentioned in his letter. What could it be? Abraham was not one given to flights of fancy. At least that was my impression during our brief meeting. He was a historian of sorts, having absorbed the oral traditions of his people as he grew up on Andros Island among the descendants of the Black Seminoles who had migrated there eight or nine generations ago. He was serious about his heritage and accepting of his people's fate. They had once, not so many years before, been known among other Bahamians as the "wild Indians of Andros." They eked out a living fishing the flats that surrounded the northern end of Andros where their settlement, known as Red Bays, hung precariously to the northwest corner of the island.

When Abraham had been a boy, the settlement enjoyed a modicum of prosperity, brought about by the abundance of sponges in their waters. They harvested the creatures and sold them to American buyers who turned them into bathroom sponges. Then, in the 1930s, a fungal infection attacked the sponges and depleted their numbers to the extent that it was no longer feasible to harvest them. The industry died, and with it the prosperity of the Black Seminoles of Andros.

I knew that Abraham had left the island many years before and worked the fishing boats out of Key West. He was now retired and protected the traditions of his people, trying to pass them down to the newer generation. The young people of Andros, even those who still thought of themselves as Seminoles, had become assimilated into the larger Bahamian culture. They did not speak the ancient language and had little use for the ramblings of an old man who would teach them of a people who, in effect, no longer existed. But Abraham persevered.

Had he come across something that could bring prosperity to his people? It sounded that way from his letter, but what could make them rich? He said he would need legal counsel to perfect their claim. But claim to what?

I would have heard from Bill Lester if Abraham had regained consciousness, and I hadn't. I'd call the hospital later to see if I could get a progress report. I suspected the only way I was going to learn what Abraham had found was if he told me. And he'd have to survive a nasty head wound to do that.

I didn't practice law anymore. I wasn't sure that Abraham had understood that. I'd told him in our one meeting that if I could ever be of help to him on Longboat Key, to give me a call. I hadn't meant legal help. In fact, I don't think I meant much of anything. My comment was more of an expression of gratitude for the help he'd given me. I had not expected to ever see him again, but I would have gladly entertained him and put him up had he come my way. It never occurred to me that Abraham would need legal help, or that he would think I could provide it.

I heard her before I saw her. A powerful go-fast boat coming up the Intracoastal. She came into view rounding the head of Jewfish Key, not slowing for the no wake signs that guarded our lagoon. She turned north, running in close to shore on my side of the water. A shiver went up my spine, a memory of another go-fast with a rifleman tugging at my consciousness. I'd been here before, a little déjà vu, but in another time and place. That day, I'd been jogging on the beach when somebody took a potshot at me. I'd survived.

Clarity sometimes comes in a flash, quick and bright and serious. I knew in that moment that somebody in that boat was going to try to kill me. I rolled out of the lounge, wishing for the pistol I'd left on my nightstand. But it wouldn't have helped. The boat slowed, came off plane, settled in the water, making way slowly. A man rose from the passenger seat, stepped back behind the driver. He lifted a weapon to his shoulder. It took me a moment to recognize it. An RPG. Rocket Propelled Grenade. Enough explosive to take out a helicopter, or my house. He was bringing the launcher into position, pointing at my patio, his face split by a grin, ghoulish in its intensity. The driver was giving me the finger. My senses sharpened, as they once did in jungles filled with the enemy. My eyes bored in on the man with the launcher. His finger was tightening on the trigger mechanism. He was about to blow me to hell.

CHAPTER TWENTY-NINE

The man was dressed in scrubs, those blue loose fitting clothes that are ubiquitous in hospitals and doctors' offices. The shirttail was outside his pants, large pockets on either side, a place for stethoscopes and other tools of the medical trade. A gauze mask hung from his neck, a cloth cap the same color as the clothes covered his hair. He wore glasses, was clean shaven, tall, lanky, and nondescript. A name tag pinned to his shirt identified him as Morgan Thomas, M.D.

He walked with purpose through the lobby, took the elevator to the fourth floor. He ducked his head as he passed the nurse's station. No one paid any attention to him. Just another doctor visiting patients before office hours, a running start on the day.

It was early and the shift change was taking place. The day shift taking over from the night crew. All the floor staff were gathered at the nurse's station, going over charts, bringing the day people up to date on what had happened overnight. Soon the lab techs would be coming to the floors, taking blood samples, getting ahead of the kitchen personnel who would bring breakfast.

A nursing assistant came out of a room carrying a bedpan, a towel placed discreetly over it, walked toward the doctor, spoke to him. The doctor nodded, a man preoccupied with his mission, bringing his life-saving skills to patients in need. The halls were quiet. A public address system broke the silence, paging Dr. Bromley. Then, quiet again, the only sound that of footsteps on polished floors.

The doctor approached the room in which Abraham Osceola lay. A Sarasota policeman sat in a chair beside the door. He stood as the doctor approached.

"Good morning," said the doctor.

"Good morning, sir."

"I'm here to have a look at the patient."

"I have to see your ID, sir."

"ID? I've just come from surgery. I don't carry ID in these clothes. Look at the name tag."

"I'm sorry, Doctor. I can't let you in without some identification."

The doctor exploded. "I'm his fucking doctor, officer. I'm trying to save his life."

The policeman looked discomfited, indecisive. He didn't want to get into trouble for keeping a doctor from his patient. Still, rules are rules, and he'd been ordered by his boss to let no one in without ID, and then only those who were on his list. "I'm sorry, sir. I can only let you in if you have identification. Even if you're on the list."

The man in scrubs didn't know about the list. He'd assumed no doctor would be refused admittance to the patient's room. "Let me see that list, officer."

The cop turned to pick up his clipboard. The doctor pulled a blackjack from his oversized pocket and hit the officer behind his right ear. The cop went down, lay still. The doctor looked up and down the hall, ready to flee if anyone came around the corner. He was alone. He reached down and grabbed the officer under the arms. He pulled him into Abraham's room, dropped him on the floor, shut the door.

The doctor, who wasn't really a doctor, looked around the room. The curtains were drawn, no lights on. The space was dim, silent except for the noise from monitors placed beside the bed. He had to get in and get out quickly. Somebody would be along any minute. If the cop wasn't at the door, somebody would come into the room, puzzled, wondering why the officer had been pulled off. Then there would be alarms sounding all over the hospital. He moved quickly, taking a small caliber pistol from his pocket. A silencer was affixed to the barrel of the gun. He would finish this quickly. One shot to the head, between the eyes, and the smart-ass Bahamian would be dead. He'd be out of the room before anybody came. If the alarm were raised, he'd keep moving, get lost in the confusion. Just another tired doctor leaving the hospital for home. The man moved toward the bed, the pistol held in front of him, his finger lightly caressing the trigger.

CHAPTER THIRTY

I was pinned to the deck of my patio, like a fly caught in the stickiness of flypaper. I couldn't move, couldn't defend myself, couldn't ward off the death that was coming for me on a peaceful morning beside a calm bay. I watched the launcher, waiting for the shot, the rocket coming my way, bringing death. I was watching a world in slow motion, the finger still squeezing the trigger on the launcher, the rocket head glinting in the morning sun, ready to launch, a look of readiness about it, a look of evil.

A rifle cracked. Close by. The man with the launcher went over backward, blood creating a Rorschach-like blot in the middle of his chest, staining the white T-shirt he wore under a black leather jacket. The launcher went over the side of the boat.

Another crack. The boat driver had begun to turn, to look for the trouble behind him, to figure out why his buddy had fallen. The bullet caught him in the neck. A look of surprise spread over his face, blood spurted rhythmically, an arterial flow that would kill him in less than a minute. He had reflexively pulled the wheel of the boat to his right when he heard the first shot. The second shot, the one that killed him, was a second later, and the man had no time to correct his course.

I watched the blood spurt from the driver's neck wound. He flopped over against the throttle assembly, his face now devoid of any expression, his mouth slack, eyes closed. He was dead, not a condition he had contemplated that day.

I looked behind me. Logan was standing in the open doorway to the patio, the M-1 still at his shoulder, a wisp of smoke escaping the barrel of the weapon. He took it from his shoulder, cradled it in his arms, looked at me and said, "pissants."

Only a few seconds had elapsed since I first saw the go-fast approaching. The M-1 was a weapon I'd bought at a gun show. I'd take it to the range and fire it sometimes, zero it in, shoot at the targets, get the kick in the shoulder and remember another time when I'd gone nowhere without an M-16. The M-1 was the weapon of the Cold War, replaced as the war in Vietnam cranked up by the M-14, which was soon replaced by the M-16, the weapon I'd carried at the end of the war.

I'd kept the old rifle in the closet of my guest room, standing in the corner, the clips on the shelf. On Saturday, after Bill Lester told me somebody had tried to kill Logan, I had inserted the clip with eight .30-caliber rounds. One of the rounds automatically chambered. The weapon was ready to fire. I engaged the safety and left the rifle in the closet.

"Logan," I said, my voice shaking with the nervous aftermath of a near death experience. "Where the hell did you come from?"

"I was bringing the rifle out to the patio. I saw it in the closet this morning and was going to ask you if I could use it at the range the next time we go. It's in pristine condition. I saw the go-fast, the idiot with the launcher, and did what they taught me to do in the infantry."

"You saved my life, old friend."

"Man, this is getting to be a habit." He laughed.

The boat was still moving slowly toward Jewfish Key. Suddenly it came to a stop. The bow had found the large sandbar that lurks off the northwestern tip of the island. The twin props were straining to push the boat farther, but it wasn't moving. It was hard aground.

I went inside to call the police. I told the dispatcher what had happened, and in a few minutes I heard the wail of a police siren, getting louder as the cruiser neared my house. I went around front to meet the officer: Steve Carey, looking tired, haggard after a long night sitting in his car.

"I was just checking out, on my way home to get some sleep. What the hell happened?"

I told him as we walked around to the back of the house. The go-fast was still straining to push over the sandbar. It wasn't going anywhere.

"I've got the boat cop on his way," said Steve. "And I alerted the chief."

"The rifle that Logan shot them with is in my living room. If you need it."

"The lab guys will probably want to take a look at it. How's Logan holding up?"

"He's okay. He just killed two men, so he's not exactly ecstatic, but he knew he didn't have a choice. Had to do it."

We walked through the patio door. "Hey Logan," said Steve. "You okay?"

"I will be."

"From what Matt says, you did the right thing. That RPG would've taken out this house and maybe a couple of others. You saved some lives today."

"Yeah. And I also took a couple."

"Had to be done," said Steve.

"I know. I'll be okay."

Steve's radio announced that the boat cop was coming around Jewfish and would be at our location in a couple of minutes. The chief was on his way.

We went back to the patio and watched the police boat idle up to the go-fast. A rigid-hull inflatable from the Coast Guard station at Cortez arrived at the same moment, coming from the north, skirting the sandbar. There were four Coastguardsmen aboard, weapons at the ready. They pulled in next to the police boat, looked at the bodies, and put their weapons away. The officer talked to the Coastie in charge and then gunned his boat toward my dock. The three of us went to meet him.

"Hey Matt, Logan," the officer called as he idled into my dock. "You guys okay?"

"We're fine," I said. "Any idea who those guys are?"

"No, but we'd like for you to come out and see if you can identify either of them. We've got the CSI guy on the way, and we'll have the meat wagon at Moore's dock in about half an hour."

"You guys go ahead," said Steve. "I'd better wait for the chief."

Logan and I clambered down into the police boat and chugged across to the go-fast. The bodies were still, one in the driver's seat and the other slumped on the sole of the boat. The driver was a big man, totally bald, wearing black pants, black T-shirt, and black biker boots. The shooter was a smaller man wearing a scraggly beard, a diamond stud in his left ear, hair in a ponytail. He wore black trousers, a white T-shirt, black leather jacket, and white sneakers. The T-shirt bore a large read splotch of blood. His eyes were not quite closed, as if he were trying to see through slits meant to keep us from knowing he was watching.

"Do you know either of these guys?" the boat cop asked.

"No," I said. "But the driver fits the description of a guy who hired one of the fisherman over in Cortez to abduct me on Sunday. The chief knows about that."

"The lab guys will figure it out. You ready to go back home?"

"Let's go," I said.

CHAPTER THIRTY-ONE

The boat cop moored his craft to my dock. I saw Detective John Kintz standing on my patio talking to J. D. Duncan.

"Logan," said J.D., "we'd like a minute for a statement. Then we'll need to talk to Matt."

"Let's go inside," said Logan. "I never did get my coffee this morning."

I walked around to the front of the house. There were three police cars parked in the street. Three uniformed officers were standing in a semicircle around Chief Bill Lester, the shade of an ancient Banyan tree protecting them from the sun. Bill was talking in low tones, the officers listening intently. Several neighbors stood near the street, watching, probably wondering what had happened. Cotty Johnson saw me and shuffled over, wearing the same housecoat she'd had on the last time I'd seen her.

"Matt," she said, "I think I'm beginning to understand why you had to give up your condo. Trouble seems to follow you." She was smiling, taking the sting out of her words.

"I hope you're not going to insist that I move again, Cotty. I'm just getting settled in."

"Ah, you can stay. I kinda like having you around."

A white Pontiac turned into our street and came to a stop behind the police cruisers. The driver's-side door opened and Jock Algren got out. He stood for a moment, surveying the crowd, a look of disquiet on his face, a man used to trouble and always ready to deal with it.

"Hey," said one of the officers standing near the chief. "This is a crime scene."

Bill looked up, grinned. "It's all right, Biggs."

"Hey, Chief," said Jock. "I don't think a uniformed greeting ceremony was necessary."

"Don't push your luck," Lester said. "I may have to run you off my island, yet."

Jock laughed. I walked up and grabbed him in a bear hug. He was six feet tall, rangy the way a marathon runner is. He had a perpetual tan, a craggy face, a bald head with a fringe of black hair. He was wearing a black silk T-shirt, black slacks, black Italian loafers, black socks, and a black leather jacket. He liked to travel in black for some reason. I think he had been taken by the hero Paladin of the TV show of our childhood *Have Gun-Will Travel*, the one in which the lead character always dressed in black.

"I'm glad you're here, Jock," I said. "We're going to need you."

"What's going on, podner?" he asked, his eyes sweeping the people standing around.

"Come on inside. Logan's here. He just pulled my fat out of the fire."

"What happened?"

"Logan killed two men who were trying to take me out."

"Shit. Is he okay?"

"He will be. He's inside giving a statement to the law."

Jock stopped. "Talk to me, Matt. What happened?"

I told him the whole story, standing in the sunshine near a bougainvillea bush, its red flowers gleaming like blood. A quiet neighborhood, filled with people I knew and liked didn't seem like a place that death would stalk on a bright spring morning. But it had. And death had come to some very bad people. It could have been me. And it would have been me if Logan hadn't picked that very moment to walk out onto the patio armed with a fully loaded M-1 rifle.

His shots had been deadly accurate, the muscle memory of the infantry sharpshooter kicking in. I doubt that he knew he still had the ability to ping a target at thirty yards. But it was there, that ability buried somewhere like a bad memory that popped up unexpectedly. In this case, just when he needed it. When I needed it.

I talked for ten minutes while Jock listened, never interrupting. I knew he was storing it all away in his prodigious brain, sorting the facts, trying to piece together the puzzle, isolating the unknowns, and deciding how we would get the information we needed.

Bill Lester walked up as I was finishing. "Bill," said Jock, "Good to see you."

"You too, Jock. I'm glad you're here."

Jock nodded his head. "Thanks. Do you know anything about this biker gang, the West Coast Marauders?"

"Some. They're based in Tampa, but they deal drugs all along the southwest coast. We've never had any problem with them on Longboat, but Manatee County has had some extensive involvement. I heard a vague rumor that they may have set up an undercover operation to infiltrate the gang last year. They rolled up a number of the members in raids, but I think the big guys stayed out of it. It might not have been an undercover thing. Maybe the cops just got lucky and I assumed it was an operation going down."

Jock thought for a moment. "Could you get me in touch with somebody at Manatee County who would know about the operation or know something about the Marauders?"

"Big question, Jock. I can try. Matt, do you remember Detective David Sims?"

"Sure."

"He knows all about Jock from that mess in the Keys last year. Let's talk to him. Maybe with Jock's government credentials they'll loosen up enough for a conversation."

"Will you set it up?" Jock asked.

"I'll get back to you as soon as I talk to Sims. But I don't want you starting a war on my island. And if you do, I don't want to know about it." He walked off.

"What are you thinking?" I asked Jock.

"We need to find the leader and cut him out of the pack. Maybe we can persuade him to help us find out what's going on and why they're trying to kill you."

"Sounds like a plan," I said.

J.D. came out the front door and down the sidewalk toward us. She was wearing jeans and a white golf shirt. Beige boat shoes. No socks. Her

Sig and her badge were on her belt, a serious look on her face, her hair in a ponytail. "Morning Matt," she said. "You okay?"

"Yeah. Detective J. D. Duncan, this is Jock Algren, an old friend." They shook hands.

"Do you live here on the island, Mr. Algren?" she asked.

"I live in Houston."

"What brings you to our key?"

"Somebody's trying to kill Matt. I didn't want to miss that."

A momentary look of surprise crossed her face before she got the joke. She laughed. "You almost did. They came close this morning."

"So I heard."

She turned to me. "You ready for that statement?"

"Sure. You want some coffee, Jock?"

The three of us walked back toward the house just as Logan was coming out the door. He greeted Jock with a handshake and a bear hug. "Good to see you, Jock. The detective here is about to grill Matt's ass off. Let's go to the Market for coffee."

Detective Kintz was waiting for us in the living room, a tape recorder on the coffee table. He stood and shook hands and we got down to the statement. J.D. was very detailed and pointed with her questions. She caught nuances and followed up on them, backtracked, asked the same question different ways at different times. She reminded me of a good lawyer boring into a hostile witness, quietly determined, searching for the truth, ferreting out the little inconsistencies that color every tale. She went over all the details of the morning's events and of the mess out on Fruitville Road. Finally she was satisfied. Kintz followed up with a few questions and we were through.

"Any luck on identifying the dead men yet?" I asked when they'd finished with me.

Kintz shook his head. "It's probably too early. The Coast Guard boat took the bodies over to the Moore's restaurant dock and the coroner's van picked them up."

"I might know who the bald guy is," I said. "If you can find Jube Smith over in Cortez, he might be able to identify him."

"We'll check it out."

J.D. stood as I got out of my chair. She shook my hand. "Thanks, Matt. I hope I didn't take too much time. I'm glad you're okay."

I held her hand for a moment longer than I should have. I tried to think of something funny to say. I wanted to hear that laugh again. Nothing came to me. It hadn't been a funny morning.

"No problem, J.D. I'll see you later."

I turned and walked out of the house. I was headed to the Market.

CHAPTER THIRTY-TWO

A uniformed Sarasota police officer walked down the hospital corridor, sipping on a cup of Starbucks coffee. He spoke to the people crowded into the nurse's station and moved on. They were too busy for idle chitchat. The cop wasn't looking forward to the day. Four hours of boredom, sitting outside the hospital room of a comatose man with no visitors. He was part of a rotation of officers who had drawn this duty. He would be relieved at eleven o'clock and would go back to patrol. Twenty-four hours of guard duty. Each officer assigned for four of those hours, the shifts juggled so that each cop only had to pull one hospital shift per day.

He raised the cup to his lips again, thankful for the caffeine jolt. He carried a paperback book in his other hand, a way to pass the time while he sat on the hard chair in the hospital corridor. He turned the corner into the hallway on which the comatose man's room was located. Something was wrong. The chair beside the door was empty, a clipboard lay on the floor. No cop in sight. He checked his watch. He was right on time. No reason for the door to be unguarded. Even if the officer needed a bathroom break, a hospital security guard would be by the door. An inviolate rule. Never leave the patient unguarded. Not even for a minute.

The man in scrubs walked toward the patient in the bed, gun ready, his cold heart pumping quickly. He'd do this fast and get out, leaving a dead body and an unconscious cop. He knew a nurse would come as soon as the briefing at the nurse's station was finished. Come to check on the guy in the bed. He wanted to be on the move by then, blending in with the night shift as they left the hospital.

He'd planned this operation with care. The timing was careful, the plan was to get into the hospital when the employees were occupied with their duties, execute the patient, and get out. He hadn't expected the cop at the door to ask for ID. His plan called for a quiet exit, the policeman ignorant of what had just happened in the room. He'd chuckled with delight at the thought of the hell the cop would pay for allowing the person he guarded to be murdered. God, he hated the pigs. He stood there for a moment, over the black man in the bed, satisfied with himself. He'd handled the officer, his quick thinking neutralizing a bad situation.

The relief officer stood at the door, his nerves beginning to agitate, sending signals to his brain. The adrenal glands sitting atop his kidneys kicked in, flooding his system with the hormone that activated the ancient flight-or-fight response. He became instantly aware of his surroundings, thought about calling for backup, realized he didn't have time. He dropped his book and his coffee. He pulled his pistol, a department issued nine-millimeter Glock, a round in the chamber. He pushed the door open with his foot, his gun held in both hands in a shooting position.

The man in scrubs heard a noise at the door, a swooshing as it opened. He turned quickly, expecting to see a nurse or an assistant or maybe a doctor. He'd have to take him out, whoever he was. He'd only been paid to kill the patient, but he guessed he could throw a little pro bono work into the bargain. He turned toward the intruder, pistol held in front of him, ready to fire. But it wasn't a nurse. It was a large man in a police uniform.

The first thing the officer saw was a crumpled cop, feet pointing toward the door. Then his brain registered a man in scrubs, his back to the comatose patient, a small pistol with silencer attached, pointing at his own chest.

The cop was a surprise the man in scrubs hadn't bargained for. Life was about to get complicated. Kill a cop and the heat of the chase became intense. Every cop in Florida would be looking for him. The thought of killing a policeman did not bother him. But cops were notorious for going after those who killed one of their own. It was probably a self-protection mechanism, a way to discourage anyone else from killing a lawman. The hell with it, he thought. It was this guy's time to go. He raised his pistol and shot the cop in the chest.

CHAPTER THIRTY-THREE

Kintz left. The cruisers in front of my house moved on. The neighbors went about their business. It was mid-morning. Quiet had returned, the nasty business of death receding into the past like the outgoing tide. J.D. was standing by the remaining unmarked police car on the street, talking into her cell phone. She closed it up and waved at me.

"Have you had breakfast?" I called to her.

She shook her head.

"We're headed for the Blue Dolphin if you want to join us."

"I'll meet you there," she said and climbed into her car.

I drove to the Market and picked up Logan and Jock. They had not eaten, but Jock had drunk a pot of coffee and Logan had nearly cleaned out the tomato juice stores. He refused to drink coffee.

We drove to the Blue Dolphin, took a booth, and ordered coffee and water and tomato juice for Logan. I made sure they sat next to each other and the empty seat was next to me. J.D. came through the door, spotted us, walked over, and sat down. Tracy stopped by to take our food orders. I introduced her to J.D.

"Nice to meet you, Detective," Tracy said. "I heard you were coming aboard. Welcome to the key."

J.D. thanked her. Tracy turned to me. "I heard there were some problems at your house this morning, Matt."

There are no secrets on our island. News, good and bad, travels fast, becomes part of the idle gossip found in every small town. The stories build on conjecture and supposition and exaggeration until finally there is little resemblance to truth. There is no animosity in the gossip, just people talking and speculating about their neighbors.

"No big deal," I said. "Somebody tried to blow it up."

"What? Your house?"

"Yep. And me too."

"Crap, Matt. You'd better be careful." She looked at Jock. "Good to see you, Jock. You ought to come around more often."

Jock laughed. "I would if people didn't keep trying to blow up Matt."

"I know what you mean." She looked at Logan. "Eggs over hard and tomato juice?"

He nodded.

She took our other orders and left for the kitchen.

I said, "The guy driving that go-fast didn't look like a biker. Do we have more than one outfit involved in this?"

"Maybe," said Logan. "We'll probably know more when they ID those jerks. If the bald guy was the same one who tried to hire Jube Smith, chances are he's not part of the biker crowd. I'm willing to bet the shithead with the launcher was a biker. He hadn't washed his hair in a month."

"You're probably right," I said. "I'd like to know what the bald guy was doing in Cortez. Could he be one of the out-of-work fishermen?"

"I don't think so," said Logan. "If he were, I think Jube would have known him, or at least recognized him."

Logan was right. People drifted through our coastal communities, staying for a short time, and moving on. Some came and found a home and stayed, but others were here for a few days or a few weeks and then they were gone without notice. They'd become regulars in one of the bars, and suddenly they didn't show up again. They'd gone back to Little Rock, or Indianapolis, or Grand Rapids. No notice of their coming or of their leaving. They were like the flotsam and jetsam found in the sea, floating with the currents, unconcerned about direction, but always moving. Maybe the bald guy was one of those lost souls, but I didn't think so. I thought he had come to our shores with a specific goal in mind. Murder. Maybe he was just the recruiter for someone else. There were always men in any town ready to kill for the right price. Sometimes that price was ridiculously low.

We finished our breakfast, talking without direction, three old friends catching up. Jock had been in Europe on some business for his agency.

His golf game was getting better. Logan was glad to be back among the living. Several people stopped by to speak to Logan, all relieved at his survival. We introduced J.D. to them and she was welcomed again and again.

"Tell me, Jock," J.D. asked at one point, "what is this agency you work for?"

"It's just one of those alphabet agencies that Washington has too many of. Not a very important one."

"Hmmm," she said. "I wonder."

Jock grinned. "How did you come to be the new guy on the key?"

"My mom died and left me her condo and I was tired of Miami. This seemed like a quieter place. I might have been wrong."

"Don't let this mess fool you," I said. "We're usually a very quiet little piece of paradise."

"I've got to go," she said. "Day two on the job. I hope nobody else gets killed today."

We paid our check and were walking to my Explorer. I'd have to take it to the body shop later. My insurance company was not going to be happy with me. My cell phone rang.

"Matt, this is David Sims."

"How are you, Detective?"

"I was doing pretty good until Bill Lester called to tell me you and your buddies were armed and dangerous again."

I laughed. "We're trying to keep it all on the island this time."

We'd had a huge mess on our hands last spring and Sims had been a big help. He was a senior detective on the Manatee County Sheriff's department. He told me that he'd heard about the problems in both Sarasota and Sarasota County and hoped it wasn't going to intrude into his jurisdiction.

"I hope not, too, David," I said. "We just need a little help from your department."

"Lester filled me in. I was surprised that he knew anything about this op. It was a closely held secret. I'm the only one in our department who knows anything about it. The feds seem to trust me since I used to be in the Secret Service."

"I think Bill just figured that if you could take down a number of the bikers you must have had somebody on the inside. I don't think he knew anything."

"That's a relief. I can't go into the details, but I did talk to the Drug Enforcement Agency, which talked to Jock's people. Since he's involved, they're willing to help. The undercover guy was a DEA agent. If y'all will go to the DEA office in Tampa, they'll set up a secure video link so that you can talk to whom you need to. You gotta go this afternoon. Two o'clock."

"Thanks, David. We'll get moving. Any problem with Logan joining us?"

"No. I told them you guys were joined at the hip."

"Thanks." I hung up and told the others what Sims had said.

"I need to go to that meeting," J.D. said.

I looked at Jock. He nodded. "I'll square it," he said.

"You'll square it, Jock?" asked J.D. "What the hell kind of agency do you work for?"

"Talk to Bill Lester, J.D.," Jock said. "He'll tell you what he thinks you need to know."

"He'd better think I need to know it all."

"He probably will," I said. "I think he's scared of you."

She laughed and waved goodbye as she walked to her car. She looked over her shoulder. "Pick me up at the station when you're ready to go to Tampa."

CHAPTER THIRTY-FOUR

We went to Logan's condo to pick up some much-needed clothes. Jock and I waited in the rental car. Logan was gone for about three minutes and came back with several changes of clothes in a large laundry bag and a bottle of Dewars in his hand. He also had a nine-millimeter semiautomatic Beretta strapped to his belt.

"Whiskey and a gun," he said, as he climbed into the car. "We're ready for war."

"You expecting war?" I asked

"Somebody ransacked my condo."

That got my attention. "What do you mean? Searched it?"

"Yeah. And they weren't subtle about it. It's a mess."

"Anything missing?"

"Nothing that I could see offhand. They might have taken my bottle of Johnnie Walker Blue, but then again, I may have drunk it. My gun was in plain sight on the top shelf of my closet. They searched the closet, but either they weren't interested in the gun or somehow they missed it."

"They didn't take my M-1 when they went through my place," I said. "They weren't just there to steal something. They were looking for something specific. We need to call the police."

"I already did. They're on the way. I also called Joy. Left her a message to get her butt over here in the morning and clean the place up."

"We'll wait for the police," I said.

"We don't have to," said Logan. "I talked to Bill Lester and he said to go on. The manager will let him in, and he'll get a statement from me later."

"What the hell is going on?" Jock asked.

"Beats me," said Logan, "but if I find the son of a bitch who did this, I'm going to string him up by the balls."

I hoped it wouldn't come to that.

We stopped by the police station to pick up J.D. and then drove to my house to get the banged up Explorer. We were going to drop it at the body shop on Cortez Road on our way to Tampa. I was alone, driving across the Cortez Bridge, Jock, Logan, and J.D. following me in Jock's rental. My phone rang. Bill Lester.

"Matt, I just got a call from the Sarasota police chief. Somebody tried to take out Osceola this morning. At the hospital. He's okay."

"What happened?"

"A guy dressed as a doctor knocked the cop at the door unconscious and dragged him into the room. It was during the hospital shift change and nobody noticed. The officer's relief showed up, saw that the first guy wasn't at his post, and went into the room, weapon drawn. The bad guy took a shot at him, but it was a small-caliber pistol and the slug lodged in the cop's Kevlar vest. It knocked him off his feet, but he got a shot off as he was going down. Plugged the intruder right through the heart."

"Shit. Any ID on the shooter?"

"Not yet. I'll let you know when we get something."

"How about those two from this morning?"

"Not yet, but the coroner will run the prints this afternoon. We should get a hit. I can't believe these guys haven't been in trouble before. Where are you?"

"On my way to Tampa, to the DEA office. Sims came through."

"Right. J.D. filled me in. She asked about Jock, too."

"What did you tell her?"

"That he was one tough son of a bitch, a good guy who had lots of pull in Washington. And that he'd die before he let anything happen to you."

"Sounds about right. Let me know if anything turns up."

"I'll call you as soon as we get IDs on these guys."

I pulled into the body shop, filled out the paperwork, left my insurance info, and climbed into the backseat of Jock's Pontiac. We pulled out onto Cortez Road, heading for Highway 41, I-275, and Tampa. The DEA was housed in a high-rise on Zack Street in downtown, a couple of blocks from the federal courthouse.

Shortly after noon, we crossed the Sunshine Skyway Bridge, suspended almost two hundred feet above Tampa Bay. A tug was pushing a large barge seaward, passing slowly under the span, the barge riding high and empty. It looked like a toy from our vantage point. Men were working on the bridge's superstructure, applying a coat of paint to the golden-colored support cables that gave the bridge its identity. I always get a queasy feeling when I cross this marvel of engineering. What if it gave way, fell into the abyss, taking me with it? Its predecessor had done that in 1980 when a ship ran into one of its supports. The span dropped, taking several cars and a bus with it. A lot of people died that day and I always thought of their horror when I crossed the new span.

We drove through St. Petersburg and into downtown Tampa. Jock found a parking lot, and we walked the two blocks back to the building where we'd find the DEA office. We left our weapons in the rental's trunk.

J.D. seemed a little surprised at all the hardware we'd tucked away. "I hope you've got permits. It wouldn't do my reputation any good to be caught with a bunch of gun-toting lawbreakers."

We were greeted by a pretty receptionist and taken immediately back to a conference room. A large video screen took up a wall at one end, hooked by wires to various computer stations. "Agent Delgado will be with you in a moment," she said. "Can I get you anything to drink?"

We declined and she left. The door had hardly closed before a swarthy man opened it and entered the room. He was wearing navy slacks, a white button-down dress shirt, crimson tie. A pistol was on his hip and a badge and ID card hung from his neck. He wasn't tall, but was muscular, like a guy who lifts weights regularly. He was smiling a toothy smile, his mouth framed by a mustache and goatee.

"I'm Dan Delgado, the special agent-in-charge of this office," he said, reaching out to shake our hands. "Which one of you is Mr. Algren?"

"That'd be me," said Jock, raising his hand. "Call me Jock."

"I'm embarrassed about this," Delgado said, "but I must ask for some ID."

"Not a problem." Jock handed him a small case holding an official looking document.

Delgado studied it, looked at us. "Gentlemen and lady, if you don't mind?" He made a gimme movement with his hand.

Logan and I handed over our driver's licenses. J.D. showed him her I.D. and badge.

"Thank you. I apologize for that, but I had to check." He looked at Jock. "I'm told that you carry a lot of weight in Washington, and I'm supposed to give you all the cooperation within my power."

"I appreciate that, Dan. Were you told why we're here?"

"Only that you have an interest in the West Coast Marauders."

"What can you tell me about them?"

"Not much. We have a deep cover agent in the gang. That's about all I know, and I'm the only one in this office who even knows that. The undercover agent reports directly to Washington. I'm about to hook you up with the man he answers to, and he'll tell you anything you want to know. However, I must caution you, nothing leaves this room. We could jeopardize the agent's life."

"We understand," said Jock. "I appreciate your help."

Dan got up and went to the console under the video screen. He made a few adjustments, stroked some keys on the keyboard, and the screen came to life. It showed a room not unlike the one we were in. There was a table with a chair at the end. It was empty.

Dan stroked again, looked at the monitor attached to his screen, looked up at us. "The supervisor will be here in a minute."

We sat, watching the empty screen. In a few moments, a man came into view. He was wearing a fake beard and had a ball cap pulled low on his forehead. He looked at the screen, grinned, and said in a southern accent, "I know. I look like an idiot. But I have to maintain anonymity. Sorry I can't introduce myself, but you can call me Bubba."

Jock laughed. "I understand Bubba. What can you tell us about the Marauders?"

"Pretty much anything you want to know."

"Let's start simply," I said. "Bubba, I'm Matt Royal, this is Logan

Hamilton, and Detective J. D. Duncan of the Longboat Key Police. I get the idea that you know Mr. Algren."

"I do indeed. We've met, although Jock won't remember me."

"Actually, I do," said Jock. "Columbia, about two years ago."

Bubba laughed. "Busted. I still have to keep the disguise on."

I said, "I appreciate your taking the time to talk to us."

"You're welcome, but I have to tell you the only reason I'm talking to you at all is that Jock's director called my boss and asked for a favor. When that particular director asks for anything, we fall all over ourselves to give it to him. The agency is a big help to us all over the world. Jock has vouched for you guys."

"I understand," I said. "Bubba, we have reason to believe that some members of the Marauders are trying to kill Logan and me and a guy named Abraham Osceola. I would think it's a contract thing, as I can't imagine why they would be involved directly in anything to do with us. Do you know if they get into this kind of thing?"

"They do. They're a bunch of murderous thugs. They make most of their money in the drug business. They import it and distribute it throughout the southeastern United States, using affiliate gangs in areas other than southwest Florida. If the money's right, they'll do contract murders. If you want somebody kidnapped, they're the go-to guys in your part of Florida."

I asked, "Who's their leader?"

"A guy names James Baggett. His biker name is Dirtbag. It fits."

"Is he in Tampa?"

"Yes. They have a clubhouse out in the country between Brandon and Plant City. You can't get in there unless you're a made member of the club. Even the wannabes have to wait until they're full-fledged members."

"How would we make contact with Baggett?" I asked.

"I wouldn't."

"But if it were necessary?"

"Mr. Royal, this is a very dangerous man. I don't think a lawyer from Longboat Key would want to tangle with him."

Jock spoke up. "Bubba, Matt here was an Army Special Forces officer in Vietnam. He won the Distinguished Service Cross there. He's been in a number of scrapes since, and is about as good as anybody I've ever seen. Logan is a former Ranger who also fought in Vietnam and then went to pilot school and went back for another tour flying Hueys. He owns a Silver Star. These guys aren't your usual civilians. I'm told that Detective Duncan is tougher than all of us put together."

"I hear you, Jock, and I know what you're capable of, but be very careful with this guy. These are really bad hombres."

"Do you have a picture of Baggett?" Jock asked.

"Sure. I'll e-mail it to Delgado. You can pick it up on your way out."

"Where can we find Baggett?" I asked.

"There's a bar called the Snake Dance Inn. It's just off Highway Forty-one, south of the Alafia River in Gibsonton. It's in an old two-story building that used to be some kind of warehouse. The building's been there for years, abandoned for longer than anybody remembers. The bar opened about five years ago. We're pretty sure Baggett owns the place. He's there every Thursday evening, holding court."

"How long has Baggett been in charge?" Jock asked.

"Seven or eight years. He apparently killed the last leader over a drug deal gone bad. They punish their members for slipups and there's only one sentence. Death."

"They sound like animals," Logan said.

"They are," said Bubba. "Anything else?"

I looked at Jock and Logan. Each shook his head. "No," I said. "Thanks a lot, Bubba."

"Keep me in the loop if you find out anything. Good to see you again, Jock."

Jock laughed. "Same here, Bubba."

The screen went blank. We sat for a moment, unsure what was expected of us.

Delgado came back into the room, handed Jock a manila envelope. "The picture you asked for is in there."

"Thanks," said Jock.

Delgado shook hands all around and showed us out.

CHAPTER THIRTY-FIVE

It was mid-afternoon when we left the office building. The sun had warmed the pavement and it was radiating heat. The day was hot for late March. The humidity had climbed and I could feel sweat breaking out. It felt more like late May. I wondered if we'd have an early summer this year, but knew that we'd probably get one more cold front before the heat closed in. It wouldn't get cold, but the front would wipe out the clouds and the moisture. We still had some good days before we had to battle the summer and hunker down when hurricanes threatened.

We got into the car and pulled out onto the street that would take us to the Gandy Bridge across the bay and south toward Longboat Key. I was sitting in the back seat next to J.D. "You were mighty quiet in there," I said.

She smiled. "I was watching the master work. Jock, I get the feeling that your agency might be more important than you let on."

"What are we going to do about this Baggett guy?" Jock asked.

I thought about it for a beat. "Why don't we go back to the key, see what Bill Lester has for us on the dead guys? We need to make some plans. We can't go after Baggett until Thursday when he should be in Gibsonton."

J.D. said, "Are you going to get the Hillsborough County Sheriff's office involved?"

"No." Jock said.

"You're not planning to go after him yourselves," she said, a hint of incredulity in her voice.

"We are," Jock said.

"Wait a minute." J.D.'s voice rose. "You're not cops. You can't just go busting into a place. A biker's bar at that. You'll get yourselves killed."

"Detective," Jock said, his voice low, a sharp edge to it, "there are some things that law enforcement is better off not knowing."

"No, Jock. You can't do this."

"Yes I can," he said with a note of finality so pointed that she didn't reply.

We drove to Longboat Key, talking of unimportant things. J.D. sat quietly, seething. She hadn't liked Jock's tone. She was used to being in charge and wasn't going to let anybody, let alone a civilian, tell her what to do. We drove to the police station and were sent on back to Bill's office. He intercepted us in the hall. "Let's grab some caffeine," he said. He led us into the small kitchen, pulled down some mugs from a cabinet and poured freshly brewed coffee. We took it back to his office and sat around his desk.

Lester picked up a piece of paper, looked at it, looked up. "I've got some IDs on the dead guys, but they don't make much sense."

"Who were they?" Logan asked.

"The long-haired punk in the boat was local. Name of Kerry Johnson. Age thirty-two. He was in the Army for a while. That's probably where he learned to use that RPG. He was dishonorably discharged after a year and sent to Leavenworth Military Prison for five years. Seems he was dealing in the arms export business. Selling stolen government weapons to some really bad people. The guns were sent overseas."

"What's he been doing since he got out of prison?" I asked.

"Mostly drugs. He did a year in the county jail for possession with intent to sell pot. He's been arrested several times on drug and assault charges, but nothing else ever stuck. He hangs out with a nasty crowd in Bradenton, but there doesn't seem to be any connection to the Marauders."

"The bald guy?" I asked.

"We can't find a connection between him and Johnson. His name was Mark Berryhill, from Lauderdale. He's been arrested a couple of times, but the charges were dismissed. Once because a witness disappeared and the other when both eye witnesses recanted their statements."

"Arrested for what?" I asked.

"Murder. Both times."

"Any connection to the bikers?" Logan asked.

"Not that we can find. The Broward County cops think he's an enforcer for one of the drug importing gangs in South Florida. The moke in the hospital was Buddy Matson. He's from Orlando. Orange County arrested him on a couple of assault charges, but couldn't get anything to stick. They think he was trying to work his way up as a shooter for one of the mobbed up groups in central Florida."

"Does anybody see any connections among the three of them or with the bikers?" I asked.

The chief grimaced, took a moment to think. "None. That's why it's so confusing. How the hell did these guys get together, or did they? We know Berryhill and Johnson knew each other because they were together in the boat. Everything else is like hitting a blank wall."

Jock sat quietly, absorbing the information. He looked up. "Got anything else, Bill?"

"Nothing. And I want to keep this close. I think somebody had some kind of inside knowledge about Osceola. We haven't put out anything public about him or that he's in the hospital."

"Wouldn't it be easy enough for somebody to call the hospital and ask about him?" I asked.

"He was admitted under a fake name. Nobody at the hospital knows who he is."

Logan shook his head. "Do you think somebody in your department is feeding information to somebody?"

"I doubt it, but anything that goes into our computers here is added to a database that is accessible by Sarasota PD and the Sarasota sheriff since the cases are involved in all three jurisdictions."

Jock looked incredulous. "You mean any cop can get to that data?"

"No," said Lester. "It's a restricted database, but the shift commanders can tap into it as needed."

"So," I said, "you're not putting these guys IDs into the system."

"Not right away," said the chief. "What did Sims have to say?"

"Sorry, Chief," I said. "We're sworn to secrecy. I wish I could fill you in."

"No problem. I understand how that works."

J.D. hadn't uttered a word since we entered the chief's office. She sat with her arms folded, a stern look on her face, staring at the floor. The chief looked her. "Anything to add, Detective?"

"No, sir."

I looked at my watch. The afternoon was winding down. Cocktail hour was upon us. "Anybody for a little libation at Tiny's?" I asked.

"I've got work to do," said J.D. and walked out of the office.

The chief said, "What's wrong with her?"

Jock said, "Bill, we may have to do a little work that you don't want to be involved in. I think your detective thinks she should be in charge and that we need to follow the book."

"I don't need to know anything else, Jock. I'll talk to her. Let's go to Tiny's."

CHAPTER THIRTY-SIX

In a way, our entrance into Tiny's was a coming out for Logan. The islanders had been concerned about the shooting and whether Logan had been hurt more than they'd been told. I thought most of the reception would be an outpouring of relief and affection for Logan.

There were maybe fifteen people in the bar when we walked through the door. Debbie, the bartender, saw us first, came around the bar and grabbed Logan in a great hug, tears coursing down her cheeks. Susie, the owner of the place, was close behind, grabbing at Logan, trying to hug him, laughing. Cell phones came out, people calling others. I figured Susie would have a big night and I didn't think Logan would be buying anything.

Everybody wanted to shake Logan's hand or give him a hug, buy him a drink. As the excitement wore down, people began to notice that Jock was in the room. He was well liked on the island, and people came up to welcome him. Soon, the place began to fill with the locals, all come to see Logan, to revel in his survival, to just be around him.

We sat and drank and enjoyed the evening. At some point the chief said his goodbyes and went out into the night. We ordered burgers from A Moveable Feast, the restaurant that shared the parking lot with Tiny's. The crowd was thinning and I suggested to Logan that we ought to go home. We were likely to have a big day tomorrow and a hangover wouldn't be of much use. Jock took a swallow of his O'Doul's and smiled. Nonalcoholic beer did not produce hangovers.

We left and drove to my house a few blocks away. We'd had a long day and we were all tired. Jock would sleep in the second guest room so that the three of us were clustered together. A defensive position of sorts. We were all armed. Jock had brought his own weapon from Houston in his checked luggage.

I didn't have an alarm system in the cottage. It really wasn't a necessity on Longboat Key, or at least it hadn't been in the past. Now I was concerned about our vulnerability in a house with so many windows. I didn't think the bad guys would give up. And they didn't.

CHAPTER THIRTY-SEVEN

The old man sat in his recliner staring through the windows to the bay. The last rays of the sunset over the Gulf reflected off it, a riot of bright colors suffusing the water. A slight breeze brought a ripple to the surface, exaggerated by the splash of a rolling fish. A trick of light gave the darkening bay the look of spun gold. The sounds of a Brahms violin concerto slipped softly from the concealed sound system.

A half-finished Scotch and water sat on the table beside him, the tumbler sweating condensation in the warm room. Donna had draped a blanket over his lap when she brought the drink, and now was in the kitchen, making him a snack. His old stomach could not handle the rich food of the dinners she'd made him over the years.

Death was near. He could feel it. He only had one more thing to do. Then he would die in peace, see what adventure awaited him in the beyond, hope it wasn't just eternal darkness, that life wasn't like a lamp, its feeble light dying into the blackness of nothingness. What kind of god would make a human being so diverse, and perverse, so intelligent, so questioning of the unknown, and then consign him to oblivion when his allotted span of years was exhausted? It didn't make sense, was not logical. The old man had lived a life of logic and enlightenment and often perversity, but he had always been a seeker of knowledge and wealth and beauty. Surely, the gods would not simply terminate all that he was and assign his rotting corpse to the carrion, the eaters of the dead, the Stygian darkness of oblivion.

The bay was black now, the Scotch finished. A plate with a sandwich sat on his lap. He nibbled at it, not really hungry. It had not been a good day. Three more dead people, and not one of them was among the intended targets. Lord knows, he'd paid enough money to get things done. He'd have to build a fire under somebody. In the old days, he'd have handled it himself.

"Donna," he called. "Come get this damn sandwich and bring me another Scotch."

The albino came into the room, shaking her head. "Sir, you know you're not supposed to have more than one drink in the evening."

"I'm almost dead, woman. A few extra drinks aren't going to push me over the edge any sooner."

"The doctor said—"

The old man interrupted, speaking loudly, agitated now. "The doctor's an ass, woman. Get me a drink."

"Yes, sir." She gave him a disgusted look, turned, and walked out of the room.

"Don't give me that look, Donna," he said, quietly, a little smile playing across his lips.

The call had come in mid-afternoon. To the throwaway cell phone he used for this operation. The Hacker had bad news. Both the men he'd sent to Royal's house that morning had been taken out. The one at the hospital had been killed by a lucky shot from a cop with a Kevlar vest. Shit happens. Sometimes bad luck intervenes. He'd try again. Other men, better men, more focused men. He'd get the job done.

The old man wanted to burn the Hacker's ass, but he didn't know who he was or where to find him. All he had was a telephone number, and he was sure that number was as temporary as his own. He'd found the Hacker through an intermediary, a private detective who had on occasion worked for the old man, one who was not afraid to get his hands dirty. He'd always been paid well. When the old man outlined the plan to the detective, an outline that was as vague as a shapeless puff of smoke on a windy day, he'd only told him he needed someone who could find out things and had the resources to get other things done.

"Are we talking wet work?" the detective had asked.

"Maybe," the old man replied. "Does that bother you?"

"Not in the least. It's just that it'll cost more."

Cost was not the old man's problem. He had more money than

almost anyone in the world. He made Forbes's list year after year. He didn't care very much if he got caught. The fun was in the game, and if he lost it at this point in his life, well, so what. He'd be dead before anybody could build a case against him. What did he care? He wanted to win, and damn the consequences.

So the detective had given him a number to call. He was told that the number had been given to him by a man in Tallahassee whose name he didn't know. The detective had called a colleague in Jacksonville, told him what he was looking for. The man in Jacksonville gave him a number in Tallahassee, probably another throwaway number. The guy in Tallahassee gave the detective a number that he then gave to the old man.

The old man knew his helper only as the Hacker. He was told to wire money to an account in the Cayman Islands. That money was probably wired to other banks in other countries with bank secrecy laws. The old man didn't know and didn't care. He wanted results. As it happened, he wasn't getting any. Not good ones, anyway.

Royal and Hamilton were still alive. He didn't know if either of them had the document, but he knew it wasn't in Osceola's possession. At least not in that fleabag motel he'd stayed in. And it wasn't in Royal's house, either. He'd ordered the Hacker to get somebody into Hamilton's apartment and search the place. He didn't hold out much hope of finding anything. The fact that the papers weren't in any of their residences didn't mean much. The only way to ensure that the documents never saw light was to kill the people who knew about them.

He couldn't understand how Royal and Hamilton kept avoiding their killers. When he'd first heard about the documents and that blasted black man who called himself a Seminole, he knew that Osceola would come to Longboat Key to contact Royal. That's what Oceola had told Blakemoore. But Royal was on vacation away from the island.

Two of the Hacker's people had gone looking for him and were redirected to Hamilton. They had waited until late in the evening, intending to simply knock on Hamilton's door and ask him how to contact Royal. They had arrived just as the cops were questioning a black man near the front of the building. He heard him say that his name was Osceola and that he'd come looking for Royal. The cops took him away. Then the

Hacker's men were confronted by that idiot security guard. Some days nothing seems to work out.

He sighed, moved a little in his chair, relieved the pressure on his thin buttocks. Maybe the Indian would die, he thought. There'd been another fuck up earlier that day at the hospital and another of the Hacker's idiots was dead. Maybe it's time for me to get lucky. That would be a sign, the Indian's death from the head wound. The end for the other two would be the final acts of a dying but resolute old bastard. He chuckled to himself and closed his eyes.

CHAPTER THIRTY-EIGHT

I was getting ready for bed. I'd brushed my teeth and undressed when I saw a red light blinking on my bedside table. It was my answering machine. I didn't use the house phone much, relying mostly on my cell. However, old habits die hard, and I'd been reluctant to give up the land line. I decided to leave it to morning, but curiosity got the better of me. I pushed the button and listened to the message.

"Mr. Royal, this is Lieutenant Charlie Foreman with the Collier County Sheriff's Department. Your name has come up in a murder I'm investigating. You're not a suspect or anything, but I'd appreciate it if you'd give me a call. I think you may have known the victim." He left his phone number.

I checked the time on the digital readout. The call had come in at a little after three that afternoon. My watch told me that it was almost ten, too late to be returning the call. I'd get in touch in the morning.

Marie had called Logan to say that she'd arrived at her sister's house and was still unhappy about being so far away. She said she understood the danger and would stay in Orlando until we told her to come home.

I went to the safe in my closet and retrieved my Sig Sauer nine-millimeter pistol. I inserted the seventeen-round clip and placed the gun on the bedside table. I wasn't expecting trouble, but strangers were trying to kill my friend and me. It never hurt to add a little safety factor to the situation. The Sig was just that.

I crawled into bed and turned out the light. The morning had started off with somebody trying to blow me up. It hadn't gotten a whole lot better during the rest of the day. Maybe tomorrow would be better. I drifted off to sleep thinking about James Baggett, the biker gang honcho. And Detective J.D. Duncan.

WEDNESDAY

CHAPTER THIRTY-NINE

I awoke from a sound sleep, instantly alert. A noise of some sort. Without thinking about it, I had slipped into the sleep of the soldier, a guarded slumber, a part of the sleeping brain alert for danger, for sounds in the night, ready to spring into action with the first perception of threat. I couldn't identify the sound at first, but it had been enough to fire up those old responses, kick in the adrenal glands, sharpen the senses.

I glanced at the clock by the phone. Three a.m. The deepest part of the night, the time when predators pounce. I lay completely still. My Sig Sauer was on the bedside table, loaded, a round in the chamber. The .38 was still in its holster on a chair across the room. I closed my eyes, trying to sharpen my hearing, straining for the sound again, trying to place what I'd heard, dredge it up from the memory banks. It came again, a small sound in the night, a slight gurgle, a swish of an oar biting into the surface. The almost silent push of a boat through water. Somebody was on the bay, close to my house, coming quietly, stealthily.

I slipped out of bed, picked up my pistol, eased myself next to the window overlooking the bay, peeked out. The dark was intense, no moon, no stars. There must be a cloud cover, I thought. I couldn't see anything. I tried to let my eyes adjust, but they were as dilated as they were going to get. My night vision was at its peak. The sound came again. Sibilant, quiet, barely audible, closer.

Then, quiet, stillness. I listened intently, my ears attuned to the slightest nuance of sound. There was nothing. I decided I'd been hearing ghost sounds in the night, sounds that weren't there. I went back to bed, but lay awake, listening. No other sound came and I drifted off to sleep.

I awoke with a start, the sound of voices, a loud angry crash penetrating my sleeping brain. "Son of a bitch," screamed Jock from the front of the house. I flinched, grabbed the Sig and ran toward the noise. I heard sounds of struggle, grunts, loud exhalations, a cry of pain.

I threw open the door to my room, hit the hall light switch, pistol in front of me, ready to shoot. Jock was standing in the middle of the short hallway wearing only his undershorts. He was breathing quickly, panting, letting the panic drain from his system. A man lay on the floor, still, his head at a strange angle. He was wearing jeans, a black T-shirt, and black sneakers. A black watch cap covered his head. A large hunting knife lay on the floor near his outstretched hand.

"He's dead," said Jock.

"Where's Logan?"

"In his room, I guess."

I heard glass break and a shot rang out from Logan's room. The door was only five feet from Jock's. We moved fast, taking up a position on either side of the door.

"Logan," I called.

"It's clear, Matt," replied Logan. "Come on in."

I pushed the door open, carefully. Logan was still in bed, his Beretta in his hand. A windowpane was shattered and another had a neat hole in it.

"What're you doing?" I asked.

"Somebody was trying to get in."

I went to the window, looked outside. Nothing. "Are you sure, Logan?"

"I'm sure."

There was a pounding on the front door. Steve Carey was calling my name. I went to open it. Steve had his pistol out. "What the hell's going on?" he asked.

"Logan took a shot at somebody trying to break in. Jock killed a guy in the hallway."

"Oh shit. I'd better call the chief."

"Let's check the back first," I said. "I think somebody was coming in by boat."

We moved toward the patio door. Three of us wearing just under-shorts, all carrying pistols. Logan was bringing up the rear. I turned on the outside floods. I could see my boat rocking gently in her slip as the breeze buffeted her. A kayak was floating just off my dock, no one in it. That was the noise I'd heard earlier. I looked at my watch, twenty minutes had passed since the boat sounds had awakened me. The sliding glass door leading to the patio was open. I knew I'd closed and locked it before we went to bed.

"I heard them coming in, I think," I said. "I couldn't see anything and didn't hear anymore, so I went back to sleep. There's a kayak out there that probably brought the guy in."

"I'm telling you, somebody was outside my window," Logan said. "He woke me up trying to get in."

"Let's go see," said Steve.

I flicked off the floods. Got a flashlight. "We're not going out there as targets," I said.

We waited for a few minutes to let our eyes adjust to the dark. We went out the front door, fast, hunkered down, pistols ready. We weren't sure if there were other men with nasty intent out there. It was quiet.

We turned the corner of the house on the side where the bedroom windows were. I saw something crumpled in the hedge that ran along the side of the house. I put the light on it. A body.

"Call the chief," said Logan.

"Let me check him first," said Steve. He went to the body, leaned over, put his fingers to the man's neck, shook his head. "Good shot Logan. He's dead."

CHAPTER FORTY

The first cruiser to arrive rolled down the street, slowing as he reached my house. No siren or blue lights. A Longboat Key Police captain parked and unwound from the car. He walked over to where we were standing at the corner of the house.

"What's up, Steve?" the captain asked.

"Somebody tried to take these guys out. Both intruders are dead. Chief's on his way."

"The dispatcher said you had a couple of dead bodies."

"One out here and one in the hall by the bedrooms."

"Show me."

We walked to where the body lay on the grass beside the house. I shined my flashlight on him. Steve did the same. The other cop knelt down, looking closely at the dead man. "I don't know him. You guys recognize him?"

"Never saw him before," I said.

"Looks like a biker," said Steve. "Got those boots, lots of tattoos on his arms. Doesn't look like he's had a haircut in a couple of years."

"The guy in the house looks about the same," said Jock.

"What happened to this one?" asked the captain.

Logan spoke up. "A noise at the window woke me up. The guy was standing there with a gun. I don't think he'd noticed that I was in the bed. Then I heard Jock scream and the one outside broke the glass with his gun butt. I figured he was coming in, so I shot him."

"Good shot," said Steve. "We've had more dead people at this house in the past two days than we've had on the whole island in years."

Another cruiser rolled up and stopped. The cop got out, came over to us. "Can I do anything Steve?" he asked.

"No. The CSI guy's on his way and I called the chief. They should be along pretty quickly. I think the excitement's over. You go on."

Both cops left and we went into the house to the hall outside Jock's room. The light was still on. Steve bent down to look more closely at the body. "You're right Jock. This guy looks a lot like the other one. What happened?"

"I heard the door to the patio and when I went to look this guy was coming at me with a knife. I broke his neck."

"Where'd you learn that stuff?"

"Here and there," said Jock. "I work for the government."

Steve grinned. "Well, that explains it."

The weak light of dawn seeped over our island, illuminating the crime-scene tape that surrounded my house. A neighbor wearing shorts and a T-shirt came out his front door to retrieve his newspaper, a cup of coffee in his hand. He glanced at the tape, the three police cars parked in front of my house, the coroner's meat wagon, the chief and I in conversation at the edge of the property. "You okay, Matt?" he called.

"Yeah, Robbie. I'm fine. Sorry for the disturbance."

"Carol thought she heard a firecracker early this morning. Woke me up to tell me about it. Was it more than that?"

"Afraid so. I'll tell you about it later."

"Glad you're okay."

Lester grinned. "I think your new neighbors are getting used to living with you."

"Who knows? They'll be coming after me with pitchforks soon if we don't get this mess cleaned up and stopped."

I'd gone over the whole thing with the chief and given J. D. Duncan a statement. Jock and Logan were in the living room giving their statements. The CSI guy had finished in the house and waited for daylight to begin his assessment of the dead man in the yard. He was meticulous in his examination of the body. He took a number of photographs, his camera flashing. When he finished, he patted my shoulder. "They came in from the patio. Busted the lock on your sliding glass door, Matt. You better get somebody to take care of that."

"Thanks. I'll get somebody in today."

Lester said, "I think I'm through here. You want some breakfast?"

"Sure. Got time for us to get cleaned up first? I need a shower. Bad."

"I noticed. The Blue Dolphin doesn't open until eight anyway."

I laughed. "Screw you, Chief."

Jock, Logan, Bill Lester, and I sat at a table in the restaurant, picking at the remainder of our food. Tracy brought another round of coffee, tomato juice for Logan. J.D. had joined us as we finished our breakfast. She ordered coffee and a plateful of pancakes and sausages and dug in like a starving lumberjack.

"Hungry?" I asked.

"Yeah. I missed dinner last night."

"We had popcorn at Tiny's. You should've come with us."

She gave me one of those looks that women seem to keep in their arsenal. It reflected disgust, humor, and patience, all in one second. As if she knew she was dealing with inferior beings, that men had not evolved at the same rate as women. She was probably right.

Bill blew over the top of his cup. "Did you get anything, J.D."

She nodded. Chewed the rest of the sausage, made a gesture that signaled she'd talk as soon as she swallowed. "Steve Carey canvassed the neighborhood and may have come up with something. The couple who live at the end of Broadway, right across the street from Moore's, heard noise a little before three this morning. Some guys had pulled into Moore's parking lot in a pickup and unloaded a kayak. They launched right there at Broadway."

"Any description?" Jock asked.

"Not much. Said there were two of them, dressed in dark clothes. The homeowner thought they were probably fishermen getting an early start. They launched the boat and paddled off into the bay."

"Is the truck still there?" I asked.

"Yeah. Stolen last night in Bradenton."

"I'm betting there was nothing to help us on either the truck or the kayak." I said.

"You got that right. No prints. Nothing. We're thinking that they knew Steve was out front, so they decided to come in the back way, over the bay."

"What about the one outside Logan's window?" I asked.

J.D. shook her head. "Maybe he was the backup in case one of you heard the other one coming in the door. Or maybe he was planning to shoot Logan as soon as he heard the intruder shoot Matt. Who knows? These aren't the brightest guys on the planet and they probably didn't realize Jock was there."

"Any IDs on the dead guys?" Jock asked.

"Not yet. We're running prints. Should have something today."

We started to get up from the table. Jock had gone to pay the check. I thought I saw something in J.D.'s face, an entreaty to stay perhaps, or maybe just a grimace at our bad manners in leaving while she was still eating. I sat back down.

"Y'all go ahead," I said. "I need to talk to J.D. I'll catch a ride back with her."

When they were gone, J.D. said, "I'm glad you stayed. I wanted to talk to you about yesterday."

"Go ahead."

"I was a little pissy and I apologize."

"Apology accepted, but you were actually a lot pissy."

She smiled. "Probably so. I'm sorry. I tend to be a bit of a control freak, and I'm still trying to get my legs under me in this new job. Then I find a strange assortment of war heroes and a shadowy government employee who seems to have a lot of power with the DEA, and they want to go off and start a shooting war, and they won't tell me what they're doing, and I get very concerned."

"You should. We haven't been fair with you."

"What's going on, Matt?"

"Jock told me last night that I needed to bring you inside. He checked you out."

"Checked me out? What the hell does that mean?"

"It means that he wanted to know a little about you before he brought you into our little circle."

Her temper flared. "Screw him. Where does he get off 'checking me out?'"

"Calm down, J.D. Jock works for one of the most secretive agencies in our government. They do a lot of things that nice people don't want to do. They do these things to protect our country, to make sure that the bad guys don't take over."

"So what? That gives him the right to dig into my personal life?"

"Only because he wanted to let you know who he really is and what we're planning to do. He had to make sure you were who you seemed to be."

She seemed a little mollified, but her dander was still up. "How deep did he go into my background?"

"Nothing real personal. He didn't look at your medical records or school grades or check porn sites for your picture."

She looked shocked, then laughed and threw her napkin at me. "I'm not on those sites, you pervert."

"I know. I already ran a search."

She laughed again. A magical sound and my heart did a little lurch.

"Okay," I said. "Here's the deal. You're not going to like it because you're a cop and cops are programmed to do everything by the book. We don't always follow the book. Hell, we don't even have a book to look at. But we do get results when we have to. Are you sure you want to hear the rest of this?"

"No."

"Then I'll shut up."

"No. Tell me. I'll forget we ever had this conversation. And I promise I won't interfere."

"We're going after the biker chief on Thursday night. We've got no grounds to arrest him, and even if we did, he'd lawyer up immediately. We'd never find out who's trying to kill us. I guarantee that Jock will get the bastard to talk."

She winced. "Do I want to know how he'll do that?"

"No."

"How are you going to get him?"

"We're going to walk into the bar he owns and ask him nicely to come with us."

"Right."

"And when he refuses, we're going to drag his ass out of there."

"Matt, I've dealt with those biker dudes. They're not going to let you walk out of a bar with their leader."

"I don't expect them to."

"How then?"

"We'll use a little leverage."

"I don't guess I need to know about that either."

"No. You don't."

She nodded.

"Where did you get the southern accent?"

"Wow," she said. "Talk about changing the conversation."

I laughed. "It's time to get onto something less serious."

"I was born in Atlanta, and moved to Miami when I was eight. I guess I never lost the early training."

"And how Jennifer Diane Monahan become J.D. Duncan?"

She chuckled, a light sound in the back of her throat, a mini-laugh. She smiled. "My dad. I think he wanted a boy. I was named for my mother's two sisters and I was meant to be called by both names, little Jennifer Diane. Typically southern, I guess. My dad shortened it to J.D. and that seemed to stick."

"You didn't turn out very boyish."

She reddened slightly, a discreet blush. "My dad was a sports nut and he took me to every kind of game ever played in a stadium. He talked strategy and tactics to the point that I probably know enough to coach a football team and manage a baseball team. But he also took me to the ballet and the philharmonic and bought me frilly dresses and told me stories of princesses."

"He sounds like a man of many interests."

"He was. I miss him a lot."

"Tell me about your folks. I only met your mom a couple of times. She seemed nice."

"My dad was an Atlanta cop. Spent twenty years on the force, re-tired, and we moved to Miami. He went to work for the Miami Beach PD and spent another twenty years there. When he retired, he and Mom wanted to find someplace less hectic than Miami, and they ended up here."

"I don't think I ever met your dad."

"Probably not. He died of a stroke the year after they moved to Long-boat. He was sixty-one years old. Ten years ago. Mom stayed on until she had a stroke last year."

"Why didn't you come with them when your dad retired?"

"Oh, I was already married and working for Miami-Dade PD."

"So Duncan is your married name."

"Yeah."

"Still married?" I asked.

"No. Divorced for ten years."

"You want to talk about it?"

"Nothing to talk about really. I married an idiot. He was a cop too. I put up with a lot for a couple of years, thinking we could make it, and then one night he punched me."

"What'd you do?"

"I broke his arm and his jaw and then I arrested him for domestic violence."

"You're tough."

"I'd been taking tai kwon do lessons since I was little. The bastard was an easy take-down."

"What happened to him?"

"He got fired and the last I heard he was working for Wackenhut as a night security guard at a rest stop on I-95 up near Daytona."

"But you kept his name."

"Too darn much paperwork to change it."

"I'm glad you're here."

She looked at me for a moment, shook her head. "Whoa, Royal. What in the world is wrong with me? I'm giving you my life story like I'm talking to a shrink. It's nobody else's business."

"I don't talk out of school, J.D."

She relaxed a little. "Your turn. Tell me how a macho soldier turned trial lawyer turned beach bum ended up in paradise."

"Just lucky, I guess. But that does touch on my favorite subject."

"What's your favorite subject?"

"Me."

"I'm not surprised. So tell me. I've spilled my guts to you."

"Don't you have work to do?"

She grinned. "I need to know more about my victim so I can work at solving the crime."

I laughed. "Okay." And I spilled my guts. Or at least some of them.

CHAPTER FORTY-ONE

Charlie Foreman sat at his desk staring at the yellow piece of paper he'd taken from Blakemoore's office. It wasn't making any more sense than it had the day before. Royal still hadn't returned his call and he'd left another message on the damned answering machine first thing that morning.

He'd taken a little time the night before to learn something about Longboat Key. There was a wealth of information on the town's Web site. It was a wealthy enclave just off the coast of Sarasota. The island was divided at its middle into two counties, Sarasota in the south and Manatee to the north. It appeared to have a very professional police department with a chief named Bill Lester.

He looked at his watch. Almost nine. Hell, he'd call Chief Lester, see if he knew anything about Matt Royal. He dialed the number he'd found on the Web site.

"Longboat Key Police Department, Officer Calhoun speaking."

"Officer, this is Lieutenant Charlie Foreman of the Collier County Sheriff's Department. May I speak with Chief Lester?"

"I'm sorry, Lieutenant. He's not in right now."

"It's important that I talk to him, Officer. It has to do with a homicide."

"I'll forward you to his cell phone."

Charlie listened to the electronic clicks coming through the phone, then the sound of a phone ringing on the other end of the line. It was answered. "Chief Lester."

"Chief, my name's Charlie Foreman. I'm a lieutenant with the Collier County Sheriff's Department."

"Good morning, Lieutenant. What can I do for you?"

"I'm investigating a homicide down here. A lawyer was shot to death in a drive-by last Saturday."

"That might not be all bad."

Charlie chuckled. "You'd usually be right, Chief, but this guy was harmless. He was the town of Belleville's only lawyer and he wasn't very good at it. There doesn't seem to be any reason for anybody to kill him."

"Where did it happen? Naples?"

"No. Belleville. A little town in the eastern part of the county, out near the Glades. I'm the resident deputy there."

"A drive-by in the Glades? I thought that was big-city stuff."

"So did I, Chief. The world, she is a changing."

"How can I help you, Lieutenant?"

"A name has come up in the investigation. The man lives on Long-boat Key, but he hasn't returned the two messages I've left on his machine. You're a small town, so I thought you might know him. Matt Royal."

"I do know him. In fact, I just finished having breakfast with him. How did his name come up?"

"I found it in a file in the decedent's office. That was the only name that wasn't somebody around here. I thought Royal might know some-thing or have some information that'll help figure this thing out."

"Did you know that Royal is a lawyer?"

"No, I didn't. What kind of practice does he have?"

"None, really. He used to be a big courtroom gun over in Orlando, but he made some money and retired early. He helps out some of the islanders occasionally, pro bono, but mostly he fishes and drinks beer. What else was in the file?"

"Not much. It was real thin. One piece of paper, and the other stuff on it didn't make any sense. The file belonged to an Indian, probably from over on the reservation. Abraham Osceola."

"Holy shit, Lieutenant. There may be a connection. Abraham Osce-ola is in a hospital in Sarasota in a coma. Somebody bashed his head in and then tried to shoot him after he was hospitalized. He's a friend of Royal's. And somebody's been trying to kill Royal."

"There *is* a connection. Tell me about Royal."

"Stand-up guy. He's a buddy of mine."

"What do you know about Osceola?"

"Nothing. He's one of the Bahamian Black Seminoles. He's not from the reservation."

"I've read about those folks. Don't know much about them."

"Look, why don't you fax me a copy of the notes in the file and let me see if Royal knows anything about it? I'll get back to you this afternoon."

"I'd appreciate that, Chief. Let me have your fax number."

CHAPTER FORTY-TWO

Professor Archibald Newman was not what I expected. He stood a couple of inches above six feet, had a head full of gray hair worn just over his ears, a gray mustache, heavy eyebrows, and a prominent nose. His eyes were ice-cold blue and a little startling as they bore into you with the intensity of a laser. Laugh lines edged each eye, softening the hardness of his face. Here was a man who worked out regularly. There was no fat, no softness that I could see. He wore khaki slacks, a long-sleeved oxford cloth button-down dress shirt, a dark blue silk tie. A stainless steel hook protruded from his right sleeve where his hand should have been.

I'd called right after lunch, identified myself, and asked if he had some time to spare that afternoon to tell me a little about the Seminoles of South Florida. Yes, indeed. He loved to chat about the Seminoles and wondered what my interest was. I was vague in my answer, told him that my friend Chief Bill Lester had heard him speak on the topic at a recent lecture in Bradenton, and thought he might be able to help me with a puzzling issue. He agreed to see me at one o'clock in his offices at New College.

The school is the honors college of Florida's State University System. It draws smart kids from all over the world to its small campus on the shore of Sarasota Bay, out near the airport. I found a parking space in a visitor's lot and followed directions to the professor's office in a building fronting on the bay.

He invited me in, shook my right hand with his left, looked at his hook, grinned and said, "Vietnam."

"Who were you with?"

"Hundred seventy-third Airborne Brigade."

"You were the first ones in. Came out of Okinawa in May of sixty-five."

He looked a little surprised. "You're right. Not a lot of people know that."

"I was with Fifth Special Forces at the very end of the war."

He looked closely at me. "Welcome home, brother."

"And you, too," I said. It was a fairly new custom among old soldiers. The Vietnam guys had faced almost as much hostility when they came home as they did from the Viet Cong. People were so against the war that they couldn't separate the soldiers who were serving their country from the animosity they felt toward the government. Many of the men who had served honorably and with valor came home and refused to let anybody know that they had fought for their country. There were no welcoming ceremonies, no thanks from a grateful nation, no appreciation at all from a people these men had served. So now, the old soldiers were welcoming each other home. Finally.

He held up his hook. "One of Charlie's grenades."

"How did it happen?" I asked. That's not normally a question I would have asked, but he seemed to want to talk, maybe share with another soldier who could identify with his loss, or at least how the loss came about.

"Charlie threw a grenade at the hole I was in. I picked it up and tried to throw it back. Apparently my timing was off. It wasn't too bad, though. I've still got my elbow." He laughed ruefully.

"They're doing wonders with prosthetics today."

"I know. But I kind of like the hook. It gives me a rakish look and the ladies take to it."

I laughed. "To each his own."

"Did you come out okay?"

"A gut full of shrapnel. But I survived. A lot of my guys didn't."

"What can I tell you about the Seminoles?" We were finished with war talk.

I handed him the fax that Bill Lester had received from a deputy in Collier County. "Does any of this mean anything to you?"

He took the paper, looked at it, looked up at me, and frowned. "What is this all about?"

"There is a man named Abraham Osceola in a coma in the hospital. He's a Black Seminole from Andros Island. I met him last year, and he came looking for me a few days back. I was out of town and somebody bashed his head in. Nobody knows why. I'm trying figure it out. A Collier County deputy found this note in a file of a lawyer who was murdered a few days ago. My name is on it. I don't know what the other stuff is."

"The Black Seminoles are real."

"I know."

"Do you know how a group of black people happened to become Seminoles?"

"Pretty much. I know the Seminoles fought a couple of wars to protect them from the slave catchers."

"Right," said the professor. "That and their land and their way of life."

"Did the Moultrie Creek Treaty have anything to do with the blacks?"

The professor nodded and told me this story.

Moultrie Creek is up near St. Augustine. In 1823, the Florida governor and federal representatives met with some Seminole chiefs and entered into an agreement that became known as the Camp Moultrie Treaty. The chiefs ceded to the United States government most of the Seminole lands in return for certain farm implements and livestock and an annuity of $5,000 for twenty years. At the end of that time the Seminoles were to agree to emigrate to the Indian lands west of the Mississippi River. The treaty also required the Seminoles to seek out and return fugitive slaves.

Most of the influential chiefs refused to sign the treaty. However, six of their number were finally induced to sign, and many of the Seminoles were required to move onto reservations on the peninsula. The reservation comprised an area of about four million acres east of Tampa Bay and south of the headwaters of the St. Johns River in modern day Brevard County on the east coast of Florida. Others simply refused to leave their land. None of them agreed to return the blacks to the government.

Slaves continued to escape from the plantations of the South and find refuge among the Seminoles. White raiders came onto the reservations and took blacks indiscriminately, including those who had been born free or belonged to the Indians. Blacks whose families had been free for generations were being returned to slavery. The Seminoles resisted and the government withheld their annuity in an effort to force them to return the blacks.

In 1826, Governor William Duval reminded a gathering of Seminole chiefs that the Camp Moultrie Treaty required the Indians to deliver to the Indian agent all blacks that did not belong to the Indians. He told the chiefs that the blacks would lead them astray in hopes of escaping from their rightful owners and that the refuge the Indians gave the blacks was causing an uproar among the white people.

The principal chief, John Hicks, agreed to bring in the runaway blacks, but only if the whites would return to the Indians blacks who had been illegally taken from them. Needless to say, the whites would not agree to this proposition, taking the position that the only blacks they had ever taken from the Seminoles were rightfully owned by whites.

There was little food and starvation threatened the reservations. The Indians began to steal livestock and crops from the white settlers, and on occasion even raided homesteads. The whites were looking for war with the Indians in order to remove them from Florida and secure the Black Seminoles as slaves. The Indians were more than willing to resist with force any attempt to deprive them of their land and black friends.

"So," I said, "that explains the references to 'Moultrie Creek,' 'large res,' and 'black sem.' The lawyer was probably making notes during a conversation with Osceola. He had been talking about the treaty, the large reservation that was promised, and how the Indians handled the Black Seminole issues. But the Seminoles refused to send the blacks back into slavery, and President Jackson repudiated the treaty."

"Sort of. Congress passed the Indian Removal Act in 1830. That law mandated that all Indians east of the Mississippi River who were living on reservations should be removed to the Oklahoma Territory. Many of the Seminoles simply refused to leave Florida."

"That reservation was a huge tract of land."

"Yeah," he said. "Most of central Florida all the way down to the Caloosahatchee River."

"What about the lawyer's notation about mineral rights?"

"No idea."

"Would there have been a will or some sort of testamentary document involved in any of the treaties?"

"I don't see how anything like that would have made a difference. Why?"

"I used to practice law," I said, "and a codicil is really just a supplement to a will. I don't think a lawyer would use that word if he wasn't talking about a will."

"I don't know. I've never understood lawyers anyway."

"If it's any consolation, neither have I," I said.

CHAPTER FORTY-THREE

I got home a little before three o'clock. Jock and Logan were at Logan's condo waiting until the repairs had been made on my house. I'd called Jay, a buddy from Tiny's, who could do just about any kind of home repairs, and he'd come right over to fix the window and repair the lock on the front door.

I listened to my messages on the answering machine. Both from Lieutenant Foreman. I knew Bill Lester had already talked to him, but he still wanted to hear from me. I picked up the phone and called.

"Lieutenant, this is Matt Royal. I apologize for not getting back to you sooner."

"No sweat, Mr. Royal. Chief Lester told me you've been dodging bad guys."

"That seems to be what I do these days. How can I help you?"

"I'm not sure. When I called you earlier, I was trying to figure out who you were and if you fit into the homicide I'm working down here."

"Bill Lester told me about that. I didn't know Jason Blakemoore. I do know Abraham Osceola, and I've followed up on some of the stuff on that piece of paper you faxed to Lester." I told him what I'd learned from Professor Newman.

"Does any of this make any sense?"

"No. Have you got a line on his killers?"

"A complete brick wall. I'd probably write it off as some kind of a random shooting by a bunch of punks from Miami, except for the fact that somebody's trying to kill you and Osceola. And Jason's office was turned upside down. I guess somehow they overlooked Osceola's file. That's a lot of coincidences."

"I agree. And I don't like coincidences."

"Me neither."

"Tell me about Blakemoore," I said.

"Not much to tell. He was a hometown boy, football hero, not too bright. Nobody could ever figure how he got into law school, much less out of it with a degree."

"Did he do any estate work, like wills, that sort of thing?"

Foreman snickered. "No. I doubt if he knew how to draft a will. He handled some overflow from the Public Defender's office in Naples, mostly misdemeanors. I doubt he ever handled a felony. I'm sure the PD wouldn't send him any."

"What about his secretary? Did she have any ideas?"

"Jason couldn't afford a secretary. He was a one-man operation. Him and his computer."

"I would think that in a small town most everybody would know him."

"They did. Me too, for that matter. I was born and raised in Belleville, but there're people here who've known me all my life and won't talk to me because I'm the law."

"Did Blakemoore have a routine? A place he went every day, that sort of thing."

"He lived in a little house on the edge of town. The same one he'd grown up in. His folks left it to him. He'd walk to work most days, have lunch at our only café, and head for the bar at mid-afternoon, stay two or three hours and go home. He was pretty predictable."

"Wife, girlfriend, drinking buddies?"

"He never married, and I never heard of him dating anybody. I don't know if he just had a low libido or if he'd slip off to Miami for some paid-for fun every now and then, if you know what I mean."

"What about Naples?"

"I didn't think he'd do anything like that this close to home. I checked with our vice people anyway, and with the Naples cops. None of their snitches ever heard of Jason."

"If there was a connection there, we'll never find it in Miami. Too big."

"You got that right."

"What about his friends?"

"Mostly guys at the bar. I don't think he ever hung out with anybody except for those afternoon stops at the Swamp Rat."

"That's the bar? The Swamp Rat?"

"Yeah. The only one in town."

"Do you think any of the people at the Swamp Rat would talk a little more freely to me than they would to you?"

"They might. If they thought you were a friend of Jason's."

"Let me think on that. I might come down and have a beer with the boys."

I thought about it for about five minutes. It would take me about two hours to drive to Belleville. If Blakemoore's friends thought I was his buddy, I might learn something they were hesitant to tell the law. I called Logan, ran it by him and Jock. They were ready to travel, but I told them I thought it would be best if I went alone. I could explain my coming to town for Blakemoore's funeral. I'd let them think he and I'd done business together over the years. I might not be able to explain why Jock and Logan were with me. I called Lieutenant Foreman and told him I would be in Belleville that evening.

I went onto the Internet and looked up Jason Blakemoore. There was quite a lot about his football career at the university, but nothing afterward. Apparently the pros thought him too small to play in their league, so his career was over, his name gone from the sports pages. I looked him up on the Florida Bar Web site. No ethical problems. I could find nothing else. He was a cipher.

My Explorer was still in the shop. I'd borrowed Logan's big Crown Vic for my trip to New College. "Can I use your car tonight?" I asked.

"Sure. We have Jock's rental."

"I'll be back tomorrow."

"Take your weapon," said Logan.

"Don't worry. I'll put the Sig in the glove compartment and carry the thirty-eight."

"Wait a minute, Matt. Jock wants to talk to you."

"Matt," said Jock, "I think it would be a good idea if Logan and I came down anyway. In case you need backup. We can take separate cars and we don't have to let anybody know that we know you."

"That might not be a bad idea," I said. "I'll be over in a few minutes.

CHAPTER FORTY-FOUR

It was dark and quiet except for the sounds from the Swamp Rat Bar. Laughter, an old Johnny Mathis song blaring from the jukebox, loud voices, all mixed together in a mélange of noise that floated on the night air, the decibel level waxing and waning as the front door opened and closed, people entering and leaving, the only sign of life in a block of empty store-fronts, two-story buildings that ached with age and neglect. The scars of failure were everywhere, a street of broken dreams, of bankruptcy and loss and age and sorrow and regrets for what might have been. Belleville was a town in its death throes. Soon it would be only a memory, an abandoned town reclaimed by the swamp from which it had been wrung. I wondered if the people in the bar knew this and were partying their way to their doom, like people in a town awaiting the plume of radiation slipping in-exorably toward them from a faraway nuclear war.

Blakemoore's funeral was scheduled for the next day at the little Bap-tist church at the end of the street, the only street that went all the way through town. I doubted there'd be many people there. The funeral was the excuse I'd make for being in town.

We are a society of rituals. Death, birth, marriage, graduations, bap-tisms, birthdays. They have grown up around our needs for validation, for celebration, and for grief. Some people die without leaving a dent in our universe. One day they're just gone and the world does not even hiccup. Others leave mammoth impressions, their lives writ large on the tablet of life. And most of us leave only a few to feel the pain of our passing, to think about us as they move ever closer to their own appointment in Samarra. I had no way of knowing if anybody grieved over the death of this small-town lawyer, but I was betting that he left no impression on the world at large.

It had rained, a quick shower passing over on its way to the Gulf of Mexico. I was in Logan's car, parked across the street from the Swamp Rat, sitting, watching the bar. I didn't know what I was waiting for, but maybe I'd see something out of place, something or someone who didn't belong in this miserable town. A biker, maybe. I knew that Jock and Logan were in the rental Pontiac on the other side of the square. They'd pulled up a couple of minutes before.

We'd put together a plan of sorts that afternoon at Logan's. We'd go in after dark and I would visit the bar, try to chat up some of the regulars. I'd tell them that I was a lawyer and that I had done some work with Jason; that I'd come to pay my respects and needed a beer. A good cover story is a simple one, and with any luck I'd pick up some information that had been hidden from Charlie Foreman.

I watched as a woman came out of the bar and turned down the street. She had tired feet. I could tell by the way she trudged the sidewalk, a woman who waited tables or worked a machine on an assembly line. Except there were no assembly lines in Belleville. She looked sixty, but probably was no more than forty, a body desiccated by too much whiskey, too many cigarettes, too many late nights. Her body language hinted of exhaustion and despair, a woman living in the present with no discernable future, not unlike this miserable town.

She passed the tavern's windows where the lights washed onto the sidewalk, the colorful neon beer sign throwing a rainbow of reflection on the wet pavement. I wondered, as I always do, about what kind of life had brought her here. When did she first smoke a cigarette or take a drink of cheap whiskey, or lose her virginity? What turned a young girl into the woman I saw leaving the bar? Then she was around the corner and out of my life forever. I'd never know the answers.

Her sojourn through my consciousness had lasted less than a minute, but I knew somehow that she had worked her way into my memory banks, back there in the brain where we store information of questionable value. Someday, way out in the future, I would hear Johnny Mathis croon the song that floated out of the bar as I sat there, and the woman would come unbidden into my memory. Maybe she was only a mirage, or maybe as I sat in the darkened car I needed something to hang onto, some semblance of humanity in a world gone crazy.

I sighed, a little embarrassed at my melancholy thoughts, glad my buddies weren't privy to them. I got out of the car and walked toward the Swamp Rat Bar, my .38 in the pocket of my windbreaker, a golf shirt under it, a pair of jeans and hiking boots completing my wardrobe.

The door to the Swamp Rat was made of heavy glass, fixed into a metal frame. It opened either in or out, depending on which direction one was moving. I pushed it open and walked into a smoky space that was narrower than it had seemed from the outside. The jukebox was loud, Hank Williams singing "Your Cheating Heart," an old song sung by a man who died too young. There was a long bar taking up the entire length of one side of the room. Narrow booths sat on the other side, seating for two. They were all empty, but the bar stools were mostly filled. I saw a vacant one down near the far end and walked toward it.

Thoughts began to crowd my brain, a sense of déjà vu, a cold fearful hand clutching at the wisps of memory. I stopped walking, wondering what was going on. Had I been in this bar before? No. Strong feelings of regret and grief and longing were settling over me, scaring the hell out of me. And in a flash a long-repressed memory took hold, came bounding to the front of my brain, and almost overwhelmed me with its power. I saw it clearly, could smell the place, hear the voices and the music. Another time. Another place. A lifetime ago. The day a boy lost his innocence and became a man before his time.

The scene that invaded my mind as I stood in the Swamp Rat Bar was clearer than the reality. Time wheeled away, taking me back many years. A vision flashed, one that I had long ago relegated to oblivion, or so I thought. A memory that I could hardly bear.

I saw a dim tavern from another time, the floor made of scarred terrazzo, no tables, a long bar running the length of the place. The stools were full. Hard-working men enjoying a drink, a little wind-down time before heading home to wife and kids and an early morning and another day of drudge and boredom. The bar was a refuge, a place to get a buzz, to think happy thoughts about what might have been, to share a tale with another soul who understood how it was to be poor and uneducated in the mid-century Deep South.

A medley of odors filled the place, stale beer, dried sweat, and cigarette smoke blown about by the anemic flow of conditioned air from the unit placed high in the wall opposite the bar. A jukebox sat in the corner, the colored lights set into its plastic face providing a look of gaiety in this essentially cheerless place. Hank Williams, now dead but still mourned in the culture from which these men sprang, crooned a ballad about cheating hearts and tears of regret.

The red brick building that had housed the bar for longer than anyone remembered was old and hunkered in a block of forlorn structures built in the late nineteenth century out near the rail yards that sustained the small town. It stood two stories tall, with a sagging veranda fronting the second floor, its brick façade dingy from lack of maintenance. It looked tired, worn out by the incessant soot produced by the steam engines that had once lived and worked in the nearby yard, and later, the residue of diesel exhaust that powered the newer behemoths that provided a small living for the men who worked for the railroad and came every evening to drink in this shabby place.

The boy stood at the door, the light of late afternoon silhouetting him. He took a step inside, letting the heavy glass door glide closed behind him. He waited for a moment, allowing his eyes to adjust to the dimness of the place. He was a child, no more than six or seven years old, his brown hair plastered to his head by the rain that was falling outside. He wore faded jeans and a white T-shirt, high-top sneakers frayed at the edges, the rubber worn down, no socks. He stood quietly, as if contemplating this strange assortment of large men.

A sliver of dread arced across his brain. He didn't belong here, didn't want to be here. But his mother was in the car parked at the curb, the old station wagon with the wooden sides rotting into mushy pulp, the burgundy metal dented and pitted with rust and age.

"Go get yore daddy," she'd said. "Go on, now. Tell him supper's ready."

The boy didn't question the order. It was the first time he'd been sent into a bar, but he sensed that it would become a recurring errand, that he would be needed again and again to herd his father home. He'd already taken a man's place in the household, listening to his mother complain about all that was wrong with her life, her poverty, her drunken husband, her lousy children who drove her nuts. He knew his father wouldn't come home, understood that he didn't want to come home to the small apartment they rented from a real estate man, where the sounds of fighting slipped through the thin walls separating the other apartments in the old house when hard men with no hope took their frustrations out on the sad-eyed women who were their wives.

The boy would eat his supper with his mother and little brother at the table in the kitchen, enduring yet another tirade as she sipped her booze and ranted about how much better her life would have been had she only married the druggist from Valdosta. He'd eat his scrambled eggs and grits and johnnycake like every other night, because the meal was cheap and easy to fix, even for a woman with a bourbon-addled brain.

As his eyes adjusted to the semidarkness, the boy saw his father at the far end of the bar, talking to the man next to him, laughing at something the man said. It was a long walk down that bar and the boy was ashamed to be making it. He knew that eyes of strangers would stare at him and the men would pity him and think his father less of a man because somebody had sent his boy into the bar to get him.

The child had been toughened by his dreary existence, by the stories his mother told of how bad her life was and his father's reminder that he'd had it much tougher when he was a sharecropper's son living on the edge of starvation in Depression-era Georgia. He would make that walk, but he knew that the smell of the place would find a permanent home in the shadowy recesses where he stored dark memories. He stood as tall as he could and stepped off.

The catcalls started. A man at the bar noticed him and said, "Boy, you got an ID?"

Other men looked at him and took up the chorus of jokes. They were not unkind men, and many of them had children the boy's age. They were just having a little fun, poking at a small human that most would have died protecting from harm had it come to that.

The boy was mortified at the not unexpected comments. He held his head high and marched down the line like a general inspecting his troops. He came to the end and stood before his father. "Daddy," he said, "Mama says you got to come home to supper."

His father looked at him for a moment without recognition as if seeing an apparition of someone he loved but didn't know had died. The boy stood fast, embarrassment creeping up his spine. His father was too drunk to see him. Then the light came back into the man's eyes. He smiled, because he truly loved his son. If he was discomfited by the boy's presence, he didn't show it.

"Matthew," he said, "want a Coca Cola?"

"No, sir. We got to go, Daddy. Supper's ready."

"Tell yore mama I'll be along directly. Y'all go on home now. I'll see you there."

"Mama says you got to come now."

His father's voice tightened. "Go on, Matthew. Do what I tell you. Tell yore mama I'll be there shortly, hear?"

"Yes, sir. I'll tell her."

The boy turned and walked out of the bar, the silence in the place more distressing than the catcalls.

Shit. I came back to the reality of the Swamp Rat Bar. A few seconds, no more than two or three, had passed while I stood rooted in a bad memory. I walked on down to the empty stool, took a seat, smiled at the bartender, and ordered a Miller Lite.

CHAPTER FORTY-FIVE

The man straddling the stool next to me was in his sixties, wore three days of beard stubble, a T-shirt stained by something dark, faded jeans. His gray hair was falling over his ears in the haphazard way of a man in need of a haircut.

"You're new in town," he said.

"Just passing through."

"Ain't no hotels around here."

"I know. I'm staying over near Naples."

He blew out some air, a sigh maybe. "Lord. What brings a traveling man into this dump of a town?"

"I came for a funeral."

"The only funeral around here is for Jason Blakemoore."

"Yeah."

"You know Jason?"

"I had some dealings with him."

"Trouble?"

"No. I'm a lawyer. We were working on a case together."

"Where you from?"

"Longboat Key, up near Sarasota."

The man stuck out his hand. "I'm Billy Joe Cuthbert. Folks call me B.J."

I shook his hand, felt the calluses of a man who was used to hard work. "Matt Royal."

"You just get in?"

"Yeah. Drove down from Longboat. I wanted to get my bearings, make sure I didn't miss finding the church tomorrow. Saw the bar and needed a beer."

"You know Jason well?"

"No. Just talked to him on the phone."

"I thought you said you were working on a case together."

"We were. Sort of. A friend of mine tried to hire Jason to help him out on a matter, and Jason asked me to lend a hand."

"You work together long?"

"No. Just the past few days."

"That's a long way to come to a funeral for a guy you really didn't know."

"I remember when he used to play football up at Gainesville."

"Ah."

"He was pretty good."

"Yeah. That was probably the best time of his life. What kind of case did y'all have together?"

"Something to do with some Seminole claims. We didn't get too far into it before he was killed."

"It wasn't about that black guy who claimed to be a Seminole, was it?"

"That's it."

"Funny. Jason was in here Thursday night talking about that one. Said the black guy was from the Bahamas, but claimed to be a Seminole. I been here all my life, knowed a lot of Indians. Ain't never seen one who was black. I figured it was some sort of scam and old Jason wasn't smart enough to figure it out."

The conversation had become inquisitorial and that raised my suspicion at first. As we talked, I began to think it was just the nature of small-town gossip, a local plumbing the mind of the visitor, adding to his stock of stories for other nights whiled away in the Swamp Rat Bar.

I finished my beer and signaled the bartender for another. "Did Jason say anything about the claim?"

B.J. shook his head. "Just said the guy had a paper that backed up the claim. Oh, and he did say something about getting a lawyer up the coast to help him out. That musta been you."

The man sitting next to B.J. had been listening to us, watching closely. We weren't talking loudly and I suspected he was having a hard time separating our conversation from the din surrounding us. I hadn't paid much attention to him, thinking he was just another local interested in the rare stranger in the town's only gin mill. He slid off his stool, threw some money on the bar, and walked toward the door. He was a big man, middle-aged, hard looking. He had ruddy skin and had accumulated some fat, but he looked powerful, a man who did heavy labor outdoors. He wore a sweat-stained ball cap with the logo of a tractor manufacturer on it, the bill pulled low almost touching his bushy eyebrows. He was wearing a checkered short-sleeved shirt, dirty jeans, and work boots.

I watched him leave and turned back to my conversation with B.J. "That probably was me Jason was talking about. Did he say anything else?"

"No. That was about it. He didn't talk a lot. Kind of a lonely fellow, if you know what I mean. A few beers every day and then he walked home. I always wondered what he did in that little house all by himself. Watched lots of TV, I guess. Sports, probably."

"Do you know if Jason told anybody else about the Seminole guy?"

"I doubt it. I was sitting on this stool like I do every day and he came in and sat on the one you're on now. We chatted a bit and after a couple of hours, he left. He was kind of keyed up, said this could be the big one for him. I think he planned to make a lot of money."

"What else did he say?"

"Nothing much. He didn't usually talk about his work, but he had a lot to drink that day. We were talking about how hard it is to make a living around here and he started talking about the Seminole guy. He got shot two days later."

"Do you know Charlie Foreman?" I asked.

"Sure. Everybody knows Charlie."

"I talked to him briefly. He said he'd talked to some of the folks in the Swamp Rat, but nobody knew anything. Did you tell him what you just told me?"

"Nah. I heard Charlie was in here Saturday night, but I went up to Pahokee to visit my sister that morning. I just got back today. I was going to call him, but ain't got around to it yet."

I changed the subject. "Tell me about your town."

We talked for another half hour and had one more drink. I used a credit card to pay my tab and left, thinking I'd gotten about all I was going to get out of the bar. It had been a wasted trip. B.J. would call Charlie Foreman the next day and then the lieutenant would have the same information I had now.

I stepped out of the bar and into the soft evening. I walked a few yards to the corner and stopped, standing for a moment on the sidewalk staring into the dark street. There were no streetlights and the only illumination was the light spilling from the Swamp Rat. The noise had subsided as the door closed behind me, bringing a relative stillness to the night. Something wasn't right. Old instincts were churning my gut, raising alarms, releasing adrenalin

What was it? I stared into the night, my vision sharpening. I saw Jock's rented Pontiac parked across the square, a shadow moving toward it. I fixated on the scene and felt the cold steel of a pistol barrel caress the back of my neck. A deep voice tinged with the cadences of the Glades said, "Come with me, Mr. Royal or sure as shit, I'll kill you."

Before I could respond, I saw the shadow stop behind the Pontiac, roll something under it, turn and run into the dark. I was puzzling it out when an explosion rocked the night. The rental shifted upward, a gout of flame shooting from the area of the gas tank above the rear axle. The car was engulfed in fire before I could move. I was cemented to the sidewalk, in shock, no more able to move than if my feet had been glued to the ground. There was no movement in the Pontiac, no one trying to exit, nothing. A second had passed before I gathered my wits and started to move.

"Don't," said the voice. I felt the pistol bore deeply into my neck. I stopped. A black Mercedes, lights out, pulled up and stopped in front of us. The rear door on our side opened. Down the block I could see people flowing out of the Swamp Rat, alerted by the explosion. The man with the voice pushed me into the car, climbed in behind me, and put the pistol into my side. The driver accelerated around the corner and raced into the night.

CHAPTER FORTY-SIX

It had been a long day and the old man was tired. He'd received a call mid-morning from the Hacker, that useless turd, to tell him that his people had once again failed to kill Royal. In fact the two men sent to do the job were dead, killed by somebody at Royal's house.

"Your biker buddies?" the old man had asked.

"No. These guys were contractors. The biker guys hired them because they knew how to handle boats." He told him how the operation had been planned and how bad it had turned out.

"You're skating on thin ice," the old man said. "I ought to fire your ass and get somebody else to do the job."

"Temporary setback," said the Hacker. "I'll get it done."

"You've had a lot of those setbacks this week. Fuck up one more time, and you're history."

The whole week had been like that. One screwup after another. He didn't understand why the men he'd hired couldn't wrap this mess up. He was sick of the whole thing.

His life was ebbing away, but not fast enough. He sat and stared out at the bay, or watched a little television, or read one of the several newspapers delivered daily to his door. Most of them weren't worthy of wrapping fish.

His gut had become so delicate that he could eat little other than some sort of mush that Donna concocted. When he did eat the rare sandwich, heartburn came with such fire that he swore he'd never again eat another. His Scotch kept him sane, but he couldn't drink all day. His fucking stomach wouldn't allow it. He did look forward to the evening. A time when he could sip his allotted two Scotches and watch the daylight dim over the bay. It wasn't much for a man who'd lived a life so full. Maybe the end time, the last few weeks of life, was the hell he deserved. Hell on earth. Did that mean that death brought nothing? Or maybe another chance, an opportunity to live a better life, to have a family, to enjoy his wealth without the burning need to see it grow?

Well, he'd find out soon enough. In the meantime, it was too late to change his fate. The gods had already written that story based on his life to date. There would be no redemption, no chance to change his eternal future, if there was a future, if there was something more than—than what? Nothingness?

Hell, he was tired of worrying about it. He'd follow through on his plan, stomp out the last people to challenge him, make one final splash on a world he'd despaired of, that he was happy to leave. Those remaining would talk about him down through the ages, regale their children with tales of treachery and deceit that made the old robber barons seem benign. In the end, all he had to leave was his legacy, and that legacy would be one that would make men tremble in awe for generations.

His phone had rung a half hour before, one of the cells that Donna would destroy the next morning. He had dozens of them. It was a foolproof way for people to communicate with him and never know his identity. He had a Web site, one that was untraceable, and had but a single page. Each night at midnight, Donna went onto the site and posted a new phone number, erasing the one from the day before. New number, new phone. She bought the phones as needed, mostly from convenience stores, never the same one twice, and always paid cash. The phones came with their own number and prepaid minutes.

He almost never talked on them. Donna would answer, take messages, and convey orders to the caller. That evening, she came to him after the phone had rung. "Turk is on the phone," she said. "He's in the bar in Belleville. Said Matt Royal came in and talked with one of the locals who knew about the document. The guy didn't know what they were or where they are."

"Ask Turk if he has weapons, and if so, what kind."

Donna disappeared and returned in a couple of minutes. "He has a pistol and some old hand grenades he got from a bent army supply sergeant. Says they're still good."

"Ask him if he'll kill Royal for ten thousand dollars."

She came back. "He'll do it."

"Tell him it's a deal, but only if Royal dies tonight. Also tell him to look out for Royal's buddies. If Turk can take them out, I'll add another ten grand a head."

Donna returned shortly, bringing another tumbler of Scotch and water. "Done," she said, as she placed the whiskey on the table next to his chair.

So he sat and contemplated life and death. He smiled to himself. Royal would go first, Royal and his buddies. If there was life after death they'd be there waiting for him. Would they be angry, relieved, happy? Or was there any such sentiment in the hereafter? Who knew? Who cared?

Turk had started the whole thing. He'd worked in the phosphate mines most of his life, traveling from his hometown of Belleville to the center of the state to dig out Florida's version of gold. His brother, who'd had some schooling at the community college in Naples, worked for the same company, but he was in lower management. He wasn't very bright, so he'd never advanced above his supervisor's position, but he worked hard and did his job in a reasonably efficient manner.

Turk, who wasn't even as smart as his brother, worked as a laborer, and held onto his job through the beneficence of the company. When he got hurt on the job, because his brother had some pull, Turk was kept on the payroll until he had enough years to retire. He owed his brother and he owed the company.

He'd returned to Belleville and lived in a dump on the edge of town out by the swamp. He'd never married, but a succession of hard women shared his bed from time to time, never for more than a few weeks.

Turk met Jason Blakemoore when he had a minor run-in with the law. One of the women hadn't taken kindly to being asked to leave, and he'd had to slap her around a bit. The bitch had gone to the law and Turk was arrested on a domestic violence charge. The only lawyer he had even heard of was Jason, so he'd gone to see him. Turk didn't have any money, but Jason made a deal for Turk to work off the fee by doing chores around his house.

Jason got the charges reduced to disorderly conduct, mainly because the State Attorney's office lost track of the woman who had complained. They had no case, but Jason hadn't figured that one out, and thought he'd done a good job by getting the state to agree to the plea.

Turk was sentenced to ten hours of community service, which he worked off during one weekend of mowing grass at the hospital in Naples. He thought Jason was a great lawyer, because even though that crazy bitch deserved to have her ass kicked, he knew the law took a dim view of such things. He figured he'd spend some time in the county lockup over it, but Jason had been brilliant and Turk was free. He happily went to work fixing up things in Jason's house.

They developed a pattern, two bachelors living in a small town. Most days they'd have a couple of drinks as the day wore down. They'd often sit at the bar at the Swamp Rat for a few drinks and then go to Jason's home for a couple more. No big deal, but Turk admired Jason's football glory and his education. Sometimes, they'd drink more than two and talk into the night.

A few days before, during one of their late night forays into the bottle of Jack Daniel's supplied by the lawyer, Jason told Turk of a client he'd seen that day, a black man who claimed to be a Seminole Indian. As if there was such a thing. But the man whose name was Abraham Osceola told a story of finding a document that would give the Black Seminoles title to much of the phosphate in Florida. It was a stretch, since neither Jason nor Turk had ever imagined anything remotely like a Black Seminole, but if there was such a document, there would be a lot of money involved. Jason could sell those rights, whatever they might be, to the phosphate industry for a tidy sum, a not insubstantial part of which would fall into Jason's pocket through the magic of the contingency fee contract. Jason would get one-third of whatever he recovered, less whatever another lawyer charged to help out.

There was only one problem. Jason had no idea of what action he should take. He could go to court, but that would probably mean federal court, and those judges scared the hell out of a lot of lawyers, including Jason. They actually expected you to know what you were talking about when you came to court. Jason didn't think he could face that kind of scrutiny. He'd never even been to county court where they heard misdemeanors. He always pled his clients out.

Osceola had told Blakemoore that he knew a lawyer up the state who was a real trial lawyer and thought he'd help them out. A guy in Longboat Key named Matt Royal. He was retired, so that's why Osceola hadn't gone to him in the first place. Jason planned to get in touch with the guy and see if they could work out some sort of division of fees that would be fair to Jason.

Turk thought the whole thing was nuts, but when he got over his hangover the next day, he'd called his brother and told him about the conversation. Maybe there was a way for them to get a part of the deal. He could sure use the money. His retirement check hardly kept him in food and booze, much less women.

The old man laughed to himself, thinking about the foolishness of simple-minded men. Turk's brother's job was not very secure. He had a new boss who expected more than he could deliver. In an attempt to ingratiate himself with the new man, and thereby keep his job, he'd told the boss the whole story. The boss sent it up the line, thinking it was all just more cracker bullshit. Within hours of Turk and Jason's conversation, the gist of it had reached the ears of the old man. And as always, he'd taken action.

CHAPTER FORTY-SEVEN

I looked at the man holding the gun. He was the one who had been on the barstool next to B.J. in the Swamp Rat. I was sitting in the corner of the backseat, scrunched against the right side door, hoping for an opening. I didn't think I'd get one. The man rested against the opposite door, behind the driver, a large pistol leveled at me. He was left handed, or at least that was the hand that held the gun. I glanced out of the windshield. We were coming up to the next corner, still accelerating. I saw a man standing in the middle of the street, a pistol pointed at the car. A flash from the muzzle, and a hole appeared in the windshield. The driver slumped over against the center console. The car veered sharply to the right, sideswiped a telephone pole and came to rest against a cinder block building that according to the faded sign painted on its side had once housed a dry-cleaning establishment.

We had not gained much speed before the driver lost control, but it was enough that the sudden stop pushed the gunman into the back of the front seat. At the same moment, I dove for him, grabbed his left wrist with my right hand, and slammed the heel of my left hand into his nose. I felt the cartilage go as a scream tore from his throat. I hit him again and at the same time banged his left wrist into the back of the seat. I could feel his grip loosening, the pain taking over his reflexes. I twisted the pistol from his fingers and slashed it across his face, drawing more blood. I pulled it back, intending to bring it down again into his face. The door opened and the man fell backward onto the pavement.

"Whoa, buddy," said Logan, leaning into the car. "You okay?"

I took a deep breath, the bloodlust draining out of my system. Sometimes, not often, and only when greatly provoked, I lose a bit of control. A red film fills my eyes and I become a man possessed by demons. I want to kill the object of my intense anger. So it was on that night. I think it was a reaction to the anticipation of my own death, and the relief that I was not going to die that day. Maybe it was the effrontery of a stranger who would put a hole in my precious hide or maybe it was just that I was stupid enough to let somebody get an advantage on me, somebody who was intent on causing my death. I am not proud of that part of me, but I live with it and usually control it.

"I'm okay. How about Jock?"

Jock leaned into the car. "Right here, podner."

"That was some kind of high noon crap," I said.

"I thought it had the right touch."

"I owe you, buddy. I don't think this asshole had my best interests at heart. How did you come to be in the middle of the street?"

"Let's get this bozo restrained," Jock said, "and then we'll talk."

I got out of the car. The gunman lay unconscious on the pavement. Jock pulled a plastic flex-cuff from his pocket and used it to secure the guy's hands behind him.

"We'd better call Charlie Foreman," I said. "He's going to be busy tonight. I thought you guys were in the car when it went up."

Jock grinned. "No, but with the car windows dark the guy with the grenade couldn't tell that."

"What happened?"

Logan spoke up. "We saw this one come out of the bar and make a couple of calls on his cell. Then he went to a beater parked on the corner and got what looked like a pistol out of the trunk. He wasn't paying any attention to us, and we figured he might be after you. We got out of the car and came over here to see what was going to happen."

They watched as the man with the phone waited by his car. After about twenty minutes, the Mercedes drove slowly down the street. He let a man off about a block behind where Jock and Logan were parked and then moved to the block just the other side of the bar. "When Jock's rental blew up," Logan said, "I figured you'd be next. It's a good thing the Mercedes turned this way. Otherwise, we'd have had to get my car and come after you."

"So," I said, "you didn't have a plan."

"Not exactly, but we improvised," said Jock, grinning. "It worked out. You're not dead."

I laughed, bleeding off nervous energy. "You'd think somebody would be here by now. The car hitting that building must have gotten somebody's attention."

"They're probably still out in front of the bar watching the rental burn," said Logan.

Less than five minutes had passed since the explosion. I was still a little shaky from the adrenalin rush, now subsiding. I'd thought my friends were dead and was sure that I'd join them very quickly. I pulled out my cell phone.

"What're you doing?" asked Jock.

"Calling Charlie Foreman."

"Hold up. I can't be identified as being part of this."

"The rental car is in your name, Jock," I said. "They'll figure it out sooner or later."

"I rented the car in a name nobody will ever be able to trace. Just being careful."

I shook my head. I could never get over my amazement at the trade-craft of my boyhood friend. Even on vacation from his world of spies and espionage and intelligence gathering, Jock had rented the car using one of the fictitious identifications he carries around with him like so much extra change. I motioned to the man lying prone on the ground. "What about him?"

"Let's take him with us," said Jock. "We might be able to pry some information out of him. Maybe that'll start unraveling this mess."

"I'll get my car," said Logan.

A siren screamed in the distance, getting louder, closer. Another took up the call, this one laced with a loud horn, coming from the same direction. Headed for the explosion, I thought. Logan disappeared around the corner and in a minute came back with his car. The first siren let out one more whoop and went silent. I heard the hiss of air brakes and then only the crackling of the fire across the square and the murmur of voices from the people gathered outside the Swamp Rat.

We loaded the gunman into the backseat. Jock joined him, a pistol in his hand. Logan started the car and drove straight out of town.

"I got around the corner just as the cops were pulling up on the other side of the square. A county fire truck came in right behind them. Where are we going?"

"I don't have any idea," I said. "Keep going straight. This road will connect us to the Tamiami Trail. We'll figure it out from there."

We traveled a couple of miles on an asphalt road that ran straight as an arrow. The dark was infinite and the sweep of our headlights revealed the flora of the Everglades pressing close. The only sound was the hiss of our tires on the pavement.

"Uh-oh," Logan said. "Blue lights behind us. A cop's coming up fast."

CHAPTER FORTY-EIGHT

The Hacker sat in the quiet of his old house, sipping a beer. His recliner was torn and poorly patched. It had been part of the furniture that came with the house when he bought it, and he couldn't think of any good reason to get a new one. He had the windows open, and could hear the hum of the insects who shared the night. The single bulb hanging from the wire over his computer was the only light in the house. He balanced an ashtray on his lap, flicking ashes into it from his cigarette.

His thoughts had turned dark with suspicion. The old man had only provided him with half his fee and a promise to pay the rest when the job was complete. Now there was some question as to whether he could finish the task.

His biker cronies had not come through like they had in the past. They were a mean bunch, men given to violence, giving it and receiving it. How in the world had a lawyer and a retired financial guy taken the best of them out? Was there more to this than he knew?

And who were these other people who'd gone after Royal? Two days in a row. The go-fast boat was a good idea, but the execution was lousy. What about the home invasion? Another fuckup, but who were these guys? The Hacker knew that the bikers sometimes contracted out their wet work, but he didn't know who they used.

The Hacker had been roaming the Longboat Key police computers. The dead men had not been identified, but the biker leader Baggett had assured him they weren't his men. Was Baggett lying? If not, then who were they?

His searches ranged far, tapping into databases of all the local law, probing the drug lords' servers. Yes, they all used computers these days, bad guys, too. They needed their information at hand in order to conduct business, make decisions, keep the drugs flowing.

The Hacker thought that the men from the boat and the break-in might have been part of one of the drug cartels. But if they were, there was nothing in the computers. That he could understand, but the cops would have any ID plugged into their database, and by now, they would have figured out who the people were and where they were from. Fingerprinting was a science and the computers that did the matches were lightning fast. How was it that the cops hadn't identified them?

He'd called the old man the night before, but the woman who worked there told him the old man had already gone to bed. The Hacker looked at his watch. Not quite nine. He got up from the chair, walked over to the computer, and pulled up the old man's Web site. There was one page with a seven-digit number on it. He picked up one of his throwaway cell phones and punched in the numbers.

The woman answered. He asked to speak to the old man. She was gone for a minute or two and came back on the line. "He doesn't wish to speak to you," she said. "He says you haven't held up your end of the bargain."

"Listen, you bitch. You tell that old fuck that I'm not finished and when I am he'll owe me the rest of the money. Tell him that if he's hired somebody else to horn in on my job, I'll take them out, too. And if he hasn't hired somebody else, he should know that there are people out there trying to kill the same guys I am. And tell him I'll find his fucking document."

He slammed the phone shut, muttering to himself. He sat back in the chair facing the computer monitor. He pulled out the neck of his T-shirt, put his nose into it, sniffed. Didn't have to shower just yet. He wasn't going anywhere anyway. He had some planning to do. He still had a rabbit or two he could pull out of his hat.

CHAPTER FORTY-NINE

"I don't think we can outrun him," Logan said.

"Pull over," I said. "Let me talk to him."

Logan flipped on his blinker and lightly touched the brakes, slowing the car. When enough speed had bled off, he eased onto the shoulder of the road and came to a stop. The cop pulled in right behind us.

A spotlight lit us up and the loudspeaker mounted in the cruiser's grille came to life. "Get out of the car. Keep your hands where I can see them."

"Do it," I said to Logan. "Jock, you stay put." He was lying on the backseat across the gunman, out of sight of the windows.

Logan and I opened our doors and got out, standing on either side of the car, hands in the air.

"Was I speeding?" Logan asked innocently.

The cop was standing beside his car, his open door giving him some protection. He had his service pistol trained on us. "Sir, somebody saw you leaving town just after a car was blown up. Called it in. I came after you."

"Deputy," I said, "my name's Matt Royal. Call Lieutenant Charlie Foreman. He'll vouch for me."

"I'll do that, Mr. Royal. Were you leaving town just now?"

"Yes," I said. "I heard the explosion and saw the fire when I came out of the Swamp Rat. I didn't see any reason to stick around."

The deputy leaned into his shoulder, speaking softly into the radio microphone that was clipped to the epaulet of his shirt. He listened, then spoke into it again. He looked up at us, still behind his door, still at least twenty feet away from us. "Mr. Royal, do you have some ID?"

"I've got a driver's license and a card identifying me as a member of the Florida Bar."

"May I see it?" He motioned me toward him.

I stood still, one hand raised, and used the other to lift my wallet out of my hip pocket. I held it up and walked toward him. I gave him the license and bar card, and he held them up so that the light from his spot was on them. He gave them back to me.

"Thanks, Mr. Royal. The lieutenant said he knew why you were here and to let you go on about your business. I take it that's Mr. Hamilton, the owner of the car." He pointed to Logan still standing by his car.

"It is. Do you want to see his ID?"

"No, sir. Sorry to bother you. Y'all have a nice evening."

He shut down the spotlight, turned off the blue lights, and drove off into the dark.

"That was close," said Logan. "If he'd looked into the car, I don't know how we'd have explained Jock and shithead back there."

"That might have been a problem."

Logan and I got back into the car. "What now?" he asked.

"The Tamiami Trail's just about a mile ahead," I said. "Turn right when you get there. I remember a pullover between here and Naples. We can stop there. There won't be much traffic."

We pulled off the highway onto a berm that ran for about a hundred feet along the road. It was grass covered and stretched several hundred feet into the swamp. A wide drainage ditch ran along the far side, parallel to the road. The black water of the ditch was broken by little red dots when the headlights shined on it. Alligators. They lived there.

Logan brought the car to a stop well off the road, near the ditch. The gunman was still unconscious. We pulled him out of the car and laid him face up on the grass. Jock found an old tin can, refuse dropped by someone with no regard for his pristine surroundings. He bent down and filled it with dirty water from the ditch and threw it into the gunman's face. He came to, sputtering, making a production of it. I thought he'd been faking it, had probably been awake for a while. I shined a flashlight into his face.

"Time to wake up," I said.

"Where are we?"

"Who are you?" I asked.

"They call me Turk."

"Okay, Turk. I've just got a couple of questions. You up to answering them?"

"Go to hell."

"Ah, tough guy, huh. I eat tough guys like you for breakfast. You really don't want to fuck with me."

"Untie me and I'll show you tough."

I chuckled dryly. "Turk, I'm not going to untie you. I'm simply going to roll you into the ditch over there and give the gators a snack."

He paled in the glow of the flashlight. One does not live in the Glades without nurturing a healthy fear of alligators. "What do you want?"

"Who sent you after me?"

"What if I tell you? What then?"

"You'll walk out of here."

"Where are we?"

"On the Trail. About five miles from Belleville. You can walk home."

"I don't know who sent me, but I know why."

"Talk to me."

"Jason Blakemoore told me about a black dude who said he was a Seminole. Said he had some papers that would make him rich. Said he'd own the phosphate."

"What phosphate?"

"All of it. All over the state."

"What's this got to do with me?" I asked.

"I called my brother about the black guy. He works for the ConFla people up near Lakeland, where I used to work until I got disabled. I thought maybe we could make a few bucks out of it. If he told his bosses, the guys what owns all that phosphate, maybe we could get a reward or something."

"Did you?"

"A little. A guy come to see me. Gave me five hundred bucks. Told me the people he represented appreciated my help and would call on me again if I kept my mouth shut. Gave me a way to contact them if I got any more information."

"Who was it that came to see you?"

"I don't know. Never saw him before or since."

"How're you supposed to make contact?"

"I get to a computer, put in a Web address and get a number from that. It changes every day. I get the number every morning, so if I need it, I got it. Never used it until tonight when I heard you talking to old B.J. I remembered Jason talking about you helping out the black dude.

"I called the number and I talked to some woman. She said they'd pay me ten thousand dollars to kill you, and another twenty thousand to kill your friends."

"How did you know where my friends were?"

"I seen 'em drive up and park. When I went outside to call the number, the car was still there. I figured that was how you got here."

"Who threw the grenade?"

"That'd be my cousin."

"What's his name?"

"Rocky Mallot. He lives in Belleville."

"Who was driving the Mercedes?"

"I don't know. I was told that some guy in a Mercedes would be there. Rocky was supposed to wait until he saw the car to toss that grenade."

"Did you kill Jason?"

"No, sir. He was my friend."

"But you didn't think anything about selling his confidential information to somebody you didn't know?"

"Jason didn't need the money, and I knew my brother. It wasn't like I told just anybody."

"What's the Web address you check out every day?"

"I don't know. It's a different one each day."

"How do you find out what it is?"

"It shows up on my e-mail."

I was surprised. "You've got e-mail?"

"Sorta. They set me up with an AOL e-mail address. I go to the library every day and look at the e-mail. Lots of stuff comes in, you know, stuff to make my johnson bigger, stuff like that. But I always get an e-mail with a Web address on it. I check it out, write down the phone number, and I'm done."

"What's the number for today?" I asked.

"It's on a piece of paper in my shirt pocket."

I reached down and retrieved the paper. "What's your e-mail address?"

He gave it to me.

"Password?"

"Turk."

"That's original."

"I didn't want to forget it."

"Let me have your cell phone," I said.

"It's in my pants pocket."

"Which one?"

"Right one."

His hands were still cuffed behind his back. I turned him onto his left side, reached into his right pants pocket and retrieved the phone. I went into its log and saw the last number he'd called. The area code was 941. The Sarasota Bay area.

I turned to Jock and Logan who'd been standing quietly a few feet from us. "Okay guys. Let's dump this turd in the ditch."

"No," said Turk, his voice rising. "You said you'd let me go."

"Yeah, but that was only if you told me everything. You're holding back."

"I'm not. Honest. I told you everything I know."

I motioned to Jock and Logan. They came over and picked him up, Jock grabbing him under the arms and Logan taking his feet. They started walking toward the ditch, carrying Turk. He was squirming, trying to get out of the grip of those about to throw him to the gators. They got to the edge and stopped. I walked over. "You sure you got nothing else to say Turk? It might mean you won't die tonight."

He was sobbing, his breath coming in gasps, fear distorting his facial features. "I swear, Mr. Royal. I told you everything I know."

"Put him down," I said. I thought Turk was scared enough now that he'd tell me anything to save his skin. I thought we'd wrung him dry. "The gators won't eat tonight, Turk."

We left him on the bank of the ditch sucking in great gulps of air. We walked off a hundred feet or so. "What are we going to do with him?" Jock asked.

"Let's untie him and let him go. By the time he gets to Bellville, we'll be back in Longboat."

Logan looked a bit perplexed. "We're just going to let him try to kill us and get away with it?"

Jock said, "Let's put him on ice for a few days. We don't want him communicating with whoever is pulling his strings."

"Should I call Charlie Forman?" I asked.

Jock shook his head. "Let me get a team out here from Miami. They can keep him for a few days where nobody will find him."

"How do you do that, Jock?" asked Logan.

"I've got lots of seniority and the director trusts me."

"What then?" asked Logan. "Anybody got any bright ideas?"

"Not really," I said. "But we have to figure out who's behind this. It could be somebody inside the police. Plus, we've still got to talk to Baggett. Thursday is his night."

"We just going to waltz into that bar and ask Baggett to tell us what's going on?" asked Logan.

"We'll have to work a little smarter than that," Jock said. "Maybe I can get us some help." He walked toward the car, pulling his cell phone out of his pocket.

CHAPTER FIFTY

We were on Interstate 75 nearing Venice, when my cell phone rang. Charlie Forman.

"Mr. Royal. I need to talk to you."

"I was going to call you, Lieutenant. I figured you were pretty busy with that car fire."

"What do you know about that?"

"Nothing. Logan and I were just leaving when we saw it catch fire. What happened?"

"Fire Marshall says somebody blew it up."

"Anybody hurt?"

"No. The car was empty."

"Glad to hear it."

"Where are you?"

"On the way home."

"We had another incident here tonight," Charlie said. "A gangbanger from Miami was shot to death. Do you know anything about that?"

"No. What happened?"

"Don't really know. He was driving a Mercedes and it looked like somebody shot him through the windshield."

"You said he was a gangbanger?"

"Yeah. He had a driver's license in his pocket. The minute we put him into the computer it lit up. He's got a hell of a rap sheet."

"Do you think it was connected to the car blowing up?"

"Don't know. Yet. Did you find out anything in the Swamp Rat?"

"Not much. I talked to a guy named B. J. Cuthbert. He knows a little about it. I think he'd be glad to talk to you."

"He's been out of town. What did he say?"

I related what I'd heard in the bar. Then I said, "I didn't think it was a good idea to meet you in Belleville. I don't want anybody to know about my role in this thing. In case I have to come back."

"Good thinking, Matt. I'll let you know how my talk with B.J. goes. I've known him most of my life. I don't think he'll fool with me."

I hung up. "I hate lying to a good man trying to do his job."

Jock said, "Sometimes it's necessary."

We had waited beside the swamp for the better part of two hours when a dark-colored van pulled onto the berm. The headlights blinked twice and Jock walked over to the driver's window. A low conversation ensued, one that I couldn't hear. Jock came back with two men who picked up Turk and put him in the back of the van. There were no introductions, no conversation with the men from the van. They left and we began the drive north toward home.

"Do either of you have any bright ideas?" Logan asked.

"I'm not sure how bright they are, but I've got some ideas," said Jock.

"Anybody got any ideas about food?" asked Logan. "I'm hungry."

"What're you thinking?" I asked.

"Pizza and beer or Chinese," said Logan.

"I meant about our problem."

Jock said, "Let me sleep on it. I may want to bring in some outside help from my agency. This thing seems to have lots of tentacles. It may be more than the three of us can handle."

We were just taking the off ramp at Fruitville Road when my phone rang again. Blocked number on the caller ID screen. Probably Bill Lester. I answered.

"Matt, what the hell is going on?"

"Good evening, J.D."

"I just had a conversation with a Collier County Sheriff's lieutenant who tells me some people were killed and a car blown up in Belleville, and you just happened to be there."

"Coincidence?"

"Don't bullshit me, Matt. Where are you?"

"I'm just leaving the Interstate at Fruitville Rd."

"Meet me on the key."

"We're going to the Haye Loft for food. Meet us there."

"Us?"

"Jock and Logan are with me."

"You could knock me over with a feather. I'm that surprised." She hung up.

We drove onto Longboat and stopped at the Haye Loft for pizza and beer. A little coconut cream pie for dessert finished our day. I chided the bartender Eric for overserving Sam, and he promised not to do it again. I thought his grin gave him away though, and Sam would not have to worry about a paucity of alcohol on Eric's watch.

J.D. came in as we were finishing. She had a determined look about her, her body coiled, stiff, her lips clamped tight, her eyes squinting. She pointed to the three of us at the bar and then to a table in the corner. There was no question about what she meant. We moved quickly like three boys being shown into the principal's office to explain some egregious breach of school rules. Jock and I had been there before. Back in high school. Only this time, I wasn't sure that J.D. wouldn't just start shooting us.

We sat at the table. She stared at each one of us in turn, sat back in her chair, shaking her head. "What were you guys doing in Belleville?"

I started talking. Told her the whole story. About the dead gang-banger, about Turk in a safe agency lockup in Miami, Jock's rental car being blown up. I explained the connection between Blakemoore and Abraham. Some of it she knew, some of it she didn't.

"We're not holding out on you, J.D.," I said when I'd finished. "We didn't expect any trouble. I was just nosing around, trying to help the local law."

J.D.'s face relaxed. "That's what the deputy said. I talked to an old friend of mine at Miami-Dade PD. They've been picking up rumors that one of the Latin gangs in Miami had been paid to kill a lawyer. The kid that pulled the trigger probably did it to get full membership in the gang."

"Why didn't Miami-Dade get in touch with Collier County?" Logan asked.

"They never made the connection until tonight. There were no reports of any dead lawyers in Miami, so they pretty much wrote off the rumor as just that. A rumor. They tied it together when Collier County ran the prints on the guy Jock shot tonight."

"Was he the one who killed Blakemoore?" Jock asked.

"Looks like it," said J.D. "The deputy found a shotgun in the trunk of the gangbanger's car. Had the driver's fingerprints on it. They can't tell for certain that it was the one that killed Blakemoore, but they think it probably was. We'll never know for sure."

"You want a drink?" I asked.

"You guys have had a long day. Go home."

"If you'll drive me home, I'll have one with you," I said.

She nodded her head. Asked for a white wine. I called to Eric, asking for another beer and a glass of wine for J.D. Jock and Logan said their good nights to us and Eric and went out into the night.

She took a sip of her wine. "I wish you'd called me before you headed to Belleville. I thought we were becoming a team."

"I should have called. I'm still not comfortable with getting a cop involved in some of the stuff we get ourselves into."

She nodded, was quiet for a minute. "I can appreciate that, but at least let me know what you're up to. I don't have to get involved."

"Agreed," I said.

"What are your plans for tomorrow night? With the biker guy?"

"We don't have much of a plan. We're going to the Snake Dance Inn and pull Baggett out of there."

"Just the three of you?"

"I think we'll have some help from Jock's agency."

"When are you going in?"

"After dark. We want them to get a little liquored up before we start anything."

"Be careful, Matt," she said. "I don't have many friends here. I'd hate to lose one."

"Count on it," I said.

We moved onto other topics, small talk, the kind that goes on in bars all over the planet every night of the year. We ordered another round and then another. It was getting late and Eric was doing what bartenders do when they're hinting that it's time to go. I paid the tab, over a protest from

J.D. that this should be a Dutch treat. We said goodnight to Eric, walked down the outside staircase to J.D.'s unmarked patrol car, a white Ford Crown Vic.

The parking lot was dark, her car the only one left. A streetlight at the corner gave us a bit of illumination. The old trees that shaded the lot hid the sky. A match flared under the overhang of the restaurant, one of the cooks having his last cigarette before locking up and going home. The shells that covered the ground crackled under our feet. The night air was cool and a hint of moisture floated about us.

She pulled out her keys. I took them from her hand, unlocked the door, opened it for her. She smiled, standing there next to me, so close I could smell her breath, a sweet mixture of fermented grapes and warm girl. She looked at me, her face inches from mine. We were like a stone tableau, immovable, frozen in a moment that seemed to last forever.

I stepped back, gave her room to get into the car. I walked around to the other side, got in, and she drove me to the village. We didn't talk during the couple of miles to my cottage. It was dead quiet. No music, no radio traffic, just the swish of tires on the pavement, the wind beating at the windshield.

She stopped in front of my house. I looked at her, stared probably, said goodnight, and got out of the car. I watched as she drove off, her taillights winking in the darkness.

THURSDAY

CHAPTER FIFTY-ONE

My phone rang a little after eight on Thursday morning. I was on the patio with a cup of coffee and the morning's paper. Jock and Logan were still in bed. I looked at the caller ID. Nestor Cobol.

"Good morning, Matt. Hope I didn't call too early."

"Not a problem. I'm halfway through the paper."

"I've been meaning to call to let you know I hired Jube Smith. I appreciate your sending him to me."

"I'm glad that worked out."

"He's got a lot of experience. I've seen him around over the years, but I didn't really know him. I knew his wife from over at the diner."

"How's she doing?"

"Not good. I put Jube to work on one of my day boats. He's home every night. Her sister stays with her during the day. I don't think she has long."

"I'm sorry to hear that."

"Matt, Jube told me something that I need to talk to you about as soon as possible. Can you meet me at the Star Fish for lunch at noon?"

"What's it about?"

"The people who are trying to kill you."

"I'll be there. Do you mind if I bring a guest?"

"A guest?"

"A cop."

"Your call."

I called J.D. Duncan. "You got time for lunch?"

"I'm pretty busy, Matt."

"Hard for a detective to keep busy on this island."

"We had two more boats stolen last night. The deputy chief thinks it's related to a ring operating all along the southwest coast."

Martin Sharkey, the deputy chief, was a good cop. He'd spent his whole career with the Longboat Key PD and had moved steadily up the ranks. He was a boater himself, and I knew he'd take a personal interest in a rash of boat thefts. Boats had been disappearing for weeks, usually the big center-console fishing boats. The theory was that they were being taken to a refueling ship out in the Gulf and then on to Mexico. A couple of ships like that, stationed at points in open water would provide enough fuel for the boats to make it to Mexico. Sharkey thought the boats were being stolen to order and that corrupt officials in Mexico had paperwork ready showing that the boats had been imported into Mexico, and bought legitimately by the new owners.

"I want you to meet some people who may have some information about who's trying to kill me," I said. "I'm having lunch with them at the Star Fish over in Cortez at noon."

"I'll be there."

Jock and Logan were going to meet Bill Lester for lunch and bring him up to date on what had happened in Belleville. Logan had talked to the chief about the ransacking of his condo the day before and found out a little more about the people who'd invaded my home. They were part of the West Coast Marauders, and both had very busy rap sheets.

Jock had checked in with his agency and they were looking into any connections emanating from Turk. He'd uploaded the information from Turk's cell phone's SIM card to the DEA and they were tracking the phone calls.

If Turk had told his brother about Abraham's document, and the brother worked for ConFla, it would be reasonable to think that someone at the company was behind the efforts to kill us. It was a big company and it might take a while to figure it all out.

My friends dropped me off at a car rental agency at the Colony Beach Resort. My Explorer wouldn't be ready for several days, and my insurance company had agreed to pay for the rental. They never pay much, so I was driving a little tin box with the power of a small lawn mower.

The village of Cortez takes up the western end of a small peninsula squeezed between the edge of Sarasota Bay to the south and Palma Sola Bay on the north. The Cortez Bridge connects the mainland to Anna Maria Island, which lies just north of Longboat Key. A shallow lagoon marked the little hamlet's southern edge and provided access to the Coast Guard Station and the old fish houses that had serviced the locals for many years. It was one of the few working fishing villages remaining in Florida, most of them long since turned into developments to house the snowbirds who came from the north every winter to enjoy the sunshine and provide a new economic engine to replace the fisheries.

Mullet was the fish of choice, the one in most abundance, the gold wrenched from the sea and bays by hard men whose forebears had fished these waters for generations. There were a few boats that went to sea, roaming the Gulf and Atlantic in search of the rapidly dwindling stocks of deep-water fish, but these days most of the men were home at night.

The Star Fish was a commercial fish house on the bay in Cortez. Boats would bring in their catch to sell and the Star Fish Company would wholesale it out to restaurants and markets. There was also a retail side where the locals came for the fresh seafood. A few years back the new owners had added a restaurant of sorts. Several picnic tables had been added to a deck on the bayside and a small kitchen served seafood, most of it caught the day before. It was an informal setting. You ordered the food at the counter and left your name. When it was ready, a server would bring it to the deck, call out your name, and deliver your food in a cardboard box. It was always good.

I arrived early at the Star Fish, ordered a diet soda, and took a seat at one of the tables. The place was quiet on a spring morning when most of the snowbirds had already gone north. I watched the bay, enjoying the view of Longboat and the other nearby keys, the mangrove islands, and the commercial boats moored to the piers. A pontoon boat idled along the narrow channel that ran in close to the shore. Several people chatting happily were seated on the seats along the rail, two of them children wearing bright orange life jackets. An older man was at the helm, his gray hair cropped close to his head. A woman about his age, four younger adults, and the kids were the passengers. A couple out with their children and grandchildren, I decided.

I watched as the gray-haired man deftly maneuvered the boat against a pier and secured it to the pilings. A slight breeze rippled the water far out in the bay, but close in to the shore the surface was glassy, mirror-like. The net camp, a small building built on stilts over the water, sat about a hundred yards out in the bay, its reflection on the still surface a reminder of the beauty found in simple structures. It had once been a storehouse for a fisherman, a place to dock his boat, dry and mend his nets, and store his equipment. The lagoon had once been full of them, but they had disappeared along with the men and women who made their living from the sea.

"Hey, Matt." Nestor Cobol was coming across the dock toward me. Jube Smith was with him. I stood to shake their hands.

"Hey, Nestor, Jube. Good to see you."

"Want to order?" asked Nestor.

"Let's give it a couple of minutes. Detective Duncan from Longboat is going to join us. How's your wife doing, Jube?"

"Not well. She's going downhill fast."

Jube's posture told of his hopelessness. It is always a blow to a man who takes care of his family to run smack into a situation that he can't control, that he can only watch unfold and know that the death of a loved one is the end result. It humbles him, makes him feel inadequate, as if he failed in his most important obligation, that of protecting his family.

I saw J.D. come onto the deck. She was wearing beige slacks, a navy short-sleeve blouse that buttoned down the front, navy low-heeled pumps, her gun at her hip and badge on her belt. When she arrived at our table I introduced her to Nestor and Jube.

We went to the counter, ordered our meals, and took our seats at the picnic table nearest the water. Jube started the conversation.

"Mr. Royal, I told Captain Cobol how we met, so there ain't no secrets. I really appreciate what you done for me and Captain Cobol advanced me some pay, so my wife's got her pain pills."

"Glad I could help, Jube, but Nestor here is the one that took the chance. I hope you don't let him down."

"I ain't going to do that."

Jube sat quietly for a couple of beats, head bowed, his face contorted in concentration like he was trying to get his thoughts in order, wanting to give me some bit of information but not sure how to proceed. Finally, he raised his head. "Mr. Royal, I heard some things from Colleen who owns the diner where my wife used to waitress. She was in there by herself about mid-morning yesterday when two men came in and ordered breakfast. She cooked it and took it to them and heard part of what they was talking about. One of them said, 'Morton ain't happy about our guys missing Royal yesterday.'"

"Did she know who they were?" I asked.

"No. Never seen them before. She described them and the big one sounded just like the guy what hired me to come get you."

"I think that guy was on the boat Tuesday when they tried to kill me. He's dead."

"I heard about that. I can't say it's the same guy, but I thought you ought to know about it."

"Thanks, Jube. I'll check it out."

We talked about fishing and local gossip while we finished our meals. Nestor and Jube got up to leave, spoke to local fisherman on their way out. I sat for a few moments, thinking about how such a beautiful day could be affected by people plotting to kill you.

J.D. broke into my reverie. "What do you think?"

"Morton may be the guy at the top of this mess. Maybe he works for ConFla."

"I've got to get back to the island, Matt. I'll run Morton through the system, see what comes up."

"I'll go talk to Colleen. She if she knows anything more. I'll let you know what she says."

We walked to the parking lot, and she left. I stood there for a moment trying to visualize what Cortez had been like fifty years before, when it was a fishing village, back before the tourists and snowbirds showed up, before air-conditioning and mosquito eradication programs and drug runners, when it was a place where men took their living from the sea, fed their families, raised their kids, lived and loved and died. Which was better? Then or now? Who the hell knew.

CHAPTER FIFTY-TWO

My next stop was Colleen's Café, a small diner housed in a four-bay strip center on the northern side of Cortez Road, across from the post office. Colleen owned the place, managed it, cooked the meals, and when she couldn't get help, waited tables. She and her husband, Pete, a Longboat Key Fire Department lieutenant, had lived on the islands for many years. They often joined Logan and me at Tiny's for happy hour.

The diner served breakfast and lunch and closed at three every afternoon. The breakfast customers were mostly the fishermen who lived in the village that surrounded the little restaurant. They'd come in early, eat and then head to sea or the bay, seeking fish and the meager money they earned when they sold their catch at the fish houses. Lunch brought a more eclectic crowd, more professional, men in short-sleeved dress shirts and ties, women in high heels. These were the real estate sales people, the business owners, and the regular coterie of tourists who had been told by the people who worked at the hotels and shops that Colleen's Café was the best place in Cortez for lunch. The daily specials were posted on a chalkboard that leaned against the building next to the front door.

It was almost closing time when I arrived. Colleen was cleaning off tables, using a large damp towel to wipe them down. She looked up as I came in, smiled, and came over for a hug. "Sorry I missed you and Logan at Tiny's the other night. I'd been so worried when I heard he'd been shot. I thought he might die and I kept thinking that I'd give just about anything to see him one more time. Then I saw in the paper that he was alive. It was one of my best days. I sort of hummed to myself all day long."

"Sometimes, when life throws you a curve ball you get to hit it out of the park. That was one of those days."

She laughed. "Matt, you'd better either give up on baseball metaphors or philosophy. Or both. You want some lunch?"

"No. I just stopped by to check up on something I heard from Jube Smith."

"Poor Jube. He's not taking his wife's sickness very well. I think he's coming apart. I don't know what he'll do when she's gone."

"It's sad. He told me about the conversation you overheard yesterday."

"Yeah. I tried to call you at home last night, but didn't get an answer."

"I was out until late. What did you hear?"

"There were two men, came in late in the morning, sat by the door, and ordered breakfast. They didn't know that we have a strange acoustic in here. For some reason I can hear people at that table when I'm all the way across the room.

"One of them said that Morton wouldn't be happy about their people missing you. I thought he was probably just talking about not finding you at home or something. Then the smaller one told the big bald guy that he had one more chance and he'd better not screw it up. 'Cept he used the F word, if you know what I mean."

"Anything else?"

"No, the big one told the little one that they'd talk more about it later."

"Can you describe the guys?"

"One was about my height, had a mustache and gray hair. The other one was bigger than you and looked like he worked out. He was completely bald, but I could see a stubble where he shaved his head."

"I don't guess you got any names."

"No, and they paid cash for the breakfast. Does this mean anything to you?"

"It might. One of the guys that Logan killed in the go-fast fits the description of the big guy, but it can't be him. The one in the boat was already dead by the time those two came in here."

"You sure you don't want something to eat?"

"I'm sure. Gotta go. Thanks, kid."

I turned and started for the door when she said, "Oh, Matt. I almost forgot. Captain Kim was in this morning and wants you to call her."

"Did she say what it's about?"

"No. I was busy and didn't have time to talk. She just mentioned that she was trying to get in touch with you. She was going to leave word with Susie over at Tiny's. She said nobody answered at your house and she didn't know your cell number." She handed me a napkin with a phone number scrawled across it.

"Thanks Colleen. Tell Pete hello for me."

"You take care, Matt."

I got to my rental and called the number on the napkin.

"Captain Kim."

"Hey, Kim. Matt Royal here."

"Matt, I need to talk to you. Can you meet me at my office?"

I laughed. "Sure. When?"

"I'm on the water with a charter. I'll be dropping them off in about thirty minutes at the pier."

"Have you eaten lunch?"

"Not yet. Busy morning."

"I'll be on the deck at the Bridgetender. Come on over and get some food in you."

"I'll be there shortly."

I sat on the deck at the Bridgetender Inn, looking across the narrow street to the bay. Kim's "office" was a group of chairs under a Banyan tree that hugged the water. It was the hangout for the guys who ran the parasailing boat and a couple of others who chartered by the hour. The City of Bradenton Beach fishing pier was to my left, a semifamous clock tower marking its entrance from the land side. A long floating dock ran along the south side and was attached to the pier by a ramp. It was a place to moor small boats.

A pontoon boat chugged along the serpentine channel leading from the Intracoastal to the pier. Captain Kim was returning from a tour of the bay with a boatload of satisfied tourists. She took our visitors out to see the dolphins, manatees, birds and other animals, and the flora that make our part of the world so special.

She was a jolly lady, the mother of two teenagers who often helped on the tours. She had once been a commercial fisher, like her mother before her and her grandparents before that. Kim had been raised in Cortez, and knew all the secrets and lore of a little village that had seen its share of loss. The sea plucked the fisher folk from this life at random intervals, in bad storms and inexplicable wrecks at sea. Sometimes the men went out and just never came back. Sometimes wreckage from their boats would wash up on a strange shore, the only clue that the sea had claimed another complement of Cortez men.

She laid the boat against the floating dock and held it steady while her passengers disembarked. She loosed her line and moved toward the little dock adjoining the office. She slipped the boat into a space on the end of the dock, fixed the lines, and cut the engine. She saw me sitting at the table, waved, and walked over. "Hey Matt. Haven't seen you in a while. Where you been?"

"Hey, Cap. I'm around. Just don't get over the bridge as often as I'd like. How've you been?"

"I'm good. Heard you haven't been doing too well, though."

"Well enough, under the circumstances."

Kim took a seat at my table and ordered a diet cola and a grouper sandwich. "I don't know if this has anything to do with your problems, but I thought I ought to pass it on anyway."

"What's up?"

"Do you know a guy named Morton? I don't know if that's a first name or a last name."

"I've heard the name." I didn't want to give away anything. Kim was tight lipped, not prone to gossip, but now I'd heard the same name from two different sources within a few minutes. I couldn't see any sense in adding to Kim's worries.

"On Monday, a couple of men, walk-ups, joined my afternoon tour of the bay. I always go around the northern tip of Jewfish Key and over by the sandbar between Jewfish and Longboat. Sometimes we'll see manatees in the area. Then I take them up into the bayou that runs into the Whitney Beach condos.

"When we went by your house, one of the men pointed it out and said something like, 'Morton says that's where Royal lives.'"

"Could have been somebody I met somewhere."

"I would've thought the same thing, but then I heard that one of the dead guys in the go-fast that came after you was big and completely bald. That pretty much fit the description of one of the men on my boat that day."

"Have you told anybody else about this?"

"No. I just heard the description last night and it made me think there might be a connection."

"I appreciate it, Kim. I'll pass this along to Bill Lester. See if anything develops."

I sat with her while she finished her meal, talking idly about the changes we were seeing on the islands. None of us old-timers liked it very much, but there was little we could do about it. We'd all lost friends who had moved to the Carolinas, driven out of paradise by the high taxes, the local government restrictions on anything that smacked of business, and the bureaucratic nonsense incurred by anybody who dealt with city hall. Pretty soon, the only people left on the islands would be the retirees who moved there and wanted things to stay the same as when they arrived. Not as things had been when working people could afford to live there, the people who fished for a living or worked the trades or waited tables in the restaurants, who were despairing of making a living under the stifling rules of the bureaucrats. The newcomers, those complaining about crowding, wanted the islands to be pristine and pure and sterile. Sort of a Disney World Magic Kingdom where trash is not allowed on the streets and the sun is always shining. They came in droves, settled into their condos, and complained about too many people spoiling the ambience of island living. To paraphrase that old philosopher Pogo, they'd met the enemy and it was them.

CHAPTER FIFTY-THREE

I parked the rental in the shade of the Banyan tree in my front yard. The house was quiet when I entered. Jock and Logan hadn't returned. I called J.D. to fill her in on my conversations with Colleen and Kim. Her voice mail answered and I left a detailed message.

I decided to walk over to Mar Vista where my friends were having lunch with Bill Lester. I needed to catch up with the chief and it was probably better to do it face-to-face. I was walking at a leisurely pace, enjoying the spring flowers and the peacocks foraging on the lawns. I was thinking about my predicament, trying to find the key that would unlock the mystery of who was trying to kill me and why.

My cell phone rang, startling me. I laughed at myself. I needed to get a grip. I answered.

"Matt," said Debbie, "where are you?"

Debbie was the blonde bartender at Moore's Stone Crab restaurant, which hugged the shoreline of the bay next door to the Mar Vista. She'd worked there for years and knew just about everybody on the key and seemed to be privy to everything that went on in our little world.

"Hey, babe," I said. "Welcome back. How was the vacation?" Deb had left the island a few days before Jessica and I had started our cruise. She had driven to Ohio to visit the many cousins that made up her clan.

"It was wonderful. Great to get away for a while, but I'm glad to be back. I need to see you."

"What's up?"

"You know those little cubbyholes we have in the kitchen where Alan can leave us notes or whatever? When I got in today there was an envelope in my cubby addressed to you."

"To me?"

"Yeah. It said, 'Matt Royal, in care of Debbie at the bar.'"

"That's all?"

"Yeah, but there's something chunky in the envelope."

"Chunky?"

"Yes, Royal. Chunky. Small, I don't know. Why don't you come by and find out what it is?"

"Are you at Moore's?"

"Yeah. I'm working a double today. Payback for all the vacation time, I guess."

"I'm a block from you. I'll be there in a couple of minutes."

The lounge at Moore's is separated from the restaurant by a wall, but you can order lunch or dinner at the U-shaped bar. The south wall is glass, giving a view twelve miles down the bay to the condo towers of the city of Sarasota. The west wall is home to a huge stuffed Tarpon, mouth open with a bottle of Jack Daniel's whiskey poked spout-first into it. Two television sets take up the corners on the north wall, usually tuned to one of the sports channels. I'd spent many an evening there, whiling away the time with good conversation with Debbie and other friends.

I was beginning to work up a slight sweat as I came through the front door, shook hands with Alan Moore, one of the owners, and passed through to the bar. Cracker Dix was at his usual place at one of the corners, sipping a glass of white wine. Debbie was not there, probably in the back making a drink for one of the late lunch crowd in the main dining room.

"Hey, Matt," said Cracker. "How are you?"

Cracker Dix was an expatriate Englishman who had lived in the village for thirty years. He was in his mid-fifties, bald, about five feet ten inches tall, and very tan. He wore a single strand gold necklace, a gold stud in one ear, a Hawaiian shirt, cargo shorts, and boat shoes. His speech had retained the memory of his native land, the accent as pronounced as it was on the first day he'd set foot in America. He was a favorite of the islanders and made his living waiting tables in the various restaurants on the key.

"I'm good, Cracker. Glad to see you." I pulled up a stool, sitting on the corner at right angles to him.

"I heard you've been having some trouble."

"Yeah, but Jock and Logan have my back."

"I heard Jock was here. How's he doing?"

"About the same as always. Drinks too much nonalcoholic beer."

"Yeah, that stuff can give you the runs. Look, I've been meaning to call you about something I heard the other night."

"What's that?"

"You know I ride my bicycle over to Cortez sometimes to Hutch's. Well, they call it Lil's now. The owner is a friend of mine, Lil Minor." He paused.

"Yes?" I said. Sometimes you have to jump-start Cracker.

"You know how it is with me. If I see a wife who looks a little lonely, I'm there for her."

"Cracker, that usually means you're in bed with her."

"If that's what they want. I'm only trying to cheer them up."

"I understand. Who's the unhappy wife in this story?"

"Lil, didn't I say that?"

"I don't think so."

"Well, I implied it."

"I guess you did."

"Her husband is not a nice man."

"What do you mean?"

"I'm not sure, but somehow he's involved with some really bad guys."

"Are you in danger?"

"Why would I be in danger?"

"You're schtuping a bad guy's wife."

"He doesn't know that."

"What if he finds out?"

He looked puzzled. "I haven't really given much thought to that."

"So why were you going to call me?"

"These guys Lil's husband hangs around with aren't, well, quite as pleasant as I am."

"Nobody is, Cracker."

"You've got a point there."

"So what about these bad guys?"

"Lil told me the other night that some guy was in the bar with her husband. They were talking about a man named Morton who wanted some lawyer on Longboat killed. Then I heard that somebody tried to take you out, so I thought there might be a connection."

"There might be. Do you know who this guy Morton is?"

"I don't know him, but Lil says he owns a bar up in Gibsonton called the Snake Dance Inn. She thinks he's pretty big in the drug business."

That was an interesting tidbit. The feds had told us that the biker leader James Baggett owned the bar. I thought they'd know better than Lil. Debbie came out of the back. "Royal," she said. "I've missed you. Miller Lite?"

"Sure. You want one, Cracker?"

"No thanks. I've got to go."

"I don't remember you ever turning down a beer."

"Lil's waiting for me over at my house."

I laughed. "I guess some things are more important than others."

"Yes they are, my friend. Take care." Cracker left some cash on the bar and made his way out through the dining room.

Debbie came back with my beer and a chilled glass. "Who's Lil?"

"You don't want to know."

"Probably not." She handed me a standard number ten envelope. "Before you ask, I don't know who left it. One of the girls found it on the hostess's desk after closing one night while I was gone on vacation."

I opened the envelope, reached inside, and pulled out a single sheet of paper and a key. The key wasn't a normal one. It looked like those you find in airport lockers, and had a number on it. The handwriting on the sheet of paper was familiar. It read:

Matthew,

I'm leaving this because I know Debbie is a friend of yours. I didn't want to take a chance on it getting lost in the mail or purloined from your mailbox at home. I'll come see Debbie if I'm able. If not, I'll probably be dead when you get this. The key is to the locker where you'll find a document that will answer any questions you may have and provide untold wealth to my people in Red Bays. Thank you my friend.

Abraham Osceola

"What is it, Matt?" Debbie asked.

"Another piece of the riddle I've been stuck in for the past week. Abraham must have been in a hurry. He didn't say where the locker is located. Did you hear about somebody trying to kill me?"

"No, but I just got back. It's probably some bartender who got tired of your cheesy tips."

I laughed. "Not this time. Besides, I always tip commensurate with the service. You should be happy with the quarter I leave."

"I might be the one trying to kill you next. Seriously, what's going on?"

I told her the whole story, everything that I knew, including the information we got from Turk. "I don't know how this letter from Abraham fits into it, but I guess I'll find out at the airport." I held up the key.

"I doubt the key is from the airport. They don't have lockers there anymore."

"You're sure?"

"I was looking for one at the airport in Cleveland a couple of years ago and a cop told me that no airport in the country had those anymore. Something to do with security."

I thought about that for a moment. "What about bus stations?"

"Got me. Guess you could check."

"I'll do that this afternoon."

"What did you find on the Web site the guy down south gave you?"

"Huh. Turk is smarter than I thought or I'm dumber. I got the Web address off his e-mail, but the damn thing is password protected. I had his e-mail password, but I didn't think to ask him about the Web site."

"Okay, I know what's coming. You want me to check it out."

Debbie had become quite the hacker over the past few years. She could pretty much crack anything on the Web. "Well, now that you mention it. You could see what you can find out about this Web site." I wrote it on the back of a napkin, handed it to her.

"I won't be able to do anything until I get home tonight."

"No sweat. I've got to find Abraham's locker and then meet a guy in a bar in Gibsonton tonight." I gave her Turk's e-mail address and password. "The site changes daily, so you probably won't be able to get it before midnight."

"Be careful, Matt. We'd miss you around here."

I grinned at her, put a ten-dollar tip on the bar, and walked out the door.

CHAPTER FIFTY-FOUR

The frigging birds were singing in the trees, a cacophonous song that was driving the Hacker crazy. Why the hell couldn't they sing in harmony? Or better yet, shut the fuck up? His head hurt from the booze the night before and his back was sore from leaning over the keyboard of his computer. Something wasn't adding up. A car had been blown up in Belleville the previous evening. The *Naples Daily News* online edition told the story, but it didn't give any details.

The Collier County Sheriff's office computers had a scarcity of information so far. The cop on the scene thought the explosion had been caused by a hand grenade. The lab people had found shrapnel that came from a kind of grenade used by the Army. The car was traced to a rental car agency at the Tampa airport, but the name used to rent the vehicle was apparently false. The only record anywhere of anybody with the name on the rental agreement was a six-year-old boy who lived in Bakersfield, California. The Hacker had checked the airline manifests for that name on any flight arriving in Tampa within a couple of hours of the time of the rental. Nothing. That was all they had.

Royal had been in Belleville about the time the car blew up. Every time the lawyer used his credit card, the Hacker was aware of it. He could track Royal's movements just by his charges. So, what was Royal doing in the Swamp Rat Bar? Who blew up the car? Was that Royal's car? If so, where did he get the documents to rent it under a name that didn't exist?

This whole mess had started with a lawyer down in Belleville. The Hacker knew that much and he knew that Matt Royal and Logan Hamilton were involved. After all, he'd been hired to kill them and the black guy who claimed to be an Indian. But he hated to be kept in the dark about an operation he was involved in. Plus, there was a lot of money riding on the successful completion of this one.

The Belleville lawyer had been killed in a drive-by. The cops figured it was some gangbangers from Miami. Maybe not. Maybe somebody else was horning in on the Hacker's action, trying to get the money. His brain was cramped from thinking about it.

Blakemoore's name had popped up in a police database that was linked to the Sarasota County computer entries dealing with Osceola and the attempts on Hamilton's life. The Hacker figured there was a connection between the lawyer's death and Osceola. He just couldn't figure out what.

He called James Baggett, the biker leader. "Who were those guys you sent after Royal in the boat?"

"They weren't my men."

"Who were they?"

"Just call them some of my associates."

"Well, your associates fucked up."

"Yeah. And they paid a high price, too. They're both dead."

"I know that. You keep fucking up and you're going to be dead."

"I'll get 'em next time."

"I ain't paying you another dime until those two fuckers are dead."

"Royal and Hamilton?"

"Bet your ass." He slammed his phone closed.

Time to call the old man.

The Hacker logged onto the Web site, got the day's phone number, and dialed it on another prepaid cell of his own. He'd long since figured out what the old man was doing with the phones. Every number the Hacker had gotten off the Web site had been assigned to a prepaid bought at some convenience store. He'd checked every last one of them.

The woman answered and he asked to speak to the man. She put the phone down and came back in a few minutes. "He is unable to come to the phone," she said.

"Then take the goddamned phone to him."

"He is indisposed at the moment."

"If that means he's on the crapper, I don't care. Give him the fucking phone."

"I'm sorry, sir, but he cannot talk to you at the moment."

"You tell that old bastard that he's got ten minutes to call me back at this number. If I haven't heard from him, I'm going to start throwing wrenches into his machine. I promise you he won't like that." He closed the phone in a rage.

The damn birds were still at it. He needed a drink, but he was all out. He'd have to drive into town to get some booze and food. He'd been laying low, hated the thought of having to deal with another human being, even that stupid nose-picking clerk at the package store.

He went out onto the front porch, the high sun making him squint. He hollered as loud as he could for the birds to shut up. Silence fell on him, but within seconds the sounds assaulted him again. He shook his head. "Fucking birds," he mumbled and went back inside.

His cell phone was ringing. He sat in his chair, picked up the phone. "Yeah?"

It was the scratchy voice of the old man, ancient sounding, weak but steady, a hint of anger. "Who the fuck do you think you are? Calling my home and making demands and threats."

"I'm the guy you need most right now, old man. Have you commissioned someone else to do my job?"

"No. You've got your job, but it doesn't seem to be getting done. If it's not completed by Saturday at noon, you're finished. Off the case. No more money. Period. You understand?"

"Yeah," he said, sullenly. "I'll get it done. Just don't forget the wire transfer to my bank."

"I won't. If you do what you've contracted to do." The phone went dead.

You old bastard, the Hacker thought. Maybe as soon as that wire transfer goes through, I'll come take care of you personally. But he knew he wouldn't. He was the brains not the brawn. He didn't care for violence, never took part in it. He just directed it.

The Hacker shrugged, got up from his chair, and walked out the door to the old beater parked next to the house. He'd have to deal with that fucking nose-picker if he wanted to get drunk tonight.

CHAPTER FIFTY-FIVE

There were two Greyhound Bus terminals nearby, one in Bradenton and the other in Sarasota. Abraham had been staying at a motel in Sarasota, so it made sense to start with the one closest to the place where he managed to get his head bashed in.

I had told Jock and Logan about what I'd learned and then left them at my house and drove the rental to North Washington Boulevard in Sarasota. I found the terminal at the corner of Sixth Street. It was housed in a rectangular, flat-roofed building, a utilitarian structure designed by an architect with no vision. Or maybe the executives who ordered it built cared nothing of esthetics and just wanted a place for the buses to load and unload their passengers. Several parking spaces were painted on the asphalt that bordered the eastern side of the building adjacent to Washington Boulevard.

On the south side, an extension of the roof hung over four long parking spaces. A bus sat in one, its door open, the driver standing by the steps leading up into the interior, wearing a uniform that included vest and tie. He smiled as I walked by. His bus was empty and the sign on the front above the windshield announced that he was heading to Ft. Myers. As I entered the building, he put the bus in gear and moved out southbound. No passengers.

I walked through the entrance into an air-conditioned space that had not been upgraded in years. There were a few people sprawled on uncomfortable plastic chairs bolted to the floor, their baggage at their feet. Most were rough looking, men and women who worked on construction crews doing the unskilled labor or washed dishes in a restaurant or picked up a few bucks as day laborers. Some were sleeping, awaiting their transportation to another place, one that would treat them better than our tourist mecca.

Gray, scuffed linoleum covered the floor. A ticket counter took up part of one wall, thick glass between the agent and his customers. A small hole covered by a metal grid was built into the glass, a place to talk through. An office was adjacent to the counter, small and plain, filled with cheap metal furnishings. A man in a uniform shirt bearing the bus company's logo was busy at a computer behind the counter. On the opposite side of the waiting room was a small alcove that held a Pepsi and a Coke machine. There were two restroom doors, one on either side of a drinking fountain. In the corner, next to the men's room, stood seven lockers in various sizes, all gray, all scratched and dirty and ancient looking. Two columns, seven lockers. Not much.

I looked at the key, walked to the lockers, and found the one with a number that corresponded to the number on the key. I tried to open it, but found that the keyhole was plugged. I walked over to the man behind the counter. "Sorry to bother you, but I don't think this key works."

"Let me see," he said. I put the key in the little tray that gave access through the glass. He looked at the key, punched his keyboard, peered at the monitor. He looked up at me. "We've plugged the locker. The dollar rental is only for twenty-four hours. If you don't get your stuff by then we plug it."

"This isn't my key," I said. "A friend left it for me to retrieve some stuff for him."

"Don't matter. If you got the key, you get access. As soon as you pay the rental."

"How much?"

He studied the monitor, looked up. "Your friend rented that locker last Friday, so you owe me for six days, but he already paid a dollar. Five bucks will do it."

I gave him the money and walked with him to the lockers. He unplugged it and left. I opened the door and found a large manila envelope with my name on it. There was nothing else in the locker. I shut the door, leaving the key in the lock and walked out, waving to the clerk.

Once in my car I opened the envelope and found another letter from

Abraham, this one several pages in length. There was also a document, handwritten in a florid style, on paper that was turning brown with age. Splotches of something, coffee maybe, marred the surface, but did not obscure any of the writing.

I put the old paper aside and began to read Abraham's letter. As I read, things became clearer for the first time in a week. When I finished the letter, I looked closely at the old document and read the exaggerated cursive used by many government scribes of the day. My heart rate shot up and I felt something akin to euphoria. I sat looking at the document, rereading it, slowly this time. I tried to decipher the signatures at the bottom. I wasn't sure, but I thought I recognized the names. I couldn't tell if the document was authentic, but I thought I knew who could help. I folded the papers and returned them to the envelope. I sat there for what seemed like a long time, puzzling it out, trying to discern some truth, separate fact from fancy. What had Abraham stumbled onto? If the document was real, if it could be authenticated in a court of law, it would change the way business was done in large parts of Florida.

My lawyer brain kicked in as I pieced together how it would play out in a federal court. Could I or any other lawyer make a credible argument that the document was genuine? What witnesses would be needed to convince the judge that the document was legally binding on the parties, that it was even real and not somebody's idea of a joke or an outright fraud? How would the court sort out the beneficiaries, the real parties of interest? A receiver would be necessary, but who could take on such a mammoth job? Could all the details of ownership built up over the centuries be unraveled? Perhaps, but it would be one hell of a fight, with very large-moneyed interests on one side and a poverty-stricken group of islanders on the other.

I turned off the flow of thoughts about legal things. The lawyer's brain is a frightful receptacle of law and facts, always churning about a case, looking for the edge that often means the difference between winning and losing. I reminded myself that I had retired from all that, turned off the spigot of issues that keeps the lawyer unsettled and tense, retreated to an island where the beer was cold, the fish plentiful, and an occasional pretty girl took a liking to me, where the most important decision I made every day was whether to make happy hour at Tiny's, Mar Vista, Moores, Pattigeorge's, or the Hilton.

I was beginning to see the edges of the puzzle that my life had been for the past week. Pieces were falling into place, the picture taking on a semblance of reality, turning jumbled pieces of the jigsaw into a recognizable whole. I still didn't know who was trying to kill Logan and me, or who had made the attempts on Abraham's life, but I now knew why.

CHAPTER FIFTY-SIX

I dialed Professor Newman. He was in and told me he'd see me if I could get to his office within the next thirty minutes. I told him I'd be there. I pulled out onto Washington Boulevard and drove north. I turned left onto University Parkway and drove past the entrance to the Sarasota-Bradenton International Airport and onto the New College campus.

The professor was in his cramped office, his feet on his desk, a journal on his lap. He held a bottle of water in his left hand. He looked up as I entered, put down his feet, and stood to shake hands. "Well, Counselor. What can I do for you today?"

"I think I found the codicil," I said.

"Codicil?"

"It's not really a codicil, but it does appear to be an attachment to a treaty. I thought you might be able to tell me what it is."

He took the document, sat back in his chair, and was quiet for a time, carefully studying the writing. "Do you know anything about treaties?"

"Not much," I said.

"I think this might be a protocol, which is sort of a supplement to the treaty of 1832. It references the Camp Moultrie Treaty in 1823, which gave the Seminoles a great deal of land in return for many of them emigrating to the Oklahoma Territory. But in 1832 some of the chiefs entered into another treaty. In this one they gave up the land reserved to them by the Camp Moultrie Treaty. Some, but not all, of the Seminole chiefs agreed to the 1832 treaty. One of the sticking points on all the treaties was what to do with the blacks whom the Seminoles treated as members of the tribe. A lot of white southerners wanted them brought back to their states as slaves.

"This 1832 treaty gave certain lands to some of the chiefs and an annuity in return for their relinquishing any claims to the reservation granted by the Camp Moultrie Treaty. This created a schism among the chiefs and led directly to the Second Seminole War when the dissidents refused to abide by a treaty they'd not been a party to."

"So the Indians got screwed," I said.

"Yeah. They always did."

"How did the U.S. government uphold the treaty of thirty-two if all the chiefs didn't sign it?"

"We won the war. There was no formal surrender, but by the mid 1840s most of the Seminoles had been transported to Oklahoma. Most of their blacks went with them. There were only about three hundred Seminoles left in Florida, and they were all pushed down into the Everglades."

"Sounds like a good lawyer might beat that '32 treaty if all the parties didn't sign it."

"Some good lawyers tried. The Seminoles filed a claims suit in 1950 seeking compensation for the whole state. The case took twenty-six years to conclude. The Indian Claims Commission found that the Seminoles owned almost all of Florida at the time of the 1823 treaty and weren't fairly compensated. The Commission assessed the 1823 value of the almost twenty-four million acres at $12,500,000. The Indians finally settled in 1976 for $16,000,000 to be split between the Oklahoma and Florida tribes. That settled for all time any claims the Seminoles had."

"But, if that document is any good, if it is a protocol to the original 1832 treaty, the blacks would have an interest separate from the Indians. One that wasn't extinguished by the lawsuit."

"Maybe," Newman said. "But remember, the blacks claimed to be part of the tribe."

"The government didn't recognize them as such. I think it'd be hard-pressed now to claim in a court of law that they were Seminoles and their claims were extinguished by the lawsuit that they weren't a party to."

"You're the lawyer, but I can't see the government trying to sort this out after all these years. The property titles alone would be almost impossible to unravel."

"Not really. All the land today would have deeds in the county courthouses showing who owned it."

"Yeah, but there're towns and subdivisions built on a lot of that land."

"The protocol only reserves the mineral rights. All that phosphate out in the center of the state would go to the Black Seminoles. They wouldn't have a right to the property on which this college sits, for instance. Only the minerals under it. There'd be no economically feasible way to mine this land. They'd have to tear down the buildings and pay compensation to the owners. The mineral rights would be minuscule compared to the value of the land and buildings."

"There'd be hell to pay from the phosphate interests. They've paid for those rights."

"Yes, but the law contemplates what it calls a 'bona fide purchaser.' Since the owner could not have known of any claims on the mineral rights, he would have to be fairly compensated for what he bought."

"That could amount to a lot of money."

"Not nearly as much as those rights are worth today. And the new owners could make a claim for all the profits made off their minerals during all the years of mining out there."

"Christ. This could open up a Pandora's box."

I shook my head. "A huge one. Can we prove that the protocol is legitimate?"

Newman studied the document for a long time. "The names of the signatories are right, I think. I can get a copy of the original treaty from the national archives and compare them."

"How long will that take?"

"I can probably get one e-mailed to me by this evening. I'm a registered researcher and most of those old records have been digitized. Do you really think you could make a case out of this?"

"I don't know. It looks as if this protocol was entered into at about the same time as the treaty. If the people who signed it for the government had the right to do that, and the Senate ratified it, I would think it's good."

"That seems a little iffy. Why would the government give away something so valuable?"

"Mineral rights in Florida at the time of the treaty were essentially worthless," I said. "There was no gold, no silver, no fountain of youth. Phosphate wasn't discovered until many years later. This was probably an afterthought. Maybe it was a sop to the Indians who were worried about their black friends. The government gave the blacks the mineral rights to all of the reservation lands contained in the 1823 treaty, and the Indians, ignorant as they were of white man's law, probably didn't know that the mineral rights were absolutely worthless."

"And the government couldn't foresee the uses for phosphate. Or even know that millions of tons of the stuff lay just under the surface."

"Exactly," I said.

CHAPTER FIFTY-SEVEN

I drove back to Longboat, musing on the vagaries of life. If the protocol was valid, then there was going to be a lot of money moved from big corporations to a small group of Andros Island Bahamians who had very little institutional memory of their Seminole ties. It was going to be one hell of a lawsuit.

Part of me wanted to suit up and do battle against the titans, go into the pit that was the courtroom and slay them with my rapier-like mind, my wit, and superior intellect. I laughed at myself. I was well out of it. I'd done my time in the courtroom and I thought I'd acquitted myself well. I'd lost some cases, but I knew that the lawyer who'd never lost a case, hadn't tried very many. I wanted no part of that circus again.

I'd been checking on Abraham regularly. The desk clerk on his floor would only tell me that there had been no change. He was hanging in, but who knew if he'd make it. He was in great shape, but he was still an eighty-year-old man. He might not survive this.

For that matter, I might not either. We were going to Gibsonton to invade the Snake Dance Inn, to try and jerk the West Coast Marauder leader Baggett out of there and get some answers. If we managed it, it'd be a close thing, and the odds weren't exactly in our favor. Jock had called in some firepower from his agency, people in debt to him, who admired him and would come without asking why. His long career had given him many friends, men who owed him their lives. These guys lived by the soldier creed of taking care of your buddy. It was one reason I admired Jock so much. He had never been in the military, but he'd been a soldier in service to his country since he joined the agency right out of Clemson University.

My service was receding into the misty distance. I'd been a soldier, and I think some of that stays with you. There's an old saying about veterans, "All gave some, and some gave all." I think the corollary to that would go something like, "When you've been part of the military, the military is forever part of you."

I was getting a little maudlin, but cheered up as I drove across the John Ringling Bridge. Longboat Key shimmered at the edge of the bay and the boats moored at the Sarasota Yacht Club gleamed in the late afternoon sun. A schooner, its sails furled, puttered under the bridge, a middle-aged couple lounging in the cockpit.

I had been having dreams of late, bad dreams, not of soldiers dead in the jungle, but of my childhood, a time cloaked in a darkness of the soul that I'd rather forget. I hadn't dreamed of that time in years, gave no thought to it, banished it from my mind. Perhaps the war memories, so vivid and bloody, had supplanted those baleful reflections of a time a child could not quite comprehend. But the incident in the Swamp Rat Bar, when I'd been thrust backward in time for a second or two, was troubling. There was a dissonance in my universe, a warping of time and space that propelled me into the past, into a time I thought I'd forgotten and didn't want to remember. A certain smell or a piece of a song would trigger the mechanism, roiling the amygdala, wrenching long-repressed memories over dormant synapses, and bringing them bounding into the present. I knew it was nothing to worry about, but there it was. I didn't want to relive my childhood, not even in snatches of memory.

My journey had been long and sometime harder than I would have liked, but in the end I had arrived at a sort of peace, living on an island among people of warmth and substance. Yet, the old demons haunted me, and on rare occasions would rise up like bile and flood my system with despair. Dark images invaded my sleep and roused memories of the depredations of my youth and of a time when circumstances beyond my control plundered my innocence and robbed me of the equanimity that every child deserves. It was those nightmares that drove me into a blackness that I feared I'd never escape. Sometimes the dreams were of war and death and soldiers gone to Valhalla, and sometimes the dreams came when I was fully awake, in the form of flashbacks to times best forgotten.

Stressful events brought the demons rollicking to the fore, but I had learned to ignore them, or to at least not allow them to take control. I brushed them aside like so much fluff and went on about my life. I took a certain amount of pride in my ability to move past these chimerical fantasies and hold the blackness at bay, fighting a deadly duel that I could not lose and continue to live. My own death lurked in the deep shadows of depression, beckoning me with its promise of relief, of peace at last. But I always won, stuffing the incubi back into the pit from which they sprang and wrenching my own happiness from their grasping fingers.

Perhaps the stress of the past few days had unleashed the long-buried demons. I'd gone from a boat-loving beach bum to a hunted man in the space of a few hours. People were trying to kill me and I still wasn't clear as to why, although now I could see the outlines of the answer forming. I hoped that the coming evening would clear away the mist, turn the shadows into substance, and give me the answers I needed to bring this mess to an end.

Jock and Logan were going to meet me at the Hilton for a burger. We were staying away from the booze until this night was finished. We needed sustenance, and on a pleasant spring evening, the outside bar would be hard to beat. I drove down the key and pulled into the hotel parking lot, parked, and walked in the back way, past the great white egret that hangs around waiting for a treat. He shuffled over a little at my approach and looked at me, waiting for me to feed him something. I shrugged at him and took a seat at the bar.

"Miller Lite?" asked Billy from behind the bar.

"Not tonight, buddy. Got some work to do."

"I heard Jock was in town."

"He is. He'll be here shortly."

"Good. I always enjoy seeing him. Logan coming too?"

"Unfortunately, yes."

Billy laughed. He had known Logan for many years. When they were younger and Logan was just back from Vietnam, they had worked together in a bar at the Tampa airport.

Logan and Jock arrived and we took a table on the deck overlooking the Gulf. We talked as we ate our burgers. Jock had called Bubba at the DEA to ask about Morton.

"What did you find out?" I asked.

"Morton is on their radar, but he's a shadow. They haven't been able to identify him and nobody has a picture or prints or anything else. Morton may not even be his name. He's tied in some way with one of the Mexican drug cartels. They think he's the southwest Florida distributor. He owns several businesses around Sarasota and uses them to launder his drug money. On paper, he's a forty-nine percent owner of Baggett's place, the Snake Dance Inn. DEA is pretty sure there's a lot of drug money being washed through that bar."

"He might be the connection between the bikers and the other shooters," Logan said.

Jock nodded. "Probably."

"Is Morton his first name or last name?" I asked.

"According to the paperwork on the Snake Dance Inn, it's both. He goes by Morton Morton."

"Like Major Major in *Catch 22*," said Logan.

Jock laughed. "Right, Logan. I didn't know you could read."

"If we can get hold of Baggett, maybe he can enlighten us," I said. "The island gossip mill has sure been full of Morton today. He must have had a couple of bald headed guys. The one Logan took out and another one still with him."

"Let's get through tonight," Jock said. "Then we'll worry about Morton."

I nodded in agreement. "I'll call Bill Lester and let him know that we're going after Baggett." I pulled out my phone. It was dark, the battery dead. Crap. "Logan, can I use your phone?"

"I never carry the damn thing. Those minutes cost too much."

Jock handed me his phone and I called Bill, got his voice mail, and left a message that we were trying to run down a witness and would talk to him later. I tried J.D. again. Got the voice mail again and left another message, telling her about the document and what Newman had said. I told her I'd catch up with her the next morning and we could try to put everything together. I also asked if she had found anything on Morton.

The sun was starting its languid dive into the Gulf, slowly sinking, its orb flattening out as it disappeared over the horizon. No matter how many times I'd seen that happen, it still caused a flutter of pleasure in my system. It was an affirmation that the world was going around, its daily progress uninterrupted, that no matter how bad things seemed, the earth kept a steady pace in its rotations. That was a soothing thought, but I reflected on the night ahead and began to wonder if I would be alive to see it happen again the next day.

CHAPTER FIFTY-EIGHT

The Snake Dance Inn was a gritty place, taking up the entire first floor of a used-up building. There was a stairway at the side leading up to a veranda that ran along the front of the structure. Four doors were placed along the front, opening onto the walkway. A couple were off their hinges and leaning against the side of the building. They were flanked by old-fashioned double-hung sash windows, some broken, the remaining glass shards standing like alligator teeth in their mullions.

The first floor had one entrance door. The rest of the façade was faded brick. Motorcycles were parked haphazardly along the street in front, interspersed among the few cars that shared the space. More bikes were in a dirt parking lot on the east side of the building. A sign identifying the place as the Snake Dance Inn hung over the door. Above the sign, a single lightbulb encased in an aluminum shade and affixed to the building by a short stanchion illuminated it. This was not a place that invited strangers. Its customers were the regulars, and in this place that meant bikers.

Gibsonton lies south of Tampa on Highway 41 just south of the Alafia River, about fifty miles from Longboat Key. It is an unincorporated hamlet that has long been the winter home of circus and carnival workers, many of whom are now retired and live there year round. It can be a rough place at times and this bar didn't add much to the town's ambience.

We'd driven north on Highway 41, turned right on Gibsonton Drive, and then left onto a side street leading to the river. The Snake Dance Inn sat in a block of decrepit buildings, long ago abandoned. It was the only place in the area with lights showing. I suspected this was on purpose, a way to keep the really bad guys separated from the elderly retirees who made their homes in the area. This part of town was simply squalid.

Jock, Logan, and I were dressed in jeans, plain white T-shirts, ball caps, athletic shoes, and windbreakers. We didn't look much like bikers and hadn't meant to. We wanted to stand out as different. We sat for a few minutes in Logan's car, trying to get an idea of what to expect. Several people on motorcycles roared up, parked, and went in. Nobody left.

"I don't see your buddies, Jock," said Logan.

"They're here."

"Can you see them?"

"No, but they said they'd be here and they will."

"I sure hope to hell you're right," said Logan.

I silently agreed with him. This was going to be interesting. We were planning to take Baggett out the front door, into the car, and to someplace to, as Jock said, have a discussion with him. I'd seen Jock's discussions before, his interrogations to be more exact, and he wasn't one to waste time with a lot of nonsense. The subject either talked immediately or Jock persuaded him to talk later. If Jock made a threat, he carried it out. It wasn't pretty, but it was effective and quick. The big problem was going to be getting Baggett out of the Snake Dance Inn.

The place was large, crowded with men and women in biker gear sitting at tables placed randomly on an ancient hardwood floor. There was an L-shaped bar across the right side as we walked in, three men behind it, dressed as their guests, slinging drinks to the women who served as waitresses. Several hard-looking men sat at the bar, drinking shots of liquor, not talking or looking around. They were dedicated to getting drunk in the quickest way possible. A woman sat at the short arm of the bar, near the corner, surveying the place. Her long blonde hair was dirty and tangled and hung past her shoulders, bangs down to her eyes, barely visible beneath a ball cap pulled low on her forehead. Her eyes were obscured behind opaque sunglasses. She wore jeans, biker boots, and a sleeveless blouse scooped so low in the front that it barely covered her nipples. She had a tattoo on her left bicep, a gaudy picture of a motorcycle, a similar one on the outside of her right arm just above the wrist. Curiously, a whimsical drawing of a yellow Vespa motor scooter was tattooed on her right breast, clearly visible in the low-cut blouse. A cigarette dangled from her mouth, smoke rising. A half-full ashtray sat on the bar in front of her next to a glass of dark whiskey. She'd been here for a while.

A number of pool tables in the back were busy with games. The air was dense with smoke, the effluvium of scores of cigarettes held in fingers, mouths, and ashtrays, giving the place the look of a foggy day. A jukebox was playing loud heavy-metal music, its raucous and discordant sounds rising above the din of conversation, the sporadic guffaws of drunken men wearing shaggy hair and lots of tattoos, and the yelps of delight from the biker girls ingratiating themselves to men who would think nothing of beating them into submission were they to dare show the slightest glimmer of independence.

Logan had stayed in the car parked at the curb, engine running in case we needed to exit in a hurry. Jock and I stood at the door, taking in a scene that wouldn't make any of the guests' mothers proud. Jock whispered, "There he is. In the back on the left."

I saw our quarry sitting at a table for four, deep in conversation with a large, shaggy man sitting across from him. Two chairs were empty. Jock and I walked toward them. Baggett looked up as we neared, his baleful stare turning to surprise when we pulled out chairs and sat down at his table.

He wasn't a particularly big man, but he looked tightly coiled, like a snake about to strike. His arms were tattooed with abstract scenes of motorcycles, a little more artistic than the average biker. His hair reached his collar, brown and greasy looking, as if it hadn't been washed in a while. He had a beard with a patch missing on his right cheek, a place where for some reason hair would not grow. His eyes were blue and he was squinting at us. A scar was visible on his left cheek, high, up near the eyes.

"Who the fuck are you?" he asked.

"We need to talk," I said.

"I don't need to talk to you, asshole."

"It would be in your best interest to engage us in conversation," I said, smiling. "Believe me when I tell you that I mean you no harm."

He laughed. "Harm? I'll have your nuts cut off before you can get out of this bar."

The man sitting at the table with us snickered. "You tell 'em, Dirtbag."

Jock was staring straight into the eyes of Baggett. "If you so much as move, I'm going to blow your balls off with the nine mil I've got pointed at them."

Baggett's face suddenly went dark, the merriment leaving as soon as it had arrived, a scowl replacing the laugh. "You'll be dead before you get to the door."

"Maybe so," said Jock. "But you won't be alive to enjoy it. You're the first to go if things get nasty."

"What do you want?"

The other man sitting at the table was still as a rock, afraid to move, his face frozen in a grimace of fear. I looked at him. "You're not going to cause us any trouble are you? I also have a gun and your balls are not safe today."

He shook his head. "Stay cool, man."

I turned to Baggett. "Do you know who I am?"

"No, and I don't give a shit."

"My name's Matt Royal."

A look of recognition crossed his face, gone in an instant, but I saw it, knew he was shocked that the hunted had become the hunter.

"I don't know that name," Baggett said.

"Yes you do, and you've been trying to kill me, and now I want some answers."

"You won't get any from me."

"I think we will," I said. "My friend here is very good at getting people to talk. What we're going to do, Mr. Baggett, is get up and walk out of here together. We'll both have our guns in our pockets and pointed at your back. It you move wrong, we're going to shoot you." I turned to the other man at the table. "Are you a member of the West Coast Marauders?"

"I am," he said, a hint of pride in his voice.

"If you don't want your leader here to end up with a slug in his head, you'll sit quietly and not move until we're out the door. Do you understand?"

He nodded his head.

"All right," I said to Baggett. "Get up."

It started out okay. We moved through the crowd near the bar, passing by disreputable men dressed in biker gear leaning against it, watching Baggett lead us toward the door. We had gotten most of the way there when I saw a glint out of the corner of my eye. A big man was moving toward Jock, only inches away, with a switchblade knife in the open position, going for the thrust to the chest, the one that would pierce the heart and kill a man instantly. I knew I didn't have time to warn Jock, and Jock had no time to respond to the blade thrusting toward him in the hand of a tattooed man.

CHAPTER FIFTY-NINE

The night is full of creepy things, ghosts and goblins and nightmares and bears under the bed. We grow out of those fears, but there always remains some atavistic suspicion of the dark, some delicate tendril of dread that skips across our minds when there is no light, when the night closes in around us and we are alone with our thoughts. So it was with the old man.

Donna had gone to bed, leaving him in his chair with one last tumbler of Scotch, confident that he could make it across the room to the bed provided by hospice. And he could do that, but he could also make it to the pantry where the booze was kept, and he had done that. Now the bottle, half-full, golden in the light of the lamp shining through the whiskey, sat on the table with the tumbler. He sipped for a while, letting the warmth of the booze warm his stomach, knowing that he would pay a price the next day, dreading the fire that would eat at his gut, reminding him that he shouldn't drink.

But what the hell. He was in his final days. Day, maybe. He knew death was close, very close. He could feel it. He only wanted to live long enough to finish the job, his final effort, and the one that would save his empire.

If anyone found out about his part in the deaths that came from that infernal black Indian's meddling in things that didn't concern him, it would be too late to prosecute. He'd beat the charge because he would be dead. There was nothing the law could do to him. He was worried about Donna, though. She was culpable, had been part of the plan, part of the orders that had gone out from this mansion by the bay. They would come for her and she would take his place in the maw of the unrelenting justice system that would grind her into nothingness.

He turned off the lamp, bringing the darkness in close, cloying in its ability to conceal the deprivations of age, the torpid state of his existence, the only illumination the rhythmic green flashing of the channel marker in the bay. He felt the mesmerizing effect from its constant repetition, each flash evenly spaced, equally bright.

His mind drifted into the past, that shadowy time of his youth, before he understood that life was brutal and that only the fiercest of men would survive and prosper. He had loved a girl then, a woman really, a slim beautiful woman with a lilting laugh and eyes that shone with a wisdom not common in one so young, a smile that lightened his heart and gave meaning to his life.

They'd met in the library of the university up in Gainesville. She was the daughter of a clothier, a widower, who owned a small chain of men's stores along the east coast from Daytona Beach to West Palm. He was the son of a man of wealth and station and, some said, ruthlessness. But the young student couldn't appreciate the decadence required to amass a large fortune. That knowledge was in his future, and when he met the girl in the library, he knew the stirring warmth of true love that perhaps only comes once in every lifetime.

In the days before birth control pills, a time of faulty condoms and mistaken understandings of fertility, pregnancy was a great risk that attended each and every coupling. The sweet girl with the lilting laugh became pregnant. When she began to show, when her belly got so big that she could no longer hide it under flowing dresses, she left school and went home to her father. He was a kind man who loved his daughter, and he took her in and cared for her and called the doctor when her labor pains came. Medicine was less refined in that time, less sure of itself, less a science and more of an art. Complications set in that were beyond the minimal abilities possessed by the doctor. The woman with the wise eyes did not survive the delivery, and the baby that was born of that glorious coupling in Gainesville was a freak, a child that should never have been conceived.

The young student had come to the house of the clothier to see his child and to bury his love. He left the child in the clothier's care, went on with his life, and grieved for what he'd lost. He never visited the child, not even once, but he sent a check every month to the clothier who raised her.

He wondered, as he often did in these final days, how his life would have differed if he'd married the girl with the wondrous smile, if she had lived, if she'd birthed a normal child, and if he'd dodged the evil that had infused his life since the day of their parting.

He wiped a tear from his cheek, cursed himself for his self-pity, and crept carefully off to the hospice bed. Sleep, that cursed state that brought him only nightmares, took him gently onto another plane of existence. Outside, in the dark bay, the channel light winked on and off and on and off, consistent in its nightly cadence.

CHAPTER SIXTY

The sound of a pistol shot quieted the crowd, but I took little notice. I was in that nanosecond between the time I saw Jock's assailant moving toward him with the knife and my reaction. A hole appeared in the temple of the man with the knife, a larger hole on the other side of his head spewing bone and blood and brain matter. He stopped cold, no movement except the fall to the floor.

Jock didn't flinch. He grabbed Baggett's hair, pulling his head back, his pistol coming out of his pocket and boring into the man's back, pushing him toward the door. I saw a bearded man wearing a watch cap and a biker vest over a long-sleeve shirt and jeans turn toward the crowd, his pistol pointing outward. Three other men spaced around the room did the same. "Be cool," said the one who'd shot Jock's attacker. "Be cool, and nobody dies." Jock's buddies had shown up.

The biker who'd been at the table with Baggett had moved with us. As I turned toward the shooter, I saw the biker coming at me, a knife at waist height, out of sight of any of Jock's men. I pulled my gun from my jacket pocket and was raising it to shoot my attacker. An arm snaked around my back, grabbing my right arm, pushing it down. Somebody was behind me, one arm around my throat and the other in control of my gun hand. I helped him out, pushing my arm all the way down to my side and pulling the trigger. The bullet entered the foot of the man behind me. He screamed and let go, but not before he ripped the pistol out of my hand. The one with the knife was a couple of feet from me, his weapon pointed at my gut. I didn't have time to pick up my gun. The guy wasn't a professional. He was a little clumsy, mad as hell, oblivious to the men holding guns on the crowd. He was trying for a kill, his rage overshadowing his instinct for survival. Surely he knew that if he got me, he would be shot down like a dog in the street.

Another biker, a big guy with a lot of gut, was coming from my left, a knife in his hand. He was moving quickly, was no more than three steps from me, arm cocked to thrust the blade into my heart.

I pivoted to my right, turning inside the right arm of the first guy, my back to him throwing my right arm over his, pinning him to me. The fat guy was two steps from me, coming hard and fast. Out of the corner of my eye I saw a figure move toward us, coming from my left. A booted foot came up, lighting fast, striking the man in the wrist. The knife fell to the floor. The booted foot struck again, so fast I thought I might have imagined the first strike. The boot caught the fat guy in the jaw, snapping his head back. He dropped like a big lead blimp.

At the same second that the boot was flying, I head butted my guy in the face, twice, quickly, stepped forward and grabbed his right elbow with my right hand. He was reeling, his nose a bloody pulp. I pivoted to my right, still holding his elbow, grabbed his right wrist with my left hand. His grip was loosening on the knife when I raised his arm, my right hand on his elbow and my left on his wrist, and brought it down forcefully onto the back of a chair. I heard the bone snap and the man cry out in anguish. The knife clattered to the floor.

I turned in time to see my booted savior smash the heel of her hand into the nose of another biker. Blood and mucus splattered. He went to his knees, holding his face, moaning in pain. The tattooed blonde from the bar wheeled again, her back to me, ready to strike the next assailant. A surprise. One of Jock's people. A gun fired. One of Jock's men put a bullet into the ceiling. The room went quiet, people stopped where they were. For a second there was no movement in the room.

The shooter, Jock's buddy, had moved toward us in the second that the action took. The biker who had grabbed me from behind was writhing on the floor, moaning, his boot bloody, a bullet hole on the top above his instep. The one from the table lay on the floor in a fetal position holding his broken arm against his crotch, blood streaming from his nose.

"Let's move," said the shooter, backing toward the door. I picked up my pistol and trained it on the crowd. The three other men were moving toward the front of the bar, each with a pistol trained on the room, point-ing in different directions, their fields of fire covering everybody in the place. The blonde moved with us, staying close, eyes darting.

We reached the front door. Logan was in the driver's seat of his car, a pistol pointed at the rear seat. Jock had pushed Baggett into the back and restrained his hands behind him with flex cuffs. Logan was making sure he didn't move. Jock was standing by the car watching the entrance to the bar, his weapon pointing toward it. He'd propped the door open with a brick. The six of us came out, slowly, one giving cover to the next guy backing out of the building. One of them had a machine pistol. He pointed it into the building, aimed high, and let off a quick burst.

"Where's your car, Fred?" Jock shouted.

"Right here, boss. The Mercury," said the man with the machine pistol.

"Give me that Uzi, and you guys get the hell out of here. I'll call you when we get moving."

Fred tossed the gun to Jock and he and the others got in the car. Jock let off another burst of gun fire into the bar's ceiling. "That ought to keep them on their toes until we're gone."

The blonde was standing next to me. "Aren't you going with them?" I asked.

"I'm not with them." She smiled.

The slight southern accent, the smile. Suddenly my brain kicked into gear, overriding my sense of confused wonder. "J.D.? Get in the car." I pushed her into the front seat.

The Mercury left, its tires squealing as they sought purchase on the asphalt of the road. I got into the front-passenger seat, squeezing J.D. be-tween Logan and me. We followed the Mercury. Jock poked the machine pistol out the window and fired another burst into the ranks of bikes parked next to the road.

"That seemed to work out nicely," said Logan. "Did you guys make any new friends tonight? Other than Blondie here."

"Watch your mouth, Logan," J.D. said, and took her sunglasses off.

He turned, squinted at her in the faint light from the dash. "J.D.?"

"Yeah. Watch the road."

"Hey," he said. "Nice tats."

"They wash off." She pulled at the top of her blouse, an unconscious attempt to cover her breasts.

Jock picked up the phone and dialed a number. "You guys go on home. I appreciate the backup. I owe you."

He was quiet for a moment, then, "I'll tell him." He hung up, looked at me. "Fred said to tell you the one that came after you with the knife was Baggett's bodyguard. There's some sort of rule that if you're the body-guard and your boss gets wacked, you die too. I guess he figured he had nothing to lose."

"He was right," said Baggett. "He's a dead man."

"You may as well be," said Jock. "After you get through talking to us, I don't think they'll want you to be their leader anymore."

"Where're we going?" asked Logan.

"We're going to drop J.D. off." I turned toward her. "Where's your car?"

"About a mile from here. I parked it and walked in."

"Show me."

She gave Logan directions and we soon pulled up behind a gray Toy-ota Camry parked in a strip mall lot. "I want to go with you," she said.

"Get out. Let's talk," I said.

We walked the few steps to the passenger side of her car. Stopped. Stood silently for a moment. I exploded. "What the hell were you doing in that bar?"

She pulled the blonde wig off her head, opened the car door, and threw it and her hat into the passenger seat. "Saving your ass," she said over her shoulder. She retrieved a man's dress shirt, pulled it on, buttoned it up, and turned back to me.

"You did that and I appreciate it. But you can't be here. You're a cop."

"Not any more. I quit."

"What?"

"I gave the chief my gun and badge and a letter of resignation late this afternoon."

"Why?"

"I needed to color outside the lines."

"What're you talking about?"

"There's some evil in the world that can't be handled by the rules."

"Talk to me, J.D. You're not making much sense."

"Have you heard about Jube Smith?"

"No."

"I tried to call you several times. Went straight to your voice mail.

"Sorry. My battery died."

"Logan didn't answer his phone, and I didn't have a number for Jock."

She was shaken, talking rapidly as if hearing the words pouring from her mouth would ease the pain I saw in her face.

"J.D.," I said, sharply. "What's the problem?"

"That bastard Baggett killed Jube and his wife, and the law can't touch him."

My heart sagged. Poor Jube. A man driven beyond his level of tolerance who'd tried to do the right thing and was killed because of it.

"What happened?" My voice sounded tired in my own ears, and I guess I was tired. Tired of death. Tired of the death merchants. Tired of the twisted people who inhabited a subterranean world that most people did not know existed. It was like another dimension, existing side by side with the one we knew, and as imperfect as ours was, the other was many magnitudes worse. A place where death was dealt without thought or even purpose.

"I was at the north end of the key checking out a car that had been broken into at the Northside Drive beach access when the chief called. Said there had been a murder in Cortez, and I needed to get over there and talk to a Detective David Sims. He said that some boat captain told him that you were involved with Jube. I tried to call, but I guess your battery had died.""

"It's okay, J.D. What else?

"I've been a homicide cop for a long time. Seen a lot of bad stuff. This was the worst."

"Tell me."

"The lady who lives next door to Jube heard a motorcycle pull up and stop. Thirty minutes later she heard a gunshot and saw a man run from the house and leave on the bike. She got the tag number. It was one of those vanity plates that said 'DBAG.'"

"Baggett's?"

"Yes. Sims ran the plate."

"Then you've got him."

"No. He called it in stolen. From a cell phone. The call came in from the east side of the county just about the time the bike appeared at Jube's."

"Could be legit."

"And he could have had someone else make the call. Give him some sort of alibi."

"You don't buy it," I said.

"Not for a minute." She took a deep breath, shuddered a little. "There's more. Did you know that Jube's wife had ovarian cancer?"

"Yes."

"She was near death. Maybe a day or two. Not long. She was just skin and bones. She was tied to the bed. Naked and gagged. Her throat was cut. There were cigarette burns on her stomach and thighs. And cuts. He sliced her before he killed her. All up and down her torso. The ME's preliminary thinking is that the burns and cuts were premortem. Her heart was still pumping blood when the bastard stuck a cigarette to her and sliced her like a raw carrot."

"How do you know it was a cigarette that burned her? Did he leave it at the scene?"

"Yes, but it was a filter tip, and he tore off the tip and took it with him. No DNA."

"Why leave the cigarette?"

"I think it was to show that he was smarter than we are. That there was no evidence. No way to tie him to the murder."

"What about the knife?"

"One of a set from Jube's kitchen."

"Jube?"

"He was tied to a chair, facing the bed. Gagged. Shot in the head. He had to watch and listen to Baggett torture his wife."

J.D. painted a scene from hell. I hoped Jube didn't have to see his wife defiled. "Maybe Jube was dead before it took place," I said.

"That doesn't match with the timeline. Baggett was in the house for thirty minutes before the shot was fired, and he left immediately afterward."

"Did you talk to the boat captain?"

"Yeah. It was the one we had lunch with. Nestor Cobol. Nice guy. Said Jube worked for him and that you'd gotten him the job. I remember Jube mentioning that at lunch."

"Goddamnit," I said.

"Baggett did it. I know that in my gut."

"But you can't prove it."

"Not in a million years. He was careful. No prints, no DNA, nothing to tie him to the scene."

"I suspect he'll talk to Jock."

"That's what I was hoping for. Can I come along?"

"This might get rough."

"I've seen rough before."

"What about your car?"

"I'll get a ride up here in the morning and pick it up."

"Okay."

We walked back to Logan's car. J.D. got in the front seat, scooted over to give me room. "J.D.'s going with us," I said. "I'll explain later." There was no objection.

"Where're we going?" Logan asked.

"Sun City." I said.

"Why Sun City?"

"That's where K-Dawg lives now."

"I know that. Are we going to visit him at this time of the night? Maggie will kill us."

"Do you remember that camp the Dawg has way up on the Little Manatee River?"

"Yeah. I think we did some drinking up there a time or two. Maybe more."

"I called him today. We'll pick up the key at his house and then take this piece of shit up there and have a nice little conversation. Don't miss your turn."

CHAPTER SIXTY-ONE

We picked up the key from K-Dawg, drove east on Sun City Boulevard, turned south on Highway 301, and after a few miles turned right onto a dirt track that ran along the northern edge of the river. An old citrus grove stretched north from the water, its trees empty of fruit. We drove for a mile or so and came to a small clearing that opened onto the river and was bordered on three sides by ancient grapefruit trees. The camp was little more than an old travel trailer set up on concrete blocks. It had a propane stove, a portable toilet, a small generator for powering lights, and bunks for four people. It sat near the river, which was more like a creek this close to its headwaters. A cleared area behind the trailer provided parking for three or four cars.

Jock dragged Baggett from the backseat, dropping him on the ground, his feet still in the car. "Get up, asshole," he said.

"I hope you've got your insurance paid up," Baggett said, "because some very bad people are going to be coming after you."

"Let me tell you something, Dirtbag," Jock said. "You have no idea what kind of bad people I deal with every day. Compared to them, those shitheads who work for you are kind of like Little Leaguers who think they can play in the majors. They wouldn't last the first inning."

Baggett was on his feet. He spit onto the ground. Jock kicked him in the back of his knee, throwing the biker onto the ground again, face first, no way to stop his momentum with his hands cuffed behind him. Jock kicked him in the ribs, twice. "Don't be spitting on my buddy's dirt."

Baggett got up slowly, his face contorted in pain and defiance and rage. He stared at Jock, a long hard stare that had certainly put fear into lesser men. Jock slapped him with his open hand. "Don't even think about it, asshole," he said. "You've got a long night ahead of you." He slapped him again. "Get into the house."

I thought I saw a momentary change in the face of the biker leader, the rage giving way to a hint of fear, maybe for the first time beginning to understand that there were people in the world who were as savage as he. He'd always been the bad guy, spreading fear, causing pain and death. It had no meaning to him. But now, he was the victim, the one upon whom the pain and fear were inflicted. He didn't like it, but here he was.

I'd seen Jock work before. He was a man of refinement who found joy in simple things like friendship or golf or the bonhomie of a favorite bar. But when necessary he could play the brute, a malicious and inhuman savage who gave no quarter. It always diminished him, depressed him, worried him that the streak of brutality was a part of him. Afterward, he would withdraw from everybody and drink too much, trying to chase the demons back into the night. He said he needed that ritual to help recover his soul. He never talked about it, except to me. I knew how much a night like this cost him, and I knew the only reason he would ever uncage the beast was to protect his country, or his best friend.

Once inside, Jock tied Baggett to a chair, pulled a small digital tape recorder from the bag he'd brought from the car, and set it on the table next to the biker. He pulled out a twenty-four-inch pair of bolt clippers "Know what this is, asshole?"

Baggett nodded, his face paling a bit. No bravado now. A man who had met his match and then some, a man now scared for his life.

Jock grinned, malevolence shooting from his eyes. "I'm only going to ask you a question once. If you don't answer it, or you lie, I'm going to cut off one of your fingers. When I finish with your fingers, I'll take off your dick. Do we understand each other?"

Baggett nodded. Jock's rough treatment had softened him, made him aware that this man holding the bolt clippers was capable of cutting him up in little pieces, one digit at a time.

"I'm going to switch on this recorder. If I have to cut off a body part, I'll turn it off so that nobody has to hear you scream and whimper like a little girl. You got it?"

Baggett nodded.

"Why are you trying to kill my buddies, Royal and Hamilton?"

"I don't know. I'm being paid to do it. I don't ask why."

That had the ring of truth. Jock accepted it.

"Who's paying you?"

"I don't know that either. He wires the money into my bank account."

"Where's your bank account?"

"Cayman Islands."

"What's the number on the account?"

Baggett gave it to him.

"If I want to get into the account, what do I have to do?"

"I've been saving money in that account for years. If you take it out, I'm broke."

"If you don't explain it to me, you're going to start losing fingers."

Baggett told us how to access the account.

"How does your boss contact you?"

"He calls me on my cell phone."

"Where's the phone?"

"In my pocket."

"When's the last time you talked to him?"

"Today."

"About what?"

"He wasn't happy about the two guys I sent on the boat to get Royal."

"They weren't your men." A statement.

"No. I hired them for that one job. None of my guys knows shit about boats."

"Did you also send the ones to the house in the kayak?"

"Yes."

"Who were they?"

"I don't know their names. A guy named Morton brought them to me."

"Who's Morton."

"An associate."

"Is he in the drug business?"

"Yes."

"Are you in the drug business?"

"Yes."

"How?"

"Mostly distribution."

"You're doing well, James. Would you like some water?"

"Please."

Jock pulled a bottle of water out of his bag, opened it, and put it to Baggett's mouth. He took several swallows, seemed refreshed.

"Where can I find Morton?" Jock asked.

"I don't know. He finds me at the Snake Dance when he needs to see me."

"I'm told he owns forty-nine percent of the place."

"He does."

"What's his first name?"

"I don't know. I think he just goes by one name. You know, like those people in Afghanistan."

"Are you telling me you have a business partner whom you know nothing about?"

"I wish I did know more about him. I've tried, but he's a ghost."

The grilling continued. Baggett had come to an epiphany of sorts. He'd understood that his only way out of this situation alive was to give up everything he knew. So he talked and talked, the trusty little recorder taking everything in.

Logan, J.D., and I had retired to the couch against the wall in the small trailer. The only decoration was a framed photograph hanging on the opposite wall. It showed five men, Logan, K-Dawg, me, and two friends now dead. I remembered the day it had been taken, thirteen years before. We'd been fishing on Art Cavanaugh's boat, caught a few, released them, and came in for lunch and a beer at Rotten Ralph's at the north end of Anna Maria Island. It had been an idyllic day, a day that sticks in the memory and always brings a little flash of joy when I pull it out and live in it for a moment. I had the same photograph on the bookcase in my house, and I knew that Logan kept his on a wall in his condo. Each was talisman of sorts, a good luck piece, a reminder of good times and an island way of life. It seemed a long time ago and far away from this dismal little trailer where a man was bargaining for his life. And I missed the guys in the picture who were no longer of this world.

CHAPTER SIXTY-TWO

An hour passed. Two. Then Jock was finished. He'd wrung all there was out of the once arrogant Baggett. Jock looked at me. "You got anything else?"

I stood. "Let's go outside for a minute."

The four of us trooped out the door, leaving Baggett exhausted, hanging against the straps that bound him to the chair.

"Jock," I said, "there's more. J.D. needs to tell you about it."

And she did. She painted the same lurid picture, leaving out no detail. I wondered if she was just being thorough or if she wanted to incite Jock, to give him the resolve to go back into that mean dwelling and pull the truth from this monster from another dimension of humanity. Maybe it worked. Or maybe Jock was picturing that poor dying woman and the dedicated husband who had to watch a horror beyond understanding. He turned on his heel and marched back into the trailer, the three of us following in his wake.

"Baggett, you piece of shit," Jock said, his voice low, menacing. He was holding the bolt clippers. "I'm not even going to ask you any more questions. Matt, put his hand on the table."

"What?" Alarm shook Baggett's body, his face contorting in fear. "I've told you everything."

"We didn't talk about Jube Smith."

I pulled a knife out of the block of knives sitting on the small countertop next to the stove and walked to the back of the Baggett's chair. "Which one do you want, Jock?" I asked.

"Is he right handed or a southpaw?"

"Right, I think."

"Then I'll take the right one."

"No," screamed Baggett. "What do you want to know?"

"Did you kill Jube Smith?" Jock asked.

Baggett stared, silent, lips pressed together. Jock nodded. I put the knife across the flex cuffs, holding his right arm.

"No," Baggett said again. "Yes. I killed him."

"His wife?" asked Jock.

Baggett dropped his head. "Yes," he said softly.

"Why?"

"I had to make an example. I couldn't let the guy take our money and not bring Royal to us."

J.D. spoke up. The first words she'd said since we walked into the trailer over two hours before. "Why did you do that to his wife?"

"It was part of the example," Baggett said.

I looked at J.D. She was standing stiffly, her chest heaving with the effort it took to calm herself. She wanted to kill him. Her body telegraphed a hatred beyond rage, beyond anything she'd ever felt before. She breathed in deeply, let the breath out, did it again, shrugged, and turned to leave.

"J.D.," I said, "what do you want us to do with him?"

"We've got his confession on tape. Let the law handle the rest of it." She walked out the door.

Jock turned to me. "Are we through?"

"I think you've covered it all. You okay?"

"Yeah. Let's get this piece of crap out of here."

Baggett was slumped in the chair to which he was tied, a look of utter defeat on his face. He'd met a man as devoid of compassion as he was and he'd done what so many others had done in the face of his own anger. He'd folded. He wasn't proud of that, but he was alive. His body language told it all, a person completely defeated, demoralized, awaiting his fate.

Jock untied the man from the chair and walked him to Logan's car, his hands still held behind him by the flex cuffs. Baggett shuffled, a man so tired he could hardly stand. The interrogation had been debilitating, both physically and mentally. He was not the same man who'd driven up with us a couple of hours before.

"Where're we going?" the biker asked.

"We're not sure, but you won't die tonight. Get in the car."

Baggett did as he was told. The three of us walked away from the car, stood under an old oak tree beside the river where J.D. was sitting on the ground, her head in her hands. She was crying softly, the sound vying with the soft murmur of rushing water. A counterpoint to the ugliness we had seen that night.

"What're we going to do with him?" asked Logan.

"I need to get him to the DEA people," Jock said. "With the tape we made, he's going away for a long time. And DEA will be able to bring down the whole shooting match. Lots of bikers will be guests of the feds for years to come. The state will probably want him for the murders."

"Can you get them to take him off our hands tonight?" I asked.

"I doubt it. Can Lester help?"

"I'm sure of it. I'll give him a call."

"Tell him what we've found out and that you just need him held until tomorrow morning. DEA will come get him then."

"Do you need Lester to check out the incoming phone numbers on Baggett's cell?"

"No. I'll send that on to D.C. Maybe we can turn up the guy pulling the strings."

"What about Morton?"

"I think we got enough from Baggett that DEA can roll up Morton and his operation, but I get the impression that Morton's pretty much small potatoes in this thing with you and Logan. It looks as if Baggett went to him for some help in taking you out, but Morton was just a subcontractor."

"Let's see what the phone numbers get us," I said. "I think we've done enough for one night. Let's get rid of Baggett and go get a beer."

"Jock," Logan said, "if Baggett hadn't talked, would you really have cut off his fingers?"

Jock was quiet for a moment, his head bowed, staring at the dirt. Then he raised his eyes and looked squarely at Logan, his face a mask of self-loathing. He nodded. Once. Then the two of them walked to the car.

I sat down beside J.D. She had gotten hold of herself. The tears had stopped. "Are you ready to get out of here?" I asked.

"Yes. That was awful in there."

"Yes."

"I wanted to see that bastard terrified. I enjoyed it."

"I know."

"That's not me, Matt.

"I know."

"That is not me," she said, spacing out the words.

"J.D., you've had a rotten day. But if not for you, I'd probably be dead."

She looked at me. Was quiet for a moment. "I never really wanted to kill anybody. Not until today. Not until I saw what Baggett did to that poor woman. The savagery of it. And making her husband watch."

"You've seen a lot of death in your job. It builds up over time. You become shell-shocked. Like a soldier who's seen too much war."

"I've always put it behind me. Sometimes, when we didn't catch the perp, I'd feel useless, outfoxed by a killer. I've seen sadistic killings, Matt, but nothing like I saw today. I think it was Baggett's making the husband watch that sent me over the edge."

"Come on," I said. "You're going to have a sleepless night, but soon you'll start feeling better. The memory will begin to fade."

"I don't know. I don't know if I can ever get back to where I was."

"You will. You'll find your way back. It'll take some work, but you'll do it."

"I hope you're right," she said, and stood up.

We walked to the car and left the clearing. I too, hoped that the worst of the memories would fade. For all our sakes.

Steve Carey was sitting in his patrol car as we pulled into the parking lot of the Twin Dolphins Marina next to the Highway 41 bridge over the Manatee River. It was almost midnight, and the last of the diners at Mattison's Riverside were leaving, sated with good food and wine.

I'd called Bill Lester to ask for help in getting Baggett to jail. I told him that we'd gotten some interesting information from Dirtbag and what J.D.'s involvement had been.

"Steve Carey's on duty," the chief had said. "I'll have him meet you at the Twin Dolphins Marina. He can take him to the Manatee County Central Jail over in Palmetto. He'll have him booked as a suspected drug dealer awaiting pick up by the Drug Enforcement Agency in the morning."

"Do you have some pretext for the jail?"

"Carey will tell them we picked up Baggett in a sting operation. If the prisoner says anything else, ignore him. He's a congenital liar."

"J.D.'s with us."

"Remind her she starts a shift at eight in the morning. She'll need to come in a little early to pick up her gun and badge."

"What about the letter of resignation?"

"That thing got lost on my desk somewhere. It probably ended up in the shredder with the rest of the crap."

"I'll tell her," I said.

We parked twenty yards from the patrol car, got Baggett out of the backseat, and walked to meet the young cop. J.D. stayed in Logan's vehicle, out of sight. "You guys trying to take my job?" Steve asked as we walked up.

"Nah, Steve," Logan said. "I got no idea how to get a cat out of a tree."

Carey laughed. "Screw you, Logan. The fire department handles that."

We made the transfer and drove west on Manatee Avenue, out toward the bridges that would take us to our little slice of paradise.

"J.D.," I said, "where do you want to go?"

"Home."

"Are you okay to be by yourself?"

She looked at me. "Don't patronize me, Matt."

"Sorry."

Her face softened. She put her hand on my forearm. "I'll be okay."

We stopped at her condo, and I walked her to the door. I stood there with her for a moment and related Bill Lester's message about work tomorrow. She seemed a little surprised, but said, "I'll be there."

"Take a day off. Bill will understand."

"I'll be at work tomorrow, Matt. Bank on it."

She went inside and I took the elevator to the ground floor. She was smart and tough and beautiful. She went to the Snake Dance to help out her friends. Or did she go just for retribution? To make sure that Baggett paid a price for what he did to Jube and his wife. It didn't matter. In the end, she was sickened by Jock's interrogation. In the end, she wanted the murdering bastard turned over to the law so that it could take its course. She was, after all, a cop.

I walked back to the car, got in, and we pulled out onto Dream Island Road.

"Think Sammy's still open?" Jock asked.

Logan grunted. "He'll be closing, but if we get there before the door's locked he'll have to stick around."

"It'll be good for him," I said. "If we don't keep him busy, he'll just go to the Haye Loft and drink."

"And if we keep him busy, he'll drink with us," said Jock.

"Exactly," I said, and that's the way it went.

CHAPTER SIXTY-THREE

The place was crawling with cops. Hillsborough County deputies were frisking people, leading them to the correction division buses, locking them down with handcuffs. Sheriff's cruisers were parked haphazardly in the street, the whole block cordoned off with crime-scene tape. The lab people were trying to make sense out of the chaos that was the Snake Dance Inn, and making little progress. The scene had been trampled by people running for their bikes, leaving the bodies of a man shot through the head and another, his forearm broken and resting at an odd angle as he lay on the floor, a large hunting knife protruding from his back.

The radio reports from the deputies and crime-scene techs were confusing, disjointed, snatches of information flowing through the circuits, adding to the chaotic situation. The witnesses all saw something different, but they were unanimous in their conclusion that the whole thing was the result of a kidnapping of a biker leader named Dirtbag.

A passerby, an elderly man who lived a couple of blocks away and walked his dog late at night, had heard the shots and called 911. A deputy on patrol was nearby and had responded within minutes. Another deputy rolled up right behind him, and together they had staunched the outflow of bikers in a frenzy to get away from a place they knew would draw cops.

Within minutes of the first deputy's arrival, several more cruisers from the area had appeared, along with a couple of Highway Patrol troopers who'd been loitering on the nearby Interstate watching for speeders. As the night wore on, more deputies arrived and the bus from Corrections had shown up. Before it was over, two more buses were needed.

The majority of arrests were based on concealed weapons, mostly knives and brass knuckles and homemade saps. A few had pistols, and some were drunk enough to take a swing at a cop. It was going to be a long night in booking.

Morton sat in the command car, watching the evening unfold. He hadn't been too concerned when he heard about the fight in the bar. It was not an uncommon occurrence, not when bikers fueled with booze and testosterone gathered. But when the report came in that somebody had kidnapped James Baggett, he started to worry. Who in the hell had the balls to walk into the mob assembled in the Snake Dance and waltz out with the head guy? From the accounts coming in, it appeared that a small army of men had been involved in the take-down, but nobody had ever seen any of them before. They did not appear to be bikers. That was the only thing everyone seemed to agree on.

He got out of the car and walked toward the small knot of lieutenants and sergeants standing beside one of the buses, talking quietly. He was in uniform, and the captain's bars on the epaulets of his chocolate-colored shirt dimly reflected the revolving blue and red lights that lit the street. The men stiffened as he approached, quieted in anticipation of their commander's questions.

"What've we got?" Morton asked as he reached the men.

They gave him what they had, theories, pieces of statements given by witnesses, what physical evidence they found. It all amounted to nothing, or not much of anything. The only theory that made any sense to the officers was that a rival biker gang had invaded the Snake Dance and snatched Dirtbag. Morton was pretty sure that wasn't the case. The men who'd taken Baggett weren't bikers. Had they been sent by the cartel? Had Baggett been skimming profits, stealing drugs? Morton was sure it wasn't a law enforcement operation. He'd have been informed of something like that going down in his sector of the county. Besides, cops didn't knife people in the back and leave them. He'd have to check on the cartel connection. That had to be who organized it, but why? And why hadn't he been informed?

He went back to the command cruiser, deep in thought. He'd make some calls, but they'd have to wait until morning. Could this thing be coming apart? He didn't think he was vulnerable. He never showed his face, except at his meetings with Baggett and then he wore a disguise. No one knew him, and of course, his name wasn't Morton.

CHAPTER SIXTY-FOUR

The Hacker sat at his computer, the alcohol coursing through his body giving him the energy he needed to find out what the hell was going on. He'd stroke the keyboard, look closely at the monitor, jot a note on a pad on the table, and move on. The information flowing through the ether was disturbing. There had been some kind of incident at the Snake Dance Inn and James Baggett was missing.

He'd tried to call the old man, but there was no answer. The Hillsborough County sheriff's computers were lagging behind the action. The last entry had been an hour before, around midnight. Surely they now knew more. The sheriff's people did not know who could have snatched the leader of the Marauders. Somebody with balls, that was for sure. The law enforcement intelligence units had heard nothing of a pending raid by anybody, good guys or bad.

The Hacker was worried. Baggett was his man, the guy he called when rough stuff was needed. If Baggett were taken out of the picture, the Hacker could not complete the task assigned by the old man and he would lose the last half of his fee. He was cloaked in anonymity, hidden behind layers of secure servers and dummy addresses. He'd never used a phone other than the prepaids. That had been tough. He'd had to leave his cocoon, his refuge in the grove, and visit stores all over southwest Florida. He couldn't buy more than two at each place, because he didn't want some clerk to remember the man who bought more phones than usual. He stuck with large discount stores, the kind of places that do a lot of business in prepaid phones and where it was unlikely that a clerk would remember a man purchasing two phones some weeks before. He bought the minimum number of minutes for each phone, and he knew that he'd lose those minutes if he didn't use them within an allotted time, usually ninety days. He was cheap by nature and only bought those that he would need for an operation. A new one for each day. New phone, new number. Untraceable.

The Hacker scanned the Sarasota and Manatee sheriffs' office computers. Nothing. He moved on to the city police departments and came up empty. He hacked into the newspapers and TV stations, picking up the bits and pieces of information that would form a story in a few hours. *Nada.*

He thought about calling Baggett, but if somebody had kidnapped him, and it looked as if somebody had, he didn't think it wise to talk to the captors. Who could benefit by taking Baggett out of the picture? The people for whom he sold drugs? Had he run afoul of the Mexicans in some way? No way to tell.

He looked at his watch. After one. He'd try the old man again in the morning. Time to go to bed. He shut down his computer, finished his whiskey, and shuffled off to bed.

FRIDAY

CHAPTER SIXTY-FIVE

On the first day of April, I was on Logan's balcony at sunup, sipping coffee and reading the St. Petersburg *Times,* one of several newspapers Logan had delivered daily. We'd decided that Logan's condo was probably a safer place for us to bed down the night before, because it was on the fifth floor and only had one entrance. We weren't sure what to expect after the night we'd had at the Snake Dance.

We'd stopped at Pattigeorge's for a couple of drinks, bleeding off the stress of the evening, and then dropped Sam at the Haye Loft. Eric or one of the other bartenders would take him home, and we didn't need any more alcohol.

I'd spent some time on Logan's computer before going to bed. Florida's secretary of state's office has a lot of information on its Web site, including most of what you need to know about corporations. ConFla was a Florida corporation and appeared to be wholly owned by a man named Walter Driggers. The main office was in Sarasota.

I was thinking that there might be a connection between the killings and ConFla because Turk's brother worked for ConFla and Turk had told him about the claim that Abraham wanted to bring against the phosphate industry. Maybe the brother sent the message up the chain of command and somebody got nervous. I could see how the amount of money involved in something like this could bring out the attack dogs.

I scanned through some other Web sites including the Securities and Exchange Commission's, but found nothing much on either ConFla or Driggers. When a company's stock is not traded on the exchanges, there is little information required by the various oversight agencies.

I Googled Driggers and found some interesting news items about him, but not much more. He was in his eighties and had never married. He had no living relatives and had become somewhat of a recluse. He lived in the most expensive home on Longboat Key, which was saying a lot. I knew the house. He had pretty much disengaged from his business, leaving its day-to-day running to some very well-paid managers. Maybe someone in top management had taken things into his own hands and was trying to suppress any documentation that Abraham had that could affect the industry. If they couldn't get their hands on the papers, perhaps they'd decided to kill anyone with any connection to Abraham. That would include Blakemoore, Logan, and me.

I moved to the archives of our local newspaper and came across an article written the year before by a young reporter with whom I occasionally shared a beer at Tiny's, Robin Hartill. She'd scored an interview with Driggers and deftly pried him out of his shell. He'd told her of his rise to immense wealth, his exploitation of the land, the mines he'd dug for phosphate. He had no apologies for the environmentalists, and to the contrary, talked of his disdain for the tree huggers, as he called them. He had no living relatives, but would not divulge his intentions for his empire upon his death.

It was late, but I knew Robin was a bit of a night owl. I called her at home.

"Hey, Matt. I've heard you're playing cops and robbers again."

I laughed. "Not my fault. Hope I'm not calling too late. How're you doing?"

"I'm fine. And you're not calling too late. I'm hoping you're ready to give me an exclusive on what's been going on around here. You know, you getting shot at and all."

"If I knew what was going on, I'd call you first. I'm wondering what you can tell me about Walter Driggers. I just read your story on him."

"He's not a nice man."

"How so?"

"He lives in that big house on the bay by himself. Just has a housekeeper slash nurse, but I got the feeling there might be more to that relationship than employer-employee."

"Why?"

"I don't know. Just a feeling. She's an albino and just about as reclusive as he is. I'd seen her at the Publix a couple of times when I was grocery shopping late in the evening, but I never made the connection to Driggers until I went to the house."

"Anything else?" I asked.

"There seemed to be a tenderness between them. I can't quite explain it, but it struck me as a little odd."

"Lovers?"

"I don't think so. It didn't feel like that. But there were definitely feelings there."

"Why do you think he isn't a nice man?"

"He's consumed with his business," she said. "He has no heirs and wouldn't tell me what his plans were for the company after his death. But he was adamant that it would survive. He said something to the effect that he'd kill anybody who got in his way. I don't think he was speaking metaphorically, either. He's as hard as flint."

"Anything else you can tell me?"

"Not offhand. Why are you interested in Driggers?"

"It might have something to do with the shootings. I'm just scratching around at this point."

She chuckled. "Right, Royal."

"Thanks. I owe you a beer."

"And an exclusive," she said, and hung up.

I went back to the computer, but couldn't find anything else of interest on Driggers. For one of the richest men on the planet, he was a shadow, walled off from the world by retainers and lawyers. Robin probably had gotten more out of him than anybody else had in years.

When I finished with the computer, Jock uploaded the digital recording of Baggett's interrogation and the contents of the SIM card in his cell phone onto Logan's computer and e-mailed it to the man we knew as Bubba at DEA headquarters in Washington. We went to bed.

Nobody came looking for us in the night. I didn't know what, if anything, to make of that, but we'd all enjoyed the quiet. Logan and Jock had gone to the Blue Dolphin for breakfast. I needed a little downtime with the newspaper and my coffee. My needs are not great.

My cell rang. Bill Lester. "Matt, I don't know what kind of ruckus you guys caused last night, but the DEA and Hillsborough County are rolling up the bikers and lots of other folks as well."

"Ruckus? What ruckus?"

Bill laughed. "It seems that somebody grabbed the biker chief right out from under the noses of his buddies last night. Is that the guy we transported to jail for you?"

"Maybe."

"It sure sounded like one of those operations our friend Jock is famous for. But I suspect you guys were sleeping the sleep of the innocent last night."

"That we were, Chief. We hung out with Sammy a bit, but turned in early."

"I hear you, Counselor. I hear you. I just wanted to let you know what's going on."

"You're a dear man, Chief. I appreciate your concern."

"Screw you, Royal," he said and hung up. I heard him snicker just before he clicked off.

I turned on the TV, seeking out the local news channel. Sometimes they had something worthwhile on. I waited out a commercial for nutritious dog food and saw a woman standing in front of the Snake Dance Inn, a microphone in her hand. She didn't know anything of substance, only that there had been a shooting there the night before and there were two dead, one from a knife wound and the other from a bullet to the brain. Another victim had been shot in the foot. I thought I knew what had happened with the knifing victim. The reporter added that a lot of people had been arrested, but there was no information concerning the charges or the names of either the dead or those in custody.

When Jock and Logan returned, I told them what the chief had said and what I'd seen on TV.

"Who do you think knifed that guy?" asked Logan.

"I don't know," I said, "but I'll bet the dead guy was the bodyguard. Baggett seemed pretty sure that he'd be killed for not keeping his boss out of our hands."

"You're probably right," said Jock. "I doubt it's any great loss."

"Did you hear from Debbie?" Logan asked.

I shook my head. "Not yet. She worked late last night, so she's probably still asleep. She tends to be a night owl."

"She needs a man," said Logan.

"Step up," said Jock.

"I'm taken," said Logan. "Why don't you step up?"

Jock laughed. "I'm kind of partial to Asian girls."

"I'll give her a call in a little while," I said. "She gets right testy when I wake her up too early. She's kind of scary first thing in the morning."

My cell phone rang. Professor Archibald Newman. I answered.

"Mr. Royal, I got the copy of the original 1832 treaty from the National Archives. It looks as if it was written by the same person who wrote the protocol. Also, the signatures are of the same people. I'm no handwriting expert, but the signatures on the protocol appear to be genuine."

"Did the archives send a copy of the protocol?"

"No. Which means that the original isn't there."

"Anything else, Professor?"

"Yes. I thought this interesting. The protocol has one other name on it that isn't on the original treaty. Abraham Osceola."

"That's interesting. That's probably my friend's great grandfather several generations removed. Why would his signature be on the protocol?"

"Maybe he was signing it on behalf of the Black Seminoles."

"Would that add any validity to the document?"

"That would raise an interesting legal question. If the blacks were part of the Seminole tribe, then it wouldn't be necessary for Abraham to sign. If they weren't part of the tribe, and Abraham was signing on behalf of the blacks, then the protocol probably wouldn't be valid because the original treaty applied only to the tribe."

"That's true," I said, "but if the blacks were part of the tribe, then

Abraham's signature could be construed as what we lawyers call surplusage. In other words, it's there, but it has no meaning. It doesn't change the original intent of the agreement."

"The government never recognized the blacks as Seminoles. Remember, back then anybody with even a drop of African blood was considered black. That's the position the government took in dealing with slavery issues."

"I wonder why the protocol wasn't attached to the treaty in the archives."

"Good question. Do you have any idea where your friend got the one I have?"

"No. Is it possible to date that paper? Make sure it is original?"

"Yes. But that takes a lot of time. I got the impression you were in a hurry to figure this all out."

"I am, Professor. Thanks for looking into this. I'll stop by later today and pick up the protocol."

"What if I asked the chemistry department to take a look at the ink? If we can get a chemical analysis of it, we may be able to figure out the time frame of the document."

"Can you do that without destroying it?"

"I think so. They should be able to just use one letter, like the "t" in the word "the." Even if that letter was destroyed, there'd be no question what the word was. The context of the sentence would tell us that."

"Go ahead. Let me know what you find out."

CHAPTER SIXTY-SIX

Sun streamed through the windows of the old man's room, the bay outside flat and smooth and inviting. Far out on the water a small fishing boat moved south, the sound of its outboard floating through the open window. A curtain fluttered briefly in an errant puff of breeze that blew from the east and a gull screamed its displeasure at another trying to steal its breakfast. The sounds died and the room was quiet, still, devoid of life.

Donna knocked softly and entered, carrying a breakfast tray. She was surprised to see the old man still in bed. He was usually up, sitting in his chair, enjoying the play of the rising sun on the waters of the bay.

She set the tray on the table beside his recliner and went to wake him. He was on his back, his mouth open and toothless, his dentures resting on the bedside table. He had lost more color and his chest under the sheet was still. Death had come furtively in the night and taken the old man to wherever his destiny lay. Donna had been expecting it and was not surprised that his life had ended. Still, it was a shock, seeing him there, lifeless, deflated, so much less than he'd been the night before.

She sat in the recliner, crying softly, her mind floating into the past, to the day her grandfather had died. She'd been in her late twenties and her grandfather was the only family she'd ever known. Her mother had died in childbirth and her father had abandoned her. Her affliction, as she always thought of her albinism, had been the defining force in her life. She'd been seen as a curiosity by the children at school and as they grew into high school age, as a target of derision. Donna became hardened to the world, her white skin an impermeable layer protecting her heart from the cruelties suffered by those who are different. She had finally despaired of finding any semblance of a normal life in the small beach town where she grew up, and retreated into the rambling house on the banks of the Halifax River, taking care of her grandfather and reading voraciously.

She knew who her father was, read about him occasionally in the papers, usually the financial pages. He sent a generous check every month, but had no other contact with her. He was a distant presence in her life, like the city of San Francisco, a place she'd dreamed of visiting, but had never seen. Yet, she had always felt a magnetic pull toward this ghostly personage, a feeling that she chalked up to some genetic convergence beyond her understanding. She often wondered if her father felt the same way.

On the day after her grandfather's death, a stranger knocked on her door. He was in his fifties, dressed casually, a man of robust good health and a gentle smile. He told her he was her father and he'd come to take her with him, if she'd go.

She went, and they never spoke of his absence from her life for so many years. He'd once told her that he'd loved her mother so much that he'd never married because no other woman had ever evoked the overpowering emotions he'd felt in the presence of the woman who had given his daughter life. There was never an apology or an explanation. She was content with that.

Over the years, she'd traveled with him, always as his companion, never his daughter. He'd told her he could not let his enemies know that he had family, because that would put her at risk of kidnapping or worse. She'd accepted that explanation, and happily served for thirty years as his nurse and helper. She was content to be in his life even if it meant standing in the shadows. She loved him and she thought that, in his way, he loved her.

Donna went to the old man, kissed him on the forehead, and pulled the sheet over his face. She called his doctor and the funeral home where they'd made arrangements. The doctor would be along shortly to take care of the formalities.

The old man had left everything to his only child. His empire was run by managers and would continue that way. Donna would never have to make an appearance. She'd issue any orders required of the sole stockholder of such a large enterprise by phone. Nobody need ever know that the housekeeper was now in charge.

There were things that had to be accomplished over the next few days. Until then, there could be no announcement of the old man's death. It was important that he appear to be in charge of the operations he'd set in motion. There was a lot to do to preserve the empire before announcing his death.

A phone rang, the prepaid that was to be used that day. She answered to hear the tight voice of the Hacker.

"Let me speak to the old man," he said.

"He's not available."

"Don't give me that crap again, woman. Get him on the phone."

"One moment."

Donna held the phone at her side for a minute, then spoke into it again. "He said for you to tell me whatever you want. He can't talk to you now."

"I'm not going to deal with some go-between. Put his ass on the phone. Now."

"He said to tell you that you'll have to talk to me from now on. If you don't agree to that, your contract is finished."

There was a moment of quiet, only the sound of heavy breathing coming over the phone. Then, "Okay, goddamnit, but I don't like it. I want to know what's going on up in Hillsborough County."

"What do you mean?" asked Donna.

"At the Snake Dance Inn. Baggett's been taken."

"I don't know what or who you're talking about."

"Baggett's my man, my subcontractor on the job for the old man."

"We don't know anything about that. Who you use to do your job is your business. We only want results."

"Well, there ain't going to be no fucking results with Baggett gone."

"I'm sorry to hear that. My employer will be, too. We'll have to get somebody else to complete the contract." She closed the phone, a smile on her face.

She knew exactly who Baggett was, but she hadn't known anything about his disappearance. She'd have to look into that. The phone rang again. The caller ID told her it was the same number that the Hacker had just called from. She ignored it.

When the cell stopped ringing, she opened it and dialed Morton.

CHAPTER SIXTY-SEVEN

In the end, the whole thing fell apart, collapsed in on itself like an imploded building. It was one of those small errors that we all make on a daily basis, the ones that come about because we're in a hurry or maybe didn't stop to think before we took some small action, an action that normally would have no consequence. In this case, it was the use of a cell phone.

I was sitting on the sofa, sipping from a cup of coffee, reading another newspaper. Logan was in the shower. Jock was deep in conversation on his phone, standing alone on the balcony, chuckling occasionally, then listening some more. He finally closed the phone and came back into the living room. The sliding glass doors were open, giving us a whiff of the salt air blowing lightly off the bay. A gull cackled in the distance, its cry taken up by others, a rising din of birdcalls floating on the breeze.

Jock was grinning. "I think they screwed up good," he said.

"What happened?" I asked.

"The DEA techies found a lot of numbers on Baggett's cell phone, both incoming and outgoing. Most of them were to or from his known associates, other bikers. Some of the numbers were assigned to throwaway phones and thus untraceable.

"We hit pay dirt with one incoming call," said Jock. "The number is assigned to a Gus Hawthorne."

"Do we know who he is?"

"A captain on the Hillsborough sheriffs."

"You're kidding."

"Nope. The call was made last night, probably about the time that the 911 operator was getting the call about the fracas at the Snake Dance."

"Do you think Hawthorne knew what was going down?"

"He was the commander of the sector that covers Gibsonton. He would have been at the scene."

"What do you make of that?"

"The feds are going through ol' Gus's entire life. They'll strip him clean. If there's any funny money or holdings or anything that doesn't fit with his salary, they'll find it. For now they're letting him sleep. He's at home in Valrico."

"Have they asked Baggett about Hawthorne?"

"Yeah. Showed him a picture. He couldn't, or wouldn't, identify him."

"What do you think?" I asked.

"I think he couldn't. I can't believe a sheriff's captain would let a guy like Baggett know who he is. He'd probably wear some sort of disguise when they met. There's a sketch artist with Baggett now, trying to change Hawthorne's appearance to match the man Baggett knew as Morton."

"Why would a cop use his personal cell phone to call a known bad guy?"

Jock shrugged. "My guess is that he panicked when he heard about the gunfire at the Snake Dance and used his own phone instead of a throwaway to call Baggett."

"Could it have been a wrong number? Just a stupid coincidence?"

"Maybe, but then he wouldn't have called the number three times in about ten minutes."

"Where do we go from here?" I asked.

"There's some more information on that SIM card. There were a series of calls from different numbers that we can't trace. More throwaways. The DEA people cross-checked the numbers with the cell carrier's records and found that some of them originated from the east side of Sarasota County. They chased down most of the throwaway numbers and found that several calls were made from them to other throwaways on the south end of Longboat or just over the bay in Sarasota. There's one cell tower on the mainland that picks up that entire area."

I was quiet for a beat. "You think someone locally is connected to Hawthorne and then to Baggett?"

"It seems that way. The techies are checking now to see how many throwaway numbers were used in that particular tower's range. So far, they've come up with several numbers, but each was used on a different day. Sometimes more than one call to or from the throwaway, but the number was only in use for one day."

"We're narrowing it down."

"Here's the kicker," Jock said. "The number that used the local tower on Wednesday is the same number that our buddy Turk called to get permission to kill you."

I sat up. "I'll be damned."

"Yeah, but that tower covers a lot of territory. We may not be able to take it any further."

I said, "Walter Driggers, the man who owns ConFla, lives on the south end of the key."

Logan rejoined us and poured Jock and me more coffee. He sat in a chair across from me with a glass of tomato juice in his hand. Jock related his conversation with the DEA and sat back.

Logan looked at me. "What do you think all this means?"

I thought for a moment. "Let's see. We've got a number somewhere near the south end of Longboat Key that was called from a throwaway phone out in East County. The same number in East County had been called by Baggett. Then, Turk called the number here, on the same day, to get permission to kill me."

"And," said Jock, "we know that Baggett is one of the bad guys and he's connected to the phone out in East County and that phone is connected to a phone in this area. We know that Turk is a bad guy and he's connected to the same phone that bounces off the local tower. Thus, there has to be a connection to the throwaway in this area to all the bad guys."

"That ain't exactly Sherlock Holmes kind of stuff," said Logan. "Any fool could figure that out."

"Right," I said. "But we also know that Turk worked for ConFla and that the owner of ConFla lives on the south end of Longboat. A man named Driggers."

"I didn't know that," said Logan.

"New information," I said.

Logan grinned. "So, the only conclusion we can come to is that the

bad guys are connected to the owner of ConFla who lives on our little island."

"Yes, but that still leaves us with nothing connecting Morton/
Hawthorne to the person we assume to be Driggers," I said.

"It's all guesswork," said Jock. "We don't know anything except that
Baggett and Turk called the same phone on the same day and that phone
may or may not be on Longboat Key."

"Round and round she goes," said Logan.

Jock gave Logan a cold stare. "Not funny. How do we turn guesses
into facts?"

"I've got an idea," I said.

CHAPTER SIXTY- EIGHT

"Hello." Morton's voice was groggy from sleep.

"Mr. Morton," Donna said. "We need to talk."

Morton came wide awake. The only woman who knew him as Morton was the albino. She'd contacted him the week before through one of his Mexican connections. His phone had rung and she was on the other end of the line. She asked to meet him to discuss a mutually rewarding business arrangement. She insisted that the meeting take place in the late evening in a public place.

They'd met in a Starbucks in South Tampa at ten on a Friday night. He was wearing one of his disguises. Not much, just a little hairpiece to cover his bald spot, a fake mustache, clear glass spectacles, a small pillow under his shirt to give him the appearance of a man of more substantial girth. He wore a faded pair of jeans and a long-sleeved checkered shirt.

He was surprised to find that the woman was an albino. She was wearing a hooded coat, so he could see nothing of her but her face. A few strands of white hair hung over her forehead. He noted that she was in late middle age, but there was nothing else to be gleaned from her appearance.

He had ordered a large coffee and was sitting at a little round table in a corner when she arrived. He was the only customer. She came straight to him, asked if he was Morton. He nodded his head, and she took the seat across from him. She did not order anything.

"I need somebody killed," she'd said, without preamble. "I understand you can make that happen."

Morton was taken aback by her directness. He thought for a moment, staring at her. "I don't know what you're talking about," he said.

"Come, Mr. Morton. Let's not play games."

"Ma'am, I don't know who the hell you think I am, but you've got the wrong person."

The woman smiled, showing teeth, evoking in Morton the image of a predator about to pounce on the hapless prey. "I know who you are, Captain Hawthorne. What I don't know is if you are prepared to provide me with your services."

It was like a blow to the sternum, sharp, debilitating, heart-stopping. Morton sat back in his chair, the air escaping his lungs in one huge draft. In all the years of his moonlighting from the sheriff's office, none of his associates had ever discovered who he really was.

The woman smiled again, this time a little reluctantly, as if she was disturbed to have upset the man. "I know about your drug connections and I know about your relationship with the West Coast Marauders. I know that you have on occasion contracted out killings for the Mexican cartels. If I was a cop, you'd be in jail now. I'm not."

Morton looked defeated, his veneer of certainty breached, his quiet confidence in himself and his anonymity lying in shambles on the coffee shop table. "How did you find out?"

"You'd be surprised at what information one can buy if one has enough money."

"I don't understand."

"Mr. Morton, I am an immensely wealthy woman. I bought the services of the best information retrievers in the world. I'm also very smart, and when I put all the pieces together, I figured out who the shadowy Mr. Morton is. Then I had you followed, just to validate my suspicions. Your disguises are very good, natural appearing, not overdone."

"What do you want?"

"I told you. I want some people killed."

"Who?"

"A lawyer on Longboat Key named Matt Royal, his buddy Logan Hamilton, and a black man who claims to be an Indian."

"Why?"

"That's none of your business. Do you want the job?"

"Do I have a choice?"

"Probably not."

"Okay. How much money is in it for me?"

"One hundred thousand dollars."

"When do you want it done?"

"I'm not sure yet. I'll be in touch."

With that, she stood and left the coffee shop. She didn't turn around or look to either side. She walked out the door and disappeared into the night. She did not tell Morton her name.

All other communications had been by phone. Early on Saturday she gave him instructions to go ahead with the kill, wire transferred ten thousand dollars into his offshore account, and promised that the remaining ninety thousand would be sent to the bank when Royal, Hamilton, and Osceola were dead. All three of them, she'd said, not just one or two. She was adamant. All three.

Now she was on the phone on a bright Friday morning when he was trying to sleep off the night shift he'd worked.

"Yes," he said.

"You have failed me. I'm not happy."

"I sent my best men."

"Okay, let's see how much you screwed up. The sniper missed Hamilton."

"Ma'am," Morton said, a hint of pleading in his voice, "my man hit him. It was just luck that Hamilton didn't die."

"And you didn't get the Indian. Why would your man hit him in the head instead of shooting him?"

"I don't know, and the man's dead."

"Dead?"

"Yeah. I sent him to the hospital to finish off Osceola, but he got finished instead."

"And the others?" she asked.

"The two men I sent to Royal's house didn't come back. Somehow, Royal killed them. I don't know what happened, but I'm bringing in some other guys to finish the job."

"Did you know that your buddy Baggett has been kidnapped?"

"My buddy? I don't know anybody named Baggett."

"Mr. Morton. Don't start lying to me or you'll be the next one to die. I know about your meetings with Baggett at the Snake Dance Inn."

Morton sighed. "Okay. Yes, I knew he'd disappeared. I was at the Snake Dance last night."

"Do you have any idea who took him?"

"None."

"You don't seem too concerned about it."

"He can't identify me. He can sing like a choir and he'll never be able to connect Morton to me."

"I'm not worried about you."

"Even if they got to me, I don't have any idea who you are, so I couldn't give you up."

"I hope not, Captain Hawthorne, or you will most sincerely regret it." The phone went dead.

CHAPTER SIXTY-NINE

The house stood like a small castle on the shores of Sarasota Bay. It was a Mediterranean Revival expanse of luxury, its stuccoed walls painted a medium beige, its roof a crown of red barrel tile. A driveway leading from Gulf of Mexico Drive wound through a hedge of sea grapes that shielded the house from the more plebian drivers who daily passed by on the island's main street. The house was built up over a multicar garage, a concession to federal rules that affected waterfront homes. Two stairways flanked the double front door, flowing downward in an arc from a small landing at the top. I took the stairs to the right and Bill Lester climbed those to the left. We met at the top and the chief rang the doorbell.

I'd called him with the information we'd learned from Jock's friends at the DEA and suggested that we talk to Walter Driggers. The chief agreed, but stressed that he had no legal authority to make the man talk if he didn't want to. He couldn't even make Driggers see us. We decided to just show up and see if we could meet with him. We were hoping that a little conversation would pry something loose.

I asked if he thought J.D. should come with us.

"She's a little shaky this morning for some reason. I've got her doing paperwork. I told her I want her to work with Sharkey on those boat thefts for the next few days."

"That's probably for the best, Bill."

A woman came to the door, opened it, and stared at us questioningly. The first thing I noticed was that she was an albino. This had to be the nurse that Robin had mentioned to me. Such people are very rare, and I'd only seen a few in my entire life. Her white hair was done up in a bun at the nape of her neck. She wore a smock that appeared to be a uniform of some kind and white nurse's shoes, the kind with rubber soles that are supposed to make your feet less tired at the end of the day. Her face was lined with the indicia of late middle age. It was a pleasant face, one made more appealing by the smile that she displayed. "May I help you, gentlemen?"

Bill pulled out his badge, showed it to her. "I'm Chief Lester of the Longboat Key police. This is Matt Royal. We'd like to talk to Mr. Driggers."

I saw a momentary tightening of her eyes, a sharpening of her concentration as she glanced at me, a slight wavering of the smile. It lasted only a fleeting moment and her face returned to the smiling visage that had greeted our arrival.

"I'm afraid that is impossible, Chief," she said, her voice draped in apology.

"Why is that impossible?" asked Lester.

"Mr. Driggers died during the night."

"Died?"

"Yes. I found him this morning. The funeral home came an hour ago for his body."

"Which funeral home?" the chief asked.

She gave him the name and address of the undertakers and we left.

As we were driving out of the residence, Lester said, "So much for your theory. If Driggers was the one after you, I'd think you're safe now."

"We have to make sure he's dead."

"I know," said the chief. "I'll make a call when I get back to the station."

"I think the woman recognized my name."

"Why do you think that?"

"More a feeling than anything. But her face changed briefly when you mentioned my name."

"You might be imagining things, Matt."

"I might be, but I don't think so."

We drove back to the station and the chief called the funeral home. Yes, they had the body of Walter Driggers.

"For reasons that I can't discuss, I need to verify that," said the chief into the phone. "I'd like to send one of my men over to get fingerprints from the body."

When he hung up, Bill turned to me. "I'll have something for you this afternoon."

I left the station and drove south on Gulf of Mexico Drive. I was going to meet Jock and Logan for lunch. The chief had begged off, saying he had a ton of paperwork to attend to. I looked at my watch. A little after eleven. I still had an hour before we were to meet.

I decided it was late enough to risk a call to Debbie. I woke her up.

"Anything on that Web site?" I asked.

"What time is it?"

"After eleven."

She groaned. "I was up until daybreak trying to crack that Web site you gave me."

"Any luck?"

"It's encrypted, Matt. The best one I've ever seen. I couldn't crack it."

"Okay. I appreciate the effort. We may not need it. Things are starting to shape up."

"Good. Can I go back to sleep?"

"Sweet dreams, baby doll," I said.

"Whatever." The phone clicked off.

I pulled into one of the beach access parking areas, took a blanket from the back of the Explorer, and walked down to the beach. I was wearing my usual island attire, T-shirt, cargo shorts, and boat shoes. I lay the blanket on the sand and stretched out on it, kicked off my shoes, and dozed in the gentle sun.

When I arrived at the restaurant, Jock and Logan were already seated. I joined them just as my cell phone rang. Caller ID told me the number was blocked. I assumed it was the chief calling, since most government numbers seemed to be blocked. I was wrong.

"Mr. Royal?"

"Speaking."

"You're a dead man."

"Ah," I said. "Nice to hear from you. Am I speaking with Mr. Morton?'"

There was a moment's silence on the other end of the line. Then a burst of laughter. "You are a resourceful man, Mr. Royal. But you're a dead man." He hung up.

If I'd told him I was pretty sure his real name was Gus Hawthorne, he'd have known just how resourceful I was. But that would have screwed an investigation, and for now, I thought the law enforcement types were right in keeping surveillance on him. If he knew he was the target, we'd lose whatever connections he had to the others of his cabal.

We were having lunch on the deck at the Dry Dock Restaurant near the south end of the key. The bay sparkled in the spring sun in hues of greens and blues and white where the sandbars poked above the surface, a panoply of iridescence. Far out, in the deep channel that bisected the bay on a north-south axis, a center-console fishing boat was cruising on plane, its wake rolling behind, providing a counterpoint to the flatness of the water on a windless day. A great white egret stood on the seawall waiting for whatever handouts the diners would offer. The servers bustled about, taking care of their customers. A quiet time of beauty and friends sharing a meal, and of an ugly threat flying on unseen radio waves from Valrico to Longboat Key.

I told them about the phone call.

"It didn't sound like an imminent threat," Jock said, "so let's eat. I've got some interesting news."

My phone rang again. Another blocked number on the caller ID. I answered. It was Lester.

"Matt, the body at the funeral home is Walter Driggers. One of my lab boys went down there, got prints from the corpse, and ran them. No question. It's Driggers."

I thanked him and hung up. I told Jock and Logan what he'd said and then filled them in on my visit to Driggers's house. "What do you have, Jock?"

A waitress appeared at the table before Jock could speak. She told us about the specials, took our orders, and left. Jock said, "The DEA techies are monitoring Hawthorne's number. About ten this morning he got a call from a throwaway that bounced off the tower that covers the south end of the key."

"That connects the dots," said Logan. "We've got Morton or Hawthorne, if that's his name, calling Baggett. Baggett calls the East County tower, that tower calls our tower, and our tower calls Morton."

I shook my head. "But we still don't know for sure the identity of the caller who's using our tower. Since Driggers was on his way to the funeral home at the time the call was made to Morton, we can be pretty sure it wasn't him."

"And," said Jock, "we haven't identified anyone using the East County tower. We can write off Driggers, I think."

"What about the woman at Driggers house?" I asked. "The albino." I told them of my suspicions that she recognized my name that morning on her doorstep.

"She's some kind of servant, isn't she?" asked Logan. "It doesn't make sense that she'd be the one making the calls."

Jock took a sip of his diet cola. "Even if she were just calling to tell Morton that Driggers had died, she has to have some knowledge about what was going on. Otherwise, how would she know how to get in touch with Morton? If the call came from there."

"We need to get into that house," I said. "My gut is telling me that it is the center of whatever is going on."

"Break and enter?" asked Jock.

"Does that bother you?"

"Nope. Let's do it."

And that's what we did.

CHAPTER SEVENTY

I eased *Recess* over the shallows, her outboards raised so that the props were near the surface. I was at idle speed, watching the depth sounder closely, fearful of running aground. The GPS receiver glowed in the darkness, guiding us to a point directly behind Driggers home. I brought the boat to a stop, released the anchor, and backed off, making sure it bit securely into the bay bottom.

We were about three hundred yards off the seawall that separated the mansion's grounds from the bay. The only illumination came from my anchor light and the faint stars visible in their velvet carpet. There was no moon.

Jock unstrapped the black two-man kayak from the bow and eased it into the water. He held onto the painter and brought it to the stern, tied it to one of the cleats. We'd borrowed it from Logan. A couple of years before, he'd decided he needed some regular exercise and bought the kayak. It'd never been used, but rested on a rack affixed to the wall of a storage room at his condo, hanging like a forlorn sea beast relegated to eternity on dry land.

Jock and I were wearing black—jeans, sweatshirts, shoes, and watch caps. We'd painted our faces with a camouflage stick and wore latex gloves. We were armed with pistols and K-bar knives, two small digital cameras, a handheld GPS receiver, and my cell phone. I'd used an Internet mapping service to find the house and made note of the coordinates. Those had been pumped into the receiver Jock carried. We didn't want to invade the wrong mansion.

We were pretty sure that the nurse preferred darkness for her forays out of the house. We had no way of knowing if she would be leaving that evening, so we'd concocted a subterfuge that Bill Lester had reluctantly agreed to. He'd called her late in the afternoon and told her that she needed to come by his office to finish some paperwork. Since Mr. Driggers had died on Longboat Key, and although his death was not suspicious, given his age, there was still some police administrative stuff to do. He said he'd have everything finished in a couple of hours, and asked that she meet him at eight o'clock that evening in his office. He would have been happy to bring them by her house, but because of other duties, he was stuck in the station for the entire evening. The documentation had to be to the medical examiner's office by nine o'clock the next morning.

Logan was parked on Gulf of Mexico Drive near the entrance to the Driggers home. He'd call me on my cell as soon as she left. He'd follow her to the police station and call me again when she headed home. The chief was adamant that he could keep her no longer than thirty minutes and he was going to have to manufacture some paperwork in the bargain.

Jock and I clambered down into the kayak and paddled toward shore, stopping twice to study the GPS receiver. We knew the house would have a security system, but Longboaters were notoriously lax about engaging them. There was normally so little crime on the island, that people didn't bother with their security devices unless they were leaving for at least a few days. If the system was engaged, we'd have about five minutes to get in and out before the cops were beating down the doors.

We stopped paddling and sat quietly. It was a few minutes before eight when my cell phone vibrated in my jeans pocket. Logan. "She just left, heading toward the police station."

We eased the kayak up to the seawall and climbed out. Jock looped the painter around a bush that hung a bit over the concrete. We moved quickly toward the rear door of the house. Jock had a small packet with him that held all the tools he'd need to pick just about any lock in the world. We skirted the infinity pool and came to the sliding glass doors that fronted it. Jock made quick work of the lock and we entered into a foyer with bathrooms opening to either side. I turned my small flashlight on, keeping the beam pointed at the floor. An elevator stood at the end of the foyer, flanked by a staircase. We took the stairs and came out onto the main floor of the house. We were in a large living room with windows overlooking the bay. Expensive furniture was scattered about on hardwood floors that probably cost a fortune. The main foyer led from the room to the front door. I moved into the foyer and found the keypad for the alarm system. It had not been engaged. We had maybe thirty minutes to find what we were looking for.

I went into the kitchen while Jock climbed another flight of stairs to the rooms above. The kitchen was large, a place for chefs to prepare feasts for large crowds of guests. I wondered if Driggers had ever invited any-body into his home. At the back of the kitchen was a door, open. I walked toward it, shone the flashlight into the room and saw an office. I entered, shut the door and turned on the lights.

There was a desk with a computer monitor, a three-drawer file cab-inet, a couple of chairs, and a cork board with bills pinned to it. This was obviously the office of the person who ran the household. I wondered if this might be the command center of their operation to wipe out my friends and me. I needed information, but I couldn't fool with the com-puter because I wasn't sure what kind of security she might have on it. I didn't want her to know that anybody had been here.

I moved to the file cabinets, opened one, looked at the files. Each one had a tab on it with labels describing its contents. I pulled two at random, but they all seemed to have to do with running the household. I thumbed through the first drawer and moved to the second. The third file in was marked as "Donna." I pulled it out, opened it, and hit pay dirt.

I read through all the documents in the file, pulled the pertinent ones out and laid them on the desktop. I used my little digital camera to pho-tograph each one. Then I put them back into the file and replaced it in the drawer.

I was about to leave when I noticed a cardboard box in the corner of the room. There were four cell phones in it. Curious, I picked up one of them and turned it on. The battery was full of juice. I copied the number off the phone onto a notepad I had in my pocket, turned it off, and re-placed it in the box. I repeated the exercise with the other three phones, turned off the lights, and left the office.

Jock was coming down the stairs. "Nothing," he said. "There's an-other big room up there that looks as if it might have been where the old man lived. There's a small kitchen with lots of pill bottles on the counter. They all have Driggers's name on them."

"I think I found what we need," I said. "Let's get out of here." We'd been in the house less than fifteen minutes.

We went out the way we'd come in and made it back to *Recess* without any trouble.

CHAPTER SEVENTY-ONE

"One day you guys are going to make me lose my badge." The chief was sitting at his desk, shaking his head. "I don't know why I let you talk me into this stuff."

Jock grinned. "Look at it this way. We're cleaning up your island. If we get this sorted out, your homicide rate is going to drop drastically."

"Okay. What do you make of these?"

Lester was pointing to the documents spread out on his desk. I'd uploaded the pictures from my digital camera to his computer and he'd printed them out. Jock, Logan, and I were sitting in chairs in front of the chief's desk, sipping fresh coffee. It was a little after nine in the evening.

I picked up the documents. "This is Donna's birth certificate, showing Walter as her father." I waved another page in the air. "This is a will, obviously drawn by the lawyer whose name is printed on the pages, and witnessed by people who probably work in the lawyer's office. It leaves everything to Donna." I picked up another document. "This seems to be insurance. It's a printout of Driggers's DNA and a certification from the lab that it is in fact his." I pulled another document from the stack. "This is a physician's affidavit attesting to the fact that the DNA result attached is that of Walter Driggers. It looks like the old man was making sure there'd be no chance of contest of his will being successful. I'll bet there's a videotape in the lawyer's office, made the same day the will was executed, that'll show Driggers completely in control of all his mental faculties. It's pretty airtight."

Logan shifted in his chair. "I take it nobody knew Driggers had a daughter. If he's leaving an empire to her, he'd want to make darn sure nobody beat her out of it. The DNA would prove that he is her father."

"Right," I said. "And Jock's contact verified that the cell phone numbers I got out of the cardboard box were all used on different days. The one used today was the number that called Morton."

"So," said Logan, "another piece of the puzzle falls into place. Those numbers bouncing off the cell tower that covers the south end of the key were coming from Driggers's house."

"Yes," said Jock, "and the call made this morning came after Driggers was dead. So Donna has to be part of this thing."

The chief rocked back in his chair. "How do we prove it?"

I sat quietly for a moment, deciding whether to tell the chief what I had in mind. I decided to hedge a little. "Maybe we won't have to prove anything, Bill. Maybe the problem will just go away."

The chief covered his ears with his hands and made a "lalala" sound. I didn't think he wanted to hear anymore.

CHAPTER SEVENTY-TWO

It was almost ten o'clock when we left the police station. Jock and Logan were going to stop by Tiny's for a beer. I told them I'd join them as soon as I secured *Recess*. We'd been in a hurry to meet with Lester after our break-in at Driggers's house, so we'd taken the boat back to its slip and tied up. I wanted to get the kayak off the bow and make sure the lines were secure and everything was locked up.

They dropped me off at my house and left for Tiny's. I went in the front door, hit the switch to turn on the dock lights, and slipped out the back. I walked down the dock and was checking the lines when I heard movement behind me. I turned and saw a man coming out of the shadows walking toward me. He was average height and was wearing dark clothes and a ball cap pulled low on his forehead. His hand held a large pistol, a forty-five-caliber semiautomatic, I thought.

"Keep your hands where I can see them," he said. He continued walking toward me.

I stood stock still, hands up in front of my chest. "What do you want?"

"I told you you were a dead man," he said.

"Ah, Captain Hawthorne," I said. I wasn't worrying about the DEA's investigation at this point. I had something much more important in mind. My life.

He stopped suddenly, a look of shock playing across his face. His shoulders sagged a little, as if he was coming to grips with a new issue, one he had not anticipated. His life as a respected cop was over. He'd be on the run for the rest of his life. If I knew who he was, others did too.

"That's right, Captain. I know and so do others. Killing me is only going to ensure you a ride to oblivion on the needle up at Florida State Prison."

"How?"

"As you said on the phone, I have resources."

"Who else knows?"

"You mean other than the Drug Enforcement Agency, your boss, and various other law enforcement types?"

"Shit."

"I'd say that pretty much sums up your situation," I said.

"That won't make any difference. You're still a dead man."

"Why?"

"I was hired to do a job."

"By the albino woman?"

"You know about that?"

"I know about a lot of things."

"Where's Baggett?" he asked.

"He's in a lockup somewhere around here. He's singing like a bird."

"He doesn't know who I am."

"No, but Donna does."

"You've got her?"

"Yep."

"She's talking?"

"Yep."

"The bitch. She's the one that set the whole thing up."

"She says you were the mastermind."

"Bullshit. She came to me. Told me she needed a couple of pansies on Longboat Key taken out."

"Did you know she was using Baggett as well?"

"I figured it out. When I saw you got a couple of his boys, I knew they were after you, too. I never asked her why she hired that piece of crap. As long as she was paying me, I didn't care."

"Did she know of your connection to Baggett? The drug deals?"

"Probably. She seemed to know everything. But we never talked about it."

"You know it's all falling apart. Why kill me now?"

"It's the principle of the thing. You're the one responsible for all this shit that's falling in on me."

I saw a slight movement behind Hawthorne, someone slipping quietly onto the dock. Jock. I hoped there'd be no squeaky boards between us and him. I had to keep Hawthorne's attention rooted on me.

"At this point you're probably just looking at prison time. A murder will put you on death row."

"I'll be dead within a week if I'm in a lockup. The Mexicans won't let me live."

"Why?"

"I know too much about their operation."

"I thought Baggett was their man in southwest Florida."

Hawthorne laughed. "Baggett did what I told him. I'm the Mexicans' man in Florida."

Jock had slipped closer and I saw the glint of a pistol in his hand. He put the muzzle to the back of Hawthorne's head. The captain flinched and started to turn his head. "Don't move an inch, podner," Jock said quietly, speaking into the man's ear. "Give your gun to Matt, or I'll spray your brains all over him."

Hawthorne relaxed a little, some of the steam going out of him. He loosened his grip on the pistol, let its muzzle point toward the dock. I reached over and took it from him. He raised his hands in surrender. "I'm fucked," he said.

I smiled at him. "That you are my friend."

CHAPTER SEVENTY-THREE

I took a rope from the boat and bound Hawthorne's hands behind his back. Jock and I escorted him to my house. Logan was waiting on the patio, a pistol in his hand. He was the backup guy.

"How did you guys get back here?" I asked.

"When we dropped you off we saw a strange car parked in front of the house two doors down," Jock said. "It had a Hillsborough County sheriff's sticker on the bumper. One of those that allows you to park in designated parking at the sheriff's office. That rang an alarm bell, so we doubled back."

"Glad you did," I said.

Jock leaned over and whispered to me. "Play along with me on this one. I've got an idea."

I nodded.

Hawthorne was quiet, trudging along toward the house. We took him inside and told him to sit in a chair across from the sofa. Jock, Logan, and I took the sofa. "Are the police on the way?" asked Hawthorne.

"No," said Jock.

"I don't understand," said Hawthorne.

"Gus," said Jock, "you need to understand something. You're either going to help us out here, or I'm going to give you to the Marauders and tell them you're the one who set up the deal to take out Baggett."

Hawthorne blanched, his face drained of color. He sat back in the chair as if he'd been hit. "Who are you?"

"I'm Matt and Logan's friend. And you've been trying to kill them. That pisses me off."

"What do you want?"

"Donna."

"I don't understand."

"You're going to help us put Donna out of commission."

"I thought she was in custody."

"Why would you think that?"

Hawthorne gestured toward me. "He said you had her."

"He lied."

"How am I supposed to help you?"

"You're going to call her. Set up a meeting."

"I don't know how to get in touch with her. She always calls me."

"We can check your e-mail, can't we?" Jock asked, a bit of steel in his voice.

Hawthorne looked as if he'd taken another blow. "You know about that?"

"I know a lot of things."

"Who are you?"

"I'm the man who took Baggett down. He was a tough guy, but by the time I got through with him, he was asking for his mommy and talking a blue streak. If you lie to me again, I'm going to start pulling your fingernails out, one at a time. Just like I did to Baggett."

I could tell by the look on Hawthorne's face that he believed him. He said in a shaky voice, "Okay, but she sets the new number at midnight. We can't do anything until then. I'm telling you the truth."

"I know you are," said Jock.

I looked at my watch. It was 11:45. "Another fifteen minutes," I said. "You'd better hope she sticks to her schedule."

SATURDAY

CHAPTER SEVENTY-FOUR

At twelve fifteen a.m., I cranked up my computer and put in Hawthorne's e-mail address. He was sitting beside me, his arms still trussed behind him. He gave me his password and I typed it in. He had a number of e-mails waiting for him, but only one from somebody called Sweetcakes. "That's it," he said as I scrolled down to the line on the grid.

I opened it. There was one notation in the body of the e-mail, a URL address. I copied it and went to my Internet Explorer, pasted the URL address in the address box, and hit enter. A Web page opened and asked for my password. Gus gave it to me and I typed it in. Another page opened, blank except for a phone number with a 941 area code. I wrote it down on a piece of paper.

"You're going to call her," I said, "and tell her you have to meet. Tell her it's important and that if she can't meet you, the whole operation is going to fall apart. Tell her you have me and I have the document."

"What document?"

"It doesn't matter. If she asks, tell her it's the phosphate documents."

"I don't understand."

"Tell her you finally figured out why she wanted me dead and if she wants the document she's going to have to pay you more money."

"What if she won't agree?"

"Then you're a dead man. You'd better be very persuasive."

I used Jock's cell phone to call the number on the Web site. His phone was untraceable, and in the event that somebody tried to backtrack on the calls, I didn't want them to find my phone in the mix. I listened until she said hello. Then I hit the speakerphone button and held the phone close to Hawthorne's mouth.

"Ma'am," he said, "this is Morton. We need to meet."

"About what?"

"I can't tell you over the phone, but it's important."

"I'm not interested in meeting with you, Mr. Morton."

"Ma'am, if we don't meet in the next hour, I think the whole operation is going to fall apart."

"Why do you think that?"

"Because, Matt Royal has the document."

"I don't understand," she said.

"Ma'am, I have Royal. He's talking, so I figured out why you need him dead. He told me he has the document."

"Then get it and bring it to me."

"No, ma'am. Sorry. We need to renegotiate."

"What the hell do you mean, renegotiate?"

"I have the document, you want the document, you have to pay for it."

"I've already paid you."

"Not enough."

There was silence on the line for a moment. Then, "Where do you want to meet?"

He looked at me. I nodded. We'd discussed this. He said, "There's an abandoned gas station on the corner of Broadway and Gulf of Mexico. Drive near the north end of the key. Drive around to the back of the station. There's a small paved area fronting on Palm Avenue. I'll be waiting for you there. Park on the side of the road across from me. My headlights will be shining across Palm, and I want you to park where they shine on you. You've got thirty minutes."

"Or what."

"Or I'll go public with the document."

"Are you forgetting that I know who you are, Captain Hawthorne?"

"Are you forgetting that I've been anticipating this moment for a long time? I've got my escape plan in place. The document will be public knowledge and I'll be gone forever."

"I'll be there." The phone went dead.

I smiled at Hawthorne. "You did good, Gus."

"What now?"

"We go to meet the lady."

Palm Avenue is a short street, only a block long. It runs south from Broadway and dead-ends into the Whitney Beach Plaza parking lot. The same lot serves Tiny's. The service station is on the corner and takes up the whole area between Gulf Of Mexico Drive and Palm Avenue, with its northern boundary running along Broadway. It had closed some months before because the young couple who ran it could not make a living and stay current with all the rules formulated by governments from national to state to county to city. The bureaucrats suck the life out of small businessmen and one by one they bite the dust. The area across Palm Avenue is undeveloped, a forest of palm and palmetto and Australian pine trees.

If Donna followed directions, she would be parked near the trees, the passenger's side of her car facing Hawthorne's headlights. Jock and I would be in the trees, while Logan lay low in Gus's car with a pistol on him. Hawthorne would be in the driver's seat but still restrained by the rope holding his arms behind him. He wouldn't look natural, but by the time Donna figured that out, Jock and I would be in her car holding her at gunpoint.

Jock and I were stooped down in the brush that grew below the trees. We were wearing our dark clothes again and camouflage paint. We didn't want any reflection when Donna turned the corner onto Palm Avenue. We watched as a late model Lexus turned off Gulf of Mexico Drive onto Broadway and then made a right turn onto Palm. Hawthorne was backed into the paved area behind the gas station. As the Lexus turned the corner onto Palm, his headlights came on. The Lexus slowed and pulled to the side of the road, directly in the glare of the headlights. The car stopped about six feet from Jock and me. Donna was at the wheel.

We moved quickly. Jock skirted the trunk of the car as I opened the driver's-side door. The overhead light in the passenger compartment came on. Donna had been looking at Hawthorne's car and jerked around quickly to see me and the gun. Just at that moment, Jock opened the passenger-side door and pointed his gun at her.

"Unbuckle and get out," he said. "Now."

She was unnerved by the quick attack and sat frozen in place for a moment. Jock put the gun barrel to her head and she moved to unbuckle her seatbelt. I backed up, my pistol pointed at her. She eased out of the car, hands in front, a gesture of surrender or maybe supplication.

"Get in the back," Jock said.

She opened the back door and crawled in. I sat on the other side of her, my pistol pointed at her side. She looked at me, smiled contemptuously, said nothing, and turned her head. Jock got behind the wheel and drove to my house. Logan followed in Hawthorne's car.

We took them inside and I used some flex cuffs to bind Donna's hands behind her. We sat her in a chair in the living room. I took Gus to the back bedroom and tied him to a bed. Logan kept watch on Donna while Jock and I cleaned the paint off our faces and returned to the living room.

Donna was getting her nerves back on track. She looked up and recognized me. "What is the meaning of this, Mr. Royal?" she asked, with just the right amount of haughty disdain in her voice.

"Donna," I said, "you're going to talk to us about why you're trying to kill Logan and me."

"I have no idea what you're talking about."

"I think you do. You tried to kill a man named Abraham Osceola. You had men trying to kill Logan Hamilton and me. You wanted the document that Osceola found. How am I doing?"

"You're not making any sense. I'm a housekeeper. How am I supposed to do all the things you're accusing me of?"

"Why did you come to meet Morton or Hawthorne or whatever you call him?"

"Mr. Morton worked for my employer. When Mr. Driggers died, I wanted to clean up any loose ends on his business dealings. Mr. Morton was one of those loose ends."

"But you knew that Morton was Captain Hawthorne."

"No, sir."

I sighed. "Donna, stop lying. I heard the telephone conversation you had with Hawthorne a few minutes ago."

"Okay, maybe I knew who he was, but I also knew that Mr. Driggers wanted the document that the captain has."

"What document are we talking about?"

"I don't know, sir. I just knew there was a document."

"Donna," I said, "I'm tired. It's been a long day and I'm not going to put up with your bullshit much longer."

"I'm sorry you feel that way, Mr. Royal. I'm being as cooperative as I can. Maybe you should bring the police in. We'll work this all out."

"The police will not be part of this." I turned to Jock. "Have you got the stuff?"

"Be right back." He disappeared into one of the bedrooms.

"What are you going to do?"

"Something the police wouldn't be involved in."

Donna squirmed in her seat. "If you let me go, I won't go to the police."

"Donna, dear," I said, "as soon as we finish with you, I'm going to give you to the police."

"I don't understand."

"You're tied to Hawthorne. He's tied to Baggett and the West Coast Marauders. I'm just not sure who the guy out in East County is."

Jock returned with a syringe full of clear liquid. "Where do you want this, Donna? Arm or thigh?"

"What is that?" A tremor had come into her voice. "What are you doing?"

"This is truth serum," Jock said.

Donna scoffed. "There's no such thing."

"I think you're right," Jock said, "but this will help."

"What is it?"

"Scopolamine. It'll make you drowsy, but it also induces loquaciousness. You'll talk a lot and probably say some things we need to hear. The only problem is that we're using a much larger dose than is recommended. It could have some lasting effects."

"Effects?"

"Brain damage is a real possibility. Paralysis, blindness. We just don't know exactly."

Fear was replacing arrogance in Donna's face. Her shoulders slumped in defeat. "Please. Don't do this. What do you want to know?"

I pulled a chair to a spot directly in front of her and sat. Our knees were almost touching. I glared at her for a moment. "Who are you?"

"I'm Donna Driggers, Walter's daughter."

"He didn't have a daughter." I wanted to see if we'd missed anything, if there was more to the story than we'd found in the documents at her house.

"Yes, he did. I have the documents to prove it."

"Where are the documents?"

"I have copies at home, and my father's lawyer has the originals."

"Any other copies?"

"Father's doctor has DNA samples from both of us."

"Anything else?"

"My birth certificate. I was born in New Smyrna Beach. It's in the records in Tallahassee."

"Why was Walter trying to kill Logan and me?"

"He wasn't."

I looked at her for a moment, staring directly into her eyes. "Get the syringe, Jock," I said.

"No. It wasn't my father. It was I who wanted you dead."

"Why?"

"My father learned that Abraham Osceola was in possession of a document that could gut his empire, give all the phosphate to a bunch of nobodies living in the Bahamas. He said it didn't matter. He was near death and I'd have all the money I needed to live on for the rest of my life."

"Then why the deaths?"

"I wanted the company. It was my birthright. I wanted to rub some people's noses in my wealth. The company represented vast amounts of money, a thousand times the amount I would have inherited from my father if the company wasn't part of the estate."

"Who is the man out in the eastern part of Sarasota County?" I had abruptly shifted my questions to another subject, an old lawyer's trick."

"I don't know. My father contacted him somehow through some old associates. I don't know how that was done. He's known as the Hacker."

"Did you have any direct dealings with him?"

"Only by phone. He thought my father was in charge, so that's usually who he talked to."

"When was the last time you talked to him?"

"This morning. Yesterday morning. Whenever. It was Friday morning."

"What did he want?"

"He called to tell me that Baggett had disappeared."

"Do you know who Baggett is?"

"Yes. He's the man that the Hacker uses for his dirty work."

"Did the Hacker tell you that?"

"In so many words, but I knew it all along."

"How?"

"I've hired the best private detectives in the state to check up on people. I want to keep my skirts clean."

"I don't think that's worked out too well," I said.

"No." A hint of desperation was creeping into her voice. "What are you going to do to me?"

"It depends on what you tell me. If you lie, you get the needle. Where does Hawthorne come into the picture?"

Donna was rattled, her eyes scanning the room, a dollop of spittle forming in the corner of her mouth. She took a deep breath. "I hired him to backstop the Hacker."

"How did you find him?"

"I knew the Hacker was using Baggett, so I had some people keep an eye on the Marauders. They led me to Hawthorne. He was using the name Morton."

"Who killed the lawyer down in Belleville?"

She looked away from me, her head down. "I don't know."

"You're lying, Donna. Do you really want to do that?"

She shook her head, looked at the floor. She knew this was the question that could put her on death row. It was one thing to plan a murder, but quite another to actually kill somebody. "Hawthorne set that up."

"Did you order him to kill Blakemoore?"

She mumbled something that I could not make out. I reached over and used my hand to raise her chin. Her eyes were downcast. She didn't want to look me in the eye. "Look at me," I said, loudly.

She raised her eyes, said one word. "Yes."

"What about the sniper last week that went after Logan?"

"Another one of Hawthorne's people. He was the one who was killed in Osceola's hospital room."

"And you ordered that?"

She looked straight at me, a last bit of defiance. "Yes, you bastard. I ordered your buddy killed."

The vehemence of that last statement rocked me back on my heels. I was looking into the face of a middle-aged woman who had fought a very visible disability all her life. Had that turned her into a murderer? I wondered at the evil that ordinary people are capable of. I'd seen it before, but it always caught me by surprise. Was it desperation or necessity or just plain meanness that pushed otherwise sane people over the edge, over that knife-sharp border that separates the good from the bad, the righteous from the iniquitous? There was no answer here, and perhaps there was no answer anywhere.

I stared at her, trying to discern some reason in her, find that spark of humanity that must reside somewhere in each of us. She stared back, her eyes hard, her pupils small pinpoints that seemed to probe my soul, her face a rictus of hate. I knew then that she would kill me without remorse, without hesitation. She was facing her own reality now, whatever that was. She knew she could not bargain her way out of this. But she tried.

"Let me go, Mr. Royal," she said, her voice flat, controlled, her breathing normal. "I've got more money than almost anybody in the world. I can set you and your friends up for life. You name the price, and I'll pay it."

I laughed. The idea was so ludicrous in my mind that I found it humorous. It was much later that it occurred to me that some people, those like Donna Driggers, assumed that all people were like her, that there was nothing that wasn't for sale. Honor was not a concept that she understood.

"No way, sweetheart," I said. "No fucking way."

"You'll regret this, Royal," she said, her voice low, defeated. "I don't understand you. You can have millions and you want to put me away for trying to protect what is rightfully mine. It makes no sense."

I shrugged. "Final question. Why? Why all the deaths?"

"I had to get hold of the document Osceola had and close out any chance of anybody knowing about it. Blakemoore knew about it, so he had to die. It was not in his office, so we searched Osceola's room at the motel. He came in while Hawthorne's guy was in the room, and got bashed in the head for his trouble. The guy didn't want to shoot him because of the noise."

"Why us?" I asked.

"I thought you either had the document or knew about it. It wasn't in your house or Hamilton's condo, so we decided it would be best to take you out. If you knew anything, you couldn't pass it on."

"I have the document and it will bring down your empire. And several others."

Donna smiled sadly and sagged against her bindings, her body taking on a posture of absolute defeat. She'd played the game and she'd lost because she hadn't understood the rules. I suspected she had suffered a lot in her life because of her albinism. I'd never know the full extent of her pain because I'd never be able to fully empathize with the pressures that made her who she was.

She would spend the rest of her life in jail. I think it was that realization that finished her off, sapped any remaining bit of hope. Her life, probably never very good, was over.

CHAPTER SEVENTY-FIVE

I called the chief, woke him up. Told him I had Donna Driggers and Captain Hawthorne and their taped confessions. He said he'd send Steve Carey by to pick them up.

When they were gone, headed to the central jail, Jock and Logan and I sat and sipped our drinks, Dewars and water for Logan, O'Doul's for Jock, Miller Lite for me. I was unwinding from the past week, thinking that it had only been seven days since I was bedding down on *Recess* on Boca Grande Island with the beautiful Jessica, sorry to see our idyll end, but anxious to point the Grady's bow north and head for Longboat Key and home. "Some week, huh?" I said.

"Yeah," said Jock. "I missed the tournament I was supposed to play in."

Logan laughed. "We probably saved you some embarrassment."

"Probably," said Jock.

There was a knock on my front door. I looked at my watch. Three a.m. This couldn't be good news. I saw Jock and Logan tense, put their drinks down, stand. If there was trouble, they wanted to be ready for it.

I went to the door, turned on the porch light, and looked through the peephole. I called over my shoulder, "It's J.D." and opened the door. "Come in," I said.

She was wearing white shorts that came to mid-thigh, a yellow sleeveless blouse with embroidered flowers around the neckline, white sandals. "I saw the lights," she said, "and figured you were still up. I heard the radio call for Carey to retrieve two prisoners from your house. I thought I'd find out what's going on."

"I thought you weren't working nights?" I said.

"I have a police scanner at home. When I'm bored, I listen to it. Heard our dispatcher call Steve. What's going on?"

"Sit down. I'll get you a drink." I went to the kitchen, poured a glass of Chardonnay and took it to her. Then I told her the story of the break-in at Drigger's house, the run-in with Hawthorne, and our subterfuge to get Donna to come to us. I related the gist of the confessions without going into detail about how we got them.

When I finished, we sat quietly. Then I asked, "How're you doing?"

"Oh, I'm fine."

"Except for being awake at three o'clock."

"I'm off today, so I can sleep in. I've been reading."

Jock stood. "I'm done," he said. "Logan, let's go home."

"I thought you were staying here," I said.

"Nope. I'm going to Logan's. His bed is softer."

I knew they were leaving me alone with J.D. I think they had more confidence in my charm that I did. They left and I got J.D. another wine, another beer for myself. "You want to sit on the patio?" I asked.

"Sure."

The night air was cool, comfortable. A slight breeze blew off the bay. The only noise was the water gently lapping against my seawall and the occasional call from one of the seabirds nesting on Jewfish Key.

"I'm embarrassed about last night," she said.

"Why? You saved my life."

"I'm a cop, Matt, for good or bad. I took an oath and I fell way below the standard that oath requires of me. I wanted to kill Baggett. I wanted him to suffer as much as Jube and his wife. I wanted Jock to take his fingers off with the bolt clippers. One at a time. I wanted to hear him scream in agony, to beg for death. And then I wanted to be the one to shoot him. First in the knee and then the other knee, then the stomach and finally, after he screamed some more, in the head."

"You could have done that. We wouldn't have stopped you."

"No. I couldn't do that. I realized that when I was watching the arragance leach out of that murdering bastard out there in the woods. He was a pathetic little pissant."

"Most criminals are."

"I know. I've collared more than my share, put a lot of bad guys away, seen a lot of bad stuff. But I never, not once, wanted to do what I wanted to do to Baggett."

"You must be very upset with yourself to find that you're just human."

"Those were inhuman thoughts."

"I don't think so, J.D. The human part is what keeps us from acting on those fantasies."

"You and Jock seem to be able to do harm to those bastards and never let it bother you."

"Jock is different. He's had to do a lot of things to protect his country. Every time, without exception, when it's over, he gets sick drunk. He's no good to himself or anybody else for days. He's never finished an operation and just gone on to the next one. It eats him up, and one day it's going to kill him."

"What about you?"

"I don't do the things Jock does. And I don't always condone his methods. But I understand the need for men like him. I've killed people. I've watched Jock kill people. I remember every one of them. They come to me in my dreams. And after a week like this last one, they'll be all over me. I won't get much sleep for a while."

"You said Jock does these things for his country. Why was he here? This isn't a national security problem."

"No. But he and I are the only family each other has. We're brothers, and Logan is our first cousin. We take care of each other."

We talked and talked. And we drank. At some point the sun began to rise from behind Jewfish Key, the birds took flight, a slight mist rose from the water, a few low hanging clouds turned golden.

"Let's go in," I said. "You've had too much to drink to drive home. I've got a new toothbrush my dentist gave me a couple of weeks ago and the guest room has clean sheets."

She looked at me, held my eyes, perhaps contemplating joining me in bed, or maybe deciding what her chances were of driving home without getting charged with DUI. Finally, she smiled. "Thanks, Matt. Where's the toothbrush?"

FINAL DAYS

CHAPTER SEVENTY-SIX

On the first Wednesday in April, Logan, Jock, Marie, J.D., and I sat at a table on the deck of the Sandbar Restaurant near the north end of Anna Maria Island. The tables were full, snowbirds enjoying the last days before they headed north, tourists storing up memories that would sustain them during the long days of work that beckoned them back to reality. The clink of silver and the buzz of conversation drifted over us, a pleasant din that did not intrude. The Gulf of Mexico was a flat expanse of green water stretching to the horizon. A beach of dazzling white sand separated the diners from the negligible surf. Two boats were anchored just offshore, close in, their occupants lounging on the sand enjoying the day. A pelican dove headfirst into the shallows, floated back to the surface and stretched his neck, swallowing his catch. Sandpipers trotted along the surf line, a frenetic pace that seemed to be perpetual. The sun was high and warm, the sky a deep blue and cloudless, the humidity low, a slight onshore breeze blowing gently at us.

We were having lunch and saying so long to Jock. He'd catch a plane out of Tampa that evening, heading back to Houston, and what he described as his reality. He'd decided to stay on Longboat Key to see the end of the string of events that had roiled our world for a week and ended in the death of people that shouldn't have died so young.

Marie had returned to the key the day after we wrapped things up. Logan was relieved to have her back, and she seemed to have forgiven me for insisting that she go to Orlando. J.D. had spent that Saturday sleeping in my guest room and then joined me for dinner at the Bridgetender Inn on Anna Maria Island. We had been a bit hungover, but relieved to be sitting over fresh grilled fish and not worried about somebody trying to kill us. I called Logan and he and Jock met us at Pattigeorge's for drinks with Sammy who was pouring them a bit stiff. Logan always appreciated that effort.

The first part of the week had been quiet. We were settling down, getting used to living without adrenalin rushes. Life was returning to the slow rhythms that made island living so pleasant. The adventure was over, and I think all of us were in hopes that we'd never have to deal with such a thing again.

Donna was in jail awaiting trial. We had recorded everything she'd said to us in my house on Saturday morning. She'd never see freedom again. She had grabbed for the brass ring of great wealth and power, and, as Logan said, been hit in the mouth with it.

Steve Carey had transported her and Hawthorne to the Manatee County Jail in Palmetto and segregated them from the rest of the prisoners until other arrangements could be made. From there, Donna was transferred to the Sarasota County jail to await trial.

Gus Hawthorne was taken to a jail in north Florida for his own protection. It didn't work out. He'd been there for three days when somebody used a homemade knife, a shank, to end his life. I didn't think he'd be much missed, and I suspect the Hillsborough sheriff's office breathed a collective sigh of relief at his passing.

Turk was in jail with his cousin in Collier County. He'd been turned over to Lieutenant Charlie Foreman, who had arrested the cousin. They would be tried for the blowing up of the as yet unidentified car.

Nobody had been able to find the Hacker. He was a ghost, a wisp of smoke that dissipated in thin spring air. All the digital trails had petered out in dead ends. The best of the tech guys at DEA and even in Jock's agency were powerless to run him down. He was just gone and there was no hope of finding him.

My friend Abraham Osceola was still in the hospital. He was slipping inexorably toward death, his ancient body responding more and more feebly. The man had done his best for his people and the cruel irony was that it was all for naught.

That morning, shortly before we left for the Sand Bar my cell phone had rung. I wasn't going to answer, but the caller ID announced Professor Newman.

"The chemistry department took a look at the protocol. It's a forgery."

"How did they figure that out?" I asked.

"The ink. The document was written with a black ink that contains an organic compound called aniline. That wasn't discovered until about 1864. It's not a permanent ink. It can be dissolved by water getting on it and nobody would be able to retrieve the words written there. It was never used in permanent documents, such as government treaties."

"Can you put a date on the forgery?"

"We could, but it would include destructive testing and take a while."

"Never mind. It doesn't matter. If the protocol couldn't have been written in 1832, then it's a forgery. Could it be a copy of an original?

"Could you prove that in court?" he asked.

"Hell, no."

"Besides, even if there was an official copy, it wouldn't have been done in a nonpermanent ink."

"Okay, Professor. I'll stop by next week and pick up the document."

"Sure."

I'd told my companions about the call. It was a sad denouement to the frantic events of the last week in March. All that death and pain, all for a forged document.

J.D. paused, a forkful of grouper halfway to her mouth. "I've seen people killed over a lot less."

Marie looked at Jock. "Would you have used that syringe on Donna?"

Jock smiled. "It wouldn't have made any difference even if I had."

"Why not?"

"The stuff in the syringe was tap water."

Marie laughed. "You're kidding. Why didn't you use a truth serum? Surely your agency has the stuff."

"There's really no such thing. At least if there is, nobody's discovered it yet."

"So you were bluffing."

"Yep. And it worked."

Marie turned to me. "Any word on Abraham?"

"Nothing new," I said. "He's still slipping."

"What a shame," said Marie. "He was trying to make things better for Black Seminoles. He thought he'd found the way to do it. A legacy for his people."

"It turned out to be a bitter legacy," said Logan.

"That it did," I said, raising my glass of beer. "To Abraham Osceola, the last Black Seminole warrior."

CHAPTER SEVENTY-SEVEN

The sun was high, beating down on us from a cloudless sky, searing the land and the people in it. Pine trees stood silently, no movement because there was no wind. There was a taste of salt in the air, the faint whiff of brine. Humidity permeated the atmosphere, a wetness that you could feel and smell. The grunts of the men hand-winching the coffin into the open grave rode the air, punctuated by an occasional sob from a mourner, a mixture of physical effort and emotional pain.

The workers wore overalls and T-shirts and sweat-stained ball caps. The mourners were clad in bright clothes with floral patterns and straw hats made from palm leaves. Most of them were elderly, the young ones having fled to Nassau to find work.

Jock and Logan and I stood with the others, all black, all Bahamian, all descendants of the black Seminoles who had found refuge from the slave catchers. They had come in the early nineteenth century as the first and second Seminole Wars pushed the Indians farther into the Everglades. Many of the Indians had accepted transport to the Oklahoma territory, to a reservation that would never be their home. The blacks among them, many carrying Seminole blood, were hounded by white men from Georgia and Alabama who wanted to return them to slavery, a condition many of the blacks had never known. They and their parents and grandparents had been born into the freedom offered by the Indians of Florida, a territory of Spain until 1763.

There was a somberness to the small crowd gathered in honor of one of their patriarchs, a boy who had grown into a man while living among them. He'd left this little village on the northwest coast of Andros Island, seeking a better life than that offered by the meager sponge beds that had survived the great fungal infections of the 1930s. But he always came home, came to visit and teach the young ones the ways of his Seminole forebears. Now he was home for good, buried in the poor soil from which he had sprung eighty years before. We were saying goodbye to Abraham Osceola.

It was the first Friday in May and as hot as a Florida summer in these latitudes southeast of Miami. The village of Red Bays had sustained this remnant of Seminole culture, peopled as it was by the descendants of those who had braved the fickle waters of the Atlantic to paddle their dugouts to freedom.

Abraham had hung on, his great body fighting for life. But it wasn't to be. Finally, the spirit that propelled him to seek a better life in Florida, to search for his people's patrimony, to give his life in the cause of his people, flagged and surrendered.

I paid for his body to be shipped home and Jock and Logan flew with me to Andros to bury him. He had no immediate family left, but his cousins had reserved a small plot of ground in the village cemetery next to his parents. And that is where we buried him on a hot day in May when the breeze deserted us and our clothes were soggy with sweat, where old people moaned in anguish and the very young wondered at the cause of such emotion.

We joined the villagers for food and drink at the little Baptist Church that seemed to be the center of activities for the town. We couldn't stay long. Russ Coit, a friend from Longboat, was waiting for us at the San Andros airport in Nicholls Town. He'd flown us over in his plane, but decided not to join us for the twenty-mile ride to Red Bays. He hadn't known Abraham and hadn't been involved in the killings. He wanted to be in Sarasota before the arrival of the afternoon thunderstorms that daily stalked the peninsula of Florida.

I was standing under a clump of pine trees that dotted the dirt yard in front of the sanctuary when the old minister who'd presided over the funeral approached me. He was stooped with age, his face wrinkled by the years of caring for his people, a large nose set off by the high cheekbones of his Indian ancestors, his skin a deep chocolate. He wore a threadbare suit, light gray, a white shirt that had been hand washed rather than laundered, a pale blue tie, and sandals. He was the keeper of the Seminole heritage, the elder who tried, mostly in vain, to impart the remnants of that fading culture to the youngsters in the village.

"You're Matt Royal," he said.

"Yes, sir."

"Abraham told me that he might call on you for help. Did he?"

"He tried, but some bad people got to him before he reached me."

"Do you know anything about the document he had with him?"

"The protocol to the treaty of 1832. Abraham made sure it got into my hands."

"Abraham seemed to think it was of great significance," the old preacher said.

"It might have been, but unfortunately we couldn't prove its validity in a court of law. I had a chemical analysis done on the ink. That ink didn't come into existence until many years after the document was supposedly written. It was a forgery. Do you know where Abraham got the document?"

"Oh, yes. It was here in the church. My father was the minister of this congregation and his father before him. I don't know who first came into possession of the paper, but it has been in my family's keeping since before my grandfather's time."

"Has anybody ever tried to make a claim under it?"

"Claim? No. I'd read it years ago, but it didn't make a lot of sense to me. I kept it because it was old and I thought someday some of the young ones might find it an interesting artifact of their Seminole ancestors."

"How did Abraham come to have it with him?"

"Abraham was one of us. He and I were boys together. He came to Red Bays every year from Key West. He'd bring money for the church and try to interest the young ones in their past. He knew a lot about the Seminoles and had made friends with many of them on their reservation in Florida. One day I showed him the old paper and he got excited. He said he thought the paper had a great significance and asked if he could take it back to Florida with him. I agreed."

"When was this?" I asked.

"In March. A little more than two months ago."

"I brought the document with me in case you wanted it back."

"Yes. We'll know it's a forgery, but there is some sentimental value in the keeping of it. It's part of our past, even if it is a fake."

I went to the rental car and retrieved a cardboard tube from my luggage. I handed it to the old preacher. He opened the tube and pulled out the document. He unrolled it, looked at it, and put it back in its holder. "To think that this very old forgery caused the death of a good man is almost too sad to contemplate."

"I think he died doing what he wanted. He was on a quest to ease the hardships of those he loved above all others."

"He was a good man, Mr. Royal."

"Yes, sir. He was."

We said our goodbyes to the cousins and left that small village out of another world and flew home to Longboat Key and all the amenities we take for granted, amenities that most of the world can only dream about. We outran the storms and landed at Sarasota-Bradenton airport at mid-afternoon. Russ suggested that we stop at Tiny's, have a few beers, and start getting our lives back on the beachbum track.

And so on a warm day in May, my friends and I sat at a high-top table in the dim recesses of Tiny's and talked of absent friends, of those who had gone to rest, each one leaving an ever diminishing hole in our hearts. We wondered who would be next, who would succumb to the blandishments of the Grim Reaper and follow him into the great unknown. We knew that the one immutable law of the universe is that each of us has his own appointment in Samarra, his own date with death. And that produced an ineffable sadness that gradually diminished in the light of warm memories told of friends who no longer graced our world.

CHAPTER SEVENTY-EIGHT

J.D. was sitting next to me, wearing shorts and a tank top, her bare feet propped on the closed hatch leading to *Recess's* small cabin. We were motoring slowly under the Longboat Pass Bridge. To our right, families were enjoying the day on Coquina Beach on the southern end of Anna Maria Island, multicolored umbrellas shielding them from the sun and giving the place the look of snow cones resting on white sand. Picnic baskets and coolers dotted the beach and a trio of teenage boys tossed a football back and forth. Across the pass, the shore of Beer Can Island was hosting the usual Saturday assault of boats, bows on the beach, stern anchors holding them against the current of the outgoing tide. More people enjoying the soft spring weather that would end soon with the first bath of summertime humidity that always fell on us in mid-May. The green water was clear and I could see the featureless sand bottom of the pass as we puttered along at idle speed in what my depth sounder told me was fifteen feet of water.

The trip to Andros Island the day before had given me a greater appreciation of my home island, of the ease with which we moved through the endless days in the sunshine, of the rhythms that pushed us along like the current of a great river, never ceasing, never slowing, never depriving us of the essentials that graced our lives in such abundance.

When we'd finished our pity party at Tiny's the day before, I went home and called J.D. "You like boats?" I asked.

"Love 'em. My dad always had a boat and I spent a lot of time on them. Why?"

"I was wondering if you'd like to join me on *Recess* tomorrow for a run down to Venice for lunch."

"Love to. What time?'

We'd agreed to meet at my house at ten o'clock. I'd put a cooler onboard filled with beer and white wine, some crackers and cheese. She showed up right on time, and we loosed the lines and shoved off.

I cleared the bridge and was passing the sign indicating the end of the no-wake zone. A party fishing boat out of Cortez was behind me and I knew the captain would be anxious to pour on the juice and get to the fishing grounds before his anglers got restless. I eased the throttles forward and the big Yamahas began to purr, the sound rising as the bow came up and then over to settle onto its cruising plane.

I followed the markers through the shoals that hugged the channel and broke clear at the sea buoy. I turned southwest angling seaward, planning to run south to Venice while staying about a mile offshore. I wanted to be far enough out in the Gulf that I didn't have to worry about the shoals that had crept out from New Pass and Big Sarasota Pass.

The water was dotted with boats, some sitting stationary while those aboard fished, some moving at slow speed, lines out, trolling for their catch, a few go-fast boats running flat-out, their unmuffled engines roaring. To the north of us a boat towing a parachute from which a tourist dangled turned slowly in wide circles. A sailboat far out on the horizon beat slowly north. The sea around us was flat, not a ripple on the surface, a perfect day to set the autopilot, put my feet on the dash, and let the boat take us toward the Venice Inlet.

In less than an hour, I began to angle shoreward, heading to the pass that would take us back inside the barrier islands. The inlet at Venice is bordered by two rock jetties jutting several hundred yards into the open Gulf. Walkways ran along the top of the jetties and people were fishing from them. I slowed as we entered the jetty area, coming off plane, the boat settling in the water. I idled just inside the pass and used my radio to hail the dockmaster at the Crow's Nest Restaurant. He gave me a slip assignment and I backed *Recess* into it. J.D. handled the lines like a pro. I cut the engines, helped her off the boat, and we walked across the parking lot and upstairs to the dining room.

On the run down, I'd told her about our trip to Andros, and what I'd found out about the forged document from the old preacher. We made small talk over lunch, enjoying the view and each other. We had a table by the large windows overlooking the pass. A small uninhabited island sat in the middle, its beach full of families and their boats, the children wading in the water. The small-boat traffic in and out of the inlet was heavy. A police boat sat quietly at the edge of the pass, the officer making sure the speed limits were obeyed and that the boats didn't endanger the people swimming near the little island.

You had to admire the police department's taste in boats. She was a thirty-four-foot center-console, sporting triple three-hundred-horsepower Mercury outboards. She'd top seventy miles per hour at full throttle. Not many boats would outrun the cops in these waters.

J.D. and I finished our meal, dawdled over one more drink, and headed back to the boat. I cranked the engines while J.D. stood on the dock to untie the lines. I signaled that I was ready to cast off, and she tossed the lines into the boat and jumped down from the dock. I eased out of the slip as she coiled the lines and stowed them in their locker.

I idled toward the jetties and waved at the cop in his go-fast boat. On *Recess* the helm seats are raised and you have to take two steps down to the cockpit. J.D. was standing in the stern watching the parade of boats coming in from the Gulf. I was fiddling with my chart plotter, dialing in the GPS coordinates for the Longboat Pass outer marker. I looked up in time to see a jet ski coming too fast toward me. I jerked the helm to starboard to miss him and was just coming back on course when the left windshield, the one in front of the passenger seat, exploded. I looked up quickly, saw a rifleman standing midway along the jetty to the left of us. He was raising the rifle to fire again. People on the jetty were scurrying out of his way. I called a warning to J.D., but she had already thrown herself to the deck. I ducked below the dash just as the windshield in front of the helm seat burst with the impact of another bullet. If I hadn't made that quick adjustment in course to dodge the jet ski, the first shot would have come through my windshield and probably my head.

I looked around the helm seat into the cockpit. J.D. had rolled up against the left side of the boat, flattened out on the cockpit floor, making as small a target as possible. I doubted that the shooter could even see her.

I had to get out of harm's way, but if I raised my head to see where I was going, I would be a dead man. I could see the chart plotter screen from where I crouched. If everything was working like it should, I could follow the icon on the plotter that represented my boat and stay in the middle of the channel until I got through the jetties. If I didn't plow into another boat, or a jet ski. I thought the radar would warn me of another boat, but I wasn't sure about something as small as a jet ski.

If the GPS system was just a few feet off today, if the satellites that tracked my signal went off-line for even a second or two, I'd pile into a jetty. No choice. I stayed down and added juice to the throttles, picking up speed, trying to get out of range of the rifleman. As I came abreast of him, I could see him pointing the weapon at me. Either he couldn't see me hunched down behind the dash or he thought I was dead. I was sure he couldn't see J.D. His angle of view wasn't right.

I saw him bring his rifle back toward his shoulder. He was going to fire again. I was afraid he had seen me and I didn't think he'd miss this time. I stood up quickly, pushed the throttles all the way forward. I was near the right side of the channel, just where I should have been. I turned the wheel hard to the left, shot toward a slow moving boat coming in. I swung back to the right, hard, got past the incoming boat and swung back to my left. I was near the end of the jetties, the open sea my safe harbor. I made a sharp turn to the right and ran parallel to the beach.

I couldn't tell if the rifleman had fired again. I thought maybe the surprise burst of speed and the zigzags had confused his aim. J.D. stood, gripping the handhold on the back of the passenger seat. "You okay?" she asked.

"Yeah. You might want to stay down there. The wind's tough up here." The shattered windshield gave no protection from the wind churned by our speed. I was running flat-out, throttles all the way to the firewall, my GPS telling me I was approaching fifty miles per hour.

"I'll hang on back here. Where are we going?"

I turned gradually toward the open Gulf, away from the beach. "We'll get back to Sarasota." I picked up the microphone on my radio. I called the Coast Guard, reported the shooting from the jetty. Told them we were okay and were headed for Sarasota. The Coast Guard radioman told me he'd alert Sarasota County Sheriff's Office and have a deputy meet us at the Marine Max facility just inside at New Pass. He said he had a helicopter patrolling in the area.

I looked back at J.D. and saw a go-fast approaching from astern. He was faster than I was and would be on us in a few minutes. "Get down," I said. "There's another boat coming up fast behind us."

I turned back forward and saw another go-fast coming my way, a bone in his teeth. He was running at high speed, his bow wave throwing water from the point where the boat sliced through the surface. He was closer than the one astern. I couldn't outrun him, I couldn't turn back, and if I ran for the beach, he'd be on me before I made it.

The sea had picked up a little, small swells that would make a high-speed run uncomfortable, but not too difficult. The boat in front was headed for me at an angle, coming in from offshore. He was about a hundred yards away when I saw a flash from the front of his boat. Gunfire. The distance and the boat bouncing on the swells made too unsteady a platform to get a clear shot at us.

I did a quick calculation in my head. If he was traveling at seventy miles per hour and I was going fifty straight at him, we'd have a closing speed of about one hundred twenty miles per hour, or one hundred seventy-six feet per second. If I turned onto a heading that would take me directly at his bow, he'd be about one hundred yards, or three hundred feet, away. At that closing speed we'd collide in a little under two seconds. Bow-on, I'd be a much smaller target.

I turned the helm forty-five degrees to port and lined up on his bow. He would not have expected this maneuver, because no sane captain would think of doing it. He'd have almost no reaction time. I was betting that he'd turn sharply one way or the other. If he didn't, we'd collide and that'd be the end. On the other hand, if I stayed on the same course along the beach, he'd quickly get close enough to kill us. I didn't know where the boat behind me was. My mind had taken a microsecond to make a decision. I didn't have time to turn and see what the other boat was doing. I'd worry about him later.

The man at the helm of the go-fast reacted quickly to my change of course. He swung out to his right, a sharp turn that pointed him out to sea. I saw the rifleman in the bow. The quick maneuver threw him off balance. As soon as I saw the oncoming boat start his turn, I turned the other way. We missed each other by feet. His wake washed under us, causing *Recess* to almost go airborne. She came down hard on the other side of the wake. I turned again, trying to line up with the middle of the wake where the water was calmer.

I heard a siren from behind me. I looked quickly. The boat that had been off my stern had lit up his light bar, activated his siren and gone after the boat I'd almost collided with. The police boat from the pass. He must have seen what was going on, followed us, and realized that the oncoming go-fast was a bad guy.

"You okay?" I called to J.D.

She was getting up off the cockpit floor. "Yeah, but I doubt I'll want to go boating with you again anytime soon. What the hell was that all about?"

I pointed to the boats. They were headed straight out to sea, the police boat dogging the tail of the bad guy. The lead boat seemed to be gaining, but it was hard to tell from my angle. I heard the beating of rotary wings coming from shore. A Coast Guard helicopter was coming fast and low, following the boats. He passed over us and within a minute I heard his loud-hailer over the sounds of my idling engines. I couldn't make out the words. The boats kept moving. Then a burst of machine gun fire and everything came to a stop. The Coasties had made their point.

CHAPTER SEVENTY-NINE

"I think we're out of it," said J.D.

"Looks like it. I don't know how much damage the boat took. I'm going into the beach."

I turned onto an easterly course, traveling at just above idle speed. We were off Casey Key, a couple miles north of the Venice Inlet. I called the Coast Guard on the VHF and explained why I was going to the beach instead of New Pass. I gave him my coordinates. He told me to get to the road on the key and he'd have a sheriff's patrol car pick us up.

I eased the bow onto the beach and cut the engines. I toggled the electric windlass and allowed the anchor to fall onto the beach and play out some chain and line. I raised the engines as high as they'd go. I hadn't checked the tide and didn't know whether it was coming in or going out. I didn't want the props bouncing against the bottom if we were on an ebb tide.

I took the stern anchor out of its locker, tied the line to a cleat, and jumped into the shallow water behind the boat. I walked out about fifteen feet and secured the big Danforth into the bottom. J.D. had grabbed her purse and was standing at the stern waiting for me.

We waded to the beach, and I dug the bow anchor into the sand. We were as secure as we could get. I'd call TowboatUS and have him come pull *Recess* back to Cannon's Marina on Longboat.

Large houses, estates used mostly in the winter months, separated the road from the beach, their lawns stretching down to the sand. I didn't want to walk through yards to get to the road, because I had no idea what kind of security the mansions had. I didn't want to get arrested for trespassing. I saw what appeared to be a beach access point several hundred yards to the south, and we started walking that way.

A small rigid hull inflatable boat with an outboard beached about a hundred yards south of us. A kid out joyriding I thought. I didn't pay him anymore attention. J.D. and I were walking and talking about the close call. We were both a little nervous and needed to bleed off some of the energy.

When we were very near the inflatable, I noticed the man sitting on the sand in front of it. He wasn't dressed for the beach. He wore jeans, biker boots, a T-shirt with a picture of a motorcycle on the front, a red kerchief, a do-rag they called it, on his head. He had a pistol in his hand, pointing at us. He unfolded from the sand and stood ten feet in front of us.

I saw it in a flash. I'd wondered how the gunman had gotten on and off the jetty with a rifle. It had been easy. He'd parked his boat at the base of the rocks, probably tied a painter to one of the stones. His rigid hull would have kept the boat afloat even if it banged into the rocks. He climbed up, took his shots, and dropped back into the boat and roared off. He'd come around the end of the jetty and had a ringside seat to watch his buddies chasing us. The police boat had probably run right by him and didn't notice anything out of the ordinary.

"Mr. Royal," the man said, "I bring you greetings from James Baggett." He raised the pistol, preparing to shoot. J.D. moved behind me, as if for protection. I felt her purse drop to the beach, hitting the back of my left leg as it fell.

"Hold it," I said. "The police will be here in a minute."

"And I'll be gone."

J.D. whispered in my ear. "When I say 'drop,' you hit the ground."

"Why are you doing this?" I asked the man.

"Because my boss told me to do it."

"Your boss?"

"Baggett."

I sighed. "How did you find us?"

"Easy. My buddy in that go-fast out there running from the law followed you from Longboat. When he saw you go into the Crow's Nest, he called me to come get you. I just live about a mile from the jetties. It was easy. I came out in my little inflatable."

"Don't do it. This can't end well for you."

He scoffed, a guttural sound, deep in his throat. "Your girl looks a little scared. Honey, when I shoot Royal here, the bullet is going to go through him and take you out too. Two birds with one shot." He chuckled at his own lame humor.

"Drop!" J.D. shouted.

I hit the sand, moving to my left. J.D. had her Sig out of her purse. It had been pointing at my back. The instant I dropped, she fired, shooting the biker through his black heart.

CHAPTER EIGHTY

On Monday, Jock Algren walked into the little room deep in the bowels of a maximum-security federal prison in Montana. He wore an overcoat against the late spring chill. He was dressed in a suit, looking like some executive or lawyer. He carried a green canvas bag over his shoulder. It was thin and narrow, about two-and-a half-feet long. The guard showed him into the room, backed out, and shut the door.

There was a small metal table bolted to the floor, maybe four-feet long and two-feet wide. A chair sat on either side. One was empty and the other contained a shackled James Baggett. He was staring at the table, showing no concern about his visitor

"Remember me?" Jock asked.

Baggett looked up. Shock moved across his face, briefly. Then he grinned. "Fuck you."

Jock sat down in the empty chair, settled himself in, reached over, and slapped Baggett's face with as much force as he could muster from a sitting position.

"Guard," yelled Baggett.

Jock slapped him again.

"Guard." Baggett was calling at the top of his lungs.

Jock slapped him again.

Baggett started to open his mouth, thought better of it, and shut up. "You can't come in here and beat me up."

Jock smiled, a cold stare adding sting to it. "I can come in here any-time I want, Baggett. I can get to you in any prison in this country and probably in the entire world anytime I want to. And I can do anything to you I want to."

"Bullshit."

"You know about the security here? Impossible to get in with any kind of weapon."

"So I've heard."

Jock bent down, picked up the canvas bag, and put it on the table. He untied the drawstring that kept it closed. He reached in and pulled something out. Laid it on the table. Grinned. Baggett blanched, the blood draining from his face, a gag reflex kicking in and making him suck in air to keep from retching.

They both looked at the object on the table. A twenty-four-inch pair of bolt clippers.

Jock sat and stared at Baggett, giving him a minute to get hold of himself.

"You came very close to losing some fingers recently," Jock said. "You'll be in prison for a long time, and I can come and go as I please. Neither your fingers nor your dick is going to be safe unless you do exactly what I tell you to do."

"What do you want?"

"Your boys tried to kill my friend Matt Royal a couple of days ago."

"You can't prove I had anything to do with that."

"I don't have to."

"What do you mean?"

"Your contact with the outside world is, as of now, completely shut off. You'll live in solitary confinement. Your meals will be brought to you. You'll get two showers a week, alone with a guard watching. You'll be allowed to exercise one hour twice a week in a room not much bigger than this. A guard will be with you. From time to time a government agent will come to ask you questions. You will answer them truthfully."

"You can't do that. The courts won't let you."

"Yes they will. You'll get used to it. But, I'm going to give you one phone call, right now. You're going to call your next in command at the Marauders and you're going to tell them that Matt Royal and his friends are to never be messed with again. You got that?"

"And what if my people don't listen."

"Then I'll come back and take some of your fingers. If anybody looks cross-eyed at them, I'll come get a finger. Do you believe me?"

"Yes," Baggett said quietly.

Jock gave him a cell phone, pulled another out of his pocket. "These phones are wired together. I'll hear everything you have to say and anything said by your buddies. Remember, any threat will be met with the death of those who make it. And my bolt clippers and I will pay you a visit."

Baggett took the phone in a hand shackled at the wrist and made the call.

CHAPTER EIGHTY-ONE

Jock called me on Monday afternoon. "Sorry to hear about your problems on Saturday. I'd be surprised if J.D. ever went on another date with you."

"It wasn't exactly a date."

"Well, whatever it was."

"How did you hear about that?" I hadn't called him.

"The date?"

"The other stuff."

"I hear lots of things."

"Well, it's over, at least for now."

"It's over forever."

"What do you mean?"

"I had a conversation with Mr. Baggett. We came to an understanding."

I laughed. "Did bolt clippers come into the conversation?"

"May have. Take care, podner." He was gone, disappearing into the ether like a guardian angel. And maybe that's what he was, after all.

AFTERWORD

History is not immutable and most of it is told from the perspective of the historian, carrying with it the personal biases and other baggage of the teller of the story. However, over many years and through the diligence of those studying the historiography of an era, the truth tends to emerge, or at least a learned consensus of that truth, of what really happened in any given time period.

In this book, I have taken some liberties with the history of a courageous people, the Black Seminoles, who lived and loved and procreated and fought and died in the Florida wilderness, seeking only the right to be left alone to live their lives in freedom. There was, of course, never a protocol to the treaty of 1832, but there was a treaty and I have tried to be faithful to the intent of that document. The Camp Moultrie Treaty of 1823 is real and I have attempted to accurately convey some of its provisions, including the ones dealing with the large parcel of land, more than four million acres, reserved for the Seminoles.

The Seminole Tribes filed a lawsuit in 1950 seeking just compensation for the acreage given them in the Camp Moultrie Treaty and taken away by the 1832 pact. It took twenty-six years to settle the case, and the Indians were paid the sum of sixteen million dollars. What a deal. That land is today worth billions of dollars, but the Seminoles and their black allies only realized a pittance.

The saga of the Black Seminoles is little known to the world at large and that is a shame. These men and women blazed a glorious trail of courage, political astuteness, and diplomacy that is a shining chapter in the history of African Americans. For the better part of two centuries, until the end of the Second Seminole War in 1842, the free black people of

Florida changed the course of history and did so with the pride and dignity denied them by the United States Government.

The Black Seminoles were fierce warriors and astute diplomats who served as the Seminoles' ambassadors to the white man. They were shrewd strategists and tacticians, often leading the war parties against the government troops. And they were men and women seeking that universal human desire: freedom.

For generations preceding the outbreak of the Civil War, black slaves had been escaping the plantations of the South and finding refuge in Florida. Often they would exchange their slavery to the whites for a benign bondage to the Indians. Other escapees lived in freedom as citizens of Spanish Florida and later as allies and friends of the Seminoles. These Seminole Negroes, as they were called, served as farmers, interpreters, spies, scouts, diplomats, and warriors. They were a proud and integral part of the Seminole Nation.

There were three Seminole wars, or one long Florida war, depending on one's perspective, that were fought primarily over the issue of fugitive slaves. In a large sense the question of ownership of the Black Seminoles was the catalyst for the wars, rather than the issue of removal of the Seminoles to the Indian lands west of the Mississippi. Indeed, the Seminoles might have acquiesced in removal if not for the perfidy of the United States government on the question of the black people who lived among them.

These blacks were the slaves, friends, allies, and, not infrequently, the spouses and children of the Seminoles. They were warriors, advisers, and tribal councilors. Little wonder then that the Indians were less than willing to give up the blacks to the slave catchers of Georgia, Alabama, and the Carolinas.

The blacks cherished their freedom; for some the first ever experienced, and for others the result of generations of their families' residence in Florida. They were willing to, and did, fight and die for the right to remain free. Many of the Seminole warriors were black, and in some cases, notably in the famed Osceola's band, made up the majority.

At least as early as 1688, the Spanish government had encouraged black slaves from the British colonies to the north to seek refuge in Florida.

Although the Spanish themselves held slaves, they were smart enough to realize that it would not be possible to entice blacks to flee British territory if they were only to exchange British slavery for Spanish slavery. As it was to the benefit of the Spanish to weaken their enemies to the north by inducing the slaves to flee, the government allowed them their freedom. The runaway slaves established communities where the authorities treated them as citizens. These communities continued to thrive during the British occupation of 1763–1783, even though the British did not welcome the runaways with the same open arms policies as those of the Spanish. During this period, the Seminoles became the protectors of the blacks who lived among them. Florida was returned to Spain at the end of the American Revolution by the Treaty of Paris in 1783.

Some of the Seminole chiefs purchased black slaves using wild cattle as payment. Forty cattle was said to be the price of a slave. However, the Seminole had no concept of what a slave should do, or how he should relate to the slave. The system developed into a semifeudal relationship rather than a system similar to the one found on the slaveholding plantations. The Seminoles' slaves lived in separate villages, and as they were more sophisticated in agriculture than their masters, they were for the most part farmers. The blacks were allowed to carry arms, and the majority was under no more subordination to the chief than was the average tribesman.

In 1821, when Florida came under the control of the United States, there were thirty-four Seminole settlements with Indians occupying thirty-one and the blacks three. The villages were surrounded by cultivated fields, and the people lived in houses constructed in the Indian fashion with palmetto planks lashed to upright posts and covered with palmetto thatch. A part of the slave's crop was paid to his Seminole master as a form of tribute, but it never exceeded ten bushels annually. At the beginning of the Second Seminole War in 1835, there were probably 1,200 free blacks and an estimated 200 slaves residing among the Seminoles.

Many of the slaves became prosperous from holdings in crops and livestock. These slaves could live among the free black population and intermarry with them. The Seminoles would on occasion also marry slaves, and the children of the marriage were free persons.

An apparently distinct class of blacks was the Maroons who had at one time been fugitive slaves from the plantations, but who had lived among the Seminoles for so many generations that their antecedents had been completely forgotten. The word Maroon was derived from a Spanish word of East Indian origin meaning free Negroes. The Maroons had intermarried with the Seminoles and were thought of as brothers and allies.

All of the Black Seminoles spoke a European language. Those who had escaped from Georgia, Alabama, and the Carolinas spoke English, and those from Louisiana and the Florida plantations spoke French and Spanish. They quickly learned the Muskogee language of the Seminoles and became valuable as interpreters. Because the former slaves had knowledge of the customs of the white man, they could advise the Indians on what to expect from them. It has been said that one of the problems with interpretation of the treaties between the Americans and the Seminoles was that the precise English of the American statesmen was translated into Muskogee by blacks who spoke the dialect of the field hand. It is not difficult to see how this could lead to misunderstandings on both sides.

After Andrew Jackson won the presidency he was able to convince Congress to pass the Indian Removal Act, which was designed to move all Indians living east of the Mississippi River to the Oklahoma Territory. It was time for the government to abrogate the treaty of 1823.

The Indians gathered at Payne's Landing on the Ocklawaha River in the spring of 1832, and on May 9 entered into a treaty signed by Commissioner James Gadsden for the United States and by several chiefs for the Seminoles. The treaty required that the Seminoles move to Arkansas and be reunited with the Creeks from whom they had separated many years before. There was however a proviso made a part of the preamble that was later to cause much consternation. The weight of authority seems to be that the proviso was a condition of the treaty. It provided that several chiefs and their black interpreter, Abraham, would travel at government expense to Arkansas to examine the country, and if they were favorably disposed to move, the articles of the treaty would be implemented. The provision seems to be quite clear that this was a choice to be made by the Indians. The Indian delegation inspected the new lands and was not happy with them. They refused to move and the seeds of the Second Seminole War were sown.

The Second Seminole War was the longest, and until then, the costliest the United States had engaged in. It began in 1835 and drew to its inevitable conclusion in 1842 when most of the Seminoles and many of their black friends and family were moved to Arkansas. The Seminoles did not surrender and several hundred of them disappeared into the trackless Everglades where they remain to this day.

After the First Seminole War and again after the Second, a number of the Black Seminoles refused to migrate to Oklahoma and instead fled Florida in canoes. They landed on Andros Island in the Bahamas, and established a settlement at Red Bays on the northwestern coast of the island. Many of their descendants reside there to this day. Well into the 1930s they were referred to as the "wild Indians of Andros." Most of their Seminole heritage has disappeared, subsumed into the island culture of which they are a part. In appearance the Andros descendants do not seem any different from the other Bahamians, but occasionally, on close inspection, one can discern faintly the features of the Seminole on the faces of these Androsians.

H. Terrell Griffin
Longboat Key, Florida